POINT BY POINT

CELIA LAKE

ABOUT POINT BY POINT

Lydia yearns to make her name as a journalist

More to the point, Lydia can't keep going as she has. There's never enough money, nor enough time. She's always scrambling, never sure of the ground beneath her or whether she can rely on anyone for help.

Galen needs to figure out who he is now.

The last year has brought too much change. His parents are rightfully under house arrest, and Galen and his brother are setting up new lives. Restoring the family business after it was nearly run into the ground by a serious of bad decisions is only the first problem.

But Galen knows people.

When Lydia asks help investigating the aftermath of an odd news story, Galen is intrigued. So are his friends in the secret society Galen has been part of since his school years. The investigation begins with a horse race, but it soon leads them from the clubs to a decadent house party to a far more dangerous gathering that could change everyone's life forever.

Point by Point is the fifth book of the Mysterious Powers series, exploring the institutions of Albion during and after the Great War. All of Celia Lake's Albion books exploring the magical community of the British Isles can be read in any order.

It is full of the power of friendship, creative solutions, horse-racing, journalism, and powerful ritual magic. Enjoy this charming romantic fantasy with a swirl of sex set in 1926 with a happily ever after ending!

Also by Celia Lake

The Mysterious Charm Series

Outcrossing

Goblin Fruit

Magician's Hoard

Wards of the Roses

In The Cards

On The Bias

Seven Sisters

The Mysterious Powers Series

Carry On

The Fossil Door

Eclipse

Fool's Gold

The Hare and the Oak

Charms of Albion

Pastiche

Sailor's Jewel

Other stories

Complementary

Winter's Charms

~

Learn more about the world of Albion and future books at my website, celialake.com.

Sign up for my newsletter to be the first to hear about future books and learn about fascinating bits of research. Happy reading!

CHAPTER 1
THE TRELLECH MOON, OCTOBER 26TH, 19

"Give me something better." Edward Morris flicked the pages back across his desk at Lydia. He was seated behind it, entirely in control of his world, and they were marked up in red ink. That part didn't bother her. She expected it, even welcomed it. He didn't waste ink on people who were hopeless. Or time.

Today, he'd called her in for notes on the last three pieces she'd turned in. None of them were breaking news, all of them were longer investigative work. She was no good at the puff pieces about fashion or ladies societies, even if some of those were every bit as cutthroat as any business conquest. Lydia had known her heart wasn't quite in the series about new approaches to apprenticeships. She'd dutifully done in-depth interviews with a dozen people, all learning desperately needed magical trades. Individually, they were all fine.

Fine. Not passionate. Not enlightening. Not a call to arms or action, to change the world.

"I assigned you to those." Edward flicked his fingers at

the papers again, and this time a little puff of magic pushed them closer to her. "I expected a spark. Kindling."

Lydia's head came up. He'd named the problem, she couldn't help stiffening against the blow of his truth. She hadn't had a better idea for something that was more than competent. "Sir." She couldn't argue, he was right.

"What would you do if you could?"

Another blow, this one stranger and unexpected. Morris wasn't a man who invited suggestions. He ran the Trellech Moon as an absolute dictatorship, which meant he held everyone from the journalists to the print-setters to the cleaners to the highest possible standards. All the time. He was demanding, driven, but he drove himself harder than anyone else.

He did not, however, ask for ideas.

She'd had a few she'd discarded. They were the kind of thing that would take time, reporting time she wouldn't have for other things. She hadn't been sure if he'd pay her salary. It was one thing to do that for a week or two, for a story that was fine. It was another thing to do it for a month or more.

"Come on. You've done good work in the past. That one about injurious apprenticeship clauses. Complicated and more risky than you told me up front, but a strong piece." He hadn't praised it like that, then. She'd contracted an apprenticeship with the harmful terms, ridden it out for a week. It had brought her to the attention of the Dwellers at the Forge, and they'd thrown their weight behind it. That hadn't come out in the final piece, of course. But she'd been able to use it to get proper advice from the Ministry, from the Guard, from several other sources. All about how to spot an unfair contract and what to do if someone you cared about ended up in one.

"Sir." She leaned back. "It would take a while. A month minimum, probably three, longer if I found anything especially good. And it would mean I'd not be available for other reporting."

He raised an eyebrow. "Stunt reporting, then? Getting yourself fully in the midst of everything? What do you have in mind?"

The idea had hit her a month ago. They'd been talking up in the upstairs lounge at the Dwellers' house, late into the night. Most of the more hotheaded of their lot had gone off somewhere for more labour debates and it had been Lydia and a handful of others. She'd been draped across one of the chairs, her foot dangling off the arm, when it had hit her.

Now she gathered her thoughts, working hard to make them line up in an orderly manner. "Sir, you remember that business with the Research Society and Lord Sisley, six months ago or so?" She hadn't reported the story.

"Not all of that came out at the time." Morris grunted. Which was another admission. "Why?"

"What's happened since? Not to them, though a follow-up is due. Various people lost power. But - who stepped into that power? Or who's tried to?"

Morris tilted his head. "Good enough question. But how do you propose to find out?" He waved a hand at her. "You don't come from those circles."

"And they wouldn't trust a reporter who did." She knew her place, as well as anyone. She went on carefully. "Might know someone who could get me entry in the right places. Maybe. I'd have to do some background research and see if he's up for it."

She suspected he wasn't. Only maybe she wouldn't need Galen to do much. Come to a few parties. Be posh. She was fairly sure he was in practice being posh these days. The family business interests were steadying out again, and the estates were doing better.

"Might doesn't get you a story." Morris flicked his fingers, and there was another little puff of air. "What's your plan?" What he wasn't asking, precisely, was how long she needed to put something together.

Lydia had a better answer for that. "Three days - starting today - in the morgue for background." It was still only ten in the morning. "Hope I can catch the person I want to ask tonight. If not, that might be a day or two." Other people didn't subscribe to the paper's schedule, after all. She looked up, meeting his eyes directly. "Thursday afternoon." Three days and a couple of hours. She could do late nights, that was fine, to pull together all the notes she'd find.

He glanced at his diary, open on the desk beside him, and scribbled a note in. "Half-two, this office, Thursday." She'd have half an hour to convince him. He always went off for the editorial discussion of the afternoon's paper and notes on the next day's stories at three.

"Sir." She nodded. He crooked his finger, and a piece of paper flew from a stack on the bookshelf on the far wall, right into place in front of him. He scrawled a note with the curving initials at the bottom. "Take that to the morgue." The cramped rooms downstairs, where all the paper's files were kept.

Lydia knew a dismissal when she got one. And honestly, that was at least five minutes more time than she'd expected. She nodded. "Sir." Then she picked up her satchel and walked out through the desks. She managed not to whistle for joy until she got halfway down a flight of stairs at the other end.

Ten minutes later, she was tucked in at an elderly table, down in the basement. The clerks were bustling around, finding things for other reporters, but she knew to stay out of the way. They each had their own patterns and paths, and magic help anyone who got in the way.

After a minute or two, the senior clerk sat down next to her. "Master Wilson." Lydia nodded respectfully. There was no sense in making him annoyed. For one thing, she'd rather not. For another, it would make her working life impossible.

Master Wilson waved a hand at the note. "Himself was generous. What's your query?"

By which Lydia knew he meant the subject, the topic. "Two things, interrelated. What happened to the people who went down in that whole mess with the Research Society last spring. Lord Sisley and all. And second, who's moving into their places now."

"Evans. Over here." That summoned a middle-aged woman, glasses perched on her nose, her hair back in an untidy bun. Lydia had seen her before, but had never actually been introduced. She appeared promptly, pulling a notepad out of a pocket in what turned out to be an apron around her waist that blended into her dark skirt.

"Sir?"

"Pyle here needs your brains. Sisley and the aftermath, you'll want to look at who took over in the Research Society, and the quiet resignations file. And then..." He reeled off a series of names. "Alder, Wrightman, Lewis, Fitzwilliam, and there's one more."

"Sutton, sir." Evans was very prompt with that.

Master Wilson grinned at her. "Just so. Go to." He then turned back to Lydia, confident she would. "Mistress Evans is here from half-eight to half-five, hour for lunch at noon.

You have her time until lunch on Thursday, but you are not important enough for overtime. See you remember."

Lydia had to smile at it, but then she did her best to be properly serious. "Of course, sir. And I know the rules. One envelope at a time. Don't mix things up. Check them in and out with her."

Master Wilson nodded. "Her desk is there." He gestured four desks down, in pride of place. It was the productive sort of slightly untidy: several piles of files were out, but they clearly had purpose. "Pencil only. We can't risk ink spills." If anyone invented a charm against ink spills that didn't interfere with the indexing charms, they'd make a fortune in certain circles.

"Of course, sir." Lydia waited for him to say something else.

He just nodded once, and got up, going briskly over to another of the desks. Lydia waited until he was gone, then drew out her notepad and three pencils - already sharpened - from her pencil case. By the time Mistress Evans came back, she was as ready as she was going to be.

"Which first?"

"Quiet resignations, please, Mistress Evans."

"Ev." The single syllable came out clearly enunciated, a moment before a thick folder was put in front of her. "Quiet resignations, last three years."

"Beg pardon?"

"Call me Ev. Are you Pyle or something else?" Her voice was brisk, but cheerful enough.

"Lydia, please. Though Pyle's fine if you'd rather."

"Not the most euphonious short names. Lid. Pile." She shrugged, amused at the wordplay. "What next?"

"Research Society, please, and then the names. I expect

I'll have a better idea once I've got through this." Lydia tapped the folder with the envelopes.

Ev left her alone, going back to the filing cabinets. Lydia quickly lost herself in the work, going through each folder and scribbling down notes. By the time she came up for air ninety minutes later, her stomach was rumbling and she desperately needed to resharpen all of her pencils.

She waited for Ev to look up and then caught her attention. When the older woman came over, Lydia cleared her throat. "Not to be a bother, but where can I sharpen my pencils?"

"You've twenty minutes to lunch. Would another pencil do you?" It would and did. Twenty minutes later, Lydia brought her satchel with her, checking all the files back in to Ev's desk, and waiting while they locked everything up. She then ducked out with a "Back at one." and went to the cheapest cafe she knew. It was a good quarter hour walk. But it gave her the chance to check in with a couple of sources along Club Way, the various staff who were out and about at this time of day on all sorts of errands. They picked up interesting information, some of which they were willing to share.

At two minutes after one, she was back at her assigned table, and hard at work again. At twenty past five, she was tidying her notes up. She'd got most of the way through the quiet resignations folder, she'd have to pick up her pace tomorrow if she could. And she'd be up all night reconciling her notes. Assuming, of course, that she could get hold of Galen for the other part of her plan. All the research in the world wouldn't help if she couldn't do that.

When she caught Ev's eye, she nodded. "I'll need that top envelope in the morning, and might need to go back to the whole thing when I've looked at the rest. More pencils."

Ev nodded. "You can come to lunch with us tomorrow, if you want."

Lydia expected it would be a bit pricier than she wanted. They got a steady salary down here, unlike her piecework by the story. But knowing more about the clerks in the morgue could be only to the good. "I'd like that. Thank you."

That done, everything handed over, she took herself off to the Dwellers. She could scrounge something from the kitchen there, almost certainly.

CHAPTER 2

THAT AFTERNOON, THE DWELLERS' HOUSE, TRELLECH

The charm light on Thomasina's lab flipped from off to on, just as Lydia was trying to decide whether to wait around. She knocked four times and knew Thomasina would come out to the sitting room when she was ready. In the meantime, Lydia could make tea and scrounge for biscuits.

She had a tenuous place here. She was not, officially, part of the club. Quite literally, in this case. She was not a sworn Dweller of the Forge. They were one of the secret societies that brought in young bright-eyed students at Schola, and then sent them off into the world to be firebrands. For one thing, she hadn't gone to Schola. She'd had five years at Dunwich instead, learning a great deal about trade and accounting. It had turned out to be more useful for reporting than she'd realised at the time.

It had been a great triumph when they'd told her she'd been clever enough, had her magic come to her fingers deftly enough, to get in. But now that she had spent time with people who'd gone to Schola, she knew there was a

9

vast gap between what they'd learned and how they'd learned and what she knew.

Despite that, over the past year or two, she had become more friendly with Martin. He was a fellow reporter, but not in competition for the same sorts of stories. Up to two years ago, you rarely saw Martin without Galen, his sworn brother since they were thirteen. They made an unlikely pairing, one from a family nearly as working class as Lydia's own, the other from one of the wealthier families in Cornwall, at least.

But then Galen's parents had interfered in a murder investigation and been found guilty of several other things. Ever since, Galen had been wrapped up in the family business and estates. He'd not been around the place much, and Lydia was fairly sure Martin only saw him every fortnight or so. Less, maybe.

Since then, Martin had asked her around more, and made sure she could come in and make use of the space, so long as she paid her tab. They were not nearly so exclusive about who could come and go as most of the clubs. She'd asked about it once, and Miriam had grinned broadly. "How are we supposed to have new interesting conversations and build connections if we're always talking to the same people?"

The Dwellers, as a society, were founded on the premise of Prometheus bringing fire to humankind. They danced around the fundamental renegade spark that made transformation possible, it made sense that they would keep reaching out. Inviting in.

Lydia had been sure Martin knew she was grateful for a warm room, where she didn't have to pay for the heat or magic it into existence. And lights she didn't have to will into shining herself, and running water on tap rather than a pitcher in her room in the boarding house. He'd lived like that for long enough himself, she knew that much.

All of which meant she was welcome to scrounge from the plates of biscuits and the general run of tea put out as a routine thing. But she didn't have the money to eat here often; they liked interesting food, rather than inexpensive food. There was nothing wrong with that, but Martin had the benefit of Galen willing to pay his tab. And Lydia suspected there was some sort of fund for assistance for members of the Dwellers, anyway. They were that sort of unremarkably generous to their own.

She shrugged and settled in with a couple of biscuits while the kettle worked up to a boil. As it started singing, Thomasina came out of her lab, closing her door and pressing her hand against the blood lock. Too many dangerous things to risk someone else getting in there, she always said. Lydia worried about what would happen if there were an emergency, but Thomasina just smiled and said she'd thought of that.

"I'm famished. If I order a meal, will you eat? My treat. I've just had a breakthrough."

"Like you have to ask." Lydia grinned and waited while Thomasina went to order. There was an arcane system of pneumatic tubes that ran through the building carrying message capsules. Thomasina wrote what sounded from the scratching like either a substantial order or a detailed one.

When she came back, she was grinning. "A bit of a feast." She was in a very expansive mood, then. She settled down in one chair with a slight bounce that shook the curls piled on top of her head.

"Anything you can talk about yet? Not on the record. I've got something else at the moment."

Thomasina shook her head. "Not today. Still too newly hatched. A week or so, when I can duplicate it a couple of times." She grinned even more broadly. "Bigger feast then." She stretched. "Let me go wash up."

Lydia waved a hand, and went back to nibbling on the biscuits, drawing a book out of her satchel to read. She'd never had an easy time reading while waiting for something to happen, but she could fall into a book at a pause like this freely enough. Thomasina took her time about it, coming back to plop down in the comfortable chair with a thump.

"And how long have you been working today?"

Thomasina yawned, amused. "Since about five this morning. And I went to sleep at midnight, so."

Lydia shook her head. "Well. Food and then sleep, right?" Thomasina kept a room here, next floor up, so she didn't have to go far when she was deeply enthralled in her work. Which was, admittedly, much of the time. "Is Galen expected any time soon?"

Thomasina tilted her head.

"It's Monday." Lydia was sure the other woman had forgotten. "About half five now."

"Might get him in an hour or two if we're going to? If you wanted to stick around. And if I haven't forgotten which week it is."

"October 26th." Lydia leaned back as one of the staff came up the stairs, and then pulled the ropes to bring food up from the kitchen below. It was indeed a feast, two trays of food, one stacked with circular bamboo baskets.

"What do you want Galen for, anyway?" Thomasina stretched her hands, as if to ease aches.

"I've got a chance at a complicated story, the sort that takes months of research, but I think I need help to meet the right people for it. I can dress up right, enough, but he really is right for it."

That got her a raised eyebrow while the food got set out. French onion soup topped with crusty bread and melted cheese. The bamboo containers held a range of dim sum. The afternoon cook here had come from Hong Kong, and many of the society enjoyed the range of small edible options.

Unusual food, in the heart of Trellech, but Lydia had found they went well with an energetic discussion and she'd come to enjoy them. And she knew how well that sort of thing worked if you were feeding an unknown number of people. And making use of whatever was easy to get at the market to keep the costs down.

Once they'd sorted out what they had to choose from, Thomasina gestured at Lydia. "So tell me about this story. Maybe I can help you persuade Galen."

Lydia tried to piece that together. "Why would you help?" Thomasina lived in her own world of alchemical formulae, brilliance, and perhaps a few too many fumes. And besides, while the Dwellers had been friendly to Lydia, it had all been about sharing information. Not trading favours. This was a big one to start with.

"Well, it sounds interesting. You know I enjoy interesting. I have to have something to keep me busy when I'm waiting for something to distil." Then Thomasina shrugged. "And Galen could use a bit of amusement."

"How is he doing these days? Do you know?" It was not the sort of thing Thomasina usually paid attention to. But she had a mind like a steel trap for things she overheard in passing, and you never knew what she'd remember.

"They were in, oh, a fortnight ago? No, it must have been longer. Middle of September, they were talking about the Michaelmas rents and what was involved in all of that. You'd make better sense out of it than I would. Anyway, he was relieved they'd made it to harvest without too many catastrophes, and looking forward to a breather. The winter's quieter. And then he and Martin and Laura went out for supper. I've been in the lab, mostly since then."

Lydia nodded. "I like Laura, the bits I've talked to her. And she and Martin seem to do well together."

"Oh, very. Living together seems to be grand for them. I'm not sure how anyone manages it. Honestly, I'd always be yelling at someone for moving my things."

Lydia snorted at that. "Me too. Though I've only ever lived with my family or the rooming house, tiny little room, all my things jammed in. No space for an extra person, which I'm sure is entirely intentional, even for a visit."

"What happens if you want to talk to a friend?" Thomasina leaned forward, snagging a bit of shumai deftly with chopsticks.

"We go down to the front parlour to be peered at disapprovingly by Mistress Pierce. Over her glasses."

"Do you pay a lower rent to make up for the disapproval? I'm certain I couldn't live with that." Thomasina took a bite, then sighed contentedly. "The food is grand."

"She's not that bad about other things. The food's quite edible, the beds aren't exactly soft, but they're not bad. She doesn't skimp on the heat in the winter or the hot water in the bath, which is a lot better than most places. At least if I can take my bath outside of the high demand hours." Lydia shivered. "I've had entirely too many cold baths in other places when I didn't have the energy to warm up the water myself. Her son does plumbing and heating and all that, which is a help. She's a widow."

Thomasina tilted her head. "Not a way I'm used to

living, but better than you had is good." She wriggled her fingers. "What does this new job mean? The one you want to get?"

"It would be a long project. The complicated things, sometimes that can be months of research, and I don't have other money to fall back on. So I can only do it if the paper backs me. Pay my salary hoping to get something amazing out of it in the long run." It felt, now she was talking about it, a little fragile, like it would shatter if she said too much.

"And what do you need to do that?"

"Luck." It came out of Lydia in a rush. "And the chance to be in the right position to make use of it. That's the tricky part. I can do hard work till the cows come home. But that isn't enough for a great story, the kind that gets people buying papers for weeks, talking about it day after day."

"And a bit of help." Thomasina considered. "Is this a story Martin would take on?"

"Not his sort of thing." Lydia shrugged. "I got my job by taking a few risks. There used to be a thing, for women reporters, back in the 1880s and 1890s. When everyone thought they couldn't, or they should keep to society events and maybe a few decorous reports on the parts of agricultural fairs that don't actually involve animals. Which shows what that sort knows about farm life."

Thomasina laughed, letting it tail off into a giggle. "And you?"

"Originally? I got myself hired by one of the big apothecaries. Not the small independent ones, you remember, there were a few people making bigger batches? In some dangerous ways, it turns out. I could keep track of what was going on, document it, get the Guard called in. Well, the Penelopes, to investigate." That was their job, after all. "And now, that kind of larger production is strictly regulated, and hard to get approval for."

Thomasina flicked her fingers. "I remember that. Awfully badly done alchemy, besides anything else." She would, of course, care about that first.

Lydia was about to say something else, when they both heard footsteps on the stairs, and Galen's voice. "Hello the lounge. Anyone up here?"

CHAPTER 3
LATER THAT AFTERNOON

Galen poked his head into the upstairs lounge, just as he heard Thomasina say, "Me. And Lydia. Though I was about to go sleep."

He came in to find both of them on the comfortable chairs, with the remains of a small feast. He grinned at Thomasina. "Breakthrough, I gather? Martin said you hadn't appeared yesterday."

She shook her head. "Lydia came round looking for you." Lydia wrinkled her nose. She was looking like it had been a long day, Galen thought. Her hair was coming down in wisps from where she'd pinned it on the top of her head. And there was a smudge of graphite or maybe ink by one ear.

"Um, yes?" Galen came over. He wasn't sure what to expect here, and he didn't entirely like that.

Thomasina waved a hand. "Help yourself to the remains. I gather there's still a lot of shrimp shumai and some of the pork buns if you want to order more." Galen diagnosed that at least some of the Jewish Dwellers had been around for tea, in some number.

"Thanks. Go sleep. Julius said if you want to come round and chat next week, he'll have time."

Thomasina nodded, and stretched as she got up, before going to the door that led upstairs to the bedrooms. Lydia watched her go, then turned her attention back to Galen, and he flushed.

"Julius?" was what she asked first. "That's your brother, right?"

"You've never met him. Don't feel badly about forgetting the name." Galen shrugged. "He had a bad facial injury in the War. He's got a proper alchemy lab set up now, on one of the country estates, and two assistants. Plus Blythe, they're engaged, getting married next spring."

"The whole, um. Thing with your parents." It was not a graceful use of words, but Galen nodded. She swallowed, trying to avoid the awkwardness and mostly failing, but not in an offensive way. "And Thomasina?"

"Different line of work, but they like talking through their research problems with each other." Galen considered, then took a breath. He had been in the office all day. He was wearing business clothes, and his tie and collar suddenly felt uncomfortably tight and formal. "You wanted to talk to me?"

Lydia took a deep breath. "I - I would very much like your help with something. Introductions, probably."

"Introductions?" He gestured. "You're a reporter. You know hundreds more people than I do."

"A specific sort of introduction." She ran her hand through her hair. Galen could see - he was finally learning to read - the little signs that she was nervous, that she was deferring to him. He hadn't expected that. She'd always treated him with amused attention before, and he wasn't sure he liked the change. She was five years older, give or take, confident, established in her profession.

"Look, back up several steps, and start there? Please?" He leaned forward to snag one of the pork buns, taking a bite. When she hesitated, he added, "I came to see if there was anyone around. I know Martin's busy. I don't have any particular plans."

"All right." She took half a minute to gather her thoughts, and Galen didn't rush her. He was, frankly, a little curious now. "I need a big story."

"Like Martin did. Only I know you do different kinds of stories. Mostly shorter and more - um. Intense?" he asked.

She nodded. "Some of the General Strike reporting. What it was like at home, in the smaller villages." Lydia swallowed, and Galen could see her preparing to launch into it, like a horse about to gallop. He waited. "I need an introduction to some people. I don't know exactly who yet, I'm still doing the research."

"And you think I can help with that?"

She bobbed her head, her hair shifting. "Rich people. With power."

"They don't - why me?" Galen was baffled, he couldn't imagine why she thought that would work. "Start further back."

"You're not saying no." Lydia said, and he wasn't sure she meant him to hear it.

"I'm not saying yes, either. I'm saying you're making no sense."

She took a deep breath, a sip of the tea, and tried again. "How much have you been following, starting last summer, when there were all those arrests? It was right around the strike. Lord Sisley, half a dozen other people."

Galen says, "I remember the strike, of course. Martin was in the thick of it. You too?"

Lydia waved a hand. "We are not talking about the strike. The strike is old news. This is new news. Potential news." She sounded very insistent.

"I remember the arrests, vaguely. We were worried about the weather. Though not as much as last month." There had been inches of snow on the ground in some places, and punishing sleet.

"The trials wrapped up in September, most all of them." That was one benefit of their Ministry, and a smaller population to deal with, compared to the non-magical community. Trials tended to be quite prompt, given the ability to require people submit to either truth-telling charms or the consequences. "And those are interesting, but they're not the point."

Galen blinked. "The point is?"

"The point is, that when you have a gap in who is in power, people step into it. I want to know who has. It's been six months. That's plenty of time for someone else to have got into the midst and begin building their own little fiefdom."

"And you think I know who it is?"

Lydia shook her head. "I think you can get invited to the sort of places where it would be more obvious."

"And," he hesitated, "bring you along with me."

She suddenly ducked her chin and flushed. "It sounds like a lot when you say it like that. I'm sorry. I shouldn't have." She stood up, gathering her satchel.

Galen reached to touch her hand. "Sit, please. I haven't said no yet. I haven't said yes, but I'm listening."

"All right. There are those trials, and there's something else. A part I can't figure out." She sat down again, put the satchel down, and swallowed. "You remember the bit - you must have - about that trial about the attack on Lord Carillon."

"Given that's Laura's brother-in-law, yes. She hadn't been at the party, but of course she was worried afterwards. All that bit about Madam Aylett disappearing in the night, leaving a couple of alchemy labs. Julius was curious about what was going on. He got some of the public reports, and he knew one of the journeymen pretty well."

Lydia's chin came up. "That," she said, "Is exactly what might be helpful. Would your brother talk to me? Or introduce me? Or something?"

"He's not terribly comfortable with strangers, I don't know. I can ask. He might tell you who to talk to, anyway." Galen shrugged. "He's my big brother, by seven years. So mostly pretty established, one of the ones who made it through the War."

Lydia nodded. "So that's one gap, where you wonder who's doing that kind of work now. Both the more hidden parts, but also the aboveboard alchemy. It's not like alchemists grow in trees."

"They'd grow in poison gardens." Galen found himself wanting to tease her. She was looking pinched.

She blinked, then snorted. "I suppose that explains why we don't have an abundance of them. Some of those are fussy plants."

Galen tilted his head. "I don't know that I ever knew where you went to school. If you did, I mean. Plenty of people just apprentice, not the Five Schools, I mean. I know you weren't." He felt himself getting more and more foolishly tongue-tied.

She tilted her head. "Dunwich. I'm actually rather good

21

at sorting out accounts, which turns out to be more relevant in journalism than it looks at first glance."

Galen swallowed. "Right. Schola, of course. I mean, that's obvious." Now he was babbling. That wasn't any help at all. "Um. Please go on?"

Lydia thankfully ignored how idiotic he was sounding. "Now, the thing about Madam A, as the papers have dubbed her - I think it's because her husband was actually rather well-liked. Also, legitimately, it's easier to make someone sound sinister if you call them by an initial. All very pot-boiler and penny-dreadful." She wrinkled her nose.

"You don't approve?" Galen leaned forward. "I thought selling the story was the thing."

Her shoulder twitched, a hint of irritation, before she deliberately seemed to settle. "Think of it as different paths in the woods that come together and part and come together and part. If you always play to the show and the glitter and the eye-catching headline, eventually you stop being true to the news. On the other hand, a lot of the news - the essential, important information people do actually need to know, or at least some people - is often fairly boring. Or at least awfully repetitive."

"So in an ideal world, you would have regular infusions of interesting new events that would give some perspective. Epic moments, turning points in human history. The General Strike, for example, the kind of thing where the impact plays out for years. And then you would have the more routine things, the shipping schedules, the financial news, the details about new inventions or products, the arts, whatever else, in amongst it."

Her chin came up, then she leaned forward. "You're smarter than you look."

Galen laughed, but he found himself very pleased by the praise. He'd always found Martin's fellow journalists much faster and wittier than he was. "Martin rubs off." That seemed safe enough to say, without causing more trouble.

"Well." Lydia seemed at a loss for words for a moment. "So, that's one area I'm curious about, but I haven't had a way to investigate it. And I still don't. Which meant I started thinking about other areas, where a follow-up might be interesting. Even important. Shining a light on something that got missed. That got me onto the serpent society, whatever they were calling it, they had their tails in many things. Fingers? I don't know what the metaphor is. And I know some of that crossed over into the non-magical community."

"And you think I can help with that?" Galen blinked. "I barely know my way around Trellech society. And by barely, I mean I have only managed to horribly insult three people this month by not knowing their family history."

"But you're still in that place where everyone sensible realises you're still new to your role, right?" Lydia was leaning forward again, rather avidly.

"Um, yes?" Galen was not at all sure where this was going. Or whether he liked it.

"That's excellent. There's space for you to pick up some sort of new interest or ask questions. Someone who was well-established, everyone would wonder if they pick up a new interest. But you're still trying things out, exploring. If it's an ordinary sort of posh interest, no one would think twice."

"What sort of interest are we thinking of here?" Galen asked cautiously. "And I don't know what I think about your theory. I mean. Lord Carillon - Laura's brother-in-law, he does different things."

"He also spent years and years outside of Albion. Before and after the War. When he came back, people had no idea what to expect except the bits they knew about. Huh. Stables, stables."

"I'm a lousy pavo player." Galen warned.

Lydia tilted her head. "You play? I mean, I've played bohort a fair bit. I'm not up to league standards, but I have a good time."

Galen considered how to explain how bohort - a game of puzzles and cleverness and magic - became immensely more complicated when you were mounted on a horse who had a mind of its own. And a sense of self-preservation, which was sometimes more relevant. It had been considered amazing training for cavalry mounts, and for the chargers knights rode into battle before that.

"It's more complicated than that as a game, but - I appreciate a good match. You shouldn't expect me to be playing."

"How do you feel about horses in general?" That had a speculative tone to it.

CHAPTER 4
THE DWELLERS' LOUNGE

"Horses?" Galen blinked at her. "I'm a decent rider. I enjoy them. What should I be thinking about horses?"

Lydia leaned back, chewing her lip. "The thing I'm wondering," she said, "Is whether the place I should look is within the magical community - or outside. If you were looking for the movers of power, where would you be looking?"

Galen blinked, but he could see the theory. "Where do you get the most leverage, you mean? Albion's trade is a good size, but it's nothing compared to the empire's. And most of what Albion produces is small scale. Crafters, not factories."

"A fair amount of grain and such, dairy, but that's a different portion of the economy." Lydia agreed. "The captains of industry, they're almost entirely non-magical."

Galen flicked his fingers. "Not all of them. But most. I agree." He swung one foot. "Which means?"

"How do you feel about horses? Specifically putting it

about you're thinking of buying a racehorse? Or a share in a racehorse?"

He let out a low whistle. "I don't know. It might look like I'm being profligate with money. I can't afford that. Literally or metaphorically."

"But you'd be willing to ask around?" Lydia's voice was more urgent.

Galen flicked one of his fingers. He never knew how to explain this part. Not to Martin, especially not to anyone else. Laura actually understood. She'd grown up with money and then seen it all slip away, and now she had no money worries, thanks to her sister's marriage. "It depends. Tell me more about what you want, and I'll explain."

Lydia swallowed. Galen saw the bobble, the way Martin sometimes got, when he asked something and then wasn't sure he should have. If he had the right to. Galen leaned forward to snag a bit more food, and give her a chance to think. When she spoke again, it was slow. "What I want is some sort of way to watch the patterns of people in the right sort of social circles. Money. Power. Social status. Horse racing seems like a place I could do that."

"Fair enough. And an easier place to get an invitation than most." He considered. It wasn't a bad idea. In fact, it had quite a bit of promise, if he could do his part. "You're right, I could pass. We have some business connections there. They know I'm near enough a country squire, land, old family, even if they can't quite place us properly. Since we didn't go to the right schools by their way of thinking."

"And will you?"

"Wait." Galen held up his fingers. "Here's the other part. I know you feel I have money, and I do. But when you have money, there are gradations of having money. Some people can spend money like water, and not run out. We're not like that. I'm still rebuilding the business. And like it or not, the estate has to pay for my parents and their housing." They were disgruntled in their house arrest on one of the smaller family estates. "My father doesn't have control over any of it, but it doesn't stop him thinking he should have a say. And we have the tenants and landholdings to think of, and I wanted to make improvements this year."

Lydia peered at him. "That's not the sort of problem I know about, no. Either part of it. So, all right. You can't just go buy a racehorse. I assume."

"Racehorses are the sort of excessive expenditure my mentor would frown on. But I can ask him about going to the races, putting it about I'd like to think about it eventually. I'd like to learn more. Maybe buy a share sometime. I can probably do that."

"Can?" Lydia let out a breath. "Will?"

"What exactly are we talking about here, in terms of time? What you need from me?" Galen gestured with one hand, realising he needed to clarify. "Martin and I have done something similar enough - bringing him along with me, vouching that he's the right sort of chap. But this would be a new set of people, mostly."

Lydia hesitated. "The obvious thing, um. Would be if you were squiring me around."

That was the obvious choice. They didn't look at all alike. She couldn't pass for his sister, or even really his cousin. But there were other challenges. "Do you know what that involves?"

Lydia squared her shoulders. "I'm up for the challenge."

"I'm not saying you're not." Galen snorted. "But - look, humour me, all right? Define the challenge. What's involved?"

To her credit, Lydia didn't charge ahead into it. She

stood for a moment, going over to put the kettle on again. "More tea?"

"Black, please." Galen leaned back and waited patiently.

Boiling the water again kept her busy for a good several minutes, and she brought the pot back, holding it carefully. While she waited for it to steep, she settled back in her chair. "You haven't escorted anyone else around to those sorts of parties."

It was a statement, not a question, and he raised an eyebrow. "How do you know?"

"I do listen to the gossip. Here, and other places. The head housekeeper at Bourne's is a friend."

Galen snorted. "Figures." That was the most posh of the clubs where he now had a membership, but also one particularly good for steady business connections. It had not been his father's favourite. "You are correct. I haven't had the taste for it. Mother was trying to marry me off well when she invited Laura out. And Laura's grand, but as she says, not a good wife for me. She suits Martin better."

Lydia looked Galen up and down. "And you're not jealous?"

Jealousy wasn't the right word. Laura had been right, of course. He knew that when she'd so gently turned him down. They'd have made a fair go of it. And then they'd both have avoided confrontation about something, then something else, then another thing. After not too long, they'd have found themselves in their own corners of their own lives. He wasn't sure what he wanted out of marriage, but it wasn't that.

"She was right, that we wouldn't suit in the long run. And Martin's glowingly happy. She's become a friend, and I could use more of those." He hesitated, then asked, "And you? No one you've been seeing."

Lydia snorted. "There aren't exactly men knocking down my door. You're enough younger. Too many men my age gone, dead, or so badly hurt that they're not thinking of marriage. An entire generation of spinsters. I don't mind it too much. I mean, I'd make a lousy housewife, now wouldn't I? I can't cook, I hate cleaning. I more than did my time helping raise my younger siblings. I don't want to do that again any time soon, at least."

Galen nodded, then asked, almost idly. "How many?"

"Five younger. I love them, but you have no idea how glad I was to move out when I did. Barely a minute to myself that wasn't at four in the morning or midnight."

"And doing both on the same day doesn't work so well." Galen offered, a bit amused.

She glared at him, holding it for the moment before she shook her head. "I am no fun when I've not had enough sleep." Then she straightened her shoulders. "So if we do this thing, if you're willing. What do I need to know?"

Galen considered. "You need to look right. I don't know how to do that. I know Laura can figure it out. You need to sound right, which you mostly do. Was that Dunwich?"

Lydia grimaced. "It was. We had elocution lessons, if we needed them, which I did. Too much of the twistier parts of London otherwise."

Galen considered. "You won't sound posh, like I do. Unless you can do that reliably, don't try. I think we should be able to fit you out as the daughter of someone who's made good money in some sort of business. Looking to marry into the landed gentry."

"Fit me out?" Her eyes went wide. "I didn't think..."

"You'll need frocks. Some number of frocks. More than

one. I don't know the details. That is why we will ask people who do." Galen shrugged.

"I can't," Her voice caught. "I can't afford that."

"My funds don't run to a racehorse. But they do run to some frocks. Or we might remake a few from the attics or something. I have attics."

Lydia leaned to look at him more closely. Galen stayed where he was. If she were asking for his help, she would get it. "There are some things here, I gather. Also in attics."

"I do not care which attics they come from, or where else, so long as they say the right things. Clothing speaks essays, at least. Sometimes novels. You want to come across as a little curious, out in the world at such things for the first time. Not an ingenue." Galen considered her. "How are you at keeping up a backstory?"

"That, I'm expert in. Newspapers, remember? I don't enjoy lying if I can avoid it. But shading the truth is fine, and a fictional father of some new money sort of background, well, I can do that."

"Martin and I have a system. Easier in this case, since I'm being myself, with the usual modifications to avoid trouble with the Pact." The oaths they'd all sworn to keep knowledge of magic away from those without it did require a certain amount of management. "Hats. I'm fairly sure you need modish hats."

Lydia laughs. "This might also be a case for gloves. I'm not sure."

Galen nods. "I can run something for a budget. Let me check this evening, and consult a bit. How quickly do we need to put this all together?"

"Don't spend your money yet. I haven't got approval. Though I might get some expenses out of Morris. The editor." She added the clarification quickly, though Galen knew perfectly well who he was, he'd heard Martin rant often enough.

"And that's what, Thursday?" Galen asked, considering.

"Mmm hmm. By then I should have a list of people I'd like to try to meet, if I can. Be around."

"That will be the complicated part, I suspect. Figuring out how to get introduced into the proper circles once we know which the proper circles are. Do you have any ideas for that?"

"Not yet. That's where the research comes in." Lydia let out a frustrated puff of breath. "If I were the sort of woman who had gone to finishing school in the Swiss Alps, it would be easy. Then I could just make noises about that. No one ever checks. So many girls are just there for a year or two, so you can be quite close in age and not overlap."

"And you know all this why?" Galen asked, suddenly amused.

"I might have investigated it as an option a couple of years ago. Different investigation, naturally. Something about cosmetics."

"Right. So you have some idea how things go. You find out the names, I'll talk to my mentor, see if he has any connections he knows about we can borrow." Galen considered his options. Alastair was going to want chapter and verse on his plans. He'd need to think about that tonight. They had their regular meeting on Wednesday.

Lydia must have seen something change in his expression. "Is he going to be angry with you?"

Galen shook his head. "Not angry, no. He's used to Martin and our exploits? Not that we've had many the past year, but he's heard the older stories. I just need to figure out how to explain what you're looking for clearly. He likes me to have a plan, and to move forward with it. I can convince him this is good practice for other things. And it's our quiet season."

"All right." Lydia sounded only modestly convinced. "Do we meet up Thursday if I get permission and backing?"

"Thursday evening." Galen agreed quickly. "I can take you to supper, if you want. Or we can do things here."

They left it at that, and at that point Lydia excused herself to go prepare for her research tomorrow.

CHAPTER 5
THURSDAY AFTERNOON, IN THE DWELLERS' ATTIC

"So, tell me the details again." They were up in an attic of the Dweller's club, and Lydia had her arms full of a billowing pile of fabric. Thomasina perched on a desk, her feet hanging off the edge. Alicia Morgan was rummaging through racks of clothes, and then fell upon a wardrobe behind one rack with a glad cry. It was like something out of a fairy tale, the poor relation getting to go to the ball.

Alicia had hair as improbably blonde as Galen did, but pulled hers sharply back. Long, still, which suggested she was actively engaged in magical work. But she used some sort of potion in it that left it sleek and shining, making Lydia very aware of all her stray wisps.

Which, honestly, was a bit how Lydia felt at the moment. She had got permission for the story, and for three months research pay to investigate, with the possibility of an extension if she uncovered enough of use. Either for her or for another reporter, which was always the trick. That wouldn't make her name, even if it might pay her bills.

Ev had turned up a large stack of references in the end.

33

Lydia also had permission to make use of her time for a bit of each week for ongoing research. At the moment, Lydia had a lot of vague ideas, and no certainty about any of it. She just could feel the pull that meant there was a story, the thing she never talked about, because either people believed her or they thought it was ridiculous. Among the posh sorts, they didn't trust it, because they couldn't use it or demand it on their behalf. She always thought it must be something like dowsing, really, but since it didn't turn up a well it wasn't solid enough for other people to take seriously.

And now she was up here in the attic, not with Laura, like she'd expected, but with Alicia, who was the undisputed queen of clothing for the Dwellers. Alicia wasn't known for being particularly fashionable, mind. She was, rather, known for her ability to dress someone perfectly for their need.

Lydia supposed that was the sort of thing they needed. She'd heard a few stories from Martin over the years about getting someone into this labour meeting or that strike, or this event or another. Often more than one. She suspected they usually had several people in on a project, depending on what it was and who was available.

It did mean they had a very well-stocked attic. Alicia was ticking through dresses. "Waist is wrong, waist is wrong, waist is... almost right. The hem's too long, but could be brought up. Hold this." Alicia thrust something made of pink and fringe into Lydia's arms. "And this is far too large, but we might remake it usefully." That one was a tightly woven velvet that felt glorious against Lydia's arm. "This one might do if you get invited to a party. No stoles or shoes or smart coats?"

Lydia blinked at the question. "None of those? Sensible

34

shoes. Wool coat that's five years old."

"Well. You're fun to dress, at least." Alicia's head popped up, considering her, then she smiled, making the comment more clearly a compliment. Or at least, not a problem.

Ten minutes later, the pile of things in Lydia's arm was over her head, and she couldn't see at all. Finally, Alicia finished. "Here, give me some of that. And come downstairs." Enough of the clothes were tugged out of her arms that Lydia could see again. Once she could move, they trooped back downstairs to the second-floor bedroom that had been set up for sewing.

A middle-aged woman with her hair up in a bun on the top of her head and glasses was settled at the sewing machine. She wore a plain dark dress, but one that was very well fit for her. Alicia waved a hand. "Anne-Marie, Lydia. Lydia, Anne-Marie. She's our seamstress, so once we get you trying these things on, and the dressmaker's dummy set to your measurements, she'll do alterations. You want to go to multiple race days, yes?"

"Probably at least three. Maybe more."

"We'll set you up for three race days, an evening party, and a day frock or two to start. In case anyone asks you to tea or something." Alicia glanced over her shoulder. "Non-magical fashion. Hidden charms are fine, nothing that would give it away."

"Oh, it is a challenge, then." As Lydia had half-suspected, the woman was French. Her accent was still fairly strong, but pleasant. "How do you wish to look?"

Lydia was about to answer when Alicia spoke first. "Galen's escorting her. They won't know his background or hers. Lydia's the daughter of some well-off but little known captain of industry. Some piece of equipment or another.

That's your job, Lydia, to work out the background. Douglas, he's in every afternoon from four to six. He can help you make sure you've caught everything."

When Lydia opened her mouth to say that she knew how to do that, Alicia looked up from where she was peering at dresses, to say, "You'll miss something. Everyone does. If you're getting our help, you get all our help."

Lydia subsided, watching Alicia hand several pieces to Thomasina for her to hang up on a rack in the corner, in some sort of meaningful order. "I didn't expect...."

"You'd never have asked if you expected. And we'd probably have told you no. We don't like people assuming. But you asked for something small, and when Galen told us more about the plan, well. It's interesting. It might lead to something more. Martin's vouched for you as clever and competent, which he doesn't say about just everyone. And frankly, Galen's getting out of practice. He should shake up his skills a bit."

Lydia thought through the implications of that. "Are you, are the Dwellers, as an organisation, just a mechanism for chaos, then?"

Both Alicia's and Thomasina's heads came up simultaneously, followed by bursts of laughter. From Anne-Marie, too. Alicia grinned. "More or less. But aimed at, mmm. The people in power who misuse what they have. There are times money is a lever. Galen's been learning that, and we respect the need for the Lords and Ladies of the Land, or that the Guard has a hierarchy, or the courts. We might argue till the cows come home and dusk turns to dawn about the specifics. But we think people should be in there and arguing to improve things. And we don't have much patience at all with selfish consumption that hurts other people."

"What does that mean about the racing?"

"Horse racing's an odd sport, isn't it? All that time and energy going into racing. Steeplechasing's better than flat, I've always thought. The horses are older. But when there are injuries, it's usually much worse for both the horses and the jockey." She shrugged. "We lost so many horses to the War, everyone's still rebuilding. It keeps many people employed, though, racing. It's skilled work that doesn't require a formal education. Oh, there's maths in some of it, but it, well. A man can make a good living at it. As a trainer or head lad, or working at a stud. The occasional woman, too."

Lydia thought through the implications of that. "And there aren't as many jobs like that as there could be."

"No. And it's a good job for some veterans. Need to be steady enough on your feet, but a horse is good for a man. And woman."

Lydia handed off the last thing she was holding, a dress of rather lovely dusty pink silk. Utterly unlike anything she'd ever worn, actually. It had the quality of rose quartz, not the rather simpering pinks she usually saw made up into dresses. "If this story doesn't pan out, maybe I can do something with that. Jobs for veterans."

"If you don't need it, might be something Martin could do a good job with." Thomasina turned around. "These last? Got them." There was a hint there that Lydia was now entrenched in a net of favours. She had asked Galen for a favour. Passing along the idea to Martin would repay a sliver of the debt. She was in over her head, and she knew it. Maybe Galen would explain it, or Martin.

Instead, she nodded. "I'm supposed to catch him for lunch next week. What do I do now?"

"Now, you go behind that screen and strip. Or don't go

behind the screen, if you don't care. What are you wearing under that?"

"A Symington Side Lacer, a slip, and..." Other underthings. It was her best set. The brassiere had been a splurge after her last big story, and she'd never regretted the freedom of movement it gave her.

"Oh, good. That would have been annoying to dig up. The side lacer's just what you want under these. We may need a different slip. Go on, then."

Lydia ducked behind the screen to undo and wriggle out of her blouse and skirt, then smooth out the layers of underthings. She hung her clothes up out of the way and let out a breath, before coming out, feeling the garters holding up her stockings more than usual.

"Mmm, you've got a splendid figure for this. The last person I had to dress like this was gloriously buxom."

"Why was that a problem?" Lydia blinked.

"Well, not a problem when it comes to my admiration. But it's much harder to alter the bust line than other parts. A hem depends on the fabric. Raising or lowering a waistline, same thing. The bodice, that's a whole remaking of the dress, and if you don't have extra fabric, it'll be a problem. Even if you do, depending on the wear." Alicia held out a rather dull-coloured navy dress. "Try this first. I know it's boring, but it will give us a sense of the way things look on you."

Lydia obligingly tried it on, then swivelled her hips side to side to get the fabric to settle into place. Thomasina came up behind her to do up the dress.

"That's not a terrible fit. Probably less showy than you need, but with the right jewellery. Do you have any?"

"Jewellery? No. Not even paste. Just a locket or two."

Alicia nodded. "No maid, obviously. Do you have

anyone who can help do your hair or your cosmetic charms? They'll need a light touch and a good eye. And I suppose you don't want to crop your hair."

Lydia put her hand up to her hair. "No. Please. If I can avoid it."

"Good to know where the lines are. Right. We'll need to sort that out. One of the staff here can help, but I want to consult. You'll need some cosmetics, and probably a hand with the hair, to get it properly smooth. A woman of property, or at least a sizeable marriage portion, she looks sleek and polished. Like she has nothing else to do."

"Um. Yes." Lydia frowned. She had known that other women had this entire routine that she'd never had either time or desire for. But now she was going to need to learn.

"I'll need time to do your eyebrows. That. Let's see. Can you get free all Friday afternoon? We should see about your hair. Not cutting the length off, but tidying everything up, doing a treatment to make it shine, trying some hairstyles to see what works best. Your eyebrows. A few other things. Your ears are pierced?"

Lydia's hand went up to her ears. "They are. I didn't put them in this morning." She swallowed. If she were going to do this thing, she'd do it right. "Friday afternoon. Tell me what to bring, and I'll be here."

That got Alicia turning around, with a tape measure in her hand, and a fiendish grin. "Oh, we're going to have a grand time getting you ready, I'm certain. Right. Frock off, I want some measurements, and then we'll have you try everything on."

Lydia closed her eyes, took a breath, and nodded, as Thomasina undid the back of the dress. "I put myself in your hands."

CHAPTER 6

FRIDAY, AT TEA TIME, MARTIN AND LAURA'S FLAT

"What have I got myself into?" Galen buried his face in his hands.

Martin was facing him, perched on a large travelling trunk they used as a table in the room he and Laura kept for writing. It was one of his favourite spots, with his legs tucked up. "You're the one who agreed."

"Don't remind me." Galen ran his hand through his hair. "It's not like I didn't think about it. But now we're about to do things. How do you do all your reporting? All I can see is all the things that could go wrong or be awful."

Martin tilted his head, the patient look Galen had come to face with a mix of anticipation and mild dread. It was the one Martin got when he was missing something. Galen was clever enough, they both knew that, but he wasn't quick like Martin was at his best.

"This is just like what we've done, you introducing me around, being charming. You're very good at being charming. And this time, you just have to let that happen. You're new to the whole racing scene, curious and interested.

Lydia will do all the actual work here. Which is the point, seeing as it's her job, not yours."

Galen sighed and straightened, letting his head bump against the back of the sofa. "Not non-magical folk. What if I say something wrong?"

Martin flicked his fingers. "First, don't borrow trouble. Second, you've done that before too, a few times. With the labour organising. That went fine. You know how to pay attention to the Silence pressing on you, and how to change the subject."

"That wasn't people standing around with drinks talking about their hobbies." Galen pointed out. Though, to be fair to Martin, he had a sense of when he needed to be talking about something else.

"Galen, your hobbies involve riding, enjoying your local landscape, and reading." Martin was amused now, clearly. "All right, so don't talk about the Dwellers. Don't talk about alchemy. Find half a dozen books that come from their side of things that you're willing to talk about. You'll be fine. Besides, it's a race meeting. Chances anyone will want to have a historical debate or deep literary analysis are on the slim side. They'll likely have a horse running, or be interested in the racing. People will go on about pedigree or racing handicaps for hours."

Galen snorted, but Martin had a point. "Lydia's counting on me." Which was the crux of it.

"What do you think about Lydia, then? What do you think she's counting on?" Martin settled back a bit, his hands now in his lap.

"I don't know her that well? She's been pleasant at parties. She hasn't reported horrible things about my family, unlike some people. But she doesn't talk much about herself."

41

Martin shook his head. "She doesn't. I don't know that much more, and we've talked for hours on and off. She works hard, and you appreciate that sort of thing. More these days, even." Galen had gone from being a cosseted and bored younger son, not allowed to do anything meaningful, to taking over the family business in, near enough, a matter of weeks. Between that and his parents' attempt to frame Martin, it had shattered everything he'd relied on. Rebuilding had, frankly, been exhausting, but it meant he knew how to work hard. And maybe make his own choices.

"All right. I won't expect personal details. And besides, she's the one who's got to make up a story for this, a whatchamacallit, a persona."

"Excellent for reporting, and she's good at it. There are stories. Gossip. Besides that apprenticeship one, where she got herself bound in an unfair contract." Martin clearly approved of something in there.

"I heard about that around the edges, but not the details." Galen flicked his finger, wanting something to do with his hands. "Tell me more about it?"

"Nearly two years ago now, she got the bit in her teeth, to use the equestrian metaphor. She was sure people were making unfair apprentice contracts. She'd heard a few rumours, I guess, pieces here and there." Martin waved a hand. "That's when I got interested in what she was doing, suggested the Dwellers might have some useful information."

Galen frowned at that. "I don't remember that. What was going on?"

"Not your line of things, and your mother was being difficult. And it was apprentice masters setting conditions in the contract that couldn't be met, or that wouldn't be met. Now, it's an oath, both directions, you'd think it would bite them as much as it would the apprentice. But some people apparently didn't worry about that."

Galen thought through that. "What kind of apprenticeship?"

"She got the idea from a talisman maker a few years before? Something that came out in another bit of reporting, I can't remember what. I was busy, you know how it is. She started paying attention, and she's got an entire network of contacts in Club Row. At least two people at Bourne's, and someone at Wishton's."

"Anyone at the Den?" The Fox House club, where Galen spent more of his time these days than he'd used to. He didn't feel like he belonged, and he probably never would. They all seemed more mature and adult and certain about their place in the world than he could imagine. But now he could go round with Alastair and meet other people in business, and make the right pleasant social noises.

"Not that I know of. If you know someone who might, that'd be a kindness. A lot of key conversations happen there." Martin looked at him more closely. "If that doesn't press too hard."

"You know my loyalty is to the Dwellers." The rest of the world, well. There were often-stuffy men and women, focused on proper marriages and making the right show while they divided up the world. And then there were those with a ruthlessly radical desire to transform it and give many more people opportunities. He knew which one he'd pick.

"Which is why we like you." Martin grinned, suddenly, then he cocked his head. "Are you getting pressure on that front? Familial?"

It seemed like the idea had popped out of nowhere, and Galen sighed. "Mother, still going on about it when I visit, of course. And Aunt Sylvia has been writing from France, making it clear she'll be taking me in hand to find a proper marriage when they get back. Whenever that might be."

His aunt and uncle had decamped for the Continent in the trial's aftermath. They kept threatening to come back, and not doing so. Galen had some sympathy for Aunt Sylvia. It wasn't her fault her brother - Galen's father - had done awful things. She'd found a garden in the south of France that was making use of her skills with plants and alchemy. Uncle Attis was lecturing at the region's Healer's College, or whatever they called it in France. Something about ongoing education, at any rate.

"So not anything new." Martin said. "Is squiring Lydia around going to make things difficult for you?"

Galen contemplated that one. To be fair, he should have given it a lot more thought when she'd asked, and he hadn't. Now, of course, backing out would be horribly messy and undermine her plans entirely. His discomfort was his own problem. "I don't know how to handle it in general. And we could run into people who know me, or know of me, at least."

"You are quite an eligible bachelor." Martin teased, his voice light, before he caught something in Galen's expression.

Galen spread his hands. "We are young. We didn't go to the War. We weren't killed or injured in it." Unlike Julius. Though Julius and Blythe really were doing well these days, and Galen wished them all the happiness they could hold. "There are plenty of young women of the Great Families who'd consider me."

Martin flicked his fingers. "And you're not interested." They hadn't talked about this for ages. Not directly, anyway. And now Martin was comfortably settled in with

Laura, here in a flat that suited them to the bones. It felt comfortable, lived in, cushioned against the ebb and flow of life.

"I don't exactly know how to put it." Galen shrugged. "Where is Laura, anyway?"

"Gone for a fortnight. She had a bit of work come up, someone who's just come back from a sanitarium. You know how she feels about that." Laura had spent a decade in and out of them, interspersed with seaside hotels, good for the lungs. Her work these days was with people who had been seriously ill, figuring out what they needed now. She was still new to it, coming up on ten months now, but she was in some demand.

Galen frowned. "Is it hard to have her gone?" He was feeling for something, and he didn't know how to name it.

"Very." Martin let out a long sigh, and then rolled off the trunk to sprawl on the other sofa, melodramatically. "I keep wanting to tell her things, and she's not here. And I have to do all my own cooking again."

"You are a decent cook, though. Much better than I am."

"Had to be. But she makes a much better poached egg than I do. And her toast never burns. I'm not sure why."

Galen leaned forward. "You have it bad, you realise."

"I have it very good, thank you. Excellently, in fact. And I still want the same for you. Which - should I be wanting?"

There was a long silence as Galen tried to figure out what to say. What he wanted was what he had with Martin. Friendship and certainty and comfort and not feeling he was doing things wrong. Someone who was all of that but also challenged him, prodded him into action. And someone who wanted the romance and other sorts of intimacy Martin didn't want with him.

Martin didn't rush him. Martin rushed him only when

it was necessary. The other times, he was quite patient. In the end, Galen shrugged. "I barely know who I am. How can I be a decent whatever, if I don't know that?"

"You've been a good friend all along. The best. What's different about this?"

Galen snorted, waving a hand, feeling like he was batting away flies. "Everything. I've known you since we were thirteen. That's different. We were both unshaped mud then, relatively speaking."

"I'll have you know I came into school with many ideas that shape me today." Martin puffed his chest up, which looked ridiculous since he was still stretched out on the sofa. Then he collapsed into rolling laughter. "Fair, fair."

Galen grinned, then he added, more quietly. "And the sort of women who are interested. They have ideas and goals, and they all involve the kind of plotting I'm not very good at, or people I don't know, and often all about money and status, and not the things I care about."

Martin turned his head with the distant expression he got when he was chasing a thought. Galen let him chase and stood up. "Can I get another drink?"

"Please. And one for me." By the time Galen came back, Martin was sitting up, looking pensive. "How much do they chase you? How do they chase you?"

Galen handed over the bottle. "It doesn't feel honest, is the problem. I'm not sure what I'd decide, about a woman who came up to me, and said, more or less, you have money, I have ideas, let's combine them. But it seems like all of them just see the land and the theoretical assets. If I can't make a go of the business side of it, what happens to her, then?"

Martin's eyes widened, and Galen went on. "And you know me, you know the Dwellers. I'd not be happy with someone who just cared about parties and frocks. Laura was right when she told me it wouldn't work between us. I need someone who..." He waved a hand. "You and I are well-yoked. I need someone who fills in the chinks in my wall, not shares them."

Martin nodded. "So. No one on the horizon, no one you can see fitting there, but you're not opposed to the idea. Just don't see any prospects."

"Do you?" Galen spread his hands, palms up.

Martin shrugged. "I have not, in fact, seen you with every woman in Albion. I will apply my investigative skills to some ideas, maybe." Galen blinked and must have looked alarmed. "And tell you my ideas, of course. Now, tell me what you've learned about horse racing. You can get some practice talking through it."

CHAPTER 7

"A pleasure to meet you, Mrs Wolling. And Mr Wolling." Galen was being charming at everyone. That was in fact what she'd asked him to do, but it was disconcerting to see him so in the midst of it. He'd been quiet on the journey. They'd taken a portal to where they could pick up the proper train line, and he'd said less and less as they moved away from Trellech.

Galen had somehow got them an invitation to join a group of magical folk, making up half the box. Lydia expected there would be sixteen in total, maybe twenty or twenty-four. There would be a fair bit of mingling with others through the course of the day. She wasn't quite sure how he'd done it, but she thought it might be some connection through his mysterious mentor. Galen had been close-mouthed about it, as if something in the process made him uncomfortable.

Now, though, he was all smiles and making all the right noises. The Wollings were greeting him, generously and cheerfully, as the Harringtons had before. Someone had pressed a glass into his hand, and offered her one as well.

48

For her part, Lydia was decidedly uncomfortable. Her frock was of much finer fabric than she was used to. Worse, her stockings were of fine silk, which meant every time she took a step, there was a slight whispering. She'd spent the entire train ride terrified she'd move wrong and tear something, despite knowing perfectly well that silk was quite strong.

She was wearing a stylishly remade deep green cloak that brought out her eyes, so Alicia had said. It had the proper charms on it to keep her comfortably warm. Even so, the air had a chill to it and an indefinable dampness that she wasn't used to. She'd kept her hand tucked into Galen's arm, smiling and dimpling and hoping her hair wouldn't come down in a tangled mess.

There was a great deal to keep track of. How to walk, how to hold herself, whether she was appropriately attentive to Galen's conversation. And she wanted to see what she could pick up. Using the proper forms of address. By the usual rules, in these settings, everyone was Mr and Mrs, or Miss for the unmarried women, as Lydia was.

Mister Wolling was in business, providing material to the Colonial Service. Some of it had to do with flasks and containers, sturdier thanks to magic that wasn't at all obvious. Some of it was proper magical supplies, she'd gathered from the brochures Ev had dug up. Tins of powders, made up rather like watercolour paint boxes, so you could flake a little off for your particular need.

Now Galen was being introduced to a Mrs Fulton, and then her husband. "May I present Miss Lydia Pyle?" Galen said. "We're so looking forward to a pleasant day out." Lydia smiled and beamed.

"Are you of the Northumberland Pyles?"

"No, Mrs Fulton." Lydia kept her voice even. "From

Lancashire. My father came up with one of those clever devices, for the new house fixtures, making things safer. I don't understand the details, of course, but they're terribly popular." Hopefully that would be read as a young woman of property and means, or at least a solid dowry.

"Ah." Mrs Fulton turned away from her. "And you, young man?"

Galen made a slight bow. "Our primary home is in Cumbria, Amberley Hall. My parents," He hesitated. This was a tricky part, and Lydia suddenly realised with a gripping fear that they hadn't discussed what made sense in this context. "My parents have retired to one of the smaller estates, and I'm tending to the family business. It's kept me quite occupied, but I admit..." He gestured agreeably. "I find the idea of a day at the races quite tempting. And perhaps sometime I'll own a horse or two myself for racing."

"You ride?" Mrs Fulton looked him up and down.

"Reasonably well in the ordinary way of things. I'd not want to risk racing, even as an amateur."

She snorted. "You've not the build for it." Galen wasn't particularly heavily built, but he didn't have the lankiness that Lydia saw on some of the steeplechase jockeys. And he was taller than they were.

Galen didn't argue, just smiled. Mrs Fulton gestured. "It's pleasant to have some young people here. My own children won't come except but once or twice a year. You might find us very boring."

Galen shook his head. "Oh, I'm sure you'd never be boring, Mrs Fulton. And there's so much to see and learn about."

She tilted her head, as if sure he were pulling her leg, but Galen looked back at her with an open pleasure at the day that wasn't at all feigned. "Well." The older woman considered. "Let me introduce you around. The other half of the box are people my husband knows, doing brickworks and some such. If they get terribly boring, do feel free to come seek me out."

As more and more people arrived, Lydia filed away name after name. She had to trust to her memory here, she couldn't afford to write things down. Galen, bless him, began making a point of collecting cards, as he could. He made it sound so easy, "I'm learning the family business, all sorts of raw materials, and my mentor, do you know Alastair Longton?"

Once he said the name, it triggered a cascade of connections. Five minutes later, somehow Galen was being cheerfully feted around the place. He was introduced to everyone with that edge of delighted camaraderie that suggested some of them had begun their drinking early in the day. It was friendly, though, which was the key part.

The luncheon went smoothly, too. Lydia made a point of deferring to the senior women at their table. That stood her in good stead, allowing her to see what they did to eat their food. There were so many little details, and she was sure she was doing something indefinably wrong. Galen kept up an amiable conversation.

It wasn't until they were moving to the last course, a board of mysterious cheeses, half of which she couldn't identify properly, that Galen got the topic close to what she'd hoped. One man, further down the table, made that muffled noise, of someone who has gossip and might be encouraged to share it.

Galen had a native talent for this. Part of her wanted to just watch him, lean in and see how he did it. How he let his charm carry the conversation, without rushing or fidgeting with it. He let it be, through the end of the meal, through the first two races.

She stuck close to him, making agreeable conversation about frocks and the weather and nodding and smiling about London theatrical events she'd never see. Then people wandered. One couple had a horse in the fourth race and went down to see him saddled up. At least half the others went with them.

Lydia found herself out on the balcony with the man, a Mr Thornley, when Galen said, "You know the Alders, then?" Mr Thornley wasn't magic, Lydia had figured that much out. He hadn't seemed to fit in, though, and sometimes those people knew the most about who else to talk to.

It was easy to fill in the details. Well-off family, or so it had been thought. They'd been up to their necks in that plot, pioneered by Lord Sisley, who had headed an empire-building snake cult, or near enough.

All the papers had settled on snake cult, anyway. It was short, pithy, and easy to fit into a banner. And it wasn't exactly inaccurate, for all those with the luxury of more characters might prefer something else. 'A private society focused on mutual benefit, with trappings of the Mesopotamian sirrush and expansive metaphysical implications'. Or so someone had called it, in an earnest letter to the editor when the Moon had not used enough words to satisfy him while explaining things.

The court cases had clarified that the former Lord Sisley had been in charge of the snake cult, so far as it went, but Lydia had her doubts about some of that. She'd had her suspicions about his actual research skills. Certainly, he'd shown no particular interest in Mesopotamia as a younger man, and cuneiform wasn't the sort of thing you picked up in a weekend. Or even a year or two.

Mr Thornley nodded, glancing at Lydia. "And the lady?" He had a posh sort of voice, that slight drawl, the disappearing R.

Lydia did her best to look pleasant and perhaps slightly dim. Galen said, amiably and lightly, "She didn't know them, not her family's sort of people. Her father's a self-made man."

"And you've got a house falling to bits." There was a snort. "I know Horace Alder. He's not a bad sort. Ambitious, though. Ambitious to a fault."

Galen glanced away, out to the racecourse. "What did he do in the War, do you know?"

That got a hollow laugh. "What the ambitious sorts with a sense of self-preservation did. He got himself assigned well behind the lines. Nice snug room in safe barracks. Did you serve?"

Galen had clearly expected this question, because he shook his head, turning to face Thornley with proper deference. "I was seventeen and a half when the War ended. My older brother served. Came home with a horrible injury, his face. But he came home."

Thornley grimaced. "Infantry, then?"

Galen paused for just a moment before he confided. "He was posted to Paris. He caught someone spying, and he got himself sent off to fix what she'd done."

Thornley gave a sharp whistle, which made a few heads below them in the stands turn. Fortunately, it wasn't that unusual a sound at the races. Something in the answer softened him, though. "I don't know the Alders all that well, but we had the next manor nearest them. You know how

53

you know the people in the area. All the social mess, dances and brunches."

Lydia knew that had not been part of Galen's youth, but he nodded, agreeably. "So you saw him in a crowd with other people."

"Just so. And they were generous enough, I suppose, if standoffish. Rarely hosted any of our set. I rode out with him, sometimes, when we were both back from school in the summer hols and bored out of our minds. We'd meet up at the boundary nearest us - a good three miles for me - and spend the day out. He went to some school I'd never heard of. Though he'd never heard of mine, so I suppose we were even up. His seemed to have less fagging."

Lydia knew the term, at least, it kept coming up when she'd helped with various other projects. Seeing to an older boy's kit, personal items, and sometimes more personal services or abuse. All right, probably often.

Galen laughed. "No, that's not a thing. I went to the same school. You know how it is, a place gets its own traditions. A bit like some of the choir schools, you don't want to mess around with what someone's good at."

Thornley peered at Galen, but apparently decided he was mostly harmless. "Anyway, I went off to university, got sent down my second year. I was no earthly good at either essays or exams, it turns out. Then the War. When we got demobbed, I ran into Horace again, in London of all places, and he dragged me along to a club. Fantastic music, and even this sort of illusionist, all sorts of sounds from all over the room? He introduced me round to some of his friends."

This was where it got delicate. Galen nodded along with the story. "Anyone you saw again?"

Thornley hesitated. "Someone Horace had been at school at. He gave me a queer turn, I have to say. There was something, I don't know. Not quite all there. You ever been to the zoo, the reptile house? In London?"

Galen was silent a fraction too long, and Lydia murmured, "I've been, several times. The snakes, they scare me a bit."

She was worried she was laying it on too strong, but Thornley nodded. "Lying there, all still and quiet, it's not like you can even see they're breathing half the time, right? And then they strike at something. He was like that, the friend."

CHAPTER 8

ON THE BALCONY, LOOKING OUT AT THE RACECOURSE

"You happen to remember a name? So I can keep well away." Galen made it sound like a minor personal failing.

"I suppose if you went to the same school, you might turn up in the same places." Thornley shrugged amiably enough. Galen hadn't been sure how well that would go over, and it wasn't as if he could stop and check in with Lydia. "Man named, what was it? Lind. Nico Lind. He always used Nico, not Nicholas. It made him sound foreign."

Galen had the sudden suspicion that Nico was short for something. Nicodemus, perhaps. He thought he'd heard someone mention a Nicomedes at one point, too. "About how old? My brother's seven years older. Maybe they overlapped."

Thornley shrugged, amiably. "I'm forty. He might have been a little younger, but not by much."

"That gives me an idea." Galen gestured. "What sort of business do you do, then? The family estates, or something else?"

"Oh, factories. Mills, mostly, weaving. Ordinary stuff, nothing fancy, but it sells well." There was a superficiality to the comment and Galen felt suspicion turn to rising anger. He'd talked enough to people from the factories to know how awful they could be to work in. That tone, he'd heard it often enough from the owners, speaking to the radio or papers. Galen knew many injuries happened because owners didn't care about safety precautions, or pushed workers too far. He also knew, from long practice with the Dwellers, that he couldn't let it show. Not now.

Now was for collecting the information, gathering up those scrap threads, and bringing information back to his friends to do something with. The coal miner's strike in May had set things shaking, and Galen hoped it would improve things in other industries. On his better days, at least. On the worse ones, he despaired of progress that did any real lasting good.

He realised that he'd been quiet a hair too long. Thornley was looking at him oddly. "It's the estates for me. We make some quite good cheese, actually, and various other things for grocers." Some of it even filtered out to the non-magical shops, as an exclusive line. That had been one of Alastair's suggestions, and it was doing well already, even just a year in.

"Ah." Clearly agricultural sales weren't of much interest to him. "You let me know if you want to expand. We might have use for wool, if you run to sheep."

"All of our current wool, such as it is, is committed else-where right now. But do you have a card on you? In case I think of something or hear from someone looking to sell? We were talking about some expansion, too." Galen had got much better at that sort of thing, with Alastair's coaching.

Thornley rummaged in his jacket pocket and handed

over a card. "Here we are." Right about then, someone called out Thornley's name, and he nodded. "Pardon."

Galen lingered on the balcony for a moment. "How do you feel about that, then?" he asked Lydia.

She leaned in to keep her voice low, he assumed. "You're quite good at this. I feel like I'm not doing my share."

"That just means you can listen more easily. I can't listen and keep track of things all at the same time. Do you need to write anything down?"

"I'll excuse myself to the powder room when we go back in. Useful place, a powder room. Do you think you could get some of that crowd talking?" It was a mixed group in their thirties and forties, at a guess. A knot of three couples, anyway, either married or long involved.

"Why them?" Galen considered his options.

Lydia smiled as she pulled back. He recognised that look. It was the same way Martin looked when he was finding his feet in a story. "The way they talked over luncheon. I think the woman in blue could be magical, but I'm not actually sure about her husband? Or her - I think that's a sister." They looked a fair bit alike, and they had the same sort of voice. "It wasn't just the accent, it was the words they used, the phrases they emphasised."

Galen nodded. "You excuse yourself, and I'll see if I can be talking to them by the time you get back." He considered what he'd heard from them at lunch. He'd got the impression they were relatively new race horse owners. That would likely be a way in.

Lydia leaned over and unexpectedly kissed his cheek, before she said more loudly. "Back in a moment, Galen, darling." All cheer and brightness. Then she went blithely off through the box, toward the door, asking something of the man by the door, one of the race course staff. Presumably, where the powder room was. Galen took his time, giving one last glance to the crowds outside, before he wandered back in.

Almost immediately, he was taken up by the group next to the one he was aiming for. "You were out talking quite a while." There was a note of prurient interest there, nosiness.

"We were trying to figure out if we have friends in common. You know how it is." Galen kept his voice even.

"Oh, goodness, who?"

"Someone my brother knew better. He had a severe injury in the War, doesn't get out much now." Galen kept his voice light. "Horace Alder."

There were murmurs. No one recognised the name, or at least admitted to it. Someone asked, "Related to why you're here?"

Galen shook his head. "Not particularly. I came because I'm curious about the racing. And maybe, as I said, buying into a share of a horse down the road, when more's settled on the estate. But my brother wondered, and so of course I said I'd ask around."

"Older brother, then?" That was Mrs Fulton, now.

"Seven years." Galen agreed. "I didn't particularly know his friends, of course. And Alder's older than that. No reason we'd have overlapped much."

That got some general agreement, and Galen was fine to play at still being quite young. He still felt it, honestly, the way he'd been too young for the war, forever on the wrong side of a dividing line between men and boys. Arguably, also on the right side, because he couldn't imagine he'd have been much good at war. But that was decidedly not the sort of thing anyone ever said out loud. It wasn't even the sort of thing he said to Martin, not more than very occasionally.

That brought the conversation around to siblings, and cousins, and a whole mess of family connections Galen didn't know and didn't particularly extend himself to keep track of. Just as he was trying to figure out how to sidle over to the other group, one man leaned over from there. "Didn't you say you were interested in buying into a horse in the future?"

"Yes?" Galen cleared his throat. "Yes."

"It's grand fun." That was one of the women, not too much older than Galen. "Do grab a drink. Felicity had a glorious idea."

Galen strongly suspected someone was now going to try and sell him a portion of a horse.

He gathered up a drink, and wandered over, continuing to look amiable and interested. As soon as he was among them, the woman who'd invited him over beamed. "I'm Prudence. This is Felicity, my sister. Our husbands, Paul and Vincent, aren't they just charming?" The men nodded, agreeable but not nearly so effusive. "And this is Merribelle and her husband, Adam."

Right about this point, Lydia came back, and Galen murmured. "I'm Galen, of course, and this is Lydia." He'd more or less caught their last names in the original introductions, and he wondered if bribing the list out of the steward was an option. Lydia might know.

"Yes, now, you were thinking about a horse, and I know you said you weren't thinking about it yet, darling, but it turns out that someone we know is just looking for other people to buy a share. Cracking good racer, so far." Prudence went on cheerfully.

Galen blinked. He let his startlement show. "I - I'd have

to learn a lot more about it. And I'm afraid most of my funds are tied up at the moment, and will be for a bit."

"No elderly rich relatives inclined to leave you anything you could borrow against?" That was Felicity. She really had extraordinarily sharp cosmetics on. From a distance, they'd simply looked dramatic, but up close, the eyebrows were precise enough to cut. Her lips had that, what was it the other papers called it? Clara Bow lips, cupid's bow. Something bow, anyway. They were very red and decidedly exaggerated, and they looked nothing like Lydia's cosmetics.

Galen shook his head. "Still trying to pick the estates out of a bit of a slump. All the money goes back into that. Though. Well. I could ask our steward how things look next season. He's been more hopeful."

"Young man," That was Paul, and he was leaning in, though Vincent was nodding approvingly. The two men looked nothing alike, one was rather tall and angular, the other the sort of broad-shouldered man who was now getting stout in middle age, but they moved and leaned much the same way. "You must make your own place in the world. You're a grown man, you can make your decisions for yourself."

Galen made a moue, a polite face. "I'm afraid there are some legal considerations for at least another year. But, please, do tell me more? Perhaps I can persuade him it would be a suitable investment. Or at least, connect me with the right sort of people, to improve the business."

That mollified the party, at least adequately. The next ten minutes contained a lot of information, some of it quite dubious, about the process of buying a share of a racehorse. The interesting thing, of course, was that there were two layers of goals. First, you wanted a horse who would race well. Winning was best, of course, especially winning some notable race. The Grand National, for example, though there were several lesser lights, as far as Galen could determine. The prize money could be substantial.

Several jumpers were geldings, he gathered, but there were some stallions and a few mares. If either of those did well, the real gem was to move on to breeding, hoping for a foal who would exceed the father or mother or both.

The other side of the coin, though, was that it was quite expensive. It wasn't just the share in the horse, but the share in the horse's costs, all the stabling fees and training, and then the races themselves. One got a chance to enjoy all the show and flurry of seeing one's horse race, and if things went well, having a grand time in the winner's paddock afterward.

It was only as that ran down, with Galen promising he'd see what was possible, and collecting the contact information for their friend who had a share going wanting, that Vincent leaned forward. "You were talking to Thornley, earlier. A word, dear boy?" Vincent was not that much older than Galen. Less than a decade, he was sure.

Galen resented the condescension more every time it happened, but he smiled pleasantly. "Yes?" Thornley had disappeared, presumably to go down to the grandstand and watch a race or two.

"Thornley's not really our sort, you know. Not entirely his fault, gather he had a bad War and all that. But he's known to have some queer ideas, the sort of thing decent chaps avoid. Not the sort of person you want to get too close to, anyway, though he's pleasant enough to fill up the space somewhere like this."

Galen considered, then said, "I appreciate knowing that." He did. Perhaps the Dwellers would need to do something about Thornley's workers, but the man had been more helpful than strictly required. If Galen could go around him, for the moment, all the better. So he would not follow the advice, almost certainly, but he liked knowing it. "Anyone you'd suggest I might spend more time with, then?" He smiled broadly at Lydia. "The both of us, of course."

CHAPTER 9
THAT EVENING, AT THE DWELLERS' HOUSE

L ydia wasn't quite sure how they ended up at the Dweller's club. Or rather, she remembered perfectly well. As they'd agreed in advance, they'd taken the train away from the racecourse. Galen's new friends had been sorry they - or at least Galen - weren't going back toward London, but instead toward Chepstow. Galen had gleefully mentioned they were staying a bit outside of there.

It was accurate enough, for all Trellech was tucked away by magical means. The distance wasn't bad, but to keep up appearances, they had stayed on the train into Chepstow, then ducked into a shabby looking courtyard near the train station, to the portal kept there for just that purpose, the easy transfer of goods and people from Chepstow and the main train line, up to Trellech.

Somehow, Galen had got her along to the Dweller's club without her paying much attention to the trip. To be fair, her feet hurt - the borrowed shoes fit well, but not well enough, and by this point in the day her feet were raw. She was still worried about the frock catching on something, or the stockings. By the time he'd tucked her into one of the conversation rooms and ordered tea, it was all she could do to not collapse.

He settled on the chair facing her. They were comfortable chairs, fully cushioned, and she was envious again of the people who just could assume this was there for them. Galen didn't rush her, though when she opened one eye to peer at him, he asked, "Food as well? I didn't want to order for you."

She let out a long breath. "Can I go change and come back? Order, I don't know. Something sturdy? Good peasant food. Unless that's a problem."

"Not a problem for me at all. I suspect it may be steak and ale pies or cottage pie or something of the kind. Anything else to drink?"

She let out a long breath. "A beer?" It didn't go with the frock, a beer, but she was going to change out of the frock. Her own clothes were upstairs.

"A beer, indeed. No preferences?" He stretched, and Lydia could hear something in his shoulder pop.

"Whatever goes with the food." She could trust to that. "Back in a few, then."

In the end, it was more like fifteen minutes. It had taken her that long to find someone who could undo the back of her dress, and then to make sure everything was hung up properly for cleaning before someone else used it. Slipping her feet back into her Oxfords, she felt the way the leather fit her feet perfectly. She'd have to get them resoled soon. Finally she let down her hair, and quickly rebraided it into a thick column down her back.

When she got back to the conversation room, the food had arrived, laid out on a cart between the two chairs.

Galen lifted a bottle. "Cottage pie and beer to go with it. Plenty for you, and some rolls as well to fill in the gaps."

"How do you do that? Go from all the fuss and formality to this?" She settled down in the chair, letting out a sigh, before she reached over to figure out her own meal.

Galen shrugged. "Martin. As with all good things in my life. I'd never had a steak and ale pie before he took me out, when we were in our last summer before school. Or half a dozen things. Eel pie, in London."

Lydia blinked. "That's dock-worker food."

"It is. We were visiting some of his relatives. They made fun of me, but I gave it my best." Galen shrugged. "A bit like you today, really."

"I'm glad you think I held up my side. I honestly felt a bit - well. Like I wasn't doing my share."

Galen took a bite or two - he was clearly hungry as well. "They have such strong opinions about what women should do, don't they? The non-magical sorts."

Lydia grunted. "There are reasons for that."

"Tell me how you see it, would you?" Galen didn't sound flippant, but Lydia peered at him, unsure how to read his tone.

"The story goes that - well. If you have women with powerful magic, and you don't teach them to use it, it warps and bends everything around them, eventually. Unexpectedly. There's a whole theory about wild magic, and about women's magic being different, and all that. I think it's rot, of course, but there's something in the core of the idea."

"Rather, yes. Whatever you think of who has the power and why, having it come out unexpectedly doesn't end well." Galen considered. "And what do you think of the rest of it?"

"I don't have strong magic. Dunwich, I did well enough, I was supposed to do an apprenticeship in accounting and business magic, all that, but I found my way into journalism, instead. I'm glad I got some education out of it. And the rights I have. Voting, being able to hold my own property. All the things the suffragettes fought for. For so long."

"And it's still rather uneven." Galen said.

"Rather. Under their laws, I'd not have voting rights for another eighteen months, until I turn thirty. Given as I don't own property, and didn't go to university."

"There's talk about expanding it further, but what's the saying? If wishes were horses, beggars would ride?"

Lydia snorted, hearing the phrase her grandmother would use. "You seem to know a lot about it. Is that because of all this?"

"The Dwellers? Oh, yes. I can probably give you a rundown on the top twenty or thirty current social ills, the positions for and against them, and what the particular points of leverage are. Not all of them are my particular interest, of course, especially right now."

She leaned back, considering him. Galen kept eating, showing no signs he was being observed. "What are your interests when you've got the time?"

Galen shrugged. "I used to turn my hand to whatever I could. But these days, I'm interested in injuries, how to make working safer. If people have to work, they shouldn't be risking life and limb and eyesight to do it. Some of the factories are particularly awful."

"I wouldn't have expected that from you." Lydia swallowed. "Sorry. That sounded awful."

Galen waved his hand. "I am rather dressed to be the callow young man of property. Still." Though he reached up and undid his tie, then the top button or two of the shirt, incongruously splitting the difference between a working man at ease and someone dressed in posh clothes. "I can't do a lot about it right now, mind, I've got obligations to our tenants to sort things out and handle things my father had neglected."

Lydia frowned, then asked because her curiosity was getting the better of her, "Is that very awful?" She couldn't imagine what it might be like, having one's parents effectively banished to their estate.

Galen took a breath and let it out. "It's decidedly odd. But I also know I'm much happier now. And so is Julius." The way his eyes lit up, it was clear how much he looked up to his older brother, how much that meant. "And we're doing better by our tenants and the business."

"How does that work, then? I realised, when you were talking to Thornley, that I should have got more of the details down." Lydia felt like she'd come up short.

Galen leaned forward, peering at her, and adding, "If you want the last roll, go to. Or they'll pack it up for you." He then went on. "You were busy sorting out who we needed to talk to, and that was grand. All that background."

"Knowing to ask about the Alders." She could agree with that.

"Exactly. What did you think of Thornley? And the conversations after?" Galen leaned back and contorted himself sideways in the seat. It was a degree of relaxation - and flexibility - that she envied entirely.

Lydia tapped her fingers on the arm of the chair. "I want to know more about Thornley now you got warned off him. What he's like, who he's spending time with. I don't know how much I can find out, given he's not our sort, as the saying goes."

"The London papers might have something. He's well-born enough. Though I'm wondering if the only reason he got sent down from university was the exams. That happens, I think, from what Alastair said in passing a while back, but it's more commonly for some sort of disorderly behaviour."

Lydia pursed her lips. "I don't know a lot about it, to be honest. What did you think about the man he mentioned, the snake-like one? It's an interesting metaphor, and I can't help but wonder if it means something."

"That," Galen said, "Is an excellent question. I can ask Julius. He might know. Or know who to talk to, at least. But whoever it is, they didn't come up in the trials, did they?"

"I haven't read all the transcripts? The paper's still getting some of them for me. They'd gone to storage already. Big bulky things like that usually do." She then peered at him. "Why do you care? I'm the one asked you for a favour?"

Galen shifted, reaching out to touch her hand. Instinctively, she realised, she wasn't at all sure he knew he'd done so. He didn't grab, he didn't take, he just rested his hand on hers, like he had dozens of times that afternoon. "Because you're doing something important, and I can help."

Lydia didn't want to pull her hand away, and she had to close her eyes and breathe before she did something hasty. "Do you want to help?"

Galen shrugged with his other shoulder. "I like helping Martin. Today seemed to go pretty well. Lending you my well-bred maleness."

"And what will your parents think if the gossip gets back to them?"

"For one thing, it might not. They ignore the non-magical as a rule. For another, well. My mother spent so long throwing eligible young women at me, she can't complain when I appear to have found one on my own."

"I'm not eligible, though." Lydia had to protest. "My family are... in a good year, they'd have been the man at the back of the private box, making sure the water for the tea was boiling. Not even the people who took the food around, that takes the sort of skills it takes years to practise." She peered at him. "Do you have a butler and footmen and things when you're at home?"

"At the moment, I have a valet with opinions, a cook, a housekeeper, three maids, and three footmen. As well as gardeners and stable hands and all that, but some of that is for the estate, not for me."

Lydia had no idea how to ask about any of this. She wanted to ask what it was like, to have someone, people, multiple people, always at your beck and call. Lydia wanted to ask how he treated them. Chances were good he was at least the tolerable sort of posh well-bred young man. She couldn't really see Martin slacking on pointing out a problem there.

"And yet you couldn't buy a horse if you wanted?"

"Well, racehorses are rather more than a year's salary for all of them." He said it apologetically. "The good ones. I asked. Also, I am thinking we should pay our people better, I'll have a look at the wages again. Mind, I gather I'm easy to work for, except for infuriating my valet by not being terribly interested in what clothes I wear. I'm a lot more inclined to sneak down to the kitchen to grab a bit to eat than ask someone to bring it to me, especially in the evening."

"What does your cook think?"

"She leaves the things to snack on in a particular place, and I take what I want from there. Works out well for everyone. If I'm not hungry, there are a few more treats for the servant's table next day."

She yawned suddenly, and that made him pull his hand back. "You must be tired. Do you want a room here, or would you rather go home? I could call a cab? They'll charge it to me, either way."

Part of her was curious about how he put that, whether that was the common practice since he was the member, or whether he'd made it clear she was his guest, or what. Perhaps both. But then she was too tired to chase that thought. "If a room would be easy, I..."

She couldn't face going back to a cold shared flat, with bumps and noises. And she was sure the beds here were as comfortable as this chair.

"Let me see to it, then. Back in a min." Galen disappeared promptly, presumably to see to it, all full of fire for this particular evening's problem.

CHAPTER 10
TUESDAY AFTERNOON, LONDON

G alen got a note from Vincent three days later, inviting him to call by Vincent's London club. He had been there a few months ago, as a guest of one of Alastair's friends, so at least he knew where the place was, and what to expect. In particular, how different it was from the Trellech clubs.

He considered that as he climbed the front stairs. There were the obvious things, of course. The Trellech clubs, whether they were as luxurious as Bourne's or as pragmatic as the Dweller's Forge, all had magic at the centre of them. Bourne's had reliably excellent workrooms, maintained perfectly. The Explorer's Club apparently had an amazing library on navigation and a storehouse of magical navigational tools to match. The Fox's Den, for all Galen didn't spend much time there, was designed to encourage negotiation between equals. It had all sorts of charms protecting privacy and making it clear who was in and who was out of the chosen group.

And of course, the downstairs staff had an easier time of it. He'd got Martin off on a rant talking through it a few months ago. It wasn't just that heating was easier, or that hot water was available in quantity. Though that was no small thing, given that the non-magical clubs still had to suffer with bedroom fires for heating, boilers for hot water, and in some cases, that water being hauled up flights of stairs to bathing rooms. Never mind about the laundry, which was an entirely different scope of problem.

The staff, too, were different. Fundamentally, in Trellech, the staff had a different education. Mostly, they'd gone straight into apprenticeship from the village schools, about the age when Galen had gone to Schola. But they were still of the same community. Albion, the magical community, numbered a quarter of a million people. It seemed like a tremendous number.

But as Galen had figured out this past year, when you left out all the children, and all the elders who rarely left their home or domestic circles, you cut it down to half of that. If you left out the people who mostly worked their farms, or rarely left the nearest village, or who were busy tending small children, you cut it down in half again.

And of course, Trellech itself was only about twenty-five thousand people, swelling to nearer thirty during the social season or major events. It was quite common to bump into the same people in your favourite cafe, or the library, or along your usual morning route. Galen certainly knew dozens of people from that, and he didn't even live in Trellech, he was only in town two or three times a week.

London, though, was seven million people. You could get lost in a crowd going two blocks. Even in the places where people might know each other, like the club he was entering, he gathered they were big enough you might only know others to nod to. People seemed to have mastered the vague nod of acknowledgement without ever bothering to speak.

Once he was inside, Galen was shown to a parlour by one of the staff. Vincent was settled in a chair, reading a newspaper that he put down as Galen approached. "Your guest, sir. I'll bring some tea."

Galen suspected that had been prearranged, as had the time. Five in the afternoon was when a man with business obligations might shake free, but far too early to be invited to a proper meal. And it also gave Vincent every excuse for cutting the conversation short whenever he liked, with a vague mention of evening plans.

"Do sit, make yourself comfortable. Your first time here?" Vincent seemed laid back, but Galen heard an odd note in his voice that suggested something else was going on.

"I was here a few months ago, with my business mentor, as guests of Gerald Fortnum." Who was a fair bit older than Vincent, well into his fifties if not his sixties, or so Galen thought. He'd not managed to figure out how to ask precisely how Alastair knew him.

"Ah, yes. Good man, Fortnum, a good man. Known to be steady. And who's your mentor?" Vincent was clearly fishing, and Galen suspected it was more than just about his finances as related to horses.

"Alastair Longton. Second son, he inherited the family property and an import-export firm when his older brother died unexpectedly. The Boer War, near thirty years ago. He's been helping me untangle some family issues."

"Entail, or something else?" It was a rather blunt question.

"My parents got into a spot of trouble." Accusing other people of murder, doing their best to frame someone, that all qualified. As well as what they'd only discovered later. "And in sorting that out, it turned out the business was doing badly. My father was persuaded to retire to one of our estates, and let me try my hand."

"And you're making a go of it?" There was a decidedly hail-fellow-well-met tone there. Hearty, overly cheerful, that's what Galen thought.

"With a lot of hard work, we might be in the black again when we see the proceeds of the harvest this year. And with a bit of luck in the weather, better next year." Galen didn't want to oversell it, but things were promising.

Of course, it helped that Galen was not inclined to take risks with investments, but to focus on staples, the things that always had a steady demand. When the business was bringing in a reliable profit, when they'd paid off all the loans, then he could see about exploring more risky opportunities, but in a measured way.

Vincent tapped his fingers together, then paused while a tea service was deposited on their table. It didn't take up much room, just the teacups and saucers, a pot with steam, and a solitary plate with a few shortbread biscuits on it. "Such a bother to talk business, isn't it? And yet, the world intrudes. I'll be mother, shall I?" He dismissed the man who'd brought it over with a nod, clearly preferring privacy to formality.

By the time Vincent had poured the tea, Galen was sure something odd was up. He couldn't figure out why, to be honest, but he was sure Vincent was nervous. There was a little shake of one hand, pouring, that nearly splashed tea. And there were looks up, to make sure no one else was close. They were all the way at the end of the parlour, in the corner, no one closer than fifteen feet in the long, narrow room.

Eventually, though, the tea could no longer serve as an excuse. Galen sipped his and did his best to look harmless and obliging. Not too obliging, but willing to listen. That was the right note here.

"Look, Amberly. You seem the right sort, even if I do not know where you went to school or who your people are. But the people I asked said you're sound. And I'm in a bit of a pinch."

Galen made a mm hmm noise, agreeable but unspecific. He had practised it for hours in the mirror at one point. He was very good at being amiably non-committal.

"I've a friend, well, an acquaintance, I'd like to impress. Sort of man who can open doors for you. And he's got a horse he's needing to sell shares of. Only all the people who might have aren't able to right now."

Galen thought he heard a note of need there, for just a moment. Vincent must be taking a chance because he saw no other options. Galen also suspected that the other unnamed people all had good horse sense. Or good business sense. Possibly both. "And you thought of me?"

"Would you at least come round and see the horse? He'd be glad to meet you at the trainer's. I could join you, bring that girl you had with you, we could go out to supper after. It's in Newmarket. There's a charming little restaurant. Quaint, but they know how to cater for our sort."

Galen suspected the place was overpriced, but possibly still tasty. Not that they were going for the food.

"I can't commit to anything, not on the spot. Just to be clear. But I'm willing to listen. And seeing the horse in the flesh is a thing, isn't it?" Galen was a perfectly competent rider, able to make sure his mount was in good health, but he wasn't sure at all what you checked for with race horses.

"Saturday, then? Pleasant day out in the country, show

up around half three, toddle round and see the horse as they settle things up for the night. And then drinks with the trainer, and off to an early supper. Country hours, you know."

Galen lifted his cup. "Usually keep them myself, so that's fine."

"I forgot you're not a city man." Vincent hesitated. "The man who owns the horse, he's high up in the City. In banking, I gather. Respectable work for a gentleman, though I gather he's considering a run for Parliament. You don't have a title lurking somewhere, do you?"

"Goodness, no. I suppose I qualify as an honourable, but only barely. Landed gentry, that's my family."

Vincent let out a noticeable sound of relief. "Oh, good. I mean." He gathered himself. "Look, there was something rather queer about things with Thornley last year. I know nothing directly against him, but there was some nasty gossip. Hellfire Club sort of things. I mean, it's one thing to have an orgy, and another to have it all hung about with horns and candles and what have you."

Galen had never been to either sort of orgy, and didn't much want to try. They had always seemed to be a jumbled mess of elbows from everything he had seen and heard. Never mind his personal lack of experience with various of the expected aspects of the thing. "I wasn't expecting to go off with him to some dark cave or cellar or what have you." He kept his voice light.

Vincent, however, didn't seem to relax. "Just, well. Aloysius Darley - same as the foundation stallion, isn't that odd, though I gather there's no relation?" He gathered himself from the tangent, which showed his nerves deteriorating. "Darley's quite a proper sort of man. He wouldn't approve of anything like."

"Am I someone he needs to approve of, then? Besides the, whatever agreement?"

"Oh, yes. I mean, he'll be associated with you. Though that's to your advantage. As I said, he knows all sorts of people. As a fellow owner, you'd have tremendous access to those people. Invited round to his private box when the horse races. That sort of thing."

Galen nodded. "Quite the opportunity. Do you have - pardon, so crass to have to ask - any idea of the sums involved? So I can consult my man of business?"

Vincent looked, if anything, a little relieved. "I have a portfolio for you, and if you have questions, well, that's what Saturday's for."

"It isn't a race day for them?"

"Not for the stable. Everyone's running on Sunday, I gather." He shrugged, as if that wasn't any particular business of his.

"And, um. Who else has shares?"

Vincent leaned down and pulled out a portfolio. Simple cardboard, nothing fancy, but sturdy enough. "I do, as it happens. That will explain things." And then he glanced at the clock, making it smooth. "Oh, goodness, is that the time, I need to change, meeting my wife for supper with some friends." He lifted his hand, summoning one of the staff to walk Galen out.

Galen had, all in all, to appreciate both the relative speed of the dismissal, and the information he'd been given. It was time to bring it back to Lydia and whatever resources she could call on from the paper.

CHAPTER II
WEDNESDAY AT TEA TIME

"The whole thing is just odd." Galen sprawled in the chair, one leg pressed up against the arm. Lydia had tucked her own foot up under her knee, since her skirt was unfashionably long but usefully full. And the other alternative was sitting primly. Given Galen's pose, that seemed the wrong mode.

"You have said that five times." Lydia pointed out. "Without actually explaining in what way it was odd."

Galen waved a hand, then snagged something off the plate Martin brought from the side table.

"Go get your own. Lydia, would you like something? There's plenty, take advantage." Martin settled down, guarding his plate like a hovering dragon from Galen. Galen, for his part, leaned over to try to snag something that looked like it had ham and cheese in some sort of dough.

When Martin batted his hand away again, Galen sighed dramatically and stood up, all in one movement. Lydia blinked at him. He didn't normally give an impression of physical prowess, he had the sort of slightly languid bearing common to the gentry. Or so it seemed, and then he moved and there was speed and intensity there. She found it distracting.

She had only recently got used to the idea he was as sharp-witted as Martin. In the visits she'd made before this particular project, he'd been quieter, more prone to listening. She'd spent more time than she wanted to admit to last night wondering how much of the change was the whole mess with his parents. And how much might be him growing up, and how much might be something else, deeper and stronger. He was something like a tree, which had needed time to go from a sapling clinging for light and ground, into something suddenly more substantial.

Martin waved a hand. "Go on, grab something. This will be a long conversation."

"How do you know?" Lydia was pushing herself out of her chair as she asked.

Martin flicked his fingers, she'd been noticing he did that a lot. "Galen, me, you. Thomasina. Miriam. And we might get a few others who like talking."

By the time she came back with her plate and a bottle of beer, she found they'd accumulated both of those. Also a third man she had seen before but never been introduced to. He was a tad bit older than Lydia. Galen and Martin were mid-twenties, Lydia was rapidly approaching thirty, and Thomasina and Miriam were about the same. Owen was thirty-five, maybe forty, the sort of man who started going grey around the temples in a dignified way.

Once they were all settled again, each with some food, Martin glanced around. "Not likely to get too many people coming through at this point. Half of them are off in London, something about the Imperial Conference."

"And you're not there?" Lydia spoke before she realised that might be rather rude.

Martin grinned. "We don't do politics, any of us. Labour rights, yes. Protective ointments and salves, yes." He nodded at Thomasina. "Literacy education and various sundry improving virtues." He nodded at Miriam.

"Also magical mayhem, in a limited and well-aimed manner." Thomasina said. "But we try not to advertise that. It worries people." Lydia blinked, and Thomasina went on. "Not bombs. There's too much risk with a bomb, even when people tell you there isn't. Think of explosives like a cat who can be coaxed into doing what you want most of the time with a bit of fish. But every so often, they're going to do the exact opposite."

"So." Miriam's voice cut through the rest. "What was odd, Galen?"

"Vincent invited me to his club, the Turf Club." Thomasina made a curious noise and Galen said, "Sports and cards, which certainly fit. Not one of their clubs that tells you a bit about the man's politics, nor one that implies military service. Though I presume he had some somewhere."

"How old is he?" Thomasina tilted her head.

"Perhaps around Owen's age? He called me young man several times, mind you, at the races."

Martin shook his head. "That's a terribly simple move, isn't it? Establishing his power in the situation. What did you do?"

"Ignore it then, but do my best to appear to take his advice seriously yesterday. I didn't want to make a scene, and it turned out to be useful." Galen shrugged, as if he were very familiar with navigating such dismissals.

"So you're going to see a horse on Saturday next. Can you conceivably buy a share?" Owen leaned forward.

Galen gestured at his bag. "I have the prospectus. They sell shares, ideally tens or better but they're considering twentieth shares, more realistically. The share pays for the fees and the horse, and if the horse wins, or goes on to stud, you make money back."

"And if the horse falls at the first hurdle and never races again, you don't." Thomasina snorted and leaned forward to snag something from a tray. "There's many ways to dope horses, too. Or just bribe the jockey, I gather."

"I got the impression that - besides being illegal - that being obvious about it was decidedly frowned upon." Galen shook his head. "So, I can't quite figure out which bit of it makes me most suspicious. Seeing as there are several choices."

Owen nodded, and said, "What do you know about the horse?"

Galen reached down to his satchel, putting his plate lopsidedly on the side table. Martin saved it from tipping with a sigh, and Galen came up with the portfolio. He handed it to Owen and reclaimed his food without any hesitation.

"One of these days, Martin's not going to be there, you know." Miriam snorted.

Galen blinked. "But I always know if he's there. It's just." He shrugged, falling quiet as Owen flicked through the prospectus.

"Let's start with the horse." Owen glanced up. "First, the horse may just not be that good, and the goal is to get people to buy into the shares, maybe split the fees with the trainer. Second, the horse they show you Saturday is not the same horse you eventually buy, so you think it looks fine, and it isn't. Third, that it's got some sort of underlying issue they know about, that wouldn't show on an independent vet exam, but will preclude racing. Fourth, that they've dosed it up so it looks grand, and normally it's weedy and failing to thrive."

Lydia blinked. "How do you know all that?"

Owen laughed. "My father's a racehorse trainer. Flat, not steeplechase, but it's the same principles. And some of his horses have gone on to it. A horse who can jump and who has good stamina can sometimes do well at longer races when they're older."

"I don't suppose we could get you to come with us as a friend?" Lydia floated the idea.

"If the trainer didn't recognise me, chances are good some of the stable hands would. Sorry, can't get away with that. But I'll tell you what I can. Can I get a copy of this to do some research on? I don't know the bloodlines like I used to, but I can write up a bit so you can sound intelligent about it, and maybe ask a few useful questions."

"Much appreciated on my part. Lydia?" Galen spoke up quickly.

"More information is good." Lydia agreed. "So if you know about racing, do you know anything about this Darnley? No, pardon, Darley. My mind keeps snaring on Elizabeth, the queen, I mean."

Owen laughed. "It does sound the same. Though she liked a good horse." He considered. "Something's nagging at me about the name too, but I don't know what. You didn't find anything in your files?"

Lydia shakes her head. "Not that turned up in the time I had. I can have another look tomorrow. Do you think there will be?"

"Horses are something we have in common. Us and the

non-magical. A shared language. So it's been a meeting place, especially around trade and finance and all that. Besides the fact that horses make an excellent conveyance of - how do I put it - changing one form of money into a more socially acceptable or less traceable one."

Galen snorted. "And socially approved, racing. More or less, anyway."

"It is an excellent way to have a lot of money show up quickly in an explainable way. We're back to nobbling a horse, mind." Owen shrugged. "So I'm very curious about what this Darley wants money for. Does he want it for what the money can do? Power or leverage? Or does he like nice things? Or shiny things."

"Some of us like money for the roof over our heads practicality of it." Miriam said a bit tartly. She didn't look at Lydia, but she didn't need to.

Martin nodded. "But there's an entire class of people who will put gilt on everything and think it splendid. And more to the point, it's often telling, what they want to do with their money. At least if they do it with gold leaf, you can get the gold back again if you really want?"

"And you can't with other things?" Thomasina shook her head. This was clearly rather foreign water to her.

"Some people spend their money on a rare potion. You take an expensive ingredient, or one that seems like it should be. And half the time, it's someone faking a unicorn horn with a narwhal or a rhinoceros or something. Or some colour of gemstone, being treated with heat or charms or foiling or whatever the other one's called. To make the stone seem a different colour." Martin shrugged.

Owen grinned approvingly. "You know your work well, Martin." he said. "Exactly. There is always consumable wealth. Potions. Wine or spirits. Also a form of potion, honestly. Whatever imported food is scarce at the moment. Things with frilly little gilding or pearls."

"It always seemed a waste of a pearl." Miriam said. "All right. So we want to find out why Darley has money or wants money or whatever. Do we know anyone in any of the banking families who might know?"

Thomasina grimaced. "My sister's seeing one of the Grindlays, fairly seriously. She might be willing to ask, or set up an appointment? I don't know what they'd share, though."

Lydia grimaced. "Probably too rich for my taste, the information."

"No harm in inquiring. Maybe they'll tell us something. Or if there's a modest fee, I can probably run to that." Galen pointed out.

Miriam shook her head. "If there's something meaningful, chances are the Dweller coffers will cover it. That's the sort of information we like to have on hand in our hoard."

Lydia blinked. "Hoard?"

"We keep our own records, not unlike your morgue, though much more piecemeal. Mostly about those causes we've taken up, or have reason to suspect we might in the not too distant future. But we do have some funding to cover fees for inquiries." Miriam laid it out neatly.

"Miriam would know. She runs the committee with an iron fist and a demanding respect for the budget." Martin waved a hand. "All right. Worth pursuing. Can you ask your sister, Thomasina, how they prefer to arrange it? One of the Scali will occasionally lend me a hand, but I think in this case the Grindlays are the bank most likely to have good intelligence."

"Why's that?" Galen looked up.

"Scali do more with our own needs in Albion. The Bardi

have a tremendous network on the continent, and the Grindlays are relatively new. By which we mean two centuries, not five. But they have done a lot with the trade with India and Africa. Though, interestingly, at least two of the shipping families prefer the Scali." Martin shrugged. "Not my usual line, but I've picked up enough."

"Right. Anything else to investigate?"

Thomasina looked up when Lydia asked. "Munitions. Something's nagging at me about the name. And I'm sure it's about munitions. Or explosives, at least." She lifted a hand when Owen was about to say something. "And it's not just because I have saltpetre on the brain. Just check, would you?"

"Is that a concern? I will, of course." Lydia said. "It's stupid to ask for ideas and refuse them out of hand."

Thomasina shrugged. "Some people think there will be another war, worse than the last. Unless everyone comes up with very threatening weapons. And the people doing the politics and the people making the chemicals are not the same people. Chemists talk. Or gossip. So do alchemists. I'll see if I can track any articles down that might give hints."

Lydia nodded. "Ta. All of you. I'm going to be very busy before we see this horse, but that's good."

CHAPTER 12

SATURDAY, NOVEMBER 6TH, NEWMARKET

L ydia and Galen had made their way to Newmarket via a portal to Cambridge. Lydia had chosen a train to Newmarket that suggested they'd come from London. They were met at the train station not by Vincent, as they'd expected, but by someone younger, in a rather dusty car. "You must be Amberly, yes? And Miss Pyle? Pardon the old beast, she's cleaner on the inside. I'm Bunny. Vincent asked me to trot along and meet you. He's having a chinwag at the stables."

Galen only understood about one word in three, but he had at least been in an automobile before. He made a show of handing Lydia into the passenger seat, next to Bunny and under the canvas roof. He took the seat at the back, with no protection from the dust or weather, though at least the sun was more or less out.

Galen had barely sat down when the engine roared to life. Galen didn't mind a train, that had a soothing sound. Even the whistles weren't too bad. But the automobile was right there, and it reminded him of some of the worst of the factory strikes he'd lent a hand at. The sound of the metal clanking, the feel of the lurking danger of a steam engine. He knew it was a fragile balance, and that at any moment, something might go wrong and it would veer off the road or have steam pouring out of every opening, or worse.

Fortunately, they didn't pick up too much speed. Bunny kept having to slow for horses crossing the road. Or twice for older women on their way back up the lane with shopping or something else in baskets.

After only about five minutes, Bunny pulled up a narrow lane some distance, a good half mile or more. There were two other automobiles visible. Galen found it easy to judge speed from a horse, and utterly impossible from the automobile.

Then Bunny was offering a hand to help Lydia out, doing something with the seat to make a little more space for Galen to climb out. By the time Galen had his feet properly under him, Bunny was ambling off into the stable yard, barely pausing to see if they were coming along.

Galen sighed and offered his arm. "Not too much?"

"An entirely novel experience, but don't let on." Lydia swallowed. "Once more unto the breach, isn't that right?" Then she hesitated. "May I dust you?" She gestured at his back.

"Show the mettle of your pasture." Galen said, quoting a bit rather further along in that speech. "Which is what we're here for, more or less. And yes, please." She patted him down with a handkerchief, hesitating for only a moment before making sure he didn't have any dust along the back of his thighs.

Once she'd done that, he offered her an arm again. They turned the corner into the yard through a gap between two buildings, about fifteen feet across. Long rows of stalls made a broad rectangle and Galen could see several dozen horses watching the goings on. It was rather a large yard, though that made sense. One didn't get deep into racing and do it on a small scale, as a rule.

Bunny had made his way over to a knot of others. Vincent stood with an older man, who must be Aloysius Darley. Darley was perhaps in his later forties or early fifties, the sort of man Galen's father had generally liked. That made Galen a tad suspicious, these days, considering everything. There were no other women there, but one other man, somewhere between Vincent and Bunny in age. As they got closer, Bunny was gesturing enthusiastically, and Vincent grimaced, like it was too much.

The last man was visibly the trainer. He looked the most at ease in the yard for one thing, and he kept glancing across the rows of stalls. Galen approved of that. It was a bit like the people he looked up to in the Dwellers, the ones long established in their professions. On the other hand, if there were some sleight-of-hand going on here with the horse, the trainer might well be in on it.

Galen put on his best manners and walked over. "Sir." That was direct to Darley. "A pleasure. May I introduce Miss Lydia Pyle?"

Vincent looked like he had eaten a lemon, or certainly something else, either bitter or sour, but Darley beamed at him. "Ah, good to see that manners are still valued."

Vincent cut in then, with a "Sir, may I introduce Galen Amberly? The Cumbria Amberlys. Miss Lydia Pyle. Amberly, this is Aloysius Darley, Horace Walter, and you've met Bunny Fortescue. And this is Allen Sykes, the trainer."

Galen smiled and nodded, committing the names to

memory. Lydia beamed without saying much. She had said that it was easier if they thought she was attractive and perhaps slightly dim. Darley nodded. "I understand you're newly come into some family money, and you're interested in taking up horse racing? It's a grand sport, the sport of kings. And of course, the late King was a fine supporter in his day. And for a young man with an interest in business, there's no better place to meet the right sort of people."

"That's what Vincent said, sir." Galen did his best to be young, eager, but still of substantial enough resources to be considered. "Some money now, the promise of more in a few years, if all goes well. I'm afraid we had rather a lot of losses in the last year." It implied that it was death duties that had done in the estate. Better to imply that rather than the much more complicated tangle of a murder, a conspiracy, and a fair bit of mismanagement before that.

"Ah, still tightly watched by some trustee, who's sure you're going to lose it all? Well, of course, one bets on one's own horse, that's a done thing, but the bets can be small. The share itself is the matter at hand. Now, I know Vincent gave you the prospectus. You must have questions."

Galen nodded. "I read through the pedigree carefully. That's a key thing with a horse, isn't it? Not just for the racing, all those comments about which lines produce reliable winners. But also, of course, if the horse stands at stud."

"Quite right, quite right." There was a note in Darley's voice now, like he'd settled into a particular mode, knowing which role he needed to take up. "Now, Crisparkle is a fine up sort. He's a half-brother to Hurry On, who was undefeated in his third year. Crisparkle's older, of course, for jump racing."

"An older half-brother, yes? And, pardon. A mixed record on the flat?" Galen did his best to look earnest and unsure.

"Ah, now, many a successful stallion's taken a while to find his stride. Much like young men, hmm?" Darley beamed, as if he'd made a grand joke. Of course, it was a comment Galen was getting rather sick of by now. "But very promising. He's taken to training well."

Galen nodded, watching the interplay between the men. Darley looked as if he were fully in control, but Victor was leaning forward a little. All the little touches Galen had learned suggested he was overeager. The trainer, interestingly, was looking anywhere but at Galen, as if he were distracted by something. Or perhaps that he was lousy at dissembling.

"I suppose the first thing is to see him, if that's possible? I've never raced, of course, but I am a rider." Galen found the reaction to that was even more interesting. Darley broke concentration for just a moment, glancing at Victor, who recoiled as if he'd been struck. In fact, Victor went so far as to cough, say, "I'll be back in a tiff," and trot back off to the driveway and the automobiles.

Darley turned his attention back. "Not the way things are usually done." He had a mild tone, but Galen felt it, the disapproval.

"Oh, pardon." Galen swallowed. "Still. I was told it was a, it isn't a problem, is it?"

Lydia squeezed his arm approvingly. Darnley shook his head. "It just means putting off our drinks and chat a bit. Go ahead, Sykes."

The trainer nodded and then gestured. One of the stable lads across the yard gestured back, and a moment later, they led out a dark blood bay. Nicely proportioned, a bit leggy, but that was likely all to the good in a race over jumps. The lad led him around in a broad circle before bringing him to stand.

The horse was, well, a reasonable sort of horse. He whuffled at the lad, flicked his tail, and looked unhappy to be taken away from his imminent dinner. He canted one hind leg, in a lazy sort of lean. Galen tilted his head, trying to place why something seemed out of place. Reasonable horse. Clearly still a stallion, not a gelding. Gelding might have been fine for a racehorse, but not if the goal was to put him out to stud after a successful enough career.

"May I go over?"

Galen glanced at Allen Sykes, who shrugged. "Don't touch him, sir. He's a bit prone to spooking."

"Of course not." Galen tucked his hands behind his back and went over to peer at the horse from several other angles. Nothing particularly wrong there. A little long in the pastern, but his hocks and knees looked solid. No obvious signs of lameness or tendency to it, though obviously there were dozens of things he might miss on a visual inspection. He smiled at the horse, then at the lad. "Thanks." Then he circled back to the others.

By this point, Vincent was coming back, carrying something under one arm. Bunny was making some sort of awkward but genial comment, then looked up at Galen. "Had enough of a look, then?"

Galen nodded. "Thank you, yes. That's a fine stallion." He glanced from Darnley to Vincent. "I suppose we should discuss the details?"

"Oh, yes. Do come inside for a drink. I understand you'll need to confirm matters with your man of business. We'll make the appropriate arrangements later." This put

Darnley back into a more amiable mood, and he swept off, as if he owned the place. They were ushered into a wood-panelled room near the door to the trainer's house, obviously kept for this sort of gathering.

A rather mousy-haired woman of an age to be Sykes' wife blinked from where she was reading a magazine. "Oh, I'll get something to go with the drinks, shall I?"

Lydia pulled her arm away from Galen's. "Do let me lend a hand, please." That was decidedly clever of her.

It did, however, leave Galen alone, where the conversation went over his head. He was sure that was entirely intentional. It was the sort of chatter people did when they didn't care that someone wasn't following, wasn't part of that particular set. Bunny was fully woven into it, which was interesting. Galen had assumed that Bunny was along with Vincent for some reason, but it became clear he was also looking into buying a share. Or rather, it was nearly a done thing, just waiting on the paperwork.

Here and there they tossed a comment to Galen, about how fine the private boxes were at this course or that one. Or what fun it would be to see friends at this race coming up. How much more fun it was, of course, if you had a winner, and got to be down in the winner's circle. Galen, for his part, smiled and nodded, and did his best to let them think he was entirely drawn in.

He was handed a drink. He drank a bit of it, and sidled off to pour a little of it into a somewhat spiky plant in the corner. From the looks of it, other people had done much the same, and the alcohol hadn't done the plant any good. Needs must, though. As the conversation wound down, and Galen had been given the promise of further information by post, Vincent looked up. "Oh, we should see about supper. You don't mind coming back to London, do you?"

Galen blinked. "We'd, pardon. You'd suggested Newmarket."

"You came from London, didn't you? No problem then. We've got two automobiles, we'll meet the ladies back at this glorious club we know. Lydia, you'll love it, I'm sure." He swept off with Lydia, leaving Bunny and Galen to follow.

CHAPTER 13
LATER THAT AFTERNOON

L ydia swallowed, glancing at Galen. "Oh, I'm not dressed for a club at all."

"You could borrow something. I'm sure Plucky would lend you something. She's got a flat nearby with two other girls."

"Plucky?"

"Bunny's girl of the moment." Vincent waved a hand. "We'll meet a few other people. And it'll give us a chance to chat some more. Show you what the good life's like."

Galen hesitated. There was no easy way out of this, was there? Lydia could see the flash in his eyes, then a slight lift of one eyebrow. She'd always wanted to do that and envied him the subtlety. But she could read the question clearly enough. "If you don't think my frock's a problem, or Plucky can lend me something. Sure. Does Galen have to sit in the back all the way there?"

Vincent laughed, a bit too loudly. "Not at all. I can take you both, if you like. Or you could ride with Bunny and let me talk about tedious dry things with Galen."

Lydia did not much like the idea of being with Bunny all

the way back, but she suspected Vincent was just as reckless a driver. Galen might get more out of him on his own. "Well, if Bunny promises to be a perfect gentleman." She got the right note in her voice, teasing but with a bit of warning.

"Oh, Plucky would have my head. Can't have that. Perfect gentleman, of course." And that was that. Bunny courteously handed her into the passenger seat of the automobile and waited for Vincent to go roaring off in a cloud of dust.

Lydia tried various lines of conversation, but the wind was much too loud, and Bunny kept shouting for her to repeat herself. The one lucky thing was that Vincent was not nearly as reckless a driver as Bunny seemed inclined to be. Bunny kept in behind him, if perhaps a bit too close, especially as they picked up speed as they got onto increasingly main roads.

It was two hours later, well into evening, when Lydia was deposited in front of a rather posh looking building. Bunny said something about taking the car to the garage. He'd be along in a minute. They'd lost Vincent's car, or rather turned off in a different direction five minutes earlier. When Bunny came back, he swept her in past the doorman, into a lift, and up to a third-floor flat.

From there, it was a flurry of activity. Plucky turned out to be a chic and sharply appointed woman about Bunny's age with raven black hair. She seemed rather brittle at first, but she turned friendly enough once Lydia made it clear she was with Galen. She and her flatmates exclaimed over her long hair - they all had short cropped bobs. But the dress she dug out looked good on Lydia. She did her best to hide that she felt utterly underdressed wearing something near enough sleeveless and made of very flimsy fabric. They reassured her it was nearly right up to the mode, and then dragged her off, giggling, back down to the street level.

Bunny had gone ahead to flag down a cab, and they all piled in, laughing and giggling, with a short drive to a row of nightclubs. It wasn't a part of London Lydia knew at all. It was nearly the opposite end of what she knew, in fact. This was all bright lights and loud noises, and people who clearly had imbibed too much already for this point in the evening.

Plucky dragged her along by a hand into a rather vast space, almost the size of a vaudeville theatre, with a balcony rimming two sides of the space. A band played on the stage, and there were tables dotted all around the edges, leaving a dancing floor of intricately fitted wood. Then Plucky pointed upward. "There's Vincent. And that's your Galen?"

Lydia had to repress the immediate response that he wasn't hers. It didn't go with the part they were playing. She nodded. "Who is that with him?" It wasn't Darley, it was someone she hadn't seen. Then something made him turn to look down at the dance floor, and she was suddenly sure it was Nico Lind.

They hadn't been able to track down much about him. That had made Galen and Martin sure he wasn't using whatever name he'd gone to school with. There were eight men named Nicodemus who might be around the right age. It had apparently been a popular name for a while, thanks to a particular singer. The Lind had proven to be the problem, and made them all suspect it was his mother's maiden name, or an assumed name, or something of the kind.

Plucky shrugged. "One of Vincent's rich friends. As opposed to the posh friends, like Bunny. Come on!" She went dashing off, pausing only to ask for a bottle of champagne to be brought to the table, and nearly dragged Lydia with her. Bunny followed along, ambling behind amiably. By the time they got up to the table, Galen was standing. "Lydia, you look wonderful. This is Nico Lind, Nico, Miss Lydia Pyle. And you must be?"

"Plucky. Bunny's girl of the moment. Don't let us interrupt you, though, darlings, there's bubbly coming, and Lydia, you simply must drag Galen down for a dance sometime this evening."

Lydia waited until Galen pulled out a chair, and by that point there was someone with a bottle and glasses. The conversation turned to something much more general, but Lydia caught Galen's eye. She wished, all of a sudden, they'd worked out signals for each other, but of course neither of them had expected to be in this particular sort of club tonight.

Once everyone had their drinks, Plucky dragged Bunny off to some friends she saw, and Vincent cleared his throat. "This might be rather tedious for you, Lydia, if you want to go meet Plucky's friends? All first rate sorts."

Lydia wanted to argue, but again, it meant Galen might get information they desperately needed. And these two men certainly would not talk about serious matters with her there.

"Twenty minutes, Lyd, and I'll come find you for a dance. How's that?" It was Galen's specificity that decided her.

"I'll hold you to that and come looking." She leaned down to kiss him on the cheek and then went tottering off in shoes that were higher than she usually favoured.

Twenty-three minutes later, she was just working around to figuring out what to say when she went over to them, when Galen found her. "Dance, Lyds? I think I won't step on your toes too much with this one."

"Of course." She waved cheerfully to where half a dozen women were sprawling across a sofa and comfortable chairs, chattering away. A couple of them eyed Galen speculatively, and then leaned in. Likely to get the details from Plucky.

"You all right?" Galen asked as soon as they were on the landing of the stairs, as private as they were going to be for a while longer. "But mind -"

That made her wonder if he thought the walls had ears. "Not quite used to somewhere this busy, but Plucky and her friends have been great, telling me all sorts of things. You?"

"Vincent's keen I buy into this horse, and so is Nico. I said I'm thinking about it, I have to check with my man of business. But that's for later, definitely. Now is for dancing."

They both flung themselves into the dance for a bit, making a good enough show of it. Lydia had picked up a bit while she had been chatting. The fashions for dances more or less crossed from the non-magical community into their own, and vice versa, but of course magic permitted some charms and additions that didn't work. And definitely not in a borrowed frock, or shoes that weren't charmed for good traction on the floors when you wanted that.

That worked until they had to stop to catch their breath and cool down. Lydia glanced up. "Do you need to get back to them?"

"Mmm hmm." Galen kept his voice low and even. "They're being very persuasive. Vincent suggested going round his club in a day or two, when I've had a chance to sort out the money end. Drinks with Nico, something like that. Different club, I think? Are you all right for a bit?"

"I'll let you know when I'm done in, but I'm good for a bit. You're still dropping me at home, though? I needn't take a cab?"

"See you to your door, of course." Galen said, amiably. She hoped he meant that as she intended, that they would leave together, and on their own. Though figuring out where the nearest portal was from here might be a trick. Probably Bedford Square, but she wasn't sure.

They parted after Galen walked her back to the knot of other women, who'd settled into cheerful commentary about everyone else's frocks. Rather to Lydia's surprise, it wasn't catty, but they had a sharp eye for fit, colour, and what had been remade from previous years.

It turned out that Plucky worked as a fit model for a couture dressmaker, and she was used to standing for hours while clothes were fitted to her. Lydia got the impression it made good money. And it explained where the spare dress had come from, as the pale green wasn't quite of a shade to suit Plucky's pale skin and dark hair. The other two girls from her flat had similar sorts of jobs that involved looking well, but also being able to be patient and take direction.

It sounded tediously boring to Lydia, but they seemed happy enough with it. Plucky commented, as they watched, that she enjoyed having the quiet. A bit of time where no one asked her anything more complicated than to move her hands or take something off or put it on, so that she had a chance to rest after busy evenings out.

Lydia kept sneaking glances toward Galen. She was obvious enough about it that one of the other women laughed and patted her on the shoulder. "You have it bad, don't you? He's right where you left him. Which, to be fair, often isn't the case around here." The woman had a bit of a lilt to her voice. She had the sort of angles to her cheek-bones and jaw that made Lydia wish she had any talent for sketching.

"Any advice?" Lydia tried to keep her own voice light.

"Men get themselves in trouble." The other woman considered. "Vincent's got a reputation as a stick in the mud. His wife is around here somewhere, with her own set. We are not her sort." She then added, "I'm Margery, by the by."

Lydia blinked. "Oh?" She must sound very naïve. "Lydia. If you didn't catch it."

"Oh, she loves flirting. She doesn't mind a bit of a pick-me-up, and she plays a fierce hand of cards. Don't play her if you want to keep your money, even if she says it's a friendly game. I'm sure that's where a fair bit of their money comes from. Vincent makes deals as a banker. One of these days they'll probably pay off."

"Why're you telling me this?" Lydia glanced over to see Margery grinning broadly.

"Oh, you seem like friendly folks. You're not them, or their set. Bunny's all right, but he'll go along with a lot of things that probably aren't good for him." Then she leaned back. "Are you going to tell them what I said?"

"Goodness, no. Why would I?" Lydia shrugged. "We barely know them. Though ta for the warning."

That made Margery laugh. "I knew I liked you. If you come round again, let me know. I'll introduce you to the more interesting sorts. Now, though." She gestured with her chin. "I think your Galen's about ready to go. Have a good night, right?" She winked cheerfully, before turning back to the larger conversation.

She was right, too. Galen came right over. "Let's find a cab back, shall we? If I'm not tearing you away?"

Lydia shook her head. She stood, making a flurry of goodbyes and air kisses tucked into other bits of the ongoing conversation, and then Galen offered his arm. The men at the table didn't even look up as they went by, but Lydia felt like someone was watching her until they were well out of the building.

CHAPTER 14
LATE THAT NIGHT AT THE DWELLERS' HOUSE

G alen felt exhausted. They'd decamped to the Dweller's house, because Lydia had missed her rooming house curfew by hours, and Galen didn't want to wake the staff at the estate either. It did no one any good, and someone would insist on making sure he was all right, lighting a fire, bringing a drink, or something of the kind.

Instead, they could collapse in the lounge, knowing they wouldn't be putting anyone out. "Do you need to return the dress? I mean." Galen realised suddenly how that sounded.

"Plucky gave me the address. I can send it back. She's sending mine on." She had given the address in London that would forward it on to Trellech.

"Do let me pay for it. Actually, ask tomorrow morning. I'm sure the staff here can add it to the pile of mail and put it on my tab. Write whatever note or label you want in your handwriting, that's fine."

Lydia let out a sigh. "I - I was worrying." She stretched.

"Actually, let me change first? See if they have something I can borrow."

"We'll both do that." Galen said. Twenty minutes later they were back, Lydia tucked into a borrowed dressing gown that was big for her.

Lydia tucked her feet up in the chair and cupped her hands around a mug of cocoa. "This is lovely. I couldn't go to sleep yet, but cocoa, that I didn't make on the hob, that's...." She shook her head. "I shouldn't get used to it."

Galen wasn't sure what to do with that. He was used to navigating the problem of money with Martin. And it was very much a problem. Martin wanted to make his own way, and Galen wanted to respect that. But he also hated knowing his friend was going without from sheer stubbornness. It was better now Martin was living with Laura.

She had good reason to keep the flat warm, and to replace things as they wore out, she needed to for her own health. Martin was earning a steady salary as a journalist, and she was as well with her own work. If the budget got padded a little by Galen or by Laura's sister and her husband, well, Martin didn't argue so much anymore.

Lydia, though, that was a distinctly different challenge. She hadn't seemed unwilling, exactly, but rather cautious, as if she expected the cost to come from somewhere else later.

Galen spread his hands. "We're doing this together, remember? And with the help of the Dwellers. Trust me, a bit of postage is a drop in the ocean."

"Everyone's been generous. You, especially, I really only expected you to make a show of it. And the clothing, and the outings, and..."

Galen hesitated, and then felt everything click for him, a rushing that he knew he had to follow. He had learned to trust these moments, to go where they led, and not just because of Martin. "You've been alone with all of it for a long time, haven't you?"

She looked up, wide-eyed, the sort of look that hid nothing and didn't try to. Like she was too tired and had faced too many challenges to keep her walls up. She nodded, once. "You..."

He shook his head. "I knew a long time ago I couldn't tell my parents most things that mattered to me. They'd ignore them or use them against me or both. It's a different solitude, but just as real. But I had Martin, and you have had no one like that." He was more and more certain now.

"Friends, here and there. But we've all moved on, different jobs, different places, different schedules." Lydia said. "It's been years."

"And it's hard to get close to other reporters - you're always out at different places." Galen said. "If not competing with each other, and some people handle that better than others."

Lydia blinked at him, then nodded. "Yes." She went quiet, and Galen didn't press. Instead, he asked, "Are you up for talking through the evening, or would you rather sleep first?"

"Afternoon and then evening, please." That decision was prompt, though the rush was followed promptly by a more leisurely sip of cocoa. "They didn't like you looking at the horse."

"They didn't. And I'm wondering why. I need to ask Owen about it, but he should be around tomorrow. As a horse, he was a good exemplar."

"It was shaped very much like a horse, yes. Four legs, head, long neck, tail. Stampy bits."

That made Galen laugh. "Horses have what's called

conformation. There are shapes of horse - or rather how the bits fit together. The back to the shoulders or the parts of the leg, or what have you. They make a difference in how they move."

"And all of that seemed reasonable? Do you know enough to tell?"

Galen nodded. "Owen went through what usually is wanted in a racing horse. This one was a bit long in the pastern - that's the bit from the top of the hoof to the fetlock."

She looked baffled, and he held up his hand, then adjusted, so his fingers were pointing down. "The horse's leg is a bit like our hand. They stand on the middle finger, or mostly on the nail of it. The tip of the finger is the coffin bone, the core of the hoof. The next two segments of the finger are the pastern.And then you get the leg going up from there. See how the angle bends, how it can extend over? That's like what the fetlock does over the pastern. And then the wrist joint is like their knee."

"That almost made sense, thank you. So a long pastern isn't good?"

"It can lead to injuries more easily. It tends to be a bit more fragile, as a structure? But this wasn't bad, just not ideal. I didn't see any obvious signs of past lameness, though some of them don't show, of course. But you can sometimes see bumps. Places the bone's got peeved is how our vet put it."

"I defer to your knowledge of horses. All right. We're not getting further on that point until you can talk to Owen." She flicked her fingers. "I feel like there's something wrong, both Mr and Mrs Sykes know it, and they're not comfortable with it. But what it is, of course, it's not like she'd say. Just she was nervous like a rabbit."

Galen frowned. "I caught that too, from Sykes. We definitely need to talk to Owen."

Lydia nodded, then set that aside, no sense fussing over it now. "What was Nico like? No, wait. Take it in order. What was the drive back like? What did Vincent talk to you about?"

Galen leaned back, then rotated so his legs were draping off over one arm. "On the way back to London - that took forever, even though we were going so fast." He worked on gathering his thoughts, which currently felt rather shaken up.

Lydia snorted. "Exactly, yes, but we can talk about automobiles later. Vincent?" She set her mug down and pulled out a notebook.

"Vincent." He shook his head. "You picked up that he gambles?" Lydia nodded. "So does his wife, and not just on horses. I get the impression they both come from money, but maybe there isn't as much there as they let on. Or at least, they're worried that there isn't."

"Where do you get that from?" Her voice was curious now, leaning forward.

"There are things you look for. Mother would always judge people about them. How well maintained their clothes are, or their things. If it's clear they have a valet."

"Do you have a valet?" Lydia peered at him. "No, wait, you said you had one, with opinions."

"Nominally, yes. But he's used to me coming and going at all hours. Mostly, he makes sure my clothes get laundered promptly, and helps if I'm dressing for a formal dinner or a dance or something like that. Ordinary everyday things, well." He shrugged. "Smaller staff now, at least where Julius and I are."

Lydia nodded, and Galen realised he hadn't explained

all of that, but now was not the time. "Anyway, on the drive up, it was one part him dropping names, only a handful of which I recognised. And one part him talking about how much good it would do me to be in with Darley and the other owners. And then one part asking more about my people and prying about the business, and what we do."

"What do you do, precisely? Or what did you tell him about that?"

"Import and export, mostly magical materia, but also some general luxury goods. Woods and mother-of-pearl and sometimes spices or something of the kind. Father had connections around Malaysia and India, and South Africa. I've kept those up. He was very interested in the import and export trade, I got the sense they were looking to get things to other places. Possibly also from. Without being noticed. Which could be about taxation and customs fees, or could be something else entirely."

Lydia considered that. "And domestic items, too?"

Galen nodded. "That's part of what Vincent wanted to sound me out about. What sort of things we produce. Of course, three-quarters of the income is magical, so it's tricky to talk about. The rest is, I don't know. Wool from the sheep, timber from the estate, there's a quarry we technically own, though it doesn't produce much these days. Tithes from the tenants."

"You realise that is rather a lot, right?" Lydia was peering at him now.

Galen shrugged. "The rest of it does better when it's well managed. Father did too much speculation. We should be back in the black when the current shipments coming in get sold through, and we've offers on a fair bit of it already, but..." He shrugged. "International trade is always a gamble, and I'm not entirely sure how much Vincent understands that."

She leaned forward. "Explain." Then as if she realised she'd given an order, she added, "Please."

"This is a partially formed theory, right? Martin and I have hammered a bit of it out, but not fully. Yet." He gestured. "Some people have a taste for risk, we can take that as a foundational premise, yes?"

"It has been widely observed, yes." Lydia smiled at that.

"Some businesses are built on the promise of endless expansion. One of my teachers at school went on about Jupiterian influences, that idea of wanting to expand and envelop as much as possible. And that in a less desirable form, that can involve swallowing up far more than we need, or can make use of, or can tend to."

"And gambling would be a form of that, being ..." Lydia frowned. "In that theory, a bit Mercurial? The element of risk, of speed of decisions to be made, tangled up with the desire for expansion and money."

Galen grinned. "Exactly. And all trade has an element of both of those, the rapid decisions and the desire for expansion. But international trade, even more so. It's often guesswork, what items will sell well when they actually arrive."

"Or whether the fad for feathers from some brightly coloured bird has disappeared, or a particular leather, or what have you."

"Exactly. We do not deal in fashion components, generally, unless they have magical use. Too rich for my blood. And Father went hot and cold on them." He shook his head. "I think that's what's getting me. Father would have liked these men, he'd be encouraging me to spend more time with them, even if it meant slacking on the business. Cultivate long-term connections, like Vincent keeps talking up."

Lydia hesitated, then she asked, her voice quiet and uncertain. "What do you think about that?"

"I'm not backing out. A bit more aware of what's going on, that's all. And I'll talk it through with people." He gestured vaguely at the house, though he presumed she knew he mostly meant Martin.

"Right." She gathered herself, a bit like a bird settling on a roost. "What did you think about Nico?"

"I'm deeply curious about Nico." Galen couldn't help feeling there were half a dozen things tugging at him. "There's something very odd there , and I don't know what. But now I've seen him, we might get a little further with the research. I can check the Schola annuals, for example, Julius still has his, or there are some other sources."

"It's a pity we don't have a photograph, or I could check with the morgue. They've got ways of matching people, even if they're using different names, though obviously it's terribly fiddly."

"If we come up with one, I'll let you know, of course." Galen stretched. "I admit, there's a lot about this nagging at me, but I don't know how to explain it. I do feel there's more going on than horse-racing and gambling, though."

Lydia nodded, then yawned, suddenly and hugely. "Let us come back to that when we've slept. I don't know about you, but sometimes I have my best insights when I'm sleeping."

Galen laughed and stood, clearing their mugs back to the tray so they could be taken off and washed. "May I walk you upstairs, then? And please, do ring for whatever you need, or breakfast if I don't see you in the morning."

She smiled, and they walked up to the sleeping rooms in agreeable silence.

CHAPTER 15

MONDAY

L ydia woke the next morning much later than she'd meant to. Though to be fair, they hadn't made it back from London until something like two in the morning, and she hadn't seen her borrowed bed until half three.

It meant, however, that it was well past eleven by the time she managed to get dressed and find something to eat. The woman who'd brought her food mentioned that Galen had already left for the day, but that she was welcome to order whatever she liked. Galen, it seemed, was a man of boundless energy, far more than Lydia. She couldn't decide if she envied that or resented it. Both, probably, the way something about the question made her stomach twist a little.

She spent the rest of the day, late into the evening, writing up her notes. The list of her current queries took the better part of two pages. That was both reassuring, for this stage in a story, and exhausting to look at. After staring at it for five minutes, she rewrote it into tidy sections, including a category for questions that crossed into multiple areas and defied order.

The next morning, she woke up with three new ideas, and spent an hour rewriting her notes into a fresh notebook, before going to the library to see if she could turn up anything on her own about the mysterious Nico. She had no luck, so she set off for the Moon's offices, aiming to meet the morgue staff after their lunch hour. Lydia timed it perfectly, in fact, coming up to the building as Ev and the others were returning.

"You wanting us, then?" Ev grinned at her. "You look like someone on a hunt."

"Please, yes. If it's not a bother."

"Himself said you can draw on us freely if we're not too busy." That was a bit of a surprise. She'd made weekly reports to Morris but she hadn't had a great deal to actually say yet. Ev went on congenially. "And I say we're not too busy for an hour or so, unless something newsworthy happens. It's been a slower week or so."

They went down the stairs, Ev and Lydia at the back of the clump. "Seasonably slow, or unseasonably slow?"

Ev stopped. "Good question. Unseasonably slow. Even with all the talk coming out of London. It makes me wonder what people are up to that we're not hearing about, actually."

Lydia nodded. "You must have a good sense of the rhythm of things." She was glad she'd asked, but now she was going to worry about what it meant, what they were missing, what was looming in the darkness. Likely at three in the morning.

Ev led the way over to her desk, gesturing for Lydia to take the one she'd used before. "What's the question, then?"

"Quite a few, but my main one for you is someone using the name Nico Lind. Magical, mid to late thirties probably, but might be a few years on either side of that. I've met him, briefly, and can recognise him if he wasn't using a glamour."

"Huh." Ev glanced up and around. "Give me a couple to pull a few things. Schola man, do you think, or something else?"

"I don't know, honestly. I'm not sure how to tell reliably if someone's not being obvious about it." Lydia started setting out her pencils and notebooks.

"There are some tricks I can teach you. Certain phrasings. I went to Alethorpe, I can teach you those more easily." Ev then nodded, and bustled off, leaving Lydia to poke at her notes.

"No Lind. I remember you were here seeing if anyone fit. So I pulled the Nicodemos files around the right age, and there's a Nicanor, Nicandros, a Nikolaus, and a Nikephoros." Ev was back promptly, given she was holding about ten files.

Lydia blinked at the list. "Those all at least seem worth checking?" Then Ev settled down next to her, handing them over one at a time. There was one, a Nicodemus who would have been about the right age to have gone to school with Galen's brother, who looked almost right. But something was different about the eyes.

She kept flipping through, and then came to the last file, about Nikephoros. First, she got to the portrait on the top. She could see how that man would look like the one she met, aged by the War and a decade and a half.

"Him." She tapped the file.

Ev leaned over to peer at the name. "Not a name I know much about. Let me see what else we've got."

Twenty minutes later, Ev had come back with five additional files. Lydia had made her way carefully through the file. It was scant, though she didn't entirely know how to weigh that properly against the rest of the morgue's collection. Three photographs. The one she'd seen first seemed to be when he finished his apprenticeship, something having to do with a specialisation in Ritual and Materia. There was one of him rather younger, beginning his apprenticeship, and one in formal uniform, early in the War.

The papers in the file were not a great deal more help. There was an announcement to go with the apprenticeship photographs, or rather a pair of them. Lydia wrote the name of the firm down, and it was a firm, though she had no idea what they actually did.

The additional files fleshed things out a bit. Parents, judging by the dates, and one small reference to two sons. What might be an older brother, but there was only one reference to him, and no file. She did, finally, track down where the 'Lind' came from. A great-uncle on his mother's side, who seemed to have lived with the family, and was referenced in a clipping from 1910 about a ball at their home.

His father seemed to have been in the empire somewhere, but it wasn't at all clear where. He might have been Army, he might have been in the Colonial Service. There was only one photograph of his mother, a retiring, formally posed one.

By the time Ev was ready to put things away, Lydia handed over the last file. "I think I've got everything useful for now. Might be back again, when I have more to dig with. Any chance of finding out more about his posting?"

Ev flipped through it, then grimaced. "See that stamp? That suggests we tried and had no luck. How critical is it?"

How big a favour was Lydia willing to spend on it, in other words.

"If you happen to hear anything, could you let me know? Anyone else looking at the file, maybe?"

Ev nodded. "That's easy enough. Anything else I should keep an ear out for?"

"Racehorses. A man named Aloysius Darley, non-magical, we're fairly sure. Nico Lind, or Nikephoros FitzWallace." That name tickled something in the back of her brain, now she said it out loud.

"Will do. If you're free Friday, stop by when we leave. Come have a drink?" Ev offered it generously, and Lydia had to force herself not to look stunned. It wasn't the usual thing, at least not with her sort of people. Lydia swallowed whatever protest, mentally swore that she'd be around. "I should be free. Come down here, or meet you at the door?"

"Down here's fine. About quarter to five."

Lydia grinned. "Ta. Friday." Then she made her way out, without quite bouncing up the stairs. If she went off now, she should be able to catch Jeremiah Aldridge at Wishton's, during his break before the supper rush. She went down the street at a good pace, veering off onto Club Row, and then turning down a small but surprisingly clean alley. Well, surprising to her, she was used to London. Here, magic did a lot to help with basic sanitation.

She was in luck. Just as she turned the corner into the back courtyard shared by four of the clubs, she heard a whistle, and turned to see Jeremiah leaning on the railing. "Wondered when you'd turn up again. Evening. Got about fifteen."

He was a broad-shouldered man, with deep brown skin. They'd known each other since they were children, growing up on the edges of the magical communities of London.

He'd ended up apprenticing as a cook, and these days he had respect and a steady income as a sous chef for Wishton's, one of the posh clubs. Every so often, one of the men - it was always men - wanted to hire him away to work for their family, and Jeremiah always refused. He preferred the greater security of clubland rather than throwing in his luck with a single family.

"Evening." She came up onto the terrace behind the building, and moved to hop up to perch on the railing, bracing her back against the wall. It was sturdy enough, especially in the corner where there was some additional bracing, making a little triangle she could perch on.

"What are you up to, then? It's what. Four weeks since you came round?"

"A story. I told you, I've got backing to chase a story." She shrugged. "Got a question."

"Might have an answer." He leaned back against the railing post, like a lazy cat scratching its back.

"You know anything about a Nikephoros FitzWallace? Or the family, the father's Augustinian and the mother is Helianthe."

"Not for you. Not for the likes of us." The reaction was immediate and fierce. "Don't you go anywhere near them." He then turned and spat over his shoulder. The sort of thing that would have had his mother rapping his fingers with a spoon, but was a traditional method of averting evil magic.

She hesitated. Pushing too hard would do no good here. Jeremiah was protective, certainly. He was enough older than Lydia, they'd always been like that. And until they both apprenticed, he was bigger, stronger, knew more, and people were far less likely to mess too much with him.

"Why?" Just the one word.

"There's nothing kind in them. Especially not now. Tell

me." It was a demand, but she supposed he had a right to ask.

"A friend of mine, posh, he's a member at Bourne's. But also one of the Dwellers." That made Jeremiah raise an eyebrow at the combination. "He's been escorting me to some horse races, trying to spot a gap in something. And this man, the son, he's turned up. Not using that name, mind."

"What name?"

"Nico Lind."

Jeremiah pivoted and spit again, this time adding a charm that flared out in a burst of light to clean the spot, as if scouring it with bleach. "Got a reputation for being focused on a goal. The family, in general, and him in particular. Cruel if he's crossed. Though I don't know how much to trust the tales. All third or fourth hand, you know?"

"What's the family like?" She'd start there, being able to put someone in context often helped.

"You know about the Fitz, right? Means someone's born the wrong side of the sheets. That can be fine, or it can mean someone will kick anyone on their way up the ladder to prove themselves. His father, in this case. That generation of the Wallaces, gather they were brutal. His father was Colonial Service, reputation for nastiness, but nothing that got prosecuted. India, I think, originally."

That was very helpful, in the awful sort of way. "Cruel magically, or something else? Nico in specific, whatever you know." She could take the father's name to the morgue in due course.

"Nothing that the toffs know about, formally? Nothing that would get him thrown out of the club." It happened, occasionally, but usually it required being caught cheating at cards, or the sort of crime that had you up in front of the judges in the Court. "But he enjoys twisting the knife. Knowing secrets. Using them to get what he wants."

"Blackmail?" It was the first thing that came to mind.

Jeremiah considered. "Haven't heard it." he admitted. "But I wouldn't be surprised. Been a couple of people give him a wide berth after being closer. The sort of distance where you're watching your back the whole time."

"Right." She said, after a moment. "I met him, briefly. I didn't like him much. He wanted to talk to the men with money." Lydia shrugged. "Not me on either count, though I had the right sort of frock."

Jeremiah obligingly whistled, and then smiled. Then he shook his head. "Won't tell you to be careful. It's your work. But don't go alone, all right? Who's with you?"

"Galen Amberly." She held up her hand. "There was a thing with his parents. I know that, I read the case. But he's a Dweller, and they have a good track record. You can't argue with that."

Jeremiah looked like he might try, then shook his head. "Take fearful risks, the lot of them, but in a good cause. And kind risks, not cruel." He let out a breath as someone called out his name from inside. "Got to go. I'll keep my ears open, send a note if I hear anything."

"Ta." Lydia hopped off the railing, and he stopped to bend down to let her kiss his cheek. "Good night!" Then she went off to her room again, to spend the rest of the evening writing up a clean and usable copy of her notes.

CHAPTER 16
TUESDAY EVENING

G alen settled into the chair in the sitting room off his brother's alchemy laboratory, waiting as Julius closed the door to the lab and went to pour tea. He had on the smaller mask, the one that covered only the worst damage on his face. The healers had found one more technique that helped over the summer, but he said the extra support felt better overall. Galen was mostly glad Julius felt comfortable enough letting more of the scarring show, at least with him. And with Blythe.

She had left them alone as soon as she realised Galen had something specific to ask about. Of course, she was sensitive to the undercurrents. She'd been their mother's companion for years, a cousin and poor relation.

But when their parents had been arrested, Julius had made it clear she had a home. More than just a place to live, it had turned out. They had made it known rather promptly they'd become close over the years. They weren't rushing a wedding, but they didn't need to.

For now, she theoretically had her own rooms, and no one commented on how easily they connected to Julius'

119

private rooms via the back staircase. Galen appreciated how sensitive she was to the fact that Galen just missed his brother sometimes. How he felt they had so much lost time to make up for, when their parents wouldn't even let Galen visit.

"The books are done." Julius had taken most of that one, along with other files for the family business. Not that Galen didn't keep on top of the number. But Julius had a far more readable writing hand, and it was tremendously helpful to have a clean copy for their ongoing records.

Galen smiled. "Thank you. But that's not what I wanted to talk about."

"I know." Julius raised an eyebrow and then passed over the tea. "Help yourself." He gestured at the biscuits. Julius himself would sip tea with other people around, but not eat. It must have been a better day because he went on, saying more than he sometimes did. "Your outings?"

"Have new fruit." Galen tried to figure out where to pick up. "I filled you in about the race horse."

Julius nodded.

"But we went to see it, and then they took us back to London - automobiles are very fast and rather loud, aren't they?" Galen glanced up to see his brother smiling. Well, the half of his face Galen could see.

"Tanks and artillery are louder." Julius said it gently enough, but Galen shivered and looked down. A moment later, Julius was reaching for his hand, patting it. "Loud is bad." Julius wanted to make that clear. "Our family. Not loud."

It made Galen snort and relax. "No, we're not. Anyway. They rushed us back to London. Someone lent Lydia a frock - it looked rather good on her actually, especially for being borrowed? Not at all, not at all our sort of thing?"

"How?" This was a softer question, encouraging Galen to explain.

"Um. Shoulders?" He gestured. "Not much on her shoulders, I mean. Mother would hate it. It was all the things she hates? Fringe and bare shoulders and clear that you're not wearing much underneath?" Galen thought for a moment how it was also like Senara Wilson before - well. Before. That didn't help at all. Lydia was nothing like Senara. And the frock had been a pale green, to be fair, not bright scarlet.

"And you?" Julius's voice was a little breathy at the end.

"I thought she looked grand. Different? But grand." Galen ran a hand through his hair.

"Did you tell her?" This was more insistent.

Galen blinked, then cast back through their conversations. "Um. Maybe not? Probably not. I should have, maybe? But we're - I mean. We're pretending to be involved. She's pretending to be an entirely different person."

"Tell her." It was not quite an order, but it had all the weight of one, an instruction from an older brother, far more experienced with women. Not, Galen reflected, that that took much at all.

He swallowed and yielded almost immediately. "I will. There's something specific I wanted to ask. A man they mentioned, who we met. Actually, two men, but you might not know the other?"

"Him first." There was a faint hint of hissing on the s, a sign Julius was getting a bit more tired.

"The other one, older man, named Aloysius Darley. He's supposed to be something big in the City, how they say it, money or banking or something like that."

Julius considered. "Magical?"

"Probably not? Vincent isn't, I'm pretty sure. But." He hesitated. "That's the other man."

"Tell." Again, not quite an order.

"He's going by the name Nico Lind, but Lydia found some information that makes it clear his name is Nikephoros FitzWallace."

Julius grimaced, first out of reaction to the name, then winced from the pain of the movement tugging on his face. He held up a hand, and Galen shut up. He'd asked last winter, when he and Julius had finally had time to talk, about what helped when that happened. Nothing he could do, it turned out. Or rather, not doing anything was helpful. Not going on, not expecting anything of Julius until the pain eased a bit.

Galen drank his tea as quietly as he could, waiting. It took a good three minutes, longer than usual, before Julius spoke again, softly and more carefully. "Knew him."

"In school?" Galen knew that tone. It meant he'd need to do more of the talking, ask questions that Julius could answer with as few words as possible.

His brother nodded. "Fox." Fox House, like Galen, like Julius. The heirs of the empire, as some would have it.

"Do you know if he was in a society?" Galen had wondered about that. Certainly, he wasn't a Dweller, Galen would have known if he was.

After a moment Julius shook his head no. "Sort who resented that."

That was a particular type, indeed. Galen had met quite a few of them. Not so much people who wished the Dwellers had issued an invitation. They often found their way to the house when they grew into themselves a bit more. Or into their sense.

There was someone from the year ahead of Galen and

Martin who'd been an incredible prankster as a student. But at that point, he had not yet learned the difference between a clever prank and a remarkably dangerous one. Or one that had risks out of proportion to the benefit, anyway, especially to innocents. Now, he was an amiable addition to their company, though you had to make sure he and Thomasina didn't get too many ideas in their heads without a moderating influence.

The thought made him snort, and Julius raised an eyebrow. "You remember I told you about Paul? What he and Thomasina get up to? I was thinking about how we pick up some people as adults who we'd not have taken as a student."

Julius nodded, then made a brushing gesture at his shoulder.

"And some people get a chip on their shoulder about it. What sort of student was he? Alchemy?" Julius shook his head no. "Ritual?" That got a nod, and so did "Materia." The sort of things a well-bred young man from one of the better magical families would focus on.

"Lydia was checking on his War record. Some of it was in his file, some decidedly wasn't. And anything about what he's been up to since. You didn't like him, though, did you? Any reason?"

Julius leaned back, considering that, taking his time. After two minutes, he waved a hand at Galen, to stay put, and he went to look out the window standing there for several minutes. When he came back, he settled in his chair, frowning.

"Heard his War went bad. Not gas. Magic. Killed most there."

Galen nodded. He didn't understand this, not enough. He'd been too young for the War, and that was a gift and a curse. Nearly everyone who'd been old enough considered him an untried lad. Julius was different. Julius had been glad he'd not been through that, but that was rare. "Secret, what happened, or was it in our papers?"

Julius flipped his hand over. "That summer." June of 1917, when Julius had been badly injured. And certainly not paying much attention to anything in the papers, even if there had been anything that made it past the censors.

"Do you know who he spent time with?" Lydia had pointed out that might be helpful information.

"Write." Julius gestured at the action with his hand. That meant that sometime, probably in the middle of the night, he'd get a list in his journal.

Galen smiled, then he leaned back. "Alastair's trying to decide if he should be furious at me. For implying I'm interested in owning a racehorse." He then went on, before Julius had to ask. "Might have an idea about the money, need to check on something. It's just that there's a trick. Or at least one trick, but I know about one."

Julius raised an eyebrow and waved a hand. "G'on."

"So, I asked Owen, one of the Dwellers, his father's a racehorse trainer." Galen said. "And - I didn't understand all of it? But that horse, the breeding he has? He should be chestnut. And he's bay. As much a bay as Romeo." Julius's much loved hunter, before the War.

That made Julius lean forward, but he gestured rather than saying anything.

"Owen's checking with his father. The horse I saw is a fine horse, I mean, no idea how he races? But there's something odd there."

"Why?"

Galen knew his brother well enough to interpret that by now. That tone to the question meant Galen should lay out the reasoning. He paused to gather his thoughts. "First, apparently, those particular horses should not have had a bay foal. Or at least it is exceedingly unlikely. And I am sure they didn't think I'd know. Which of course, I didn't but that's why friends, allies, and informative experts are good to have in your life."

Julius snorted, but nodded.

"They are pressing me to decide. We didn't manage drinks yet - something came up yesterday. Alternately, they want me to think they are much more important than I am. I would have been very peeved to get to London and find they'd cancelled."

Julius lifted a finger, and Galen added. "They sent a note to the club." There was a cover club, more or less, a place where men of Galen's station could be members, all quite private. It meant those outside the magical community could send round a message, as Vincent had, and Galen would still get it promptly. Fortunately, he'd left a request that if anything came in for him on short notice, they should pass it along by journal.

That reminded him, though. "I don't know what that means about Lind. Or Fitzwallace, whatever we're calling him."

"Lind. Habit." That was the instruction of his brother, who had done his share of intelligence work, and Galen would certainly respect that. He nodded.

"Lind. He must have figured out I'm magical, but I don't actually know that. Vincent wouldn't have told him, Bunny isn't. And you and I look alike, but if you didn't know him well, and it's been a decade or more, well." He shrugged. "We'll have to keep trying."

Julius looked up at that, meeting Galen's eyes, then gathered himself. "Dangerous." It wasn't telling him not to.

Julius had never made Galen feel like the younger brother, forbidding him from doing things. But he had experience Galen didn't. The kind that made a difference.

Galen nodded. "Dangerous. But it's…" He frowned. "I agreed to help Lydia a bit on a lark. It'd been a while since Martin and I got up to anything smaller, not like the General Strike. He's been busy. The strike work was important, but only briefly dangerous. A lot of it was just gruelling."

He hadn't gone into it with Julius before, but in the strikes, Martin was on far more solid ground. Galen had learned to hang back, carry things, hold signs, and pass out sandwiches and flasks of tea, without being actively posh at anyone. It was a challenge.

Julius raised an eyebrow. Obviously, he'd caught some part of that. Galen said, as mildly as he could, "I want to get this right. Especially as it seems we have stumbled into something queer. I didn't like the way Lind felt. And there's something odd about Darley. I'll be careful, and we have resources they don't know about."

That got a nod, and Julius then gestured. "Tell about the grounds." They settled into a more comfortable report of what Galen had seen in his rounds of the property and tenants in the last fortnight. By the time Blythe came back an hour later, Galen had settled into reading aloud to his brother while Julius prepared several materials for his next alchemical experiment.

CHAPTER 17
SATURDAY, NOVEMBER 20TH, AT THE RACES

"**R**eady?" Galen leaned in to murmur at her. She was done up in yet another tailored frock, this one of a deep green that Lydia rather coveted. Galen had looked her up and down when she'd turned up to meet him. She thought he'd approved, at least, but she still felt like she was wearing a costume. Or perhaps not exactly a costume, but like something she wanted to grow into. She felt like she was staggering around in her older sister's good shoes, at any rate.

"As ready as I'll get." They had talked out the plan for today. Lydia would see what she could pick up from the women, while Galen got lured into agreeing to buy into a share in Crisparkle. Let himself be lured. He'd decided to play it that way. When they'd talked about it last night, he felt it might give them more scope later.

As they walked in, Lydia couldn't help thinking back to what had kept her up last night. Certainly, some men - more men than women, anyway - enjoyed having power for the sake of power. Certainly plenty of people like money, or else what money could buy. Even if she thought many of them hadn't ever been truly poor, not like her family had.

But what she'd kept coming back to, again, was that there was something they were missing. Something lurked in the back of her head. Were these men up to no good? Probably. At least, the bookmakers would give decent odds. The sort of thing a horse that had consistent form might expect. Not every man was nefarious, nor was every woman a saint. She certainly wasn't the latter, and she was fairly sure Galen wasn't the former. Or Martin, or various of the other men she saw regularly socially.

The question, though, was perhaps more about what sort of race they were running. If it were about social status, the sort of things that would be Lords and Ladies of the land among magical folk, that was one sort of challenge. And not one that she and Galen were as likely to figure out, honestly. Galen was well-born, but there was a chasm between his family and those circles near as deep as the one between her family and his.

If it were about, oh, industry and factories and making a lot of something apparently necessary, they might well not figure it out either. The Dwellers knew more about that sort of thing than many magical folk. But there was a difference between understanding the labour issues and understanding the engineering side of it all. Not, of course, that labour wasn't relevant to the money, but it wasn't the only factor.

Lydia supposed it could be about magic, or about access to magic. At least for some of them. Or about some other sort of influence, the ability to make trades in different places, perhaps, and make money. Or the ability to influence markets. That might bring together both status and money, and some people liked that combination above all else.

Well. Her job today was to gather up whatever wheat she could from the gossip, rather than the chaff. They were introduced around - about half the same people as last time, including Vincent and Felicity. A moment later, Bunny and Plucky came in. Lydia could see an immediate chill from Felicity and Prudence. Plucky went off to talk with several other young women, dragging along another young man. She wriggled her fingers at Lydia as she went, as if amused by the whole thing. Clearly, the frock had got back to her safely.

"I gather you met Plucky." Felicity definitely disapproved.

"Last week, yes. She was very kind, and lent me a dress." She glanced after Plucky, then tilted her head. "Is there something I ought to know?"

"Oh, she's just not our sort, darling. Loud and flashy. Bunny finds her amusing right now, we wish he'd settle down properly." She waved a hand. The men were gathered out on the balcony, leaning on the railing and discussing something. Possibly even horses.

"Can I ask a bit more about Bunny, then? And of course, you all. Vincent and Galen were talking ever so much, last week, I didn't get a chance to get to know him better." As she hoped, that got somewhere.

Vincent and Bunny had gone to school together, and had been posted not far from each other during the War. Vincent had been an officer in the trenches for some of it, but he'd been invalided out relatively early on, with a posting well behind the lines after that. Some sort of injury, not discussed, clearly not terribly obvious to the casual observer. Lydia felt her mind wander over the possibilities.

The more genteel forms of shell-shock, perhaps, or a manly injury, a proper token of a soldier, now largely healed. The sort of thing that got articles and stories, unlike the far more complex injuries of many. Including Galen's brother.

Though having seen Vincent's public records, Lydia suddenly wondered whether it had been one of those intentional injuries. Shooting himself in the foot to get him out of the worst of the Front. There was something about him, in their interactions so far, that made her suspect he had three or four reasons behind each choice.

Bunny, it seemed, had been the one to introduce Vincent to Aloysius, and Aloysius had introduced Nico to the mix. That gave them a better chain to explore. Lydia hadn't been able to turn up much about Aloysius Darley beyond the very public information. He was on the board of this business, and that charity, but even those were fairly uninformative. One was about food, and the other had something to do with transport, trains, she had assumed from the fact the prospectus had a train on the masthead.

And so, of course, they couldn't avoid inviting Bunny along sometimes. And thus, also Plucky. Felicity and Prudence might disapprove, but they were not monsters about it. There were laws of civility at play. It came out, a little later, that they were daughters of a rector, a well-off man from an excellent family. They had gone to good schools, including somewhere in Switzerland for polish, before being presented at Court.

Lydia vaguely followed all of that, but she'd have to do more rummaging tomorrow to make sense of half of it. After Lydia ventured a few more questions, she heard "And who are your people again?" That was Prudence, who seemed to have a somewhat more suspicious nature than

Felicity. Or perhaps she was less directly dependent on Galen's good will.

"Papa's in business. He did really quite well. And Galen - well, we met, and really, he's so self-possessed."

"Not in the War?"

"Oh, no. He was just too young. Turned eighteen that next year. His brother fought though, poor man. Badly injured, his face." Lydia hated using that as a topic of conversation, but it was the thing that fit here, and she braced herself for a reaction.

"My." Felicity seemed to consider half a dozen things. "Vincent will want to know. He's very devoted to making sure veterans have access to proper resources. I'm sure that's not a problem for Galen's brother, but there might be people in his unit who could use a hand. Services." The idea of it seemed to settle her.

Lydia supposed that a clergyman's daughter - she wasn't quite clear on the difference between a vicar, a rector, and a parson - would be inclined to charity. Or at least the proper show of it. "I haven't had a chance to meet Julius yet. He's - well, he doesn't see people outside the family."

"Ah." That got a cool, searching gaze from Felicity. "Well. We'll just have to introduce you around to more people, won't we? Make sure you meet the right sort."

Lydia nodded, hoping one or the other of them would expand. After a moment, Prudence nodded at her husband. "Paul was in London, managing supplies. He had a terrible fever as a boy, and his heart just wasn't up to it, the doctors said." Lydia suddenly wondered how true that was. Some men bribed their way out, or their fathers bribed their way out. She wondered if it had caused a split between the sisters. Having one husband in the midst of the fighting, and the other safe on this side of the Channel.

"I would love to meet some more people. I - well, Papa kept me at home. My mama died when I was young, and I think he couldn't bear to send me away to school. I had a governess and all that, but it's not the same at all." Also, it was a far simpler lie to keep straight. That got them off on a good twenty minutes of where she'd grown up. She'd picked a spot near where an aunt had a farm. She knew the local landscape enough to talk about it. And she knew there were a couple of newly-rich men who'd bought up properties in the area, none of whom were particularly socially notable.

Believable lies. For someone whose lifework was in finding the truth, her job involved rather a lot of them. This offering at least got Felicity and Prudence talking about what social events Lydia might find of interest. That, of course, led to questions about Galen. "Vincent's explained a bit, but of course you can't trust a man to fill in all the details of a someone's background. However did you meet? And what is his situation, exactly? Vincent said there had been some oddity with his parents?"

Lydia had, thankfully, asked Galen what she should say if the question came up. Otherwise, she would have been caught entirely flat-footed here. "His parents, well. Some unfortunate business decisions, and some legal trouble. The actual estate businesses are doing well, steadily, but they're not flashy. I don't know all the details, of course, but he's mentioned wool and cheese and various other goods like that. Not manufacturing." Lydia dimpled. "That's more my father's line. But Galen has a mentor who's been helping him sort out the import and export trade his father had been exploring. More cautiously, but more steadily."

"We'd gathered Galen is not overly inclined to gamble." Felicity said, glancing at Prudence. Lydia remembered the comments Margery had made at the club. That Felicity ran with a notably fast set and was a terror at cards, while Vincent was more conservative but not with banking deals. Perhaps Paul was a gambler.

"He's cautious. And still under the thumb of his mentor, though now they've got through the harvest, I gather he's got a bit more money to play with. He is very interested in that horse..." Lydia let her voice trail off expectantly.

"Oh, Vincent will be very glad. And honestly, it's such fun. Getting to be in the winner's circle, and all the drinks and cheer. Really quite thrilling, and you meet so many of the best people." They kept using that phrase, as if relying on it to get Galen to join them. Assuming everyone wanted to win. Whatever Galen wanted, Lydia wasn't at all sure it could be summed up that simply.

"So who would you suggest we meet this time round? Honestly, you've been so kind, and so has Vincent, but we still barely know anyone."

"What are your own interests, then? Besides Galen?" Prudence teased, there. "You do keep looking at him."

Lydia flushed. "Well, he's easy on the eyes, isn't he?" He was wearing a sharply tailored suit today, with a bright pocket square and tie of deep purple. It was a rather striking contrast to his hair and skin, but somehow it worked for him.

"Well, if your family approves, I will say he's been good-humoured when I've seen him. And tolerant of Bunny, which not everyone is. Well. We know all the people here. You might want someone who can take you in hand, intro-duce you to some of the older matrons in society. You must

- pardon, dear. I gather you don't have a mother or aunt who can help with that sort of thing."

Lydia ducked her chin. "Oh, I'm afraid not." She had a mother, and plenty of aunts, but it was true they were no help with society introductions. Cooking eel pie, yes. Doing laundry, yes. Society events, no. Other than perhaps cleaning up afterwards.

CHAPTER 18
SATURDAY AFTERNOON

Galen found himself neatly cut away from the others by Vincent and another man. Bunny was occupied elsewhere, nearer the door to the balcony. Vincent leaned on the railing, racing form in his hand.

"Nico thought you had promise." Not a subtle man, but Galen hadn't expected that. "He'd like to have lunch with you, get to know you better, if you're willing. And if you're ..." He waved the paper at the horses. "Willing with the horse."

"The two things come as a set, then?" Galen kept his voice light. "I'm considering the horse."

"Your man of business isn't being too difficult? Or, no, you said a trustee."

Alastair wasn't either, but it did well enough here. "Cautious man, about some things. And there's my elder brother to think of."

"Felicity said, yes." Vincent said. Galen suddenly wondered if Lydia had, or if Nico Lind had passed something along. It would make a difference which. Though

135

there was no reason Vincent might not have found out through some other means.

"Badly injured in the War. His face, he's not able to do the public side of things anymore." Galen kept his voice even. He'd talked through this with Julius. Well, mostly talked at Julius, who had said a few words. He'd written out rather more in the charmed journals. Julius much preferred that for extended comment, for all the obvious reasons and some less obvious ones. Like the fact he'd be up in the middle of the night, with pain. Writing a long note to Galen was a pleasant distraction, apparently.

Vincent nodded. "I'd gathered. Nico mentioned knowing the name." Well, that at least gave Galen fair warning.

"It matters that - well. That he doesn't worry too much. About the family property, about me." Galen shrugged, trying to get the right mix of mutual worry and careless-twenties into it.

"Ah, well. You just need people to show you how things are done. And if you make a good impression on Nico, doors would open for you. Aloysius, too, especially if you're looking to expand a business. Nico said you came from the right sort of people."

Galen nodded and took a breath, glancing out over the racecourse. It at least was convenient to have it right there, being a visible distraction. He was milking every chance he could get to think through things. With any luck, Vincent would assume he was cautious about the horse - which he was - and not judging what to say about any of the rest of it. "I want to do well, you know? Get the estates on a good footing. Make it so Julius doesn't need to worry."

"And your parents won't interfere?" Vincent pressed at that a bit more.

"No, no. That's not the problem." Galen let himself sound distracted. His parents were, to some extent, unable to be nearly as much of a problem as they wanted to be. He made a brief visit once a month to deal with the household accounts with the steward. Sometimes he saw one or the other of his parents, rarely both on the same day. They had their own interests or lack of them. But mostly, they were a pit of bitterness and frustration.

Galen should feel more filial, and he just didn't. He didn't wish them ill. He didn't know how to be with them, and maybe he never had. He certainly knew he couldn't expect them to give him anything he actually wanted. His aunt and uncle were doing slightly better with that, checking with him and with Julius, but it wasn't the same thing at all. And they all knew it.

Vincent shifted, slightly, leaning more now. Galen knew enough that it was meant to put him at ease. Being who he was, being a Dweller, and Martin's friend, it just made him suspicious. "It's not everyone who gets this kind of opportunity, you realise."

Galen nodded. "I'm quite aware. And it's on generous terms. Just..."

"It's time to be a man." Galen wished, suddenly, that people thought well enough of his skills to feel they needed to be subtle. Vincent clearly didn't. His parents didn't. Rather a lot of other people didn't.

He didn't mind Alastair being blunt; that was part of the arrangement. Martin knew he'd pick things up. Julius had learned it quickly. Lydia - well. Lydia seemed to assume he was competent, though Galen wasn't entirely sure why.

But taking insult here wouldn't do any good at all. "Ah, but that's the question, isn't it? What kind of man am I?

What kind of man do I want to be? I'm certain I'm still figuring it out."

He was pleased with that answer, and even more pleased when Vincent turned to blink at him, unsure what to say to that for a good minute. Then he shrugged. "Well. We can introduce you to the best people. The interesting parties."

Galen nodded, let the sentence fade away a bit. "I admit, I'm curious about Nico. How, well, I'm sure you're the right person to tell me." Also not subtle, but Vincent puffed up in pride, rather noticeably. Decidedly not subtle. "How do I make a good impression on him?"

"You made a decent start last Saturday." Vincent said, waving a hand. "It's not everyone he'll have a drink with."

Galen shrugged. "Oh, I'm sure he thinks I'm a stripling. Not good for much yet. Or - well with horses, it'd be a yearling. Possibly some promise, but no way to test it yet."

"Oh, I think we can call you a three-year-old. Old enough to be racing on the flat. Not over fences, yet. That takes seasoning." Vincent relaxed a bit, as if having a framework for this helped. "He's not just thinking about this horse, of course."

"I assumed it wasn't just the horse." Galen agreed. "You're all taking it very seriously, of course, but I could tell there's more weight behind it."

"Rather." Vincent turned, leaning more on one elbow so he could watch Galen closely. "I'm at a bank in the City, of course. And Aloysius has his fingers in several projects. Nico, well. Nico has an eye for the future. Where investment might be most profitable. What to avoid. The things a man with business interests might care about."

Galen had always been told that - with a few carefully managed exceptions - future-telling was a dubious practise at best, especially when it came to markets. Certainly, omens and prophecies existed, and a fair number of them were accurate. But the more accurate ones usually had some personal element. Not an agreeable but fairly unre- markable horse. "Many a man would be." he agreed. His father, for one.

"That takes some boldness, though. Some risk. I've had some long-term bets riding on Nico's recommendations. Bit of a bobble last spring, but everything's settled down."

"Any particular reason why, the bobble?" Galen wondered, suddenly, if that had to do with Sisley and the trials.

"Oh, one of the twitches of the market. A horse has a bad day, everyone panics. Next time out, they might win. That's the draw of it, isn't? You'll find out that you need to ride out these ups and downs. Plenty of things in the soup, and then you can ride whatever rises to the top."

It was a terribly mixed metaphor, but Galen nodded along. He - or more likely Lydia or Martin - could dig into the details later. "And Nico?"

"Nico's got a gift." This was unabashedly wanting some of that for himself. "And he's lucky. He has a steady stream of picking winners. Both on the track and elsewhere and it's skill, not just luck."

"Huh." Galen made a properly non-committal noise. "All right. So how do I impress him?"

"With chaps who were in the War, well, your service would tell him a lot."

Galen nodded. "Not an option, here." He wondered, too, what that had got for Vincent.

"Or your school. Who your people are. I don't know all of it, of course. He knows people I don't, different side of the City, and all that."

And how. Galen kept from snorting. "So the fact he placed my brother, that doesn't hurt."

"Absolutely not. The biggest thing, though..." Vincent paused as a race began, in a tumult of the starting pistol and the thunder of hooves. One of the horses pulled out in front rather early, faltering later in the race, with another two coming up close behind. They battled it out into the last stretch, almost neck and neck, until one finally pulled ahead by a hair.

"Well." Vincent sounded pleased at something.

"You have a bet on?"

"Not that one, but it's a good sign for later." He didn't explain, but returned to the earlier conversation. "You have to understand that Nico's looking for a mix of things. Potential. Someone who can learn how we do things, without needing too much handholding or explaining. And he thinks you might qualify there. But also someone with the right sort of mettle."

"And what sort's that?"

Vincent waved the racing form. "Yours isn't a Colonial Service sort of family, are you? Or Army, outside of the recent?"

Galen shook his head. "County squires like I said. Travel in the country, my parents did a Grand Tour, but nothing much beyond that."

"Pity. That's the right sort of thing. A view to the strength of the empire, that always goes over well with Nico, and some of the other people he knows."

Galen had one of those moments where he felt himself split in two. One one hand, there was what other people assumed about him, by how he said certain words, and the clothes he wore, and which clubs he belonged to.

And on the other, there was what he'd chosen. The

Dwellers, and Martin in particular. The people who got used up and discarded by empire. The people who'd died in the mud of the trenches and in the dust of Africa, who'd gone to sea and never come home. And all the people who'd died in mines or factories, or because of them.

At the moment, though, the way to help them was to learn more. He cleared his throat. "Well. Never really had the opportunity to do that sort of thing. Even most of the current business is rather domestic. We're looking for export trade, of course, everyone sensible is."

Vincent nodded, then turned more serious. "The way to impress Nico is to - well, talk up that sort of interest. How you'd like to hone yourself, become one of the best and brightest of your generation. And we're looking to you, all you who were too young to fight, to fill some rather big shoes."

Galen wished he hadn't put it that way. People kept saying that. He couldn't ever fill Julius's shoes. Julius was still wearing them, even if he never saw more than a handful of people. For another, he'd been truly heroic. And not just when he'd gone off to set something to rights he'd found out about, something that had likely saved dozens or hundreds of lives. At least for a bit longer.

"Very big shoes." It was the right thing to say, so Galen said it. He could hate himself for it later. "Does that mean taking risks?"

"Perhaps." Vincent glanced over, then focused on the racecourse again. "But the clever sort of risks. Perhaps you know something that would be useful to Nico. He wants to have lunch, this week. And if that goes well, perhaps a house party. You'll meet rather more of our set."

Suddenly, certainly, Galen got the sense that Vincent was none too sure of his own place in that knot of people.

Or at least, that his place was not as stable as he pretended it was. Galen couldn't tell if it had to do with money, or with some other aspect, but there was something there that caught his attention and wouldn't let go. Before he could continue the conversation, however, Felicity came out on the balcony with a fresh drink for Vincent, and Galen slipped away to see if Lydia needed anything.

CHAPTER 19

LATE SATURDAY EVENING AT THE
DWELLERS' HOUSE

"Did Vincent suggest that if you were a very good boy, we might get invited to a party?" Lydia settled back in what was rapidly becoming her usual chair in the lounge. Then she clapped her hand to her mouth. "That came out differently than I meant."

Galen snorted and slung one of his knees over the arm of his own chair. He really did find the most absurd ways to sit. If sitting were the word for it. It was more like a sprawl, half the time. "Well. Depends what kind of good boy you mean."

They were, at least, alone for the moment, though Galen was apparently expecting at least Martin and Thomasina to appear in the next half hour. Possibly Owen or a couple of the others. Which reminded Lydia of another question, even more awkward.

"What did he mean, then?" She'd start there. It was a sensible journalistic inquiry.

"If I make the right show of things at lunch. Which apparently means a - mmm. Playing up my interest in the empire. Expansion thereof, implied. Though honestly, where does one expand to? That's the question?"

Lydia nodded, and then frowned. Something was nagging at the edge of her mind. "Can we come back to that?" she asked.

"Of course." Galen leaned back, without an apparent care in the world.

"What else could Vincent have meant?" Lydia asked.

"Sex, drugs, sex and drugs. We can probably rule out enchantments, alchemical potions, or anything like that, though honestly, the distinction between alchemical potions and drugs is rather nebulous? Julius has a whole bit about it." Galen waved a hand, rotating from the wrist without lifting his head.

Lydia asked, before thinking about the implications. "And the sex?"

"You know, I can't decide about that one. You hear stories about house parties. I mean, the sort of house parties thrown by people who are known to like drugs, extravagant gambling, and so on. And Thornley had that comment about a Hellfire Club, which usually implies sex and dark magic, however you define that."

It didn't answer Lydia's question. "Have you?"

"No. And I don't exactly want my first time to be - well. Like that." Galen said it straight out, though he still didn't lift his head. Then a moment later he did, peering at her. "You're very good at asking questions people answer. It must come in handy."

The utter good-natured amusement in his voice was about the only reason she didn't burn up in embarrassment. She grimaced, and he must have caught her expression. "Most people assume things. I'd rather be asked."

"If you assume things, you get them wrong." Which was a point of pride for her. It always had been. She wanted to know the actual thing, not the assumption. Then she offered. "I have. But I'm not interested in an orgy." It seemed fair, but she really hoped he didn't ask about it. Then she tilted her head. "You must know people say things about you and Martin."

"Oh, they do. Sometimes they even say them to our faces. Not here, people know better. Also, various of our lot have made it clear that's not on. Not about us, not about anyone." Galen shrugged, the shoulder nearer her, and let his head fall back over the arm of the chair again.

"And you're not."

"When people kept assuming, we talked about it. He's not interested, not in men. Laura, yes, very much so, and I wish them everything good." There was a note there, the way he leaned into the comment, that made Lydia wonder if Galen had been interested, even if he'd set it aside.

Lydia was also struck by how two people could say the same words, and have them come out sounding utterly different. She'd talked once to a woman whose husband had left her. Left her and three young kids, all under the age of seven, to run off with a secretary. She'd washed her hands of both of them and wished them very happy very far away in a tone of voice like a vengeful queen. She must have had a powerful thread of magic to her, because he'd gone to India not long after, taking the other woman with him.

When Galen said it, though, he meant it. These were people he cared for, and he wanted them happy. So she asked, "It's that simple for you?"

That got his head up. "Why wouldn't it be? If Martin had been interested, it'd be different. But he isn't, and I.

145

Well, I'm not interested in someone who isn't interested back. Turns out. Only no one has been." He shrugged. "Even Laura. Mother tried to marry me off, she was the last attempt."

"Oh." Lydia wasn't even sure how to ask about that. "What happened?"

"There was the murder, and Martin got accused, and it was all horribly tangled. Laura was very clever and sensible. And she was sensible enough to look at me and tell me I needed someone else."

Lydia frowned, and wished she could see Galen's face. He had an odd hollowness in his voice. "That - um." She wasn't sure how to respond.

"She said I was loyal and kind and thoughtful and a good friend. And it helped to hear that eventually. But she thought I needed someone who'd inspire me to be brave. Like Martin does, actually, he always has. You know the Schola houses well enough, right?"

Lydia nodded. "It's required, for making sense of the lot of you." she said. "You're Fox House, right?"

"As a proper scion of my sort of family was supposed to be. Though I was rather second tier compared to some in our year and the year above. They ignored me amiably, most of the time. And especially once we were Dwellers. There's a certain protection there, no one wanted some fiendishly ingenious prank turned on them. Mind, it's a lot of work keeping up that reputation for future generations of students."

"I suspect you have some stories," she agreed. "But Martin?"

"Martin's a Boar. Charging in, determined, stubborn. He's not bad at some of the martial magics, actually. But he's better at - how do I put this?" Galen lifted himself bodily, slid into a different position in the chair, now mostly upright but leaning forward, one foot tucked under the other knee.

"Are you completely unable to sit in a chair?" It came out of her again, before she could think better of it. That kept happening with him.

He glanced down. "Currently? Apparently? It changed after my parents and things. I can do it when I'm being formal, but if I - well. If I like who I'm with, you take your chances."

Lydia waved a hand. "The furniture will probably survive. Martin. Charging at things."

"More, I worry about him surviving." Galen ran his hand through his hair. "Mostly he's very deliberate about what he charges at? His writing. The strike work. Figuring out how to get information that helps people stay safer. But Laura's right, he needs moderation, and I need bucking up. Or something. Inspiration. The fire coming down from the heavens." He gestured vaguely at the other side of the room. Lydia craned her neck, to realise there was a large and somewhat faded mural of Prometheus carrying a reed with fire down to share it with humanity. The central myth of the Dwellers, she'd learned that much long ago.

"And what do you worry about?" Galen blinked at her, visibly startled. She spread her hands. "Besides the estate?"

There was a twitch of his shoulder. "People don't ask me that. People assume they know what I'm good for. The thing is, I don't feel good at much. We have the estate, but we're not Lords of the land. The land's not bad, the tenants would manage. Maybe we'd sell off the big houses. It would be a failure in many people's eyes, but it's not a crisis." His shoulder twitched again. "I'm always too young or too late or too inconsequential to do anything important."

"I begin to see," Lydia said, "Why Laura thought you needed someone to help you buck up. You think you don't live up to that, either, do you? Or your friends here."

He hesitated again and it was like that moment of a fox caught out in the open, by someone it knew could be a threat. Lydia had seen one a few times in parks, coming home late from a political meeting. "No. I don't."

"Well. Martin couldn't help with this. What we're doing. Or most other people. You know how to make the words go right. You can make the proper show. And honestly, coming across like you're a bit young and new to things is exceedingly useful. They keep telling you things, had you noticed? Well, you did, you're the one who pointed out how unsubtle Vincent was being."

"I had noticed. And I suppose that might be a help with Nico. Certainly it's the safest way through. And the most useful for you. Make him spell out what's on offer."

"That's an interesting trick, isn't it? I wish I knew better what they'd asked in the trials for Lord Sisley and all." She waved her hand in a circle. "We're back to the expansion and empire part."

"We are." Galen shifted positions again, this time shoving himself into the back corner of the chair and pulling both feet up on the seat with him, his arms around his legs. It made him look very young indeed, especially when he rested his cheek against his knee. Lydia swore to herself she wouldn't let a hint of that come through. "What do you mean about the trials?"

"So. I can more or less understand why there wasn't a trial on the other side. Non-magical." She waved a hand. "I gather the actual trial was about stealing antiquities and threatening people in the process. Not about the snake cult. That just came out as part of it."

"But being in an expansionist secret society is not actually against the law. Ours or theirs. Well, see also Club Row, here. We're not the only ones with ideals and projects." Galen considered. "Nico's not in a society, and I'm sure he'd have wanted Dius Fidius."

"Your ideals are less expansionist than Dius Fidius, mind." That was the sort of society and club Lydia was sure Lord Sisley had wanted to belong to as well, made of the notable leaders and holders of power. The similarities did leap out at one. "Not that I know a lot about it, just the rumours."

"That's not hard." Galen pointed out. "All right. So they could try our folks, such as they were. Sisley and the others. And it's a scandal, but it's a short one. Longer than Mother and Father, but most people have already moved on, and it's only been months."

"But - do we think that's what Vincent is up to? And Nico? And other people? They're clearly up to something."

Galen considered. "I don't like the feel. I mean, I don't exactly have a broad experience of things. Not like this? But there's something off. They're trying to be very persuasive, which suggests they're desperate for fresh blood. Or new money. Or both. But I don't think they're just after my money, even if that's the obvious thing they're going for with the horse."

"And it's possible that Sisley and all didn't know everyone involved. When you read the pulps about this sort of thing, it's all masks and cloaks and secret passwords. No one knows everyone else involved."

"Well, that's just sensible organising." Galen said it like it was a matter of fact. "If you work on a cell structure, then if one of you gets arrested, the amount of damage it does to your plans is limited."

At that point, they both heard a mess of people coming up the stairs, talking loudly and at speed.

CHAPTER 20

TUESDAY, NOVEMBER 23RD, AT NICO'S CLUB

G alen settled into the chair, and made a point of looking around. Not gawking, but taking the place in. It was, in fact, what he and Lydia had expected. There was dark wood panelling with the sort of patina of age that only happened when the wood was properly tended for decades.

He could smell the faint but pervasive scent of wood polish, lemon and beeswax. It was, of course, the middle of the week, an unfashionably late lunch, so the place was rather quiet. There were two men at a table near the door, a good twenty feet away, and one solitary man at a table halfway down the room. But that was it, in a space that might comfortably have held thirty or forty.

Nico gestured. "A pleasant place, isn't it? The light is rather good this time of day. For all it's the guest dining room, a few members prefer it for that reason, at least when it's not busy." His tone was light, as if he were making every effort to be charming.

"Thank you for the invitation, of course." Galen settled his hands on his lap, and looked back at his host. Nico was sharply dressed, in a suit made for the City and all its expectations, and Galen was sure he'd see polished shoes if he could see Nico's feet. Galen was less well-tailored, himself, but similarly dressed.

"Well, it seems sensible to get to know each other better, doesn't it? Vincent thinks you show some promise." Nico leaned forward. "And I am interested in that promise."

It was rather more blunt than Galen had expected. He flushed, it wasn't like he could stop himself, but then glanced up. "I'm flattered, of course, but not sure why you've both taken an interest."

"May I be honest?" Nico sounded charming now, enough that Galen knew to suspect magic. He didn't think Nico would do anything too overt, not here. He must be bound by the Pact as well as anyone else in Albion, anyone with magic. Certainly anyone who'd had enough magic to be at Schola.

"Please." It was a sensible way forward. He didn't expect Nico to actually be honest, but it would be informative what he did share.

"You've been done badly by. A whole lot of us have been. We were promised the world, the shining fruit, ready for us to reach for. And what did we get? My generation, we got a war, a horrific war." Nico glanced away, and Galen was sure this was artifice, now. Even if it had something real, down at the roots, the man had learned to use it like a dagger. "I'm sure your brother doesn't speak much of it. Most of us chaps don't. But I swore, after some of what I saw, I'd never let it happen again. Not to me and mine."

Galen nodded once, silently. He wasn't sure how to answer that. Finally, he said, "I was too young to fight. And now, no one thinks I'm worth much. Not tested the same way."

Nico coughed. Galen couldn't tell if he was covering for feeling that way, or for some other piece of the puzzle. Then he murmured "Pardon," and went on smoothly. "Well, blaming you for it isn't the way forward now, is it? We need your generation to step up, certainly. So many losses, people who would have taken on our goals and progress."

For a moment, Galen wondered if Nico could possibly know about his membership in the Dwellers. It wasn't something they advertised broadly, as a rule, it made them too much of a target. But it also wasn't secret and there were quite a few ways someone might come across current members. "What's your aim, then?"

Nico tapped his nose with his finger, the classic sign of someone getting something right, but needing to wait. "Threefold, really. First, if we can be of mutual assistance to each other, I'd like to figure that out. And I suspect we can be." Again, he was spreading the charm thick. "Second, you're a young man making his way in the world. Perhaps I know people who might be useful connections. Business, other areas of your life." He nodded. "Miss Pyle seems rather taken with you."

Galen had no idea what to do with that at all. Was Nico picking up on something there that Galen hadn't noticed? Or simply Lydia's act? Or was he implying Galen could do better? Galen gave up, and blinked. "Beg pardon? I'm not sure what you mean by that."

Nico laughed, loudly enough he attracted attention, and waved a hand. "My. You are amusing." It had a definite sense of 'entertaining puppy' to it, but he went on. "I'm married. My wife stays at home. She doesn't care for crowds." There were volumes there, to be teased out, but knowing he was apparently married, perhaps Lydia could find records. Then he leaned forward. "The sort of wife a man chooses can open doors for him. Or close them."

"And Lydia?"

"Do you care for her?" The question came back, rapid fire. Yes, Galen did. Not the way Nico likely meant. Certainly, for the purpose of her story, he seemed likely to be her access to things.

"She's good fun. And sensible. Practical. I know where I am with her." He was making her sound like an efficient secretary, which was not right at all. Also, he wasn't at all sure he knew where he was with her or with anyone. But damned if he'd let on about that to Nico.

"I suppose she's got some money to be settled on her. Nothing so crass as a purely fiscal exchange, these days, though there are plenty where that was more or less what was going on. My parents were an arranged match. It worked out well enough." There was a slight shrug of his shoulders. "Choosing for magical potential, rather than wealth, in our case."

Galen nodded. He wondered, all of a sudden, about the family connections. A beneficial match to his father's family would have set up expectations of Nico and his father both. The way those carried down the generations could be entirely poisonous.

"I gather there were some family complications. I get the papers, of course, though I spend most of my time these days in City matters." Strongly implying the non-magical sorts. Galen wondered, suddenly, if that were because all the likely prospects in their shared community knew better, or if Nico felt he couldn't actually be competitive there. If that were the case, why on earth not?

Instead, Galen nodded and gave the expected answer. "Quite a few. My brother's settled into alchemical research.

I'm taking on the estate management and some of my father's business interests." He let himself shrug. "That has kept me quite busy this year, though it might ease up over the winter."

"Well, that brings us to the third matter. A young man should have interests outside his work. An older man, too." Nico included himself in the latter category with a sweep of his hand.

"Not just horse-racing." Galen offered it as the answer to an exam. He was fairly sure that was the intention, anyway.

It got him a broad smile. "Precisely. Racing is a fine way to meet people, to make some connections. It is a largely unobjectionable place where people from various walks of life might come across each other. That is a tool, not my interest."

Galen nodded, then gave the cue he felt was expected. "And your interest?"

"On the regular, I get together with a select group, a few people who, like me, are seeking more than drugs or parties, jazz clubs or gossip. Those things are fine here and there, but they're no good day in and day out."

Galen made himself pause and take a sip of his drink. It wouldn't do to be too eager, or to be too casual. He had to find the place somewhere in the middle. He thought, suddenly, of what Lydia would do, how she'd tilt her head, ask a question. Not make an assumption. "You must have some goal. Not a cause, precisely, but something that brings you together?"

Nico laughed rather warmly. "Oh, we do. I would be pleased to have you join us, meet some of the others, in a relaxed setting. I'll talk to the others, see if we can find a suitable event. Tell me, were you considering buying in to Crisparkle?"

Clearly, the one hinged on the other. "My man of business doesn't approve of it, but as Vincent's pointed out, a man has to live his own life." Galen said. "A half share, mind, I can't manage a whole." He'd already got the idea that Vincent and Felicity needed money, but Nico's interest implied it wasn't just them. The question was why. It was entirely possible Nico was just greedy.

"That's plenty to get you in on the fun. So you'll be at the race meeting, next Saturday?"

Crisparkle was racing for the first time then. "Both of us. I'm meeting Lydia that morning. We'll take the train together."

"I feel like I should know her family, but I suppose it's a common enough one, Pyle." He shrugged. "I do appreciate your attention to the details. It's so ever much easier to manage things when people aren't sloppy about the Pact."

That made Galen sit up and take notice. Mentally, at least. He couldn't tell if that was a threat, a warning, a practical statement, or all three at once in one great untidy knot. He managed to keep his voice even. "Has that been a problem with others?"

Nico shrugged. "Not for long."

Right. Definitely a threat. Whatever else it was. There was a pause as the next course was brought over. As the waiter left, Galen glanced after him. "The staff here are very good, aren't they?"

"They know their place." It wasn't exactly dismissive. But it gave Galen a very clear sense that Nico divided the world into people who aspired to be like him, and people who wouldn't ever come near that.

"May I ask a bit about your service in the War?" Nico's

eyebrows raised, and Galen went on quickly. "My brother was wondering if you'd had any overlap." There were two ways this could go. Nico might just answer, or at least give some of it. Or Galen would end up reeling off what he could share.

"The trenches, for a good while. And just behind them, for some time. Then I got sent off elsewhere." His lips went tighter, and Galen could read the signs of something personally awful there. "The magical attacks were increasing. The problem with distinct lines of magic, with different approaches, is countering them becomes near impossible. We overlap, certainly, with Germany, with Italy, with Spain or Hungary. But there is too much variation."

Galen rather thought that variation, being able to respond to it, made you stronger. He knew, however, that was an unpopular opinion with most of the upper classes. How could you excel if the rules kept changing on you? More to the point, how could you out-compete the rest of the world if they knew things you didn't, and could use them?

Here, he just nodded. "Julius wasn't in the trenches much, but he said the sense of being pinned down was - awful for everyone, worse for some kinds of magic."

"Quite." It was a single echoing word, bracketing the sorts of emotions no well-bred man of Albion would ever admit to having. Then he twitched his shoulder. "My family line has some magics, some practices, that fit my interests. I've picked up a few others, as you do. That, in large part, is what our select group explores."

Before Galen could ask anything further, he spread his hands. "Now, that's quite enough of that. So I can introduce you to the best sorts, tell me more about the business interests."

Galen gave in to the inevitable. This, at least, he had ready answers for. He didn't show all of his cards, even most of them. He and Alastair and Julius had plans for the business, good ones. But they had talked through where introductions might actually be helpful. Then Galen had run the same lists by Lydia and Martin, and several of the Dwellers, to see what would be useful there.

By the end of their luncheon, Nico had half a dozen likely candidates, and promised to see about some introductions next race day.

CHAPTER 21
SATURDAY, NOVEMBER 27TH AT THE RACES

"Galen! Come to watch our horse race? He's in the third. You must know that. They're just starting the first now. We'll save the champers for later, but here, come get a drink."

Vincent was all visible bonhomie from the moment they stepped inside the private box. Today, it was just the share owners and their wives or the ladies in their life. Lydia kept a hand tucked firmly into his arm as they got a drink. They'd both thought someone - Felicity, Prudence, one of the others - might want to steer her off. Fortunately, her excitement about seeing Crisparkle race was an excellent excuse for her to stay glued to his side.

Today, at least, no one was trying to split them up immediately. Lydia and Galen ended up on the balcony with a dozen other people. Not all the part owners were here, apparently, but between the ones who were, they owned a fair portion. Three legs, the head and neck, as one of them put it. But not the barrel or the hindquarters, and there was some argument over the shoulders and withers.

159

The people themselves were an interesting mix. Galen was noticeably the youngest, though Lydia supposed most people his age didn't have a sizable amount of money to spend however they wanted. She hadn't been entirely sure how to ask about that, how much risk he was taking. She didn't even know exactly what numbers were involved. Whether it was the sort of sum a young man might lose gambling in a particularly bad week, or whether it was enough to buy a house in Trellech. Though, she supposed, for the particularly high gamblers, those two could be the same number.

She did not know how to live like that. Either amount would have changed her family's life, in huge ways, for years. Better food, a larger flat. The current one at least had indoor plumbing. That was a joy of the magical streets in London. But it was still cramped and made of awful angles to live with. It only wasn't filled with smoke because her da was grand with a drawing charm for the chimney.

Here, though, she smiled and nodded. Galen made a point of introducing her to everyone. He was friendly, solicitous, and she found herself getting far too used to someone paying attention to her. Her glass never went dry, she always had a place to sit if she wanted one. He angled himself so she wouldn't be jostled.

It wasn't just the physical things. He made a point of including her in the conversations, and of redirecting them when a topic wandered far astray, into something she couldn't comment about. Or at least not without blowing their cover. There were certainly a number of political comments where they were both biting their tongue.

He'd even been grand that morning when he'd met her at the train station. "You look smashing." It was all eager and earnest. "You know, I realised I'd never said. You make the clothing look wonderful. Even that frock you borrowed from Plucky. I know the other things, they were able to fit them to you, which has to help."

She had, in fact, been feeling self-conscious about the fact her frock was a much brighter blue than she'd normally ever consider. And that over it she wore a cape with vivid red and gold ribbon around the edges. His cheerfulness had made her smile at him, in a complicated twist of relief and wishing he hadn't had to say that to make her feel better. "Thank you."

He'd then grinned. "Julius pointed out I hadn't actually told you. About Plucky's frock." He was, at least, a man who apparently took correction well. She hadn't actually thought anything of it at the time, but it felt good that he'd noticed, at least eventually.

Now, she listened to him amiably chatting with a friend of Vincent's about ancient oaks - apparently a reasonably safe topic. Not the oaks themselves, in this case, apparently one had nearly dropped a limb on someone's head.

"Oh, there you are. Galen, darling. And Lydia, of course. Can we pull you away for just a moment before we settle in for the race we're all here for?" Felicity was bright-eyed. Perhaps a bit too much so, but very well-dressed in a sharp frock of deep golden wool peeping out from under a strikingly black coat. Utterly impractical, and yet Lydia rather coveted it.

"Certainly." Galen turned, letting Lydia find her place next to him. Felicity drew them off to one corner, perching on a chair while Vincent came to join them, his hand cupped around a tumbler.

"We had the most delightful idea, coming down here

this morning. We're having a house party, a proper Friday to Monday, next week. Do say you'll come, both of you. There's a ball on the Saturday, a winter theme, but I'm sure you can throw something together."

Lydia was sure she couldn't, and she honestly wasn't even sure the Dwellers could stretch to that kind of thing. Galen, however, beamed. "Oh, that's most kind. I'm pretty sure I can shake free. Can I let you know by post or telegram?"

"Oh, telegram, darling, soon as you can. Tonight, if it's not too much bother, or tomorrow at the latest. So we can make sure everything's ready. And the theme's really quite fluid. I mean, nothing tasteless like children's stories, but I'm sure you can come up with something."

Lydia swallowed a lump in her throat. "I'll need to check as well, but how kind." She squeezed Galen's arm. "And we should talk about clothes."

"Tonight." Galen promised. "I do have an idea, actually."

"See, it must have been meant." Felicity swooped in, kissing them both on the cheek. "Come along, Lydia, dear, I want to ask you something."

Lydia did not want to be parted from Galen, but she suspected this was where Vincent would clarify that he was involved with Nico's select few. A private home, a country house, would make a good place for that kind of thing. And Galen had the address now, for the telegram, since they were going to be there tomorrow. Lydia could do the necessary research.

Well, do the research and collapse into a pile of nerves at the idea of keeping up this show for three days. The ball was the easiest part, if Galen could sort out fancy dress. It was the rest of it, the meals and the amusements. Lydia suspected that whatever Felicity arranged, it would not be straightforward and easy to manage.

"Now, it will be such a grand chance for you to meet some of the better sort. Tell me, will you be bringing a maid?"

Lydia froze, though briefly enough that she hoped Felicity didn't notice it. "I'd prefer not, if it's not a bother for you?"

"Oh, I'm sure we can have one of the housemaids lend a hand with your hair and your frocks. And it means less sharing in the servants quarters. They always imply it's awful."

Lydia thought that entirely sensible. Servants in a great house had next to no privacy as it was, often sharing cramped rooms in the attic with others. Cramming more people in wouldn't help anything. She just murmured. "I'll let you know when I confirm. Your invitation is so kind. But do you have any particular suggestions about the ball? Anything you'd prefer I avoid?"

That got a lot of pleasant chatter. Lydia was fairly sure Felicity was going for some sort of ice queen motif, all brilliant clear sparkle and cutting edges. Likely an excellent chance to show off whatever diamonds she owned. It made Lydia wonder why Galen was so sure he had a solution. She asked about who would be there.

"Oh, fifteen, now, with the two of you." Felicity tilted her head. "Would you prefer to share a room? It might be more convenient, otherwise you'll be at opposite ends of the house, I expect."

Not a question one routinely expected from a clergyman's daughter, but on the other hand, Felicity went rather against that grain in a number of ways. Lydia coughed. "Let me check with Galen." Though given the choices, she would cheerfully sleep on a chair or even the floor, in order not to be so far away from him.

"Ah, darling. The secret of a happy marriage is deciding what you want to do and doing it anyway." Which made one wonder, honestly, what Felicity got up to while Vincent was doing things with Nico. Suddenly, Lydia wondered if there was a whole women's side to things, and whether she would hear about it from Felicity in more private. Felicity just beamed at her. "You're quick. You'll catch on."

Before anyone could say anything further, Vincent and Galen came back. Galen had an odd look on his face, as if he were very busy thinking about something. As soon as they got closer, he held out his arm to Lydia. "Would you rather go down to the ground level to watch, or watch from up here? I've said I'd rather give someone else a go at the winner's paddock if it comes to that." With so many owners, not all of them could troop down at once.

Lydia considered. "The balcony gives a good view, and we don't have to fuss with the crowds."

"Quite right." Vincent was all rather noisy cheer now. "More drinks all round, no worrying about pickpockets and other scoundrels." An entire group of them filtered out to the balcony with fresh drinks. Half the party went down to the ground level to find a place by the course itself. From there, things happened really quickly.

The horses lined up, their jockeys standing out in bright coloured silks. "That's ours, the yellow and red." Rather like a venomous snake, Lydia thought, the warning colours. They certainly stood out against the background. They all gathered up in a row, waiting for the start, like wriggling bees.

Then the race was off. There was a huge flurry of chaos, one horse getting left well back. The others stretched out along the field, shifting and looking for the best place. She could barely make out the colours of the silks, though someone had a radio on with the announcer explaining what was going on.

The fences seemed, suddenly, very high, the way the horses flung themselves up and over them. Some horses - including Crisparkle - seemed to just gather themselves and bound over, more like a gazelle than a horse. Others struggled, their knees dragging through the brush. Lydia had vaguely followed racing, but she somehow hadn't realised until now how big the fences were, how closely the horses ran together.

The race was not as long as some, but by the time the horses approached the finish, there was one out in front. Galen's was - she thought - in a knot of four horses going neck and neck, and then there was a clump stretching back. One of those stumbled and fell, but both horse and rider came up promptly, standing on all their feet. Lydia let out a sigh of relief, and shifted her focus back to the frontrunners. She found Galen's horse was neck and neck with another, the other two had fallen back at least half a stride.

There was cheering and also people holding their breaths, both at the same time, which made for an exceedingly odd counterpoint to each other. As the horses crossed the finish line, their bit of balcony went quiet, straining to hear the results. When the announcer called out "Crisparkle in second, by a neck," everyone started cheering, and she could hear someone open champagne.

"Oh, that's grand." Vincent looked relieved, the kind of relief that suggested he had bet money on it, and probably more than he should have. Which was another interesting detail, if it were true. If the horse were a fraud, Vincent would know, and not bet, surely?

Galen turned to her, beaming. "There we are. Brilliant, isn't it?" He shifted his arm around her waist, this time, which let him pull her gently out of the crush of people celebrating. It was definitely a help, but somehow it brought home, in all the ways, how she was so distant from anything he'd known.

CHAPTER 22
SATURDAY EVENING, AMBERLY HALL

As they found their seats on the train, Galen glanced up. "Could I convince you to come back home with me for a bit? We can feed you, of course, properly." She'd only had nibbles at the party. Galen himself was starving, and he'd eaten most of a sandwich, in quarters, between being introduced to people.

She blinked at him. "Costumes?" she asked.

"Exactly. Do you mind if I see if Martin or Laura's handy?"

Lydia shook her head. "No. Just." She hesitated, and Galen waited to see what she'd say. "Today was an awful lot. And the invitation."

"It was. And frankly, I'd rather talk about that somewhere we won't have other people coming in, being noisy. We can hole up in the library after I rummage to see if I can find what I remember."

She nodded, and then leaned her head against the window, letting her eyes close. They had about half an hour before the station they wanted. Galen took the time to write to Martin and Laura, as well as to Julius and Blythe, to warn them he'd be bringing Lydia by. His friends had visited before, though they met up far more often in Trellech, but Julius always wanted to know if someone new was coming. A new friend, that was a way to put it.

Lydia had handled herself superbly today, even though there had been point after point where she must have been out of her depth. That house party invitation. Galen wasn't sure he wanted to go either, mind, but it seemed the only way forward.

Forty-five minutes later, they were walking from the portal up to the house. Lydia stopped short. "You're not serious."

Galen grimaced. "Pardon." He gestured. "Stately home, Georgian model, not nearly as big as it could be, but still rather immense."

"And how many people live here?"

"Me. Julius. Blythe - they're engaged. I mentioned that. More house staff than we really need, but we didn't want them to be out of work. A housekeeper, cook, three maids." He ducked his chin. "All the woodwork takes a lot of dusting and polishing, even if no one's actually using it. Three footmen. And a valet for me. A couple of kitchen maids. And a host of gardeners and groundskeepers."

He gestured. "Julius has a laboratory off the back. It used to be the ballroom. Bedrooms on the first floor. Mine's that one, here at the front. Several of the staff live out, these days, there are cottages on the estate. A lot of the rest of it is in dustsheets and such. We use the library, and one of the breakfast rooms, and sometimes the music room. But it's entirely a lot."

"The fact you said 'one of the breakfast rooms' implies

others, yes. That is, by definition..." She let her voice trail off. "You do know what kind of place I live in? Where my family's from?"

"I've visited Martin and his family, and listened to him. So yes. The idea of that much space, does it make you a bit, um, agoraphobic?"

"That's open spaces, not large houses." The note in her voice, a bit more teasing now, was reassuring, at least. "I don't know if there's a word for being terrified of large stately homes."

"It'll be worse at the party." Galen stopped walking, about twenty feet from the front steps. "If you aren't up for it, there's no shame. We can call the whole thing off."

Lydia shook her head, squaring her shoulders. "I'm terrified, but that's no reason to cry off." She swallowed. "Show me what this kind of house is like. Can I get a proper tour, so I understand how things fit together? The public spaces, and..." Lydia grimaced. "Would it be an awful bother to see the other spaces? The servant's hall?"

Galen consulted his watch. "We've got about forty-five minutes before Martin and Laura get here. They wrote while you were napping. Let's put our things in the library, and I'll show you around."

Five minutes later, they were standing in the dining room. "And where we're going for this party is bigger?"

"Decidedly so. I - well, I can look that up in the library. Now we've got the address."

Lydia blinked at him. "Do I want to ask why you might have a book that tells you about other people's houses?"

"Because it turns out that a lot of scandal happens at these things. It's much easier to have the kind of scandalous romance you want, and not the utterly embarrassing sort, if you know where the bedrooms are. Then you just have to know which bedroom you want. But knowing where the stairs are, also often helpful. Hence, a book. Someone - someone in the magical community, with a very, very good memory. He got himself invited to an amazing number of places over his decades as something of a rake, and he wrote it all down."

"And people haven't changed things?"

Galen snorted and gestured. "Keeping up a place like this is expensive even before you get into death duties. We tend not to knock down perfectly good walls that are still standing up. Change the furnishings, sure. Julius's lab needed renovation and protection charms and all that. But the footprint is basically the same."

"All right. So. Breakfast room for less formal meals. Dining room, more formal."

"We'll figure out a time to practise that this week. Though if it's a large party, that's usually less fuss. Especially if there's a ball. That might just be nibbles and finger foods. It is perfectly acceptable to ask a maid for a bit of toast and tea in your room, or an egg or something simple like that, if you're starving. Which - tea?"

"Tea." Lydia sighed, and let him steer her back to the library, which was quite comfortable.

As soon as they were settled, there was a knock on the door. Blythe opened it. "Galen, Julius found what you remembered. And he asks..." She nodded, once, at Lydia.

Galen hadn't expected that at all. "Lydia, pardon. Would you like to meet my brother?"

"Oh. Oh!" She sounded unsure at first, but that second sound was pleased, even eager. "If it's not a bother. I admit, I'm curious, the way you talk about him." Then she grinned. "Look up to him."

Galen could feel himself flushing. Blythe snorted, and said, "Moment." She disappeared out of the library again, leaving a pile of fabric on one arm of the sofa. A moment later, there was a knock on the door.

"Come in, please." Galen stood, and Lydia, after a moment, followed suit. Julius was wearing the larger mask today, the one tinted to match his skin.

He nodded at Galen, and Galen took his cue. As Julius came over, he said, "Lydia, my brother Julius. Julius, this is Lydia. Thank you for rummaging out the fancy dress. I'm hoping some of it suits."

Julius nodded, then took Lydia's hand, and bowed slightly over it. Very precisely, carefully, the way Galen could hear, he said, "Welcome."

Lydia smiled back at him. "Galen speaks so glowingly about you. And your work, though I'm sure I can't follow the alchemy."

"Neither can I, half the time." Galen pointed out.

Julius smiled, the half of his mouth that was visible tilting up, and his eyes crinkling. "Learns well." He then gestured at the clothes. "Explain?"

Galen knew that meant both explain to Julius why he'd wanted them, and to Lydia what they were. "We've been invited to a country house party. And um, we could use your advice. Blythe, you too? It's a very fast set, even by current standards. And the lady of the house, as it were, has made it clear we either share a room, or we'll likely be at opposite ends of the house."

Lydia nodded. "I wasn't sure how much of a problem that would be, but ... seeing this, which I gather is rather smaller, I'm. Well."

"On the scale, this house is quite modest, for the sort of place it is. All one block, bar the ballroom and what is now

Julius's office space."

Julius raised an eyebrow, and Galen said, "I was just going to fetch it." He glanced at Lydia to make sure she was all right, and then went to rummage for the book. It was up on a higher shelf, which meant finding the stepstool, and by the time he came back, Julius had said something that had made Lydia smile.

As Galen laid the book out, he started thumbing through it, matching it against the card Vincent had given him with the house's name and location. "Here we are. Thornwick House, Sussex." He then opened the page. "One country house, long and narrow version." He gestured. "See, here are the bedrooms. There might be more bathing rooms and loos than this shows, but I wouldn't count on it."

Lydia took a breath, then let it out. "How do you want to handle that?"

"I am fairly sure there will be some sort of chair or sofa or what have you. Or there are ways to cushion the floor. You, of course, will have the bed. Though we'll have to figure out something if there's a maid coming in to light the fire, which there certainly should be in November." He waved a hand. "My valet is used to my eccentricities, and - well. It would do him some good to have a purpose to his gossip, I suspect. He doesn't always approve of my taste, and I'm fairly sure he'll think our hosts are tacky, but there you are, obligations to live up to."

Lydia blinked at him. "You don't have to sleep - oh, you're ridiculous. We can work something out." She sounded not offended, at least, at the idea.

Galen spread his hands. "Your choice, and your comfort. Besides, you'll be putting up with a great deal of difficulty during the social events. You should at least have the most comfortable sleeping arrangements."

Julius snorted at that, then added, "Point." Galen grinned at him. Julius then nodded. "Welcome. Anytime." That was to Lydia, and a clear sign of Julius's approval. Galen wasn't sure what had brought that on, and he certainly would not ask in the moment. Then he gestured at the clothing.

"Right. Clothes." Galen had to explain that part. "Remember that Mother and Father had those photographs, from - you must have been five. The winter party? There's a set of robes, sort of timeless historical, but they're warm - houses like that will be chilly, this time of year, most likely. And I thought they'd flatter."

Blythe nodded, and went and pulled out a frock. It was made of deep green, with delicate embroidery in gold picking out holly branches dotted with tiny red berries that gleamed with colour. "I thought it might suit your colouring?" Julius offered, carefully, to Lydia.

As Blythe brought it over, he could see Lydia's face change. She reached out to touch it, and the velvet shifted under her hand. "I don't think your mother wore it more than the once. Charmed to avoid crushing, and that colour is a magical dye, but nothing that risks the Pact."

Galen nodded and left them to it while he went to rummage for the other outfit. This was a solstice theme, a deep gold that picked up the shade of his hair. Gores and the lining of the sleeves matched the frock, and the embroidery helped the neckline stand out.

Julius considered. "Classic. They, brash?"

Galen nodded. "They are. But I have put myself forward as a tad more conservative."

That made Julius snort again, the sound he made instead of laughing, this time. "Will do." He then gestured.

Blythe nodded. "If you'd like to try it on, I can show you where to change. And I'm glad to do the adjustments for you."

Galen nodded encouragingly at Lydia, and she let Blythe lead her off.

CHAPTER 23
SATURDAY EVENING

Lydia followed along as Blythe led her up a rather elegant staircase, then into a room at the top. "Guest room," she added. "Pardon, did Galen explain anything?"

That, at least, Lydia could do something with. "A fair number of things. That you live here with Julius, you're to marry sometime. That you've been fond of each other for a good while, that you used to be his mother's companion."

Blythe grimaced at the last bit. "Much better now. Julius has two alchemical assistants. I handle most of the office work. If what he's doing takes off like we hope, we'll need to hire someone else. Well, maybe multiple someones, set up a proper workshop as well as his current laboratory, but there are outbuildings we could use." She nodded. "He's been curious about you."

"Julius?" Lydia blinked. "Why me?"

"Because of how Galen talks about you." Blythe turned away, moving to separate the parts of the costume and hang them up on several hangers from the wardrobe. "Here, try those on - you might need a hand with the last layer. Let me get my sewing kit, so I can make the adjustments."

She slipped out, leaving Lydia utterly unsure how to read what she'd just heard. She shrugged, undoing the frock she was wearing and laying it over the chair. Then she slipped into an undergown of what felt like the finest linen, then the overgown, which fell around her in gentle folds. She was contemplating how to get that on, which she was not at all sure about managing properly. It had a line of fabric at the back of the neck, not quite a ruff.

As she was trying to decide, there was a knock on the door. "Blythe."

"Come in." Once Blythe had closed the door again, she nodded approvingly. "It's not cutting edge fashion, but you don't want that, anyway. It's so easy to get wrong, and that sort of set will notice every bit. And it's harder with fancy dress. This is classic, you can wear it like that, if you want, but try the overgown."

The overgown, in fact, made the outfit. It created a spray of what looked like evergreen boughs that framed her face that were mostly embroidery work, but with a touch of an illusion charm. "Oh, my. You wear it much better than she did." Blythe was very cheerful about that. "Let me just take in the waist a bit. And can you lift your arms comfortably? I can adjust that too."

They went through the contortions Lydia was getting used to now, to make sure the dress fit as it should. "Right. We'll have it thoroughly cleaned and ready for you. Do you need other clothes?"

"Probably, but the Dwellers have helped with that so far?" Lydia felt it was a rather weak response.

"Martin and Laura got here a couple of minutes ago. That's why I was so long coming back. She may have something, too. And Galen said you wanted a look belowstairs, how the back stairways and such work?"

Lydia ducked her head, but Blythe seemed to treat it as a reasonable thing. "Yes, if it wouldn't be a problem for your staff."

"Oh, I suspect they'd quite like getting one over on the sort of people who would disapprove. I'll give you a tour when you've had something to eat and a sit down. Galen's rather abashed he forgot about feeding you earlier."

"I was full of questions. It's not his fault." Lydia came out with it, before she realised she was defending him. And she perhaps hadn't even had to do that.

Blythe hesitated as she finished putting things away in her sewing kit. "Don't break his heart, all right? If you can avoid it." She straightened up, and her hand was on the doorknob before Lydia found words.

"Wait, don't what?"

"Don't break his heart, please." Blythe turned back, puzzled, now peering at Lydia.

"I didn't think I could." Lydia got it out, mostly without stammering. "He's. He's been very kind. Generous. And I didn't expect that. I was asking a favour, this project, and it's taken up so much time."

"Pah. It's the quiet season. You've been doing a lot of the research work, which is entirely fair. And it's - it's been very good for him." Blythe considered. "I've known him since he was tiny. I mean, lived with him, known him. Not really an aunt, or an older sister, but I've seen him in a lot of stages of his life. The last year has been tremendously hard on him."

"On all of you, surely?"

"Oh, plenty of change for all of us. But for Julius, for me, it's been a freedom we didn't think we'd ever get. And the pleasure of figuring that out with each other, and that's a proper joy." Blythe nearly glowed with it. She was not a beautiful woman by current standards, or even striking. Her complexion was the sort that magazines would describe as washed-out and faded, all tones of pale brown and beige. When she talked about Julius, though, her eyes lit up and she shone with her affection.

"Galen?" Lydia wasn't sure how to ask or what to ask.

"He had all these responsibilities come down squarely on his shoulders. Julius can advise, but he never had a hand in the business, either. And he can't do any of the meetings. Their father - well, both their parents - wanted to keep them wrapped up in cotton wool and padding. Then Martin's been busy. Galen's so pleased he's been getting more writing opportunities. But it means that the person he relied on to talk to about things hasn't been handy. They love each other, they'll always be there for each other. But it takes more planning than it used to."

Lydia tucked much of that away to think about later. Probably at two in the morning. "I like what I've seen of Martin. And how they are together. Trusting." She hesitated. That was too mild about Martin. "Let me try that again. Martin at the Moon, he's very practical, no-nonsense. Professional, more than that, he's easy to work with, which isn't something you can say about everyone. Seeing him more with Galen, though, they're so easy with each other. Sure of each other. You've seen how Galen is about plates when Martin's around."

That got a flashing smile. "That's the thing people who like them notice. I wanted a bit of that loyalty for me, and I think other people should have it too." Blythe shrugged. "Just. I know you have to put on a show for this investigation, but I don't know what Galen feels about it. Other than that he likes you and trusts you. Enough to invite you home."

Lydia frowned, thinking through. "Is that why Julius came out? I didn't expect that."

"Bright woman." Blythe lit up again. "He's heard a fair bit about you, the past weeks. Of course he was curious." She shrugged. "And I suspect that not turning away from Julius is, well. I can't imagine Galen getting close to anyone who would be rude or dismissive like that. But I think he had to see it, before..."

Lydia wouldn't ask what came after. She could fill it in. Galen wouldn't let himself get too close to anyone who would hurt his brother. She could only assume she'd done well enough. "I - I don't know a lot about his sort of injury. But I hope I've learned a bit about how to treat people who have been hurt, at least avoid making it worse if I can."

"That will do well enough to be getting on with. And much better than their parents, though that's not a high bar." Blythe brushed off her hand. "Come on, you need tea. I need tea, actually." With that, Lydia was bustled off downstairs. The library had new people in it - Martin and Laura - as well as a cart of tea sandwiches and scones that Laura was putting out on a table. There was no sign of Julius.

"Here we are, then." Blythe said. "The dress will be grand. She looks glorious. Galen, I'll fit yours tomorrow, shall I? Do you need me to stick around?"

Galen shook his head. "Julius went back to his study, and he said he's got something for you to help with when you get a chance? Thanks, for..." He gestured. "The everything? Lydia, are you all right with it?"

"It's a beautiful frock." That was true enough, and she

could be enthusiastic about it while being baffled by everything else. "Thank you, Blythe."

"Why don't you come stay here the night before. We can make sure you're properly packed up. Do you have the right sort of suitcase? Hatbox?"

"Um." Lydia shook her head. "No." She hadn't had to think about that before. This entire process was bringing up quite a lot of things she hadn't had to think about before.

"Right. I'll pull some things out of the attics. They'll be older, but fine. We can spruce them up."

Laura offered, "If you want posh, I can borrow Lizzie's luggage set? They're not travelling until at least spring."

"Oh, please. That'd be quite the thing. And consult on what ought to be in it, please? Including underthings."

That was also baffling. "Um. I know they affect the fit of the frocks, but - why?"

Blythe spread her hands. "If you don't bring a maid - we could lend you one, but to be fair, they're all good girls, but none of them has much experience as a lady's maid. Which means one of their maids will unpack for you."

"Or my valet."

Martin raised an eyebrow. Galen rearranged himself in the chair, leaning against a corner. "Willet has opinions, but he is good at unpacking things."

"Isn't that going to shock them? And surely, they'll just send a maid to be nosy."

Laura laughed. "See, Lydia, you do know how to go about this. They will. All right. Let me borrow Lizzie's posh luggage, and - Galen, do your funds stretch to a few days of nice underthings?" She then named a number that sounded absurd to Lydia, before adding. "That's silk. And tiny little stitches no one can see."

"I can't."

Galen shook his head. "If we're going to do the thing right, we'll do the thing. I can go without book money for a month."

Which made Lydia blink at him. "I don't want you to go without. And there's the horse, and the everything."

"We think we can fit up your clothing easily enough - we were talking about that before you came down. You have shoes that will do, a frock for the fancy dress. I have clothes for all that sort of thing. So it's just the underthings and a few scarves or whatever."

"Which I can lend you. Jewellery?" Laura contemplated Lydia.

"There are family pieces. I'll go to the vault tomorrow. We're not married, or even engaged. No one will expect diamonds and such. But there's some nice semi-precious pieces, artistic and interesting, but not extravagant."

Lydia glanced from one to the other. "All right." She let out a breath. "You've got the bit in your teeth, isn't that the saying? You'll help make sure I won't look foolish?"

Galen shook his head. "You won't look foolish. And I'll be right there. If worst comes to worst, we make a short ramble to the nearest portal - there's one about three miles away. Together."

Laura said, dryly. "Pack comfy shoes, just in case. I had to do that, after - well. Whatever's going on at this house party, it won't be that." When Lydia blinked at her, Laura said, "The goldwasser, that golden potion that everyone was - well. It made you dream of things. Very addictive. A whole party of that."

Lydia had no idea how to ask more about it. Galen caught the expression and said, immediately. "Come sit here, by me. The sofa is all yours. And eat. Please. It's been a long day."

He was so very earnest about it that Lydia couldn't refuse. Besides, she was truly starving, and the food looked amazing. Everything was elegantly set out, but there were hearty sandwiches and hefty scones, and lashings of tea. Once she was settled, and she had a bite of an excellent cheddar and chutney sandwich, she swallowed. "All right. Tell me what to expect."

CHAPTER 24

FRIDAY, DECEMBER 4TH, IN SUSSEX

"Ready?"

Lydia shook her head. "No. But I need to be. Here we are." The train was slowing. As soon as it stopped, Galen got the carriage door open and hopped down, offering Lydia a hand. He glanced down the train to see Willet, his valet, wrangling the luggage. There were three suitcases and a hatbox, though to be fair, one of the suitcases was mostly the costumes for the ball.

"Someone is supposed to be meeting us."

As they came around the corner of the station, they spotted Bunny in his memorable motor car. This time, however, the roof was fully up. "Your man can ride with you, Galen, or wait for the next run, your choice."

"With me, please, I'd rather he be able to see to the unpacking. Willet?"

Willet was settling the luggage onto a rack at the back, and nodded. "Moment, sir."

Galen had come to a comfortable enough detente. Willet had been second footman under his parents, and a promotion to valet was quite a coup. Willet disapproved of the lack of suitable occasions to show off his skill. This, though, this was the first house party he was attending entirely because of Galen, and the first as a proper valet. He'd certainly been around for others, though, and Galen was hoping he'd gather some useful information from the servants' hall. Once he slid into the back seat of the auto, Galen joined him, letting Bunny make sure Lydia was comfortable. They took off at good speed, though not quite as much as in Newmarket.

It was not exactly a long drive, perhaps twenty minutes, but that meant it was quite a fair distance from the train. Galen was suddenly very glad there was a portal somewhat nearer, just across the estate at Monk's Gate. Quite an old one, he gathered, pre-dating the Pact. The house, when they pulled up the drive, fit the rambling and lengthy floor plan. It was pale brown and beige stone, but he could see several Edwardian repairs.

The house had, he gathered from his and Lydia's research, belonged to Felicity's side of the family, an aunt or grandmother or something of the kind. Lydia said nothing, but when they piled out of the automobile, she took his arm and leaned in while Bunny was making sure the luggage was unloaded without scratching the paint. "Rather large."

"I'm glad we said we'd be in together." Galen still wasn't sure how that was going to go, but he was sure he'd rather know where she was, and be able to write Willet if he needed to.

As they came up to the front steps, now trailing Bunny, there was Felicity. "Oh, goodness, right on time." The way she said it, it was as if they'd been slightly rude. "Though, I suppose if the train was running on time, the way Bunny drives, I shouldn't be surprised. Come in, come in. I suppose you want to freshen up. The trains are always all over soot." She swept in and up a staircase to the right, which curved around the short wall of the main entry hall, and up to the second floor.

Galen barely got a chance to glance at the artwork and decorations. He was not an expert at it, but it did tell you a bit about a place, or the people. Felicity went on, at a quick pace, a good three-quarters of the way down the main hallway, before abruptly disappearing into a hall or doorway to the left. "Servants are in the West Wing, you'll be along up here." She went up another flight of stairs, before turning left again, into an oddly shaped but surprisingly large room.

It did, much to Galen's relief, have a plausible sofa tucked under the window, as well as a sizable bed. "Loo just down the hall, there, and a bathing room down at the far end of the hallway." She waved a hand, dismissively. "Your valet will sort out the scheduling, I'm sure. I'll be sending one of the maids up to help with your hair, of course." She nodded at Lydia. "Come down for a drink as soon as you're settled. Back downstairs, through the entrance hall, right through the sitting room, and then we'll be in the drawing room on the right."

With that, she swept off again, without seeing if they had any questions.

Once she was gone, Lydia let out a long breath, then brushed her hands, going to the windows and door. "Mind if I?"

Galen blinked. "Oh. Right." Some sort of privacy enchantment. "Better you than me."

Lydia nodded, then cupped her hands, murmuring something, and then clapped them together sharply three times. She didn't explain herself, just got down on hands and knees to peer under the bed. Then into the wardrobe, and finally she moved to open up each drawer of the dresser and bedside tables. Then she grimaced at something.

Lydia stood, coming to the door to the room, clearly focusing on what she was about to do. She tapped the door in a specific rhythm. She then traced a pattern with her finger, before going to each of the walls and repeating it, as well as at each window. "Right. We should check every time we come in, that something hasn't been added."

"Teach me that?" Galen knew a handful of methods for checking that there was no magical object in the room. Or rather, to highlight the ones that were. He had one of the magical journals tucked into his suitcase, in a hidden compartment, and a few things in the toiletries case, but nothing at all obvious.

Lydia demonstrated once, then again, until Galen had the knack. "Much appreciated." Then he settled on the sofa, while he gestured for Willet. "Go ahead and unpack, Willet." He glanced around. "I suppose we can use - by which I mean I can use - the door of the wardrobe to change behind, or give you some privacy or whatever."

She grimaced. "I hadn't quite got that far. How do we do this?"

"You get cleaned up. I get cleaned up. We look sharp. We go downstairs through this labyrinth and stick together. I expect they'll want to pull me aside to talk about things, but other than that, I don't want to be on my own."

"You don't want? My. Martin was right about you needing a bit of bravery." Lydia hopped up onto the bed before adding. "Do you use a stepladder to get into this?"

Willet turned, rummaged under the foot, and wheeled out a small set of stairs. "Ma'am." He gestured. "Sir, as we discussed last night?"

Last night, when Lydia had arrived at the house, they'd talked through what they could plan on. Willet had a list of things to listen for, or even nudge the conversation toward, if he could. The financial state of the household, who else they were connected to, how frequently Nico or Aloysius were guests. They had a list, at any rate, which Willet had duly memorised.

Galen sighed. "I think we just do the thing. And see how it goes."

"That is not at all reassuring." Lydia glanced at the bed. "There's plenty of room here. You don't need to sleep on the sofa. I'm all right with it."

Galen glanced at the bed, at Lydia, then at the other end of the sofa. The sofa was entirely safe to look at, fortunately. Not like anything else in the room, including Willet. Then, very carefully, he said, "I'm not sure I am."

Willet coughed. "I'll go see about my room, sir. And perhaps a screen for dressing. It would be handy with the costumes tomorrow." He slipped out of the door. He had opinions about Galen's life, though if he had opinions about Lydia in specific, he had not yet mentioned them.

Galen let him go, then glanced over at Lydia. She looked like a picture of innocence, without saying anything, which did not help at all. Either. "I've said I don't have experience. And they're going to expect me to."

"If you were going to have vapours over it, last night would have been a great deal more convenient." Her tone wasn't acerbic, exactly, more amused. "What are we going to do, then?"

"Well. I was going to sleep on the sofa. Defer any complications of that sort until...." Until when, that was the question. He found Lydia interesting, intriguing. Clever, determined, all the things he wished he did better at. And she appeared to not hate his company. Though to be fair it was hard to tell at the moment, seeing that she was invited along on this thing because of him, and it was her story. And her possible long-term success as a journalist, in her own right. He swallowed.

"Sofa." Her voice was softer now. "I know I can rely on you. Where either of us sleeps doesn't matter."

He wished it did. Then he coughed. "We should wash up, and change, and go down. I'll see if I can find the loo. There's a basin there? And maybe Willet will rummage up a screen or something."

"I just need to change my frock, it won't take long. And wash my face." Galen nodded. He took his time down the hall, peering at paintings and decorations. When he came back, Lydia was indeed in a new frock, this one in a vibrant blue that brought out the colour in her eyes. He changed his shirt and jacket while she at least appeared to focus on reading a book, aimed the other way.

"Right. Down we go."

From the moment they turned into the drawing room, it was name after name. Felicity and Vincent, Prudence and Paul, Bunny and Plucky, they knew. Nico, apparently on his own. Which made Galen wonder how deliberate that was. That left six others to make up fifteen, introduced in passing as Abby, Charles, Merry, Oswald, Enid, and Perks.

Galen suspected Abby was also magical, and perhaps Perks, but it was damnably hard to tell. It sometimes helped if you could get the conversation round to schooling, because the ways they ducked the conversation were often similar. Whether someone had gone to Schola or apprenticed. But where Felicity had been privately educated, and Vincent and Bunny were themselves, it left little room.

The drinks were also generously poured, which meant Galen also had to be careful not to get drunk. Or even tipsy. This was no place to be muzzy-headed. It meant he poured a fair bit of his drink into a potted plant, poor thing, but it would probably survive. He did learn a bit more about the house. Felicity promised them a tour of the house and gardens tomorrow during the day. It had been significantly renovated by her aunt and uncle.

Galen almost didn't catch it, but he could have sworn he heard Felicity say they were on an extended trip overseas, and that they were just living there temporarily. What that suggested about finances and the family, well, that was another problem for Lydia's research, most likely.

Finally, the gong rang for dinner. It was relatively informal. Not everyone paired up by precedent, but Merry and Oswald drew Lydia off with them to the far end of the table. It left Galen up with Felicity, Nico, Vincent, and Perks. The conversation left him feeling entirely unmoored. He could follow only about one sentence in eight about Vincent and his work in the City. Perks apparently did something in the decorous sort of trade that was appropriate for a gentleman of high standing, and of course Nico was enigmatically Nico.

Galen could only occupy himself by watching the reactions. He was especially intrigued by Felicity and Nico. They had seemed to barely talk at the races, but here she was teasing and laughing. He was paying her due attention as the hostess, but there was something else there. Galen knew he wouldn't spot an affair if it hit him over the head, but it didn't quite feel like that. And yet, there was obviously something more than geniality going on.

CHAPTER 25

FRIDAY EVENING

Lydia got through supper without drawing too much attention to anything she did wrong. This was not the most nerve-wracking part of the whole production. The theoretically looming snake cult certainly topped table manners as a worry.

However, she found it exhausting to keep on top of every detail, worrying about which tiny gesture might give her away as a fraud. All the others at the table used multiple forks and knives and various other accoutrements without bothering to look at them. Watching the others helped. And Galen was near enough she could glance at what he was doing.

He kept making sure she had something she had to respond to when there was a new course, so she could see what other people did before she followed suit. Or he just as quietly made a point of which piece of silverware he chose, letting his hand linger over it while he replied to someone.

She couldn't stop thinking about earlier, about how he both did and didn't want to share a bed, even with no promise of particular pleasures. He certainly wasn't like other people she'd been to bed with. Not that there was a long list there, just three men. But they had been, each of them, in a bit of a hurry about it. She wasn't interested in that again, or in stroking anyone's ego. And she certainly wasn't interested in someone who wasn't actually able to be a partner.

Which is what made things with Galen so complicated. She'd watched him carefully last night, after what Blythe had told her. If Galen were lovelorn, he was doing a grand job of hiding it. Most of the time. And then he'd come out with something like this afternoon, about not trusting himself to share a bed.

She might, at this point, have a reasonable sort of map of what Galen would likely do if he had to rise to a challenge. But she had no actual idea about what he felt about any of it. He was more a man of his class and education than he wanted to be, she suspected. They all kept their emotions rammed down to the bottom of their souls.

These two things kept her more than occupied through supper, along with tracking the conversation for anything that might be useful later. Afterwards, there was a general migration toward the ballroom. There were various pieces of furniture around the edges, a table for cards, and someone put music on a gramophone. Several others started dancing, the twisting and kicking that was all the rage, and that Lydia had no idea how to match.

Galen brought her a drink and settled next to her on a bench. "I suspect they're going to try and separate us a bit. Or that..."

"We talked about this." They had. Lydia and Galen knew what their mutual goals were. They had magic, which was rather a lot of reassurance right now, even if Nico also did. Possibly some of the others.

Not a minute later, someone came up and tugged at Lydia's hand. One of the other women, Enid. "Come outside, it's not too cold yet, especially if we're dancing. And you must try this." She pressed a glass, a tumbler of something, into Lydia's hand, taking away what Galen had brought her and setting it aside, balanced precariously on a ledge.

Lydia let herself be dragged. She couldn't put up too much of a fuss, or they'd get suspicious. More suspicious. Enid tugged her along to one side of a long pool. "Do you know the Charleston? Or the Black Bottom? Anything like that?"

"Two left feet." Lydia said, demurring. "I'm sure I'd kick someone. Or fall on my face."

"Best place to try it right here. Nice soft ground, it hasn't frozen yet." Enid did a couple of steps, then called up to the ballroom. "Bring the gramophone out!"

Five minutes later, a good half of the party was out on the grass by the gazing pool, a long shallow oval of water, maybe a foot or two deep. There were no signs of anything like fish, and honestly, Lydia thought it could do with a good cleaning. It was all over greenery and water plants. Before she could think more about it, though, Enid began demonstrating steps. Slowly at first, and then faster.

"There, see, you're getting it." Enid beamed at her. "Does your boyfriend dance?"

Lydia blinked, then said. "Oh, Galen? Not like this, I don't think."

"You don't know?" Enid blinked at her. Her eyes were wide, and Lydia got a look close enough to be fairly sure Enid had taken something. Her pupils were very large.

"Not the sort of thing we've done together? Just the partnered dancing, foxtrot, a fast waltz. Dancing with each other. He's ..." She glanced back toward the house. "He's had a lot of responsibility." She also suddenly thought that what Enid was showing her was more about dancing at someone, like it was a challenge. Certainly it required a flourish of athleticism, with the speed and the high kicks some of them were doing.

"Oh, pish. You'll see Vincent out here, and he's a banker in the City. If he can dance, so should Galen."

Lydia felt there was something inherently off about that logic, but she didn't argue. "Can you show me that thing with the knees?"

"This thing?" Enid bent down and crossed her hands from knee to knee, then straightened up, and did a series of wide kicks.

"The first one." That kept them occupied for a bit. Well, mostly it kept Enid occupied with laughing, but Lydia didn't mind about that. Being laughed at because she couldn't dance was about the safest thing she could think of right now.

When Lydia came up for breath finally, most of the rest of the party was out near them. Even Galen, though he was standing talking to Vincent, further back. Lydia took a sip of a drink - a small one, but she was blindingly thirsty. Suddenly, there was a bit of pushing and shoving among the men on the other side of the pool.

One of them, Charles, had been showing off, at least that's what it seemed like. He and Oswald got into a bit of a competition, each trying more and more absurd kicks and twists and various manoeuvres. The dancing got wilder and wilder, then Oswald stepped forward, and shoved Charles, sending him teetering toward the pool.

It was the sort of moment where you knew exactly what was going to happen, and could do nothing to prevent it. Lydia backed up a step or two, but not far enough to avoid the splash - and Enid got soaked by the wave of water.

No one moved for a moment, and then Galen stepped forward, almost running, when Charles didn't immediately stand up. He waded into the pool, got an arm under Charles' shoulder, and they staggered out to the side, collapsing on the ground near Lydia.

Galen looked up, as if reacquainting himself with where Lydia had got to. "Lydia, can you find Charles's man? He'll want clean clothes, something warm, the water's frigid."

"I'll get Willet, too." Lydia brushed her hands off and went off to go find them. It was not simple. First she had to find a maid, then the maid had to go see if they were downstairs, then try upstairs. She came back looking furious, the way someone who was in service, at the mercy of others, had to repress it. "He'll be done in a minute, ma'am. And Willet faster."

Lydia hesitated. She shouldn't, she knew she shouldn't. The sort of person she was pretending to be wouldn't notice. Wouldn't bother saying anything. She gestured, with a "Do you have a moment?" and the maid nodded, tightly.

They found a spot beneath the curve of the stairs. "Are you all right?"

"Miss." There was an offended note. Lydia was being decidedly improper.

"Look, you know I'm not like them. It's probably obvious to you."

The maid looked her up and down and nodded. "Yes. Half a dozen ways, miss, if you don't mind my saying so.

Mostly things they won't notice. Or they assume you're new money. You don't know how things are done."

"Well. That's all right then." Lydia grimaced. "Can you tell me, tomorrow? Anything I can change."

"Yes'm." Again, that tight angry sound, just a hint.

"What happened?"

"Bellow. Um, Master Charles Bellow's man. The staff is old-fashioned here, we belong with the house, not the Paxmans." That was Vincent and Felicity. "We use the last name, below stairs. Mr Willet is Amberley."

"Ah, right. I can likely follow that." Lydia agreed. "Did he hurt you?"

"Not more than a grab, but he's got a nasty pair of hands, him. And a foul temper. I know how to use my knee, miss." The maid looked at her, searchingly, and said. "Beg pardon."

"Men with money get plenty grabby and worse." Lydia said, firmly. "Good." She hesitated. "Felicity said she'd lend me a maid tomorrow. Can that be you? Would it help if I asked? Said you'd been helpful with something?"

"I'd be glad to, Miss." That was a little more distant, as if the maid was putting herself back together. "I'm Netty, miss."

"Netty. I'll see what I can do about that. And - um. When I'm in my room. I can give you a card, if you ever need a new place. Or want one. I know someone could help."

"Very kind, miss." Netty hesitated. "The staff here is good. And it's usually quiet. It's Mrs Paxman's aunt's house, she's abroad for another three months. They'll borrow some flat or something then. I don't think they like being out in the country much at all."

"So, not as well off as all that, then." Lydia said it out loud, if mostly to herself.

"Miss." Netty was trying to look resolute, but the corner of her mouth twitched. "You shouldn't say things like that, miss. The walls sometimes have ears. Not here, but the rooms. Sometimes the hallways."

"Quite right. Well. I'll ask for you tomorrow. Thanks for lending a hand." And with that, Lydia nodded, and strode off back to the pond. As she came out, she could see two people coming out from a different door. Willet was trotting ahead, with a towel and a couple of blankets in his arms, and the other man was slinking along behind him.

Her shoes meant she couldn't rush, so by the time she got back to Galen, Willet had offered him a towel and a warm blanket. Lydia could see her cue and coughed. "Come along, Galen, darling. You should change properly, warm up by the fire. Your feet must be soaked."

Galen took a step and grimaced. Willet said, "I'll come see about your shoes, sir, soon as I've helped Mr Bellow's man see him to his room."

"Goodness, what a lot of fuss." Felicity had come up. "Do ask for anything you need, hot drinks or the sort of drink that makes you hot. And do come down, Galen, when you're warmed up? Or I'll have to come along and check on you."

Lydia wondered whether Felicity meant it, or whether she did right now, but might get distracted. Surely she remembered that Galen and Lydia were sharing a room.

As they walked off, Galen keeping the blanket around his shoulders, he nodded at Nico as they went by. "Very heroic." Nico's voice had a twist to it, like it was defining Galen a certain way, and perhaps finding him wanting.

Once they were back inside the house, Galen started to

speak, but Lydia shook her head. "Not until you're in front of our fireplace." When they got to the room, he opened his mouth again, and Lydia held up a finger. She checked for magical items again, and this time, there was something new. Under her bed, there was an unexpected glow. She considered, then used a bit of newspaper to push it where she could see it.

Galen considered, letting the blanket drop. He toed off his shoes by the door, then gestured at her hatbox. Lydia saw his idea immediately, and she took the hats out, leaving them on top of the dresser. Galen scooped up the stone without touching it. He covered it with folds of the towel and closed the box again, before sliding it under a corner of the bed and tucking the blanket around it for extra muffling.

It would probably do, especially if either of them happened to talk in their sleep. It did not, however, make Lydia inclined to say anything at all.

CHAPTER 26

SATURDAY MORNING

G alen had not wanted to talk last night. Besides the problem of finding the enchanted stone, he had, frankly, been exhausted. The strain of putting on the right show was one thing. He'd expected that. But the shock of the cold water, and then how the rest of the men would have been fine letting Charles freeze, apparently.

He had wondered, at three in the morning, whether the War made them like that. Or whether they had been like that already and the War made them more so. Julius didn't talk much about what the War made him. Not the physical injuries, certainly. But also not the emotional ones. Betrayal, a deep call to honesty, a jot of heroism.

Julius had come out of it, though, resolute about making the world better. His recent experiments were helping rather a lot with infected wounds, an alchemical mix of honey and herbs and several other things he wouldn't explain while he was still experimenting. It wasn't showy; it wasn't posh parties; it wasn't being lauded in the papers or on a racecourse. But it actually mattered.

It also gave Galen a lot to live up to. He'd meant what he'd said to Lydia about wanting to make sure things were steady for the tenants. They couldn't just up and leave the land, if he messed things up. He wanted to make it so they had more trades and more options. Or perhaps help selling on the extra of whatever they harvested or made. He was constantly aware of the expectations.

And on the other hand, a fair bit of his generation seemed entirely willing to lounge around at a house party, drink and take drugs of various kinds, and be idle. It was better, he supposed, than a snake cult with ambitions, but it was equally venomous.

He had slept on the couch, though wrapped up in several blankets, and with a warming charm to boot. At least his feet had thawed, and Willet had promised that his shoes would be properly tended and ready. He suspected that Willet had been up late managing it, but he gathered it might get him some sympathy below stairs. Possibly also some gossip.

By the time he woke up, it was half-past nine, and Lydia was propped up in bed, wearing a shawl, and reading a book. When he stirred and rubbed his eyes, she waved a hand. "Morning. Willet came up. Do we want breakfast up here, or downstairs?"

"Here, please, if you'd ring?" He rubbed his head. "And one of his headache powder packets? I should go find the loo."

"Of course." She grimaced. "Are you warm?"

"Better, thanks." Galen unburied himself from the blankets and found his dressing gown and slippers waiting for him. "Might be a bit. I'd like to have a wash if no one's using the bathing room."

"I'll be here."

Twenty minutes later, after he'd sluiced off his feet and legs again, and as much of the rest of him as he could manage with a damp washcloth. That done, he came back to their room to find a large tray of breakfast items. Toast and marmalade and an egg cup. Not a full breakfast, but it would do well enough. Willet was waiting, the shoes prominently in front of his wardrobe.

"Brilliant, Willet. Any news from the rest of the house?"

"There's some talk of a billiards game after luncheon, sir. Mister Paxman inquired if you'd be up for a chat after luncheon. That is at half twelve."

Galen nodded. "Of course, if you'd take a message to him. I - what's the weather like?"

"Pleasant for December, sir, and sunny. If you wished a walk before luncheon, I believe you could have a quiet one. Much of the house is still getting going."

"Right." Galen glanced at Lydia. "Walk?"

Five minutes later, they were out the door, with directions on how to make their way through the walking paths on the property. Lydia waited until they were halfway through the gardens and unlikely to be either overheard or spotted. "Are you really all right?"

"I was going to ask you the same." Galen ran his hand through his hair. "Nothing's obviously wrong? Only."

"Only it's got this sort of oily film all over it. I don't trust the drinks, but you can't not drink."

"Wine's safer than cocktails." Galen said immediately. "Not that you can't add things to it, but it's more noticeable if someone does."

"I don't suppose you know - no, we can't use any useful charms, can we? All the ones I know have lights or something of the kind. Obvious to other people."

"Quite. I checked the water pitcher this morning, but."

He shook his head. "I wouldn't put it past someone to use something to make people more biddable. And I do not know what will happen when Vincent has a chat."

"Vincent and Nico both, do you think?"

Galen shrugged one shoulder. "I suspect Vincent, maybe both of them together, but then Nico wanting to get me alone. He can't talk about the magical bits with Vincent around."

"Who else do you think?" Lydia tilted her head. "Wait, you must have a journal."

"Only way to do modern magical business. Despite the expense, so very useful. Mine's in the secret panel in my suitcase. Why?"

"I'd love to know if there's any information on the others here. I wish we'd known the names in advance, and it's Saturday. Minimal staff at the paper's morgue."

"Fortunately," Galen said, "The Dwellers never sleep. Or at least the house never does. I'll write a note and see what we get back. Maybe we'll get lucky and someone knows them or went to school with them. When we get back, and we might hear something by supper and the party."

Lydia nodded. "And we shouldn't talk about - well. Anything."

"No. I'll wrap the charm stone up when we go to bed, but we can't leave it like that, Nico might check on it."

"You really should have had the bed last night." Lydia stopped and turned to Galen. "You were soaked to your thighs." Then she blushed. "Um."

"It is Victorian ladies who weren't supposed to have legs. I believe, in the bounds of propriety, you may notice I have them. And besides, you were doing things with your own knees last night. I noticed that."

She blushed darker. "Enid was trying to teach me to dance. I mean, that kind of dancing."

Galen made a slight bow. "We'll have more of that tonight, then. Of varying forms."

Lydia hesitated, looking down and away, then back up. "Not just because it makes the right show?" Her voice cracked slightly as she spoke, and Galen did not know what to do with that. Well, he also could not sort out how he felt, which did not help at all.

There was an awkward silence, the kind that stretched on and on, before Galen found himself plunging into a different sort of pond. Far more metaphorical. He reached to take Lydia's hand, looking down at both their hands, then back up at her face. "I don't know how to have this conversation."

It was the truth, but it made her laugh. Her eyes crinkled, and the sound rolled around. When she stopped, she took a breath. "Blythe said I shouldn't break your heart."

"Do you think that's likely? Does she think that's likely?" The words came out in a rush.

"She seemed to think it might be a reasonable concern. On the other hand, it likely matters more what you think." Lydia squeezed his hand. "I don't want to. For the record."

"Right. Oh. Good. I'd rather you didn't. Rather no one did, honestly, it seems awful? But you in particular." Galen was definitely babbling now, and they both knew it. He looked away, trying to figure out what to say that might be sensible.

In that silence, Lydia said, "I do like you, Galen. Not just because you're helping me so much. And you're kind about it. Most people aren't. Their helping comes with leashes and expectations and pity or expected gratitude, and you don't do any of that. And I liked you even more, seeing you wade in to help Charles last night, when none of the other men did anything."

Galen shook his head. "They didn't think much of it. I don't know if you heard, but one of them - Oswald, I think - muttered about how he should just buck up, it wasn't like it was the War."

"Huh." Lydia didn't like that, visibly. "Not any patience with him."

"No. And the War was far worse, I mean, those of them that were in the middle? But - a cold pond's not much good either. I was really worried he was going to go face down in it, from the cold and drink and whatever. The shock of it can do things to your heart."

Lydia was watching him, chewing on her lower lip.

"Yes?" He didn't know how to make sense of that.

"A thing I very much like about you, Galen. I want to borrow it like a cloak, how you treat other people. Loyalty and kindness." She squeezed his hand again. "You wanted to help. Last night, it was your first instinct. And how you are with Willet. You treat him like a person."

"Martin would have my head if I didn't." Galen pointed out. "It's his doing."

"Martin might give you a mirror, but you choose to look in it. And to hold yourself to his standards, the things he respects, rather than, rather than theirs." She gestured back toward the house.

Galen swallowed and closed his eyes. A moment later, he could feel a kiss on his cheek, and Lydia was right there, up close. He hesitated for a moment, then brought his other hand to rest at her waist, right at her hip. Before he could decide to do anything else, she asked, "May I kiss you?"

It was ridiculous, out here in this field, when they had other things they should focus on. "Yes. I. Please."

He'd read about kisses. Had a few himself, nothing that he felt explained the mystery of them. Certainly, he'd heard a fair bit from Martin. This was nothing like that. She was delicate at first. Maybe it was figuring out his height, maybe she didn't want to rush him. He didn't know whether he should be grateful for that, or feel ashamed she felt she needed to.

Then, the sensation of it, the closeness of it, the warmth, all of that swept over him. She tilted her head a little differently. And then there they were. Kissing was like riding. It had a rhythm and a dance to it, and it was something he was suddenly sure he could learn. Probably faster than he'd thought. It was certainly something he suddenly wanted to do a lot more. His hand tightened on her hip, her other hand broke free from his to go round his shoulders. They stood there, kissing and kissing until both of them had to pull back to breathe.

Her eyes were gleaming, a stormy deep blue, and she blinked at him before grinning. "There. More of that later. When we get the chance. We should probably keep walking, though, to put on the right show at luncheon."

Galen swallowed, trying to gather himself. His head was swirling, and his body was answering all those needs in ways he'd never really figured out how to deal with properly. He coughed. "Um. Yes." He then took her hand again. "Walking. I think I remember how to walk."

It took a stumbling step or two, but then they kept going, to make a large loop of the grounds, before coming back for luncheon. The women whisked Lydia off after that.

Galen was left with Vincent, in a wood-panelled study, the sort of place that he suspected Vincent only used for show. He should have been focused on every detail of what Vincent said, but it mostly flowed over him.

It began with the sort of praise that would make any sensible person suspicious. That Galen was a pillar of his generation, he was the right sort, he was clever and appealing. That his tastes matched theirs so well. The implication, of course, was that these were the proper tastes, Galen should be praised for having them.

And then Vincent turned to the idea Nico saw him as a good prospect, and Galen should see about taking up the offer Nico was offering, there would be a time to discuss that tomorrow. It came across as an order, but the sort of order you got from a second-in-command, unwilling to upset his commanding officer. Or afraid to.

Galen knew he should keep his attention on their goal. He nodded, and made agreeable noises, and asked for advice, while the rest of him was caught up in when later might be, and what Lydia had in mind.

CHAPTER 27
SATURDAY EVENING

The party that night was more or less what Lydia had expected. Chaotic, loud, and full of people. There were another thirty or forty people here at least, all posh voices and drawling accents, the kind of thing she had to listen closely to.

She spoke well enough now, at least, but it wasn't like that.

The costume was more or less the right thing. And Netty had done a glorious thing with her hair, commenting that it had been a while since she'd got to enjoy working with long hair. Bobs were very modern, but they gave so many fewer options. In the end, she'd ended up with braids twined around her head. They anchored a collection of golden holly leaves and gleaming red berries. It was like a crown, but so sturdily fixed in her hair she could have flipped upside down and they would never move. Galen looked grand in his costume. As she'd though, the golden yellow flattered him rather than washing him out.

Of course, those feelings of confidence only lasted until they got downstairs to the ballroom. Instantly, Lydia felt overdressed compared to the number of women who were wearing the thinnest of straps on their dresses. Felicity was wearing something that seemed to stay up invisibly, with a slit that went almost to the top of her thigh. Despite that, though, it was very much an ice queen motif, a pale silvery blue with beading that looked uncomfortable to touch, never mind embrace.

As they took a break from the dancing, Galen murmured, "Drink?" She knew he'd get one that was safe, and make sure it was, so she nodded. She'd let the trays from the servants pass them by. He disappeared, leaving her alone in a corner of the ballroom, shifting her hips slightly from side to side in time with the music.

One woman came up to her. "You're Lydia, aren't you? Felicity said you're from Lancashire. Where about? My people have been there for ages. Poppy Crewe."

"A bit north of Blackpool. Daddy bought the house when I was small." Lydia smiled. "You?"

"Oh, quite near there! Do you know, you must know…" She considered. "Well, there's Tansy Parker. She must be close to you. And Thip Walker. No?"

Lydia shook her head. "I'm afraid I didn't get out much until recently." This was, frankly, what she'd been afraid of. "You know, governess, kept at home. A short leash?"

"And now you're at one of Felicity's parties. However did you manage that?"

"Daddy's busy." Lydia shrugged. "And Galen's - well, Galen's the sort Daddy approves of. Oodles of ancestors." She tried to get the tone right, but by the way Poppy responded, something wasn't going the way Lydia wanted. The other woman backed up a step, eyeing her.

"Well, Galen is a fine sort of man, I suppose." Poppy shrugged. "But does he know what he's getting? I'm more and more sure you're putting us on. Pulling one over on him. On Felicity."

Lydia felt her mind scrambling. "Just because I don't know the same set you do? Come on. Not moving in your circles, but you're not the only people in the world." It was far more aggressive than she'd wanted to be. Pushy. That was not a place Lydia felt comfortable at all most of the time.

Poppy's eyes narrowed. "And Plucky likes you. I never like anyone Plucky likes. She's got no taste at all." She seemed to be gearing up for something else when Galen came back, offering Lydia a glass.

"Do you know where she comes from?" Poppy demanded, stamping a foot and making bells somewhere on her dress jingle.

Galen blinked a little slowly. "Beg pardon?"

"Do you know where she comes from?" Poppy repeated it, the pitch rising.

"Yes, I do. Haven't visited there, but that's nothing out of the ordinary. Modern life, and then there's all the racing."

"Racing." Poppy's eyes narrowed again, into slits this time. "Oh. Felicity said." Then her eyes went wide. "Oh." It was as if she'd realised some desperate mistake, because she took two large steps back, then spun, and disappeared into the crowd.

"I'm fairly sure she's now going to ask all her friends north of Blackpool if they know me." Lydia said, nodding at the drink. "Thank you for turning up when you did."

"I didn't much like the way she was looking at you." Galen dropped his voice to near a whisper. "And you saw…"

"Yes." Lydia sipped her drink, but couldn't think what else to say. Or at least, what else to say, here and now?

The party swirled on around them. Lydia caught glimpses, here and there, of a little knot of people. Nico, talking seriously to Vincent, at one point, and Vincent listening intently. And then Vincent having a word with Felicity and Prudence. Poppy grabbed them after that, gesturing energetically, and glancing over her shoulder until she spotted Lydia.

Felicity, at least, seemed to be trying to calm her down, offering a drink, until Prudence pulled her out to dance.

She'd noticed a few people filtering away when Galen tapped her arm. "Upstairs?" She nodded, and they slipped out of the ballroom, back along the hallway. When they got into the upstairs hallway, Galen whispered in her ear, "Play along." A moment later, he had her pressed against the wall, one hand on either side of her shoulders, looking at her. They were far enough down the hallway to get some warning of anyone coming closer.

"We have a chance to put on a show. Let them hear a bit. If - it's a lot to ask."

She immediately saw his point. And yes, it was. "How?"

"Both of us, in bed. I promise I'll be a gentleman. Not do anything you don't want. But we'll have to make it sound right. And you'll need to help with that." He kept his voice a low purring murmur, the kind of tone that meant with sweet endearments and enticements, not a bloody-minded plot.

"Oh, I know you will." She let her breath out in a rush, then leaned her head back, as she heard someone coming up the stairs. That couple - Abby and Perks, not Charles - giggled as they went by, half stumbling into Abby's room.

"Well." Galen glanced after them. "Can we do this?"

She deliberately twined her arms around his shoulders. "Let's, please." She raised her voice just enough to carry, as

Perks came to close the door. Perks glanced at them for a bare second before they heard running footsteps as the door swung shut, and a sudden squeal and creak of bedsprings.

Galen was visibly caught between shock and bemusement. She pivoted, tugging him along with her, letting her hands slide down his arms so she could curl her fingers under his and guide him. "Come along, Galen, do."

It made a splendid show. It was a pity no one was about to admire it, but if there were charms to overhear, at least it would sound good. Once they were in the room, she pushed the door closed, and then turned the lock for good measure. "We don't want anyone disturbing us, do we?" she said, before she moved to her side of the bed, rummaging for a notebook and stub of pencil. Easier than a pen in bed, for certain. She held them up, and Galen nodded back at her. "You need a hand out of that dress, darling?" he asked.

"Please. Undo it at the back, would you? And I'll help with your cuffs. No need to get Willet up here. Or what was her name? It's gone out of my head." Getting in a bit more protection for Netty could be all to the good.

They couldn't draw this out too long. He undid the row of tiny buttons up her back, the kind that required a maid. He stepped away to let her shimmy out of the dress and hang it up, leaving her in a silk slip. Lydia regretfully removed all the sharp ornamental holly from her hair, feeling the braids to make sure she hadn't forgotten any. He undid his cuffs and collar, then glanced at her, before shrugging out of the shirt. Galen ducked behind the wardrobe, grabbing pyjama pants as he went by, and she rummaged for a light dressing gown.

They were overheard, not watched. At least she was pretty sure of that. Though it was November, and their bed had curtains. Closing them was certainly a good idea, so she went to do that while Galen finished changing and setting his own costume out on a hanger.

When he joined her in bed, he was shivering a little, and she immediately moved the covers so he could get in, then wrote a note. "If I need you to stop, I'll tap you twice on the hand or where I can reach. You do the same."

He took the notebook and made a little check mark. "You looked glorious in your frock. And your hair." He reached out a hand to touch one curl, hesitating for a moment before he made contact, but she smiled at him, encouragingly. Then he wrote, "I don't know how to make this sound right."

She nodded at him and mouthed, "Follow my lead." Louder, more clearly, she said, "I know you were a bit shy about having people so nearby. Not nearly the same as when you're at home, the wing to yourself. And last night, darling, you weren't in shape for anything. Cold does - well, it doesn't do men any favours, does it?"

Galen blushed at that, rather scarlet, but he managed a weak smile at the end. She was, she was sure, rather bolder than other women he'd been around. Or at least differently bold? She couldn't tell, and she certainly couldn't ask. But he was the one who'd proposed this, and they had a way to communicate when it was too much.

When he'd recovered a little, he coughed. "Certainly not me at my best. But the door is locked, we don't have to worry about anyone barging in, thinking it's their room. And I do - well. The way you looked tonight." His fingers shifted, to brush her cheek with his thumb. "I couldn't keep my eyes off you."

The bashfulness, the delight in his voice, those were entirely real. Lydia smiled. "Even with all the other women there? They were rather more fashionable." A woman wanting reassurance, that was entirely normal. She hesitated, over commenting on the way her body was not the fashionable sort right now, not nearly enough flat planes.

"Perhaps. But I like your curves." He blushed again as he said it. "I suppose I've never said that before."

She laughed, let herself enjoy it. No, he hadn't. "You haven't, no, but I rather like hearing it. Do say more about what you like, then. And I'll return the favour."

Something in that lit him up. "Oh, I like that. Fair-minded of us, isn't it? And there's something about being somewhere new that loosens the tongue." He let his hand shift, tentatively, to her shoulder, and she nodded to encourage him. "I do like your curves. Solid, there. I know where I am with you. And that's the thing, isn't it? A good party is one thing, a bit of fun. But I don't want the floor slipping away, under my feet."

"You've had a bad year or two." Which, well, would give Nico a hook, if he chose to use it, but she knew Galen had already brought up enough of it to intrigue. "And I do like keeping you company." She held out her own hand, palm up, asking if she could touch. He hesitated, then drew it toward him, kissed the top chivalrously, and then set it down on his shoulder. On bare skin. He inhaled, suddenly, and she remembered again how new this must be to him.

And that this was not at all how he'd expected things to go.

She leaned into him, and said, more loudly. "I'm glad to show you. You know that. Be here and be real." She hesitated, and it came out in a giggle. "Me and my curves." Before he could do anything, she dropped her voice to a bare murmur, right next to his ear. "We should kiss, or make it sound like that. And then roll into something more active. If you can make the bed sound right, I can make the other noises."

He shivered under her touch, but he nodded. "You and your curves. And your pleasure. Mustn't forget about that."

Lydia should warn him, really, that wasn't what men like him were supposed to worry about, at least not in public. But while it might get him teased, she couldn't bear to talk him out of it. Whatever this was, though, it couldn't last. And she wasn't really in a position to suggest changes to his behaviour, she was the one intruding in his world. More to the point, they had a plan to follow through on right now. She smiled at him and tilted her head, encouraging the kiss.

This, at least, they had done before. He had clearly thought about it a good bit in the interim, about what angles might work better. And about how to best get his hand in the small of her back, giving her something to arch against. One of his legs slipped against hers, and she could feel that this was working him up, but he made no motion about that. He just focused on kissing her. Not touching her anywhere else.

She wanted the kissing to go on forever, but that would cause him a great deal more teasing, a great deal more suspicion. He had to be seen as the right sort of manly man for this to work. Or at least not the wrong sort. Reluctantly, after several minutes, she pulled back with a little squeal. "Oh, my, you're so ready, aren't you?"

Galen sucked in a breath. "Oh. Oh, yes. Are you?"

Ridiculous man. She nodded, then gestured, and mimed at him. She pressed the flat of one hand against the top of the other, as he might be on the bed, and that she would match it. He took a breath, rolled over onto his stomach, and braced on his elbows, and began this ridiculous charade. As he got going, she started making all the proper sort of gasps and squeals, mostly just wordless noises. Those were easier, they gave less away, and they'd certainly be far less embarrassing in the morning.

As he kept going, she gestured at him, to pick up the pace. His own heavy breathing might not carry to the listening stone, but it matched her well, and well. Plenty of men weren't very articulate in the midst. It built and built, until he groaned, and she was suddenly entirely sure he'd climaxed.

She, well. Lydia had complicated feelings about all of it. When it was safe for her to have a bath, she would likely have to do something about that with her own fingers. She let out a couple of louder squeaks, then a pitched sigh, a "Oh, oh, yes."

It was nothing at all like she wanted, and yet it made her want a great many things now.

He twisted his head to peer at her, and she patted his shoulder, mouthing "Rest" at him. He let his head fall to the pillow, shivering slightly, and she tugged the blankets up over his shoulders, avoiding touching him.

She waited until he was sound asleep - it didn't take long, only a couple of minutes - before she let out a sigh. Lydia slipped out of bed, and said, near the device, "Of course you're asleep." in fond frustration. Once she had it tucked back up into the hatbox and padded by wrapping, she found a blanket and a warmer robe. That done, she curled up in the sofa to read and maybe fall asleep herself.

CHAPTER 28

SUNDAY MORNING

The next morning, Galen woke with his neck stiff, and the rest of him aching. At first, he felt foggy-headed, and then suddenly everything came rushing back to him, and he pushed himself upright.

Lydia was lying in bed, reading, curled up on her side, facing away from him, but the movement must have alerted her, because she pushed up on one shoulder. She was wearing a dressing gown, with her braids coming down around her shoulders. "Galen." She gestured, indicating the listening charm was out again. "Willet brought up breakfast, have some tea?"

She was so matter of fact about it. He rolled over and sat up, pulling one leg up as he tried to catch his breath. "Last night."

"You knew exactly what I wanted and needed." Her voice was very firm now, and insistent. She didn't reach to touch him, but she didn't pull away. "And we'll have other chances, right?" She went on, briskly. "Willet said Nico wanted a word, before luncheon. I thought I'd have a bath while everyone else is getting moving." She hesitated, and said, "Kiss, for the morning?"

He swallowed, but nodded, for all his mouth felt like cotton wool. She leaned into him, encouraging him, pulling back to whisper in his ear. "We'll talk more, properly private. Are you all right?"

That, the fact she asked, that almost broke him open, and he did not know what to do with that feeling. He rubbed his cheek against her shoulder for a moment, nodding. Then he kissed her again. The kissing still felt so new, but at least they'd worked it out. It wasn't scrambling for purchase and fearing he was going to fall screaming off a cliff. Finally, she pulled back. "I'll let you get dressed. Be back in half an hour, give or take the hot water?"

He nodded. It gave him time to pull himself together. By the time she came back, forty-five minutes later, he had dressed. Then he'd thought about charm-cleaning the bed, decided against it, checked on the listening stone, eaten some of his breakfast, stared out the window, and sipped some tea. Lydia came back with a glow about her, something very satisfied. As he blinked up at her, she kissed him on the cheek and plopped down on the sofa next to him. "Well. Supper tonight is supposed to be just the people staying. And I gather there might be some games this afternoon. Everyone else seems to be sleeping in, though."

He wanted to go for a walk with her, somewhere private enough they could really talk, but there was a looming appointment with Nico. "I should find Nico, I suppose." he said. "You all right for a bit?"

"There's a library downstairs. I'll be fine. I suspect it's not occupied." The other guests had not seemed terribly inclined to literary amusements, no. Or mornings, even late mornings.

When Galen came downstairs, he inquired whether Nico was available. "Mister Lind is in the office, sir, if you want to go on through?" He was led to a door off the drawing room. The footman knocked. "Mister Amberly, sir, as expected."

Nico was sitting behind a large wooden desk, looking as if he were entirely at home in someone else's office. If Galen hadn't known better, he would have sworn that Nico lived here, that this was his demesne. It wasn't, Galen knew it wasn't, but the impression was so strong.

"I hope you and Lydia had a pleasant night? No untoward interruptions once you got upstairs?"

"Very pleasant, thank you." Galen made himself settle in the chair on the other side of the desk. "She's a cheerful sort. Obligingly so."

"I gather you've been on a short leash, old chap. In a number of ways. Financially. With the ladies. Your other opportunities."

Galen shrugged. That cut closer to home. It was, however, also accurate. "A fair bit. It's been a bad year or so. We may speak privately?"

Nico got a slow grin. "Oh, quite privately. All the ways I know about."

Galen nodded. He trusted that the oaths and promises coiled around the Pact would remind him, if they could by chance be overheard by someone without magic. "You must have done your research by now, and know the situation with my parents."

"And your brother. Rather unfortunate, all round, really. And now here you are, needing to live up to expectations. I presume that besides Miss Pyle's other visible attributes, she comes from some money? Not the sort that she's mentioned, but something of the kind."

"Sufficient resources, yes." Galen settled back uncomfortably. He let it show. Not that he trusted himself to hide it, but letting his uncertainty be visible might help. Since he was going to do that, anyway.

"Oh, you're not in trouble, Galen. Not at all. I want to offer you an opportunity." Nico held up his hand smoothly. "Not asking for any further money, though there will be some investment opportunities down the road, if you're so inclined. No, you're exactly the sort of young man with potential we're looking for."

"We? You and Vincent?"

Nico laughed, as if that were the most amusing thing he'd heard in a month. "Vincent's very good at what he does. And he's certainly a generous enough host. But not very much like Vincent." He spread his hands. "I and a select few gather for a spot of benefic magic. You're a Schola man. You did well on your exams." That was a telling detail about the research Nico had done. "You know your ritual theory well enough that working in unison with others has a magnifying effect, properly managed. We gather for an increase in prosperity. Our own, of course, but the good of the empire."

Galen listened intently, trying to memorise the words as well as the tone. "The empire?"

"Oh, yes. We're just starting on a part of that now. Besides those of us who can call on those blessings, make them real, send them out... well, we have those like Vincent and his set who can carry them along. Into the halls and offices of the City, in the Colonial Service and Army. All the places we can touch."

"And the goals? Besides, well, increase?"

Nico shrugged, elegantly. "Power. Distributing power as we see fit. We know better, we are better, we were born and bred for this." He hesitated, as if making a decision, and Galen suddenly did not trust that hesitation at all. It was deliberate, designed to pull him in. "The War was hell. You have a sense of that, for all you didn't fight. Most importantly, we want to make sure that never happens again. That the empire is so strong, so shining, so resilient that we will never be locked into a deathmatch on every front again."

"You had mentioned a little about your group. I gather something has changed a bit?"

"Several of them were in attendance last night. And Perks. Abby is quite aware of us, mind, too."

Galen was suddenly glad he and Lydia had made such a show of it last night. "And what does Perks think of me?"

"Callow youth, ridiculously sentimental, that bit about fishing Charles out of the pond. He'd have been fine. But Perks sees a certain amount of promise in you. As do I, or we'd not be having this conversation. You are untested, ritually speaking, but that's an easy enough matter to tend to. Will you join us next Saturday? See how you get on with the magic?" He made it sound like a day in the park. Which, of course, made Galen even more suspicious than he'd already been.

"I'm flattered." He tilted his head. "Where? When? And what's involved?"

"You have a journal?" Galen nodded. "I'll send round the generalities, the preparation, tomorrow evening, and the address an hour before. Arrive when we reach full dark. I trust you can do the proper calculations."

Not terribly late, then, at this time of year. "Near a portal, I'm assuming?"

"Oh, yes." Nico's voice was purring now. "Though a rather remote one. Private land, very well placed for what we want. The portal is just outside the boundary. Someone will meet you."

Galen nodded. "And what should I plan on for the evening?" He kept his voice even. A hint of nerves showing wouldn't be bad, but he wanted to come across as reasonably eager, not wondering what he'd got himself into.

"The ritual, oh, about an hour or so. Food and drink afterwards. Of course, don't tell Lydia anything about it. We have some women take part, but only those who have proven themselves." He waved a hand. "Friday will be all men, for the ritual itself."

"Not your wife, then." Galen said.

"Not our wives." Nico got a sudden grin. "Ladies given to personal entertainment, sometimes. Or does that shock your little provincial heart?" Ah, there it was, the thorn amid the flattery, just enough to goad him to prove himself. At least Galen recognised it easily.

Galen made himself shrug one shoulder. "I'm not inclined to wander. To be honest, my mother flung enough eligible young women at me I find being chased on brief acquaintance a flaw rather than an enticement. I've known Lydia for a bit, in other settings."

"Ah." Nico steepled his hands. "That tells me something about you, yes. I can see how that might be. And you said your parents were more than a little restrictive."

"Kept me close to home, yes. Especially after Julius came back." Galen shrugged. "I understand it, I suppose. I didn't like it, it couldn't have lasted. But I can see why they felt as they did."

Nico shifted at that. It wasn't quite relaxation. The man was far too guarded for that, too precise in the implications of his movements. But he approved, and he let that approval show. "A man in your position might go one of three ways. He might run wild, given the chance, which you clearly haven't done. He might become more rigid, fenced in. Or he might become open-minded. Seeing that his family had a reason, even if he doesn't wish to continue like that."

"Quite." Galen shrugged slightly. He was more sure Nico hadn't turned up his association with the Dwellers, or at least not made sense of what it meant. He considered playing a hand. "What you all are up to? There was that whole mess. I didn't follow the details, busy with my own things. But Lord Sisley, and that lot?"

"Oh, no." It was the kind of place where many men might have said, 'Merlin, no'. Galen caught the slight pause and wondered what Nico usually said in such settings. "Or rather." He considered. "Sisley and his lot were an arm of the thing. Like Vincent and his friends are. We have several circles. It is the inner circle I am inviting you to meet, the elite I am inviting you to visit. Three additional circles of magicians, two now. Sisley led one, and we are working up a replacement."

He did not, Galen notice, make any suggestion that Galen might suit there, eventually. Instead, Nico went on smoothly. "And then three circles, those are incapables, who you won't ever meet. We keep things strictly separate. Rather a lot simpler when someone trips up, don't you know?" The use of the term for those without magic told Galen everything he might want to know about what those people were for. Even, apparently, Vincent, who might well have been sharp enough to spot it and feel unsure of himself. Fuel for the magic, in one form or another, or messenger boys taking items out into the world.

On the other hand, parts of this were sensible management. Galen knew from the Dwellers about the strength of individual cells for various activities, about being able to swear he knew nothing, even under the Silence oath. It was also cursedly annoying, though the part where Nico was inviting him to the most central of the three groups was promising. "Oh, that makes sense." He tried to sound amiably eager.

Nico nodded. "We won't be making certain mistakes again. Those last three circles that help support the work, as I said. Getting talismans and effects and what have you out to the empire, or carrying messages, or acting on our behalf in all their places."

"And how does Darley fit into this? It was clear to me Vincent wanted to be on his good side."

"Aren't you clever." It was praise, but again, it had that tinge of Nico taking the opportunity to dig the hook in a little deeper. "Darley has a great many connections we are hoping to make use of. And money. And tremendous strokes of luck. Of course we'd rather those benefit us, rather than others." He made a casual twist of his hand. "The horse is a show of good faith. He's asked for that. Something tangible to cement the relationship. You understand, of course."

Galen nodded slowly, trying to figure out how to ask more questions without letting his own caution show. It was clear he wasn't going to get an explanation of the truth of the horse. "And of course, money is a help. Both for its own sake, and I suppose you have rather large aspirations. Reaching out into the empire, that takes resources, surely."

"Entirely clever." Nico's eyes narrowed for a moment, and Galen made himself hold still, keep breathing. It was far too much like a snake considering striking now. "Are you sure you don't know what we're up to?"

"Nothing but what I've picked up from you and Vincent.

And buying into Crisparkle would help prove to Darley and whoever else that your association is indeed profitable, right? But - well. I did get the impression that Vincent and Felicity were a bit lacking the ready money."

That was the right thing to say, and Nico threw back his head and laughed. "He's been sure you were so dazzled by the show you wouldn't notice. But I suppose being kept on a short leash makes some things more obvious, doesn't it?"

More that years discussion with Martin and the other Dwellers made some things absurdly easy to spot, but Galen shrugged agreeably. "Vincent has made a good show of it. It was the eagerness to bring me in, when I don't come with much money myself, that tipped me off, more than anything."

"Indeed." Nico steepled his fingers, signalling an end to that line of question. "Are there other matters we should discuss?" That was a neat trick, too, leaving it to Galen to decide what he dared ask.

Galen nodded. "I suppose there's nothing else you can tell me about the ritual now?"

"No." Nico shrugged. "You understand. Initiatory experiences, and facing up to the challenge of the moment, seeing what you're made of. Especially since you weren't in the War. It builds trust."

Whose trust was the question. When Galen said nothing further, Nico nodded. "If that's all, we might as well get on to luncheon. I think Felicity wanted a croquet match in the afternoon, or perhaps something inside if it actually rains. Come along, we'll find a seat."

CHAPTER 29

"And the horse is - well, there's something about the horse. Probably not actually the bloodlines it's supposed to have that's a common enough issue. But not exactly newsworthy." Editor Morris flicked through his notes and the ones Lydia had given him, one more time.

Lydia waited, uncomfortably, not sure where to look. Galen sat next to her, on one side of the table in the meeting room, while Edward Morris sat on the other, papers spread out. He was tapping his pencil on a corner of the notepaper. At least it wasn't his pen. When he got supremely distracted, he blotched ink everywhere, and three people would have to get it out of the wood and clothing.

"This isn't enough." Morris glanced up at Lydia. "It is thorough work, so far, and at some risk to yourselves." He nodded at both of them. "But it is not illegal to have private rituals. If it were, I suspect all of Albion would be in gaol. It is not illegal to want to make money. Or to do things that are in poor taste. Likewise. It is not even illegal to use the non-magical as patsies and catspaws, within the bounds of the Pact."

Galen smiled at that. Lydia caught his lips quirking up. He was being really very patient, coming along to this meeting on the Tuesday. They'd got back to his home later than planned on Monday. She had needed to get back to her rooming house, so she hadn't been able to talk it through with him. Just meet him this morning.

"And some of these people have no magic, and they are not our concern, legally. And more to the point, under the Pact." Morris shook his head. "We are reporters, not the bearers of justice. Well, reporters and investigators." Galen got a nod there.

"Sir," Galen cleared his throat. "I've been glad to assist, of course."

Morris nodded and turned his attention fully onto Galen. Lydia was glad to have a break, but she wasn't sure what Galen would think of it. "Go on."

"Can I ask what the options are here?" Galen spread his hand. "Is this an end for the investigation? Having something of a personal stake in it now."

Morris nodded. "What do you think about all of this? Pyle laid it out well, of course." Lydia basked briefly in that praise.

Galen gathered his thoughts, rather visibly. "I wasn't in the War, but I - well. I can see how men might come back from that, and want enough power they would never have to fear it again. It won't work, it can't possibly work. But I can see why they're trying."

Morris let out a hollow laugh. "And why won't it work?"

"Not enough people. Not enough reach." Galen shrugged. "I did, as it turns out, do reasonably well on my Ritual exams, though for some odd reasons. I mean, we're assuming there aren't hundreds of people in each of these circles. Sisley and all, that was, what, two dozen?"

Morris pulled a folder out from under his notepad, flipping it open. "Three circles of fourteen each. The trial brought out Sisley's circle. One turned up in a terror at the Guard demanding to confess."

Galen frowned. "An oath pressing on him, then? Something particular? And none of them mentioned Lind?"

"Likely. They handled that in closed court." Morris shook his head. "Does it matter?"

"Not exactly." Lydia glanced at Galen and considered. He was, in many ways, acting more like a Dweller than she'd seen him before. At the house party, he had been playing the innocent. And not so much play as all that, sometimes. He seemed honestly to be as good-hearted and kind as he'd come across. Shy, certainly not full of bluster and false pride. But now, he was more calculating. Not in the way Nico was, or Vincent, where you knew there were plots afoot.

No, this was something more strategic, seeing the pathways forward, picking and choosing as he went, in what looked at times like a glorious headlong rush over a cliff. But they somehow kept working.

Galen fell quiet. Morris went on. "I can't ask you to go to that meeting, you realise. You are not one of my reporters. You owe me nothing. And there may be nothing there. We are not a scandal sheet. Knowing that there is a larger group might be enough to monitor them. You have more names for us. Perhaps in six months, or a year, we will have something we can use."

Galen's chin came up. "First, sir." It was a very polite formality, but it had an edge to it. "You cannot tell me to go, but you cannot order me to stay home. Second, if I do not go, they will be sure something is up. Lydia will come under greater suspicion. I'm fairly sure we've got away with things so far because she didn't go to Schola. The usual methods of tracking down information among Nico's sort won't work nearly as well for her. But that will only last so long."

Lydia had had that thought early that morning. Well, the second one. She had suspected Galen was going to insist on continuing. Morris opened his mouth, and Galen sailed on, undaunted.

"And third, sir, I have my own reasons not to want to see that sort have all the power." Lydia had a rush then, of his friends. Of Martin and Marian and Thomasina and Owen, all people who came from the professional classes, perhaps, but not posh land-holding families. Galen leaned back, using the tricks Lydia had long since learned to recognise. All the shifts of someone who knew he had some power in the conversation, and was going to make everyone else work to convince him.

It looked good on him. As much as Lydia disliked that trick, it looked very good on him. Utterly different from the way he'd looked Saturday evening in bed, but just as good.

Morris tapped his pencil one last time, then set it down. "There is one option I would not normally suggest. If you take it, you will need to see it through."

Galen shrugged. "I'm willing to do that." There was a steel to him now, something Lydia couldn't begin to put into words. She wondered, for a second, what he would say about it, if he could.

Morris nodded, and then stood, rather abruptly. "A minute." He strode out of the meeting room, calling out for one of the runners. Then he was borrowing a pen and paper from someone's desk and writing up a note, causing a flurry

227

of motion and activity just outside the door. Galen glanced over at him, and just waited.

Lydia cleared her throat. "Thank you."

He tilted his head, not entirely looking at her. "For what?"

"Being willing." Lydia gestured with one hand, incoherent. "For a lot of things."

Galen shrugged, as if he were about to say something. Then he stopped, and instead, said, "What do you think he's doing?"

"Message to someone."

At that moment, Morris handed the message off, and came back in, brushing off his hands. "The gathering is on Saturday. We'll be discussing it in Editorial tomorrow if things go as I think. Pyle, be there, whatever the other plans involved. Amberly, you as well, if possible."

"The other plans, sir?" Galen kept his voice even.

"Anyone with my job and some longevity builds up a certain black book of people in the halls of power. In this case, one of the Guard."

Lydia watched a series of expressions go over Galen's face. She could read him well enough to be sure there was something complicated there.

"Which one, sir, may I ask?" Galen's voice was a hair strained, flat, but not too noticeably.

"Hippolyta FitzRanulf." Morris was rummaging through his papers, and he missed the expression on Galen's face, like a portcullis dropping suddenly, before Galen gave his face over to polite readiness like a mask. "I'll get someone to bring some sandwiches. She'll likely be half an hour or so, given time to get across town and back, if she's there and available." He wiggled a hand. "Messenger, so that if she's not handy, the clerk can redirect it."

Galen nodded. "Sandwiches, thank you." He waited until Morris had swept out, closing the door behind him, then closed his eyes and let out a long sigh.

"You know her?"

"She's the one who investigated that murder. And nearly accused Martin. She doesn't like the Dwellers one bit."

"Well. Blast." She wanted to say several other things, not suited for the offices where she worked, even if newspaper folk were creative with their swearing. "How much of a problem is that?"

Galen shook his head. "I suppose it's my comeuppance, back to haunt me." He swallowed.

Lydia reached out to cover his hand with hers. "Are you sure?" She was asking both about then, and about now.

"My discomfort doesn't matter here. Not much, anyway. Sorting things out, so they don't get to hoard the power they want. That matters." He grimaced. "And to be fair, Captain FitzRanulf has a thing about people hoarding power."

"What's she like? And how can I help?"

"Very formal. Straightlaced. You know, hair back in a tight bun, and her uniform perfectly tailored? I found out after that she's a by-blow to the Ranulfs, which I suppose explains a lot. Starting with the name." He then blinks. "Oh, well. I suppose we could look at her and at Nico as two different ways that goes, couldn't we? If his father was the same."

"Oh." Lydia tried to get her head around that. "I still can't believe people actually do that."

"Some of them. Apparently. Anyway, she's been in the Guard since she started her Apprenticeship, has a solid reputation. Mostly she deals with murders or deaths or

229

what have you, which I suppose explains why Editor Morris would want to be on good terms with her."

"Well, sometimes the press can be a help in that kind of thing. Getting information out, encouraging people to come forward. And a murder is, like it or not, always good for our sales."

Galen grimaced. "I suppose it would be." He waved a hand. "She doesn't hate all the people with power? She respects Lord Carillon. Laura's brother-in-law. But maybe he's an exception. And it's not like I have much power in the scheme of things."

"But you are, at least, coming across like someone who might want it." She peered at him. "We haven't really talked about your discussion with Nico. I didn't like to take the risk."

"Quite right." Galen shrugged. "Feeling me out. He didn't come out and make it obvious he'd been listening in Saturday night, but he - well. I'm clear he was. Though whatever he heard helped convince him you're obliging, I am a young man who likes my pleasures, even if I'm a bit provincial about them. Saturday's events apparently include some sort of entertainment of the more personal kind afterwards, for those that want it."

"Well, you know all the penny-dreadfuls about the aftermath of arcane ritual acts and the implications for maidens in the vicinity? It's a staple of the genre."

It made Galen smile and relax, visibly. Lydia was delighted with it. He took a longer breath, then said, "I don't expect the thing to be pleasant, though I'm also assuming that whatever I see Saturday will be..." He shrugged. "Well."

"Yes?"

"Something to bind me to them. Some sort of oath or

obligation or ritual experience. Possibly something humiliating, that they can hold over me."

"Are you worried about that?" Lydia twisted in her chair. "You've already done so much."

"It's not enough. It's..." Galen grimaced. "This is what the Dwellers are for. I've never really been the arrowhead. I'm always back making sure things are working smoothly. But this, this I can do. I'm in the right place to do it. If I didn't, I'd hate myself for the rest of my life. Or rather, I'd hate myself for a bit. Then I'd turn into someone like my parents, who took the easy way out, again and again. I would destroy myself, and destroy any good I've been for Martin, and ..."

Lydia said, softly, "You have been very good to me, and for me, and I hope for more of that to come."

That made him look up, wide-eyed. "Oh." He swallowed. "I can't talk about Saturday night right now. I mean."

"No. Quite." It came out sounding a tad prim. "Not this near my colleagues, please."

"Later. I promise. Sometime later, when we can." He ran a hand through his hair. "Could there be tea to go with the sandwiches?"

"There should be. Let me go see what's up. I'm more usually the one sent to arrange them." Lydia stood. "I won't be far, back in a moment."

Galen nodded and picked up his pen, fiddling with it slightly.

CHAPTER 30
TUESDAY AFTERNOON, AT THE HALLS OF JUSTICE

Galen waited, impatiently. Just when he thought someone might have arrived, a messenger came back, and Editor Morris came in with a note immediately after. "Captain FitzRanulf asks if we could go round to the Halls of Justice. She has someone she wishes to consult who can't come here. She promises it will be worth my while, though. Do you mind?"

Galen was not at all sure he wanted to go into the Guard Hall or any of the Halls of Justice, but he had committed to this thing. He would see it through. At least the conversation about it. Whatever he thought about Captain Fitz-Ranulf - or probably more importantly, what she thought about him - there were limits on what she could do to him in this circumstance.

And Lydia would be right there, which made him feel better. If she were there, she could get help, tell people. Persuade people. She was rather good at that, without being brash about it. Just relentlessly determined.

They wrapped up in coats and gloves, and had a brisk walk down through the main square, then off to the Guard

Hall. One of the apprentice Guards met them there, and escorted them in through the private courtyard of the Halls of Justice, along an interminable hallway, and into a meeting room. It was simple, well proportioned, with a large rectangular table in the centre. There were eight chairs around it, a fireplace, and the sort of disarmingly pleasant chestnut wood panelling and white plaster that made Galen think of country houses.

Three people sat at the far end of the table. Galen recognised Captain FitzRanulf immediately. She was in her full uniform with her hair pulled back, but she had set her hat and outerwear on a coatrack in the corner. One man seemed to be an aide or apprentice, younger than Galen but in his twenties. The last man had auburn hair, but Galen's impression of him was interrupted when he wheeled his chair back from the table and around toward them.

"Thank you for coming down here. As you can see, rather a bother to get across town, especially on market day." He gestured. "This is Captain FitzRanulf, and Edwards, my apprentice."

"I've met Captain FitzRanulf previously, sir." Galen kept his voice polite. "Captain." She nodded at him, and he had no idea what she thought.

"I know Morris, of course. And you two are?" The man gestured, then went back to his place at the end of the table, looking at them expectantly. He made some slight gesture, and Edwards stood up. "Of course, sir. Back in a tick." It was that, in the less formal mode, that made Galen hope this would not be entirely awful.

"Galen Amberly, sir," Galen said.

"Lydia Pyle. I'm a reporter, working for the Trellech Moon." She nodded at Morris, who went around the table, settling down next to Captain FitzRanulf. He leaned in to whisper something quietly to her.

"Amberly. Ah, yes." Galen braced himself for a comment about his parents, but instead got, "You look a good deal like your brother about the eyes, has anyone told you? I gather he's doing much better these days." It rather notably wasn't a question.

Galen couldn't help smiling at that. "Much, sir. May I let him know you inquired?"

"Oh, certainly. Actually, I might see if he's willing to consult about something. Right, yes, where are my manners?" Galen was utterly sure this man had not forgotten for a moment, but he was glad to play along with the scene-setting, whatever it was in aid of. "Griffin Pelson. Very long title, entirely uninformative, please call me Griffin. What I actually do is work with the Guard and Ministry about issues related to significant property, inheritances, institutions, and so on. Edwards has gone off to get one more person, Captain Orland, who deals primarily with cases related to family and inheritance."

Galen had met Antimony Orland dealing with his parents' case. "Captain Orland oversaw some matters around my parents, sir. I appreciated her explanations, and her deftness with some of the magical work."

"Ha! And you are highly intimidated, as all sensible folk should be. There will also be tea in a moment. Whatever else we are today, it will be civilised." He settled back, glancing from one side of the table to the other. Captain FitzRanulf was giving nothing away, though she was at least not scowling. No one asked Galen anything. Everyone just waited.

Two minutes later, Captain Orland came trotting in, brisk but with her hair flying in wisps that fell out of her bun. She was wearing a vest, blouse, and skirts rather than the full Guard uniform. She was comfortably middle-aged, but the sort of middle-aged that suggested she climbed small mountains in her days off.

The informality was a contrast to the way she'd been during the trial, but closer to how she'd been with Galen afterwards. He'd been so grateful at the time that she had been willing to explain what she was going to do until he felt sure he understood. She had a passion for the work, clearly, and that must help. "Pardon, hello, yes. Oh, goodness. Galen Amberly. What have you come across, then? And who are you?"

Lydia introduced herself, and Griffin gestured. "Explain why you wanted to speak to someone, please."

Editor Morris began laying out the proposal Lydia had made, what seemed like months ago. He followed it with a pithy summary of the events so far. That ended up with "Amberly and Pyle spent several days at a house party, and Amberly has an invitation for a bit of ritual magic next Saturday." He left out the embarrassing details of Saturday night, other than that from all accounts Galen and Lydia were doing a good job of seeming to be happily partnered.

In any other circumstance, Galen would have been admiring the skill with words - well, the man was the editor of the largest paper of Albion. As it was, he wasn't sure what to do. All four of the others looked varying degrees of intrigued and something Galen couldn't name. Griffin was the most obviously interested, FitzRanulf was withholding judgement, and Orland was scribbling notes.

"What are your impressions of Lind, then?"

Galen gestured at Lydia to go first. She promptly said, "I don't care for him or the feel of his magic. I've not come across someone who felt like him much. A few times, doing interviews. Knowing there are dozens of things he's not saying, and most of them are rather unpleasant." She named someone to Morris, mouthing it across the table. Galen didn't quite catch the name, but Editor Morris nodded as if that meant something to him. "But he also wasn't interested in spending much time with me."

Galen nodded. "I have the decided feeling of being courted. Like he'd spent time thinking of what would be most enticing to me. Playing on the fact I was too young for the War, what he knew about my brother, my parents." It was no use hiding it. If Griffin didn't know the details already - and Galen would eat his hat if he didn't - everyone except possibly Edwards could give a full and detailed explanation.

"And you think there is something desperately wrong there." Griffin tapped his fingers together, thoughtful.

"I do." Galen swallowed. "When we talked to Editor Morris earlier, he pointed out that nothing that has been proposed so far is illegal. Secret societies exist. I'm a Schola man. I'm in one of them. Certainly, people may get up to a number of things I don't like on private property, and do regularly. As our recent adventures show."

Something in his tone made Captain Orland snort and relax a bit.

"That is a problem, yes." Griffin considered. "Hippolyta called me in because of several complications. The War did a number on so many of our institutions. The Guard, but also the Halls of Justice. Not so much our judges, but the ... the rest of the supporting structure, as it were. A combination of cases that set new precedent, deaths of a few key people being groomed to succeed to positions where institutional knowledge is critical." He waved a hand at himself. "Some who can't serve as originally intended."

Galen inclined his head slightly. "Sir." He swallowed, then decided he'd ask his questions, come what may. It was necessary. He could feel the tug, the rhythm of it, somewhere deep inside him. "It can't be that they want me for money. They have to know by now how scant that is. We're getting things on the right track, but there's a fair bit to do before we're fully solvent. I bought a share of the horse, but that's all the luxury spending for a bit."

Orland looked up and raised an eyebrow. "What did you sell?"

Galen had known that was coming. "That awful painting in the back of the gallery, the one that near glowers at everyone? Turns out to be by the great-grandfather of someone who's aiming at membership in the Albion Inheritance, and she has more money than taste."

Lydia blinked at him. "You never said."

"I implied it came from the estate. Which it did. Unfortunately, we don't have so many paintings we actually want to get rid of, given the choice. That one dropped in our laps, and Julius and Blythe agreed we could use it for the horse. The estates are doing better, though, enough." His chin came up, and Lydia reached to put her hand on top of his.

"And the horse?" Griffin had caught onto that.

"I'm pretty sure it's a lure. We can't chase it down further, what's wrong with it, without tipping our hands. But one of our contacts is pretty sure it's - a horse of different breeding. Might well win races, but he doesn't command the sort of bloodlines you'd expect at that price."

Griffin shrugged. "A lure, as you say. Not a bad one, for sorting out who asks awkward questions and who doesn't." He waved a hand at Galen. "Or who leaves off asking soon enough."

237

FitzRanulf had stayed silent through this, but she cleared her throat, and everyone got quiet. "You do realise how dangerous this might be. If they don't want your money now, it's more likely they want or need you for the ritual work."

Galen looked straight at her. "I had figured that out, about at the point when they asked me to the house party. Saying it out loud is a tad more challenging."

Her lips quirked, hinting at a smile, and she inclined her head. "I admit, that is not a challenge I've ever particularly faced. Why are you willing to consider it?"

She was leaving it open for him, then. She knew he was a Dweller, but he wasn't sure anyone else did. Galen swallowed, and then said, "Sirs, captains. I am oathsworn, and glad to be, as a Dweller at the Forge. When presented with men and women who want even more power, without a plan for using it beyond personal benefit, well. I am perhaps obligated to charge ahead."

There was a brief silence, then Griffin said, his voice all seriousness. "And how can we trust you will do as we agree? Not put your fellows first?"

Galen shrugged slightly. He let all the way he'd been brought up show, a man with money and good family, and all that meant or might mean to others. "Sir, if I gave up my fellows or my oath, you would never trust me. And you would be right. More to the point, I would never trust myself again. I will not give up my friends, who challenge me to be better in the world."

He then nodded at FitzRanulf. "It made things difficult for Captain FitzRanulf in the past. As my friend explained then, our oaths oblige us to an accurate accounting to the authorities, when asked."

"Also," Griffin pointed out, "If we get you under oath in

a courtroom, we will know if you are lying, at the very least."

"Our oaths are often rather ruthlessly practical, yes." Galen relaxed a hair, keeping his gaze open, to take in the table. Editor Morris was looking very thoughtful, Captain Orland was leaning back, and Captain FitzRanulf was poised and not giving anything away.

"I think," Griffin said, "We may proceed with a plan. Galen, can we prevail on your time two mornings this week - ideally, without breaking your fast - to go through some of the ritual possibilities? Myself and Antimony. Lydia, you would be welcome if you're available and Galen wishes."

Galen nodded. "Wednesday and Thursday, by preference?" It would give him a day to gather himself before answering that particular summons.

"Come by the front door at half-nine. About two hours each time, we can run to lunch afterwards."

They were dismissed a couple of minutes later to wander out into the mid-afternoon mist. Editor Morris strode back off toward the paper, and Lydia went with him, though she looked a tad sorry to leave him. Galen sighed and went to find a portal back to the house, hoping he had, in fact, done the right thing.

CHAPTER 31
THURSDAY AFTERNOON, THE DWELLERS' HOUSE

"So, tell. What was it like?"

It was Thursday afternoon, not long after lunch. Galen sprawled in his favourite chair, legs over one arm. Martin was leaning forward, having pulled his own chair round. Lydia was on the other side, where she could at least make sure Galen had something to drink when he ran out.

He'd come out of the session looking utterly exhausted. She'd been at the first one, but she'd had to miss this morning's thanks to various meetings at the paper. Working her way through a lot of additional research material in the gaps between them took forever.

"A lot. It was a lot." Galen swallowed. "I, um. I turn out to be not bad at some of it? It's not like Ritual class in school, what we were doing."

"Also, I was lousy at Ritual, and a bad influence, I'm sure." Martin pointed out.

"Never." Galen shrugged. "Captain Orland is very thorough. And so is Griffin. Did you find out more about him, Lydia?"

"He has quite the reputation as a problem-solver, but not the sort who makes the news. Glad to let other people take the credit. Some sort of injury in the War, confidential. He's a solicitor by training, and was in line to be a judge, but I gather there's some fussing about whether he can adequately handle the magical workings for it."

"He was certainly in the midst of it today. Some adaptations - it was one of those chalk on the floor things, but he had me draw some of it, and Edwards did the rest. He was very smooth and precise at the ritual work itself. I could feel it, right off." Galen rearranged his legs.

"So, what can we do to help?" Martin leaned forward again.

"Are you worrying, Martin? That's my job, usually." Galen sounded teasing, more than anything. Fond. Lydia envied that sense of fondness, rather a lot. The way they were easy with each other, in a way they weren't with anyone else. It was selfish to barge into that.

"Well, you don't seem to be doing it." Something in Martin's tone brought Galen's head up, and then he pushed himself upright.

"I'm taking the thing seriously, but it's tricky since I don't know what to worry about specifically. I mean, yes, ritual magics. But which variety of them? That's part of what they've been walking me through."

Martin let out a sigh, and collapsed back in his seat, rather as if one of them had to be slouched and the other upright, in alternation. "Lay it out for us, then. So I can decide what I'm worrying about properly."

Galen nodded. "When it comes down to it, there are five things that they might want. Besides the obvious power. They said that one. We don't have to guess about it." Galen held out his hand, ticking them off on his fingers. "Money.

Which they know they're not getting from me, so that's out. Influence, again, not very likely."

"You know us." Thomasina had been sitting cross-legged in the chair at the other end of the seating. "Do they know that?"

"Probably not, but we can't rule it out." Galen admitted. "You never know what gossip has got around." He waved a hand. "But not the most likely choice. Or I think - and Griffin and Captain Orland agreed - they'd have treated me differently a couple of places."

Martin considered, then nodded. "Fair. Go on." He was more visibly distracted now, worrying at a frayed patch on one of his shirt cuffs.

"So, the other options are that they want me to owe them a favour, unspecified. Hook me with the benefits, take the cost later. Possibly with a spot of blackmail."

"That one is slightly less of a worry, since we hope there won't be too much later involved, right?"

Galen coughed. "Well, that's the idea. But binding ritual magic, that's a trick, isn't it? Oaths made under coercion are still oaths. Though Captain Orland said that if they did, and if they were tried and convicted, they could make them undo it. Probably."

Lydia cleared her throat. "I don't like the sound of that 'probably'."

"She explained the options." Galen looked up, suddenly very earnest. "They might be able to undo whatever it is. I mean, that's half of what the Penelopes are properly for, as investigators. Undoing magic, especially the sort that wasn't terribly well designed in the first place."

"So now we're hoping they're incompetent ritualists?" Martin waved a hand at Lydia, including her. "Definitely not on."

Galen looked slightly abashed for a moment. "Anyway, we don't think that's incredibly likely this first time? Captain Orland thought it was more likely they'd want to use my energy, my magic, to fuel whatever they're doing. That's why I'm so, well." He waved his hand. "She was testing how easy it might be, what I could do to protect myself, without being too terribly obvious."

"Oh, that's an interesting problem!" Thomasina said cheerfully. "You want to be the opposite of a catalyst, don't you? An inhibitor. But not too obvious about it."

"More or less, yes. You can see the trick? But they'll also probably not kill me the first time or anything like that. I mean. Logistically speaking, that would be horribly complicated for them."

Martin nodded, slowly, as if he were thinking through something. Lydia didn't know how to read him well. For that matter, she wasn't doing so well with Galen right now. He was being more guarded, or somehow quieter. He glanced up and then grinned. "That's me practising, Lydia. For the record. What Captain Orland taught me. Being an inhibitor. It's hard work. Against my nature, she said, seeing as how we..." He gestured at the house. "And you, for that matter. Inclined to be catalysts."

Thomasina chortled, clapping her hands in delight. "I will convert you all to alchemy. I'm sure of it."

"Not a huge stretch for me." Galen pointed out, before focusing back on Lydia. "You're thinking. Martin's thinking."

"You said five things." It came out of Lydia's mouth before she could think of anything else. "What's the fifth?"

Galen let out a breath. "Them offering a deal I can't refuse. That I'd do anything for. Helping Julius - even though we're pretty clear everyone has done all they can, at least unless someone develops a new technique? Threatening you." He gestured at Lydia. "Turns out that ... would be quite effective. I'm glad you weren't there today, actually."

Lydia curled her arms around her stomach. "Oh." It sounded hollow to her, and it must have sounded worse to Galen, because he shifted, leaning toward her, holding out his hand. "Are you, are you feeling guilty that I'm doing this?"

"I am the one that asked you." It felt horribly exposed to be talking about this here. In front of other people. Even if it was Martin and Thomasina, who had some right to hear it.

"And I am the one who said yes. I knew when I did it might lead to some unexpected places. And it's not as if I didn't know about the possible snake cult going in. I mean. That was part of the original premise." He was trying to tease and reassure, and it was almost working. Mostly, the earnestness in his voice, in his eyes, was working.

"I can't go with you." She grimaced. That just sounded pitiful.

"No, but you can be waiting for me, so I know where to come back to. You can help me think through and make sure we've talked about the best options for each of the things that might come up. You can take what I give you and tell the truth and shame the world."

"You have a lot of faith in me." She looked down at their clasped hands.

"I do. Because you've been observant and steady and clever and determined. And I like all those things very much."

She heard Martin's inhale before she registered the rest of it. Galen saying that, here, in front of his friends. She didn't know what he meant by it, especially after the mess on Saturday they still hadn't talked about. But she wanted to, very much, now.

"Do you?" Lydia made it half a question, half a comment.

"Mm-hmm. Look, let's start with what Martin is dying to sort out - all the possible protections. He's used to the shoe being on the other foot. Usually I'm the one wanting to hang him about with talismans and charms and what have you. Not that that will work this time."

"It won't?"

"Fair chance they'll make me strip when I get there, or search me, or... whatever. Whatever I do, it has to not show. Magically, visibly."

"Knots in your hair." Thomasina's voice cut through Galen's. "Granny magic. Very effective. Might want a needle for it, but we can do it where it won't show."

"There we go. More like that, please. We'd wondered about protective charms painted in oil on the skin but there's a chance that might react if they do some sorts of testing or magic."

"Soles of the feet?" Martin suggested. "Or small, in the back of your knee?"

"That might work." Galen agreed. "I like the hair, though. I wish I knew more about the instructions, but of course, that's the sort of detail they wouldn't tell me until the very last minute."

"It helps set up the anticipation, certainly. And gives you less time to find an alternative." Lydia waved a hand. "Do you have anyone here who can do sympathetic protection workings?"

Martin, Galen, and Thomasina all said in unison, "Nan."

"Nan?" Lydia had not met a Nan, she was pretty sure.

"She's mostly in London, doing protections for the

political work there. Strikes, too. I don't know how busy she is, but I think this qualifies for bothering her."

Martin waved a hand. "I'll go track her down tomorrow. Do you have a photo and all on hand?"

Galen tilted his head. "I should in my closet here."

"Closet?" Lydia was now baffled.

"Oh, right, we haven't shown you that. Up in the attic, anyone who might be here overnight without notice has a closet. Half a closet, more like a cupboard, but deep enough for a suitcase, a hatbox, and a couple of boxes. We all keep things we might need on short notice handy. When we were here after London, that's where my pyjamas came from."

"You might have told me sooner." She pointed out, amused. "What does she need?"

Martin was the one who answered. "Photograph, signature, ideally three drops of blood, nine strands of hair, and whatever other personal bits and bobs you're willing to share. Nail clippings work well. In a tidy little envelope, of course. Very sanitary. She uses those to make a connection to you while in the protective circle. It doesn't always work. She might decide the interference from the ritual is too much, but it might give us warning if you're in a bad way." Martin considered. "What happens if you are?"

Galen spread his hands. "There will be some support from the Guard. Probably at our house. I'd not bring them here, and that's private. And if they do need a blood link for some reason, well, Julius is handy." He added to Lydia. "Useful for tracking."

Lydia leaned back. "You've all done this before." She was still trying to take that in. She was used to the paper talking about things like that. People generally treated reporters well enough. Until they didn't.

But she could usually carry a locket that would alert the office if something went wrong, or she was badly hurt. They loaned them out freely enough. Even if, in her more cynical moments, she was sure they went to the expense of maintaining them because a reporter getting hurt meant a good story. Probably with the sort of headlines that sold a lot of papers.

Galen nodded. "We have, um. Routines about it? Practises? Customs. I like customs. We fling ourselves down from heaven, bringing fire and forging iron. It's not the safest pastime, so over the centuries, we've figured out how to - how to take care of each other."

Lydia nodded, slowly. "All right. How about you talk me through what the options are? And we can figure out what might work here. Besides..." She gestured. "Nan."

"You'll want some more food and another drink." Galen said. "A fair number of them are Thomasina's invention or improvement, and she will be glad to tell you all about it. And why she's brilliant. Which she is."

In someone else's mouth, those words might have been catty or nasty. Galen, though, just sounded honestly delighted, like he was thrilled to have such a clever friend.

For a moment, Lydia didn't know what she felt. And then she knew. She'd fallen in love with him, somewhere before this, what she was feeling wasn't new. Even if she hadn't yet spotted the moment that changed everything for her. But this made her love him more. It was a depth and a breadth she hadn't known she had in her. She took a breath, hoping no one saw how shaky it was, and then went to fetch fresh drinks for both of them, and another round of food.

CHAPTER 32
THURSDAY EVENING, IN THE DWELLERS' TEMPLE

By mid-afternoon, everyone else had other places to be. Lydia had research she wanted to do, and he couldn't go with her. They'd agreed she should come for lunch tomorrow, so they could talk things out more, but that seemed a long time away. The other Dwellers had gone off to various plots, and Martin had had a meeting he needed to be at.

Galen hadn't wanted to go home. Julius would listen to him. He knew that, down to the foundations of his life. But he wasn't sure he had words for what he was feeling now. And some of it, he was sure, might be painful for Julius. Galen had this sense of being courted, as a young man of potential, even if they just meant to use him.

And some part wanted that welcome. That desire. All of that was still new to him. There was, he had discovered, a seductive difference between being invited to things because he was from the right sort of family and being invited for himself. The former was interchangeable with dozens of other people he knew.

Even though he knew it was false, or at least built on

hidden principles, even though he had friends who loved him among the Dwellers. He supposed there was someone somewhere who could explain it.

Now, though, it made him climb up to the glassed-in roof at the top of the building that looked out over the forge in the back of the building. It was well set off from the main house, both for safety and noise reasons, though of course any number of protective and sound-muffling charms helped there. And with the neighbours.

Part of him wanted to go down there, to make something real and solid. But it was late to begin anything meaningful. It wasn't safe to work the forge alone, and certainly not in the mood he was in. Instead, once he had climbed all the stairs up, he made his way to the symbolic forge, set off to the east of the space. He lit the lanterns and then pulled over one of the wood and iron benches. Every piece here had been made by a Dweller, every piece touched by hands who'd shared his oaths. He found comfort in that, though he'd not yet found a piece he was willing to add.

It wasn't religious, not exactly. He didn't pray here for guidance, or make bargains. Well. Not often. When Julius had first come home from hospital, he'd spent the better part of a night here. Galen had curled up in front of the flames, willing to offer anything to help his brother. Nothing had, or at least nothing that wasn't made of a long slow path and brutal stubbornness.

Now, he just closed his eyes, and leaned his elbows on his thighs, and tried to settle his mind. He was so lost in thought he didn't hear footsteps. The first thing he heard was "Dweller at the Forge, how is the fire?" Martin's voice, but very careful. The world outside had gone fully dark, just the lights from the nearby houses flickering.

Their standard phrase, going back hundreds of years in some form. Asking how he was, the status.

He shrugged. "The foundry door is open." Which meant that things weren't as bad as they could be. But all of them knew to read it as things being really rather awful, or at least possibly so.

Martin patted his shoulder. "Minute."

He disappeared back toward the drinks cabinet, and the snacks left out in stasis. Galen sighed, and stood, moving the bench back and instead pulling out two thoroughly stuffed wool pillows for them to sit on. Martin preferred them, and - well, he'd been on that bench for a while. Parts of him had gone numb.

"Here." Martin thrust a tankard in his hand, filled with a cider Galen liked, a matching mug in his own hand. "Budge over." He settled down, legs akimbo, focused on Galen.

"Thought you had a meeting?"

"You've been up here a while. No one saw you leave, so I took a chance you were still here." Martin shrugged. "If you were willing to wear a charm that let me find you, it would be much easier all round."

Galen grimaced. "Sorry."

"Hey." Martin was more insistent now. "It is weird. Shoe on the other foot. Though I'm getting a much better idea what I put you through. I'm not going to talk you out of doing this. And you're being sensible, and taking good advice. I'm going to worry, you're my best friend in all the world. But we'll do this together, the way we always do."

Galen closed his eyes and shivered suddenly. He felt a lump in his throat, and he couldn't speak, couldn't swallow, couldn't do anything.

Martin watched him, then set his drink down, and slipped an arm around him, tugging Galen to lean on his shoulder. It was always odd, and a little awkward, but Galen let out a breath.

"You're really messed up, huh?" Martin spoke quietly. "About this thing on Saturday? The preparation?" Galen didn't say anything, but Martin knew, Martin always knew. "Something else."

"Something else and all of it." Galen found his voice, more or less, but he was whispering now, a rumble. "Shouldn't I want all that? The parties and the shine and the - they made me feel wanted."

"Ah." Martin was quiet and Galen was suddenly desperately afraid he'd bollixed everything, forever. He tried to pull away, and Martin's hand clamped down on his side. "Don't you dare." Galen stopped moving, trembling with it now. He felt caught. "We are going to work this out, you."

That last part made it possible for Galen to take one breath, then another. "I don't know how to do this."

"What, exactly, are you choosing to do here?" Putting it that way, bring it back to the choice, that was so like Martin, and it was also what Galen needed.

He cleared his throat, fumbled for his mug of cider, and took a sip. Maybe it would ease things just enough. "They want me to be like them. My parents would approve. Young man, good breeding, enough money, at least in a few years. Chasing pleasure."

"And?" Martin's voice was even, like a thread leading him through a labyrinth.

"In my better moments, I know I don't want that. Not like that, anyway. Not at that cost."

"Cost to whom?" Oh, it was going to be the Socratic

mode, then. Galen cursed their Trivium teachers for making Martin so fond of it. It was cursedly useful, even while it was deeply annoying.

"To me. To others. To them too, but I don't think they see that." Saying it out loud, though, that helped. More than a bit.

"Good. That you're seeing it that clearly." Martin considered, then his next question was, "What does it show you about what you want?"

That was sharp and hard, and of all people, Galen didn't know if he could tell Martin this. "I feel like I have to earn my place. Not be that man. Money, blood, land, all of it. You - we've talked about this. About how most of the Dwellers are more like you, more like your father's side, anyway. Professionals. Skilled workers."

"We've talked about that. Better positioned to see all the ways something could improve. We're in the guts of it, over and over. Seeing the places it's gone wrong." They had talked about this. "You see some of it, too. What it does to your tenants, what it means for what you can sell on at what costs. You were talking about timber last month."

Galen shrugged slightly. "Still. I - all of this with Lydia is bringing it out. The house, the money, the everything."

"And?" Martin was gentler now. "Have you talked to her about it?"

"Not nearly enough. Some of it came up while we were at the house party. And we didn't have privacy, and we had to make everything look right and she was so kind about it and I feel awful and what if she never wants to do anything with me ever again?" It came out as one great long run-on sentence. He sounded about five years old and offended by a toy.

"Oh." The first sound was breathy. "Oh, you've got it

bad, don't you? That's - well. Talking. Very good place to begin, talking. You come from very different places, but so do Laura and I, and we work it out."

"Work?" Galen picked up on that verb tense.

"Work. Ongoing project. We had a confusion - that's what we call them, confusions. Not argument, not a fight. We're not angry at each other? We're just coming at something so differently we can't see the other side. Anyway, this was about how we handle some bills. She's got her own hangups from when they didn't have money. I've got mine, and you know those well enough." He waved his free hand. "Talking. Highly recommended by all the best people."

That made Galen smile and snort once. "It's. I mean. Why would she want me? Given everything."

"Galen, my brother. The way she looks at you? She's wondering the same thing about her. Which probably means you're a good match for each other. At least worth figuring out, trying it out. Did you - um. Whatever you did at the party? Notice how I'm not asking. I think if I ask you for details right now, we won't talk about anything else. But was it good?"

Galen couldn't begin to explain it anyway, not without a couple of days and a lot more sense of himself than he was managing right now. But he nodded. "It - she made me laugh. She made me feel good about things. She's got more experience. Not that that's hard."

Martin waved a hand. "Experience can be got. When you want to. All right." He paused. "Are you worried about getting hurt? With her? Saturday?"

"Not more than anyone else. Which is to say, a lot, sometimes?" Galen said. It felt better to say it out loud, again, though Martin surely knew it. "Saturday. Yes. I mean.

There'll be someone from the Guard available if there's any sign of things going wrong. But how do we know that will work? That I won't be on my own?"

"How do you feel about that, then?" Martin shifted slightly, to better peer at Galen's face.

"Last night, it was mostly that if I got hurt, at least it would mean something. I wouldn't be useless." It came out as a hiss at the end, almost inaudible.

Martin was quiet for a long pause, enough for a dozen breaths. When he spoke, his voice had that fierceness to it. "What do you want to do with your life, then? Now you have more choices? You could back out of this. No one would blame you."

Galen swallowed. "I can't. I've seen." He gestured feebly with his hand. "I know there's rot there. At the centre of the empire. And we shouldn't even have an empire. I mean, how can anyone sensibly think about an empire? Make good decisions about it?"

Martin shook his head. "Big question." he agreed. "All right. You're going to do this. Which is what we all knew this afternoon. What else can we help with?" He hesitated before going on, his voice clear and insistent. "You want good things, Galen. Trust yourself. And you are our friend. Not just mine, but - everyone here. And everyone's been - well. This has been so good for you. Seeing you figure out how you can use the things you're brilliant at to do something that matters."

Galen looked at the shrine fire, then held up his mug, letting the light bounce off the metal. "You're not going to stop me. Ask me not to."

"No." Martin listed his own tankard and clinked it slightly. "Help you. I'll tell you if you're being foolish, but you're not, not here. You're being brave, and brave looks good on you."

Galen didn't know how to answer that, how to go on with it. So he nodded and took a long drink from his mug, trying to trust that it would work out somehow for the best.

CHAPTER 33
FRIDAY EVENING, AT GALEN'S HOME

Friday night, Lydia came out of the portal to find Blythe waiting, wearing a densely woven wool cloak. She held out her hand for Lydia's suitcase while holding up a lantern in the other. "May I?" Lydia blinked at her, then down at her hand, then handed it over. It wasn't heavy, and Blythe seemed determined to be helpful.

"Good evening?" Lydia wished that hadn't come out as so much of a question.

"Good enough. Galen's fretting a bit. I thought you could use a spot of advance warning. We're having comfortable food tonight. I'll be eating with you for the last bits of logistical planning around having a couple of Guard in our sitting room, and then I'll leave you alone." It all came out in a clipped tone that Lydia first thought was annoyance with her, but then realised must be worrying for Galen.

Lydia was not sure how she felt about either part of those plans, honestly. They were both complex, but for entirely different reasons. Even in the dim light of the lantern, she was certain it showed on her face.

Blythe went on, deliberately. "Galen hasn't said much about the house party. Not - anything private. Except, given that I've seen him grow up, I know there was something there. Can I be a beneficent aunt to you, or to him? Should I be prepared with handkerchiefs?"

"I think that's something we have to talk about. We haven't had a chance. He's been exhausted, or busy, or..." She shrugged one shoulder. "Tonight, maybe, unless he thinks it would distract him too much."

Blythe paused. They were only about twenty feet from the house now. "Is he going to be all right?"

"How on earth can I answer that? He's going off into a den of a ritual magic cult, with three days' preparation."

"Three days and all his years since he joined the Dwellers." Blythe pointed out, crisply.

Lydia shrugged, now feeling a bit defeated. "I don't know what that involves, not really. And besides, he's said himself, the more dangerous parts usually aren't his."

"No, but walking into a room of posh men who are sure they rule the world? That, he's got some experience with." Blythe let out a breath. "I'm worried. Julius is worried. But we also know Galen is sensible, he has practice in difficult situations. And he has his friends."

"Which includes me." That part, at least, Lydia was very clear on. "I'm not going to weep on his shoulder tonight. I'm pretty sure, anyway. Or tomorrow. No promises about after."

Blythe snorted. "That's fair. Let me show you your room, and then we'll have supper."

Supper was, in fact, a tad awkward. Julius joined them for

conversation, but did not eat or drink. That made sense, and he seemed used to it, but Lydia thought it must feel very lonely. Though perhaps less lonely than he had been for years.

Galen wasn't quiet, exactly. He talked through what they knew, one more time, the preparations, the Guard. But he was decidedly subdued. Once the meal was done, Blythe and Julius stood. "We'll be around tomorrow, of course, but keep out of your way."

Which left Lydia alone with Galen. They sat, silently, awkwardly, until she said, "Where would you feel comfortable?"

He looked around. "I suppose we should let them clear up, too. My - would you mind my room? Is that too much for you?" Even if it were, Lydia wouldn't have said so. Not tonight, not tomorrow, and probably not Sunday, either. Instead, she followed him upstairs.

It wasn't what she'd expected. They turned down the hall to the front of the house, on the first floor, looking out over the expanse of lawn. Or she assumed it did, since it was dark out. The room itself was all white and shades of a shadowy blue-grey, the sort of colour that was called slate. It was like a quiet ocean, or a cloudy sky, but it had a luminousness to it or a reflective quality she found restful. There was an enormous bed sticking out from the far wall. A sitting area with a sofa and two comfortable looking chairs were closer to her, in a deeper grey-blue, strewn with a couple of decorative blankets. Galen gestured. "Have a seat. Drink? I've, um. Tea, wine, and maybe cider up here."

She should probably choose tea, but taking the edge off her nerves seemed like a good idea. And if it were wine, she could pace herself properly. "Wine, please? Red if you have it."

Galen nodded and went over to a drinks cabinet tucked

in beside a desk. Lydia claimed one end of the couch, not least because she wanted to see where he sat. When he came back with two empty glasses and an opened bottle of wine, he appeared to consider his options. "May I?" Lydia nodded.

A moment later, he'd poured a glass and settled down next to her, before pouring the other and tucking one foot under his other thigh. "This is - odd, isn't it? For you too?"

Something in his tone, a mix of bafflement and earnestness, made her suddenly relax. "Oh, Merlin, yes. Both of us. Right. That's better, then."

Galen let out a breath and then lifted his glass. "To mutual confusion, and to sorting some of it out." It was a fair toast, and she sipped her wine, while he took a longer sip, then set the glass back down on the low table by his knee. "How do we start that? The house party? Tomorrow? Some other thread I'm not thinking to mention?"

"Chronologically speaking."

"I, um." Galen looked away from her, as if he couldn't say this while looking at her. Or perhaps near her. "That night was awkward. But you were kind, after, and that made it easier. Thank you." His voice rose at the end, like it was a question.

Lydia's thoughts swirled and rushed at her. A proper response would be to thank him. Even to demur, that it was only what was proper. If proper could be applied to faking sex. Instead, she did her best to reach for the sentence that tugged at her. "I would like to do that again. Properly. With you. At some point." She held up her hand. "Not tonight. Not tomorrow, probably. It's the sort of thing that should be given its own space? Not crowded."

Galen looked at her, and he smiled. He had a charming smile when it was real. His eyes crinkled, and there was something shining about him. "Oh." He leaned forward, peering at her. "You really would? I don't know a lot about what I'm doing."

Lydia felt that the done thing here was probably to shore up his masculine insecurities. That was not a skill she'd ever chosen to gain. It wasn't even one she had but didn't mention, the way she didn't admit to being able to do her own typing quickly and accurately. If you did that, everyone asked you to do theirs instead of your own work. Then his eyebrow shifted, and his voice was cautious. "Should I appear with flowers?"

"Goodness, no." That made him smile again. That was better. "I don't - I don't know what to do with your interest, to be honest. I've more experience in bed. Or not always bed, um. Apprenticing leads to some curious locations. So does journalism."

Galen leaned forward. "You can't drop a comment like that and not give me some detail. Barns? Hot air balloons? Second parlours? Wardrobes? Orangeries? Though honestly, it's a tad hard to get privacy in an orangery."

Lydia gaped at him for a moment, then shook her head. "You're ridiculous, Galen. You do know that. And, what, may I ask, is an orangery?"

"It is a place, common to certain types of country houses, where one grows oranges. Also, arguably, lemons or limes or other citrus. Glassed in, usually."

"That would make it a rather exhibitionist space, yes." She let out a breath. "Barns. And the usual range of storage cupboards. I don't recommend them. The cleaning supplies smell awful half the time, and for some reason it's always me that bangs my elbow on the mop."

She looked away, blushing suddenly. Before she could figure out what to say, Galen's fingers brushed her hand, then cupped up under her fingertips. "And you're not seeing anyone now." There was that vulnerability again.

"No. Not for some time, actually." The end of her previous whatever you called it had been painful, and not just on the personal level. Galen must have caught some hint of that from her face or her fingers. He squeezed gently.

"A cad? I'm not actually much of a duellist by absolute standards, but I can hold my own with the sort of people who aren't either."

That made her snort. "Pen is mightier than the sword, in this case. Or the image worth a thousand words. Photographer, no longer working at the paper, off doing portraits and fashion shots. Pays vastly better and the hours are regular."

"And the cad's surrounded by women who, I hope, ignore him."

Lydia blinked at that. "You don't approve?"

"Of someone—" He stopped and caught his breath. "You didn't mean me to see. Pardon."

There were two ways this could go. She could ask and they could build something together. Or she could refuse, and that would be the end of it. "See what, please?"

Galen let out a long breath. "Sometimes, I just know how people fit together. It's not clairaudience or whatever you call it. It's just knowing. Martin says it's fitting together hundreds of pieces quickly in my head. It doesn't, I can't rely on it. It's not the sort of thing you can do on demand. But sometimes I see it. It's why I didn't argue with Laura when she said we wouldn't suit. It hurt, but she was right, and the sooner I figured that out, the better for everyone. Especially Martin."

"And me?" Lydia held her breath now, not sure what

he'd say. But she knew that sense, it was what drove her to her best work. Finding the thread of it, using that delicate line to follow. She'd been so cautious about ever talking about it, knowing what the Schola educated thought of such things, that it was strange and giddy to hear him say he understood the same thing.

"You want somewhere you can belong. Not just a relationship, a marriage, a man. More than that. People. No one should tie their lives up with just one person. How can that possibly work out forever?"

That said volumes about his parents. And whatever other family he had. Also, he was absolutely right. She looked up to find him watching her. It wasn't a hard gaze, the unpleasant stare she'd had at the house party. It was something soft, someone looking out over the landscape, and seeing all that was right with the world. "You do see." She swallowed hard. "What does that mean?"

It rushed through her head that he had that. He'd somehow found that. Not just Martin, though she expected that sorting out Galen and Martin's relationship would be a puzzle as long as she spent any time with either of them. But other people, too. How he was with Blythe and Julius, even though she knew, factually certain, that that was new to him. To them, too. The Dwellers, and how they talked to him. Galen made light of his contributions, even before this, but they saw him as worthwhile. And not just for money or influence. Steadiness to go with the pleasantries and the charm.

"It means." He paused. "The simple part is - I can see how you like being around the Dwellers."

"Yes, but." She did like it. Lydia loved how she learned something every time she visited. How people were glad to talk about their passions, they didn't hide them. The food, the different kinds of food, as well as its abundance. They shared. That was how it felt. She didn't feel poor or behind or lacking when she was there. Even though she knew she was, in all sorts of ways that mattered everywhere else. "But that's a school society."

Galen snorted, as if she'd said something tremendously funny. "It's not just born of Schola. We'd be giving up so much if we were. Let Dius Fidius be short-sighted and resolutely posh. We know better." Then he caught something in her expression again, and his voice got gentler. "We can invite people in. There's a process, but Thomasina and Miriam and several of the others have already suggested it. You."

Lydia blinked hard, then she could feel the tears welling up. She put her free hand up to her face. "I told Blythe I wouldn't...." Before she could get the last words out, she found herself tugged closer to him. He pulled her against his shoulder, while he rummaged in a pocket and produced a clean handkerchief.

It took her several minutes to gather herself. Galen didn't fuss at her, didn't interrupt her, didn't expect her to be done. When she finally shifted, he was watching her intently. "We'll talk about that. After tomorrow, all right? But they like you. Not just because you listen to Thomasina go on, though that's actually an excellent sign. And much appreciated." Then his voice shifted again. "I like you. You make me want to be brave and shining. Not a knight, I'm not made for that. But, I don't know. A compass."

"A sundial," Lydia suggested. "Pointing out the time and the place, steady as a rock."

Galen considered that, his eyes half closed. "Something like that. You make me want to reach for things. Be active about it, not just supporting other people's ideas. And it terrifies me and it thrills me, and Martin's the Boar, he's supposed to go charging at things." That last bit sounded entirely put out at the universe, so much so that it made Lydia break into giggles.

"You two make each other better, too." She knew that, as well as she knew anything in the world. Then she took a chance, reclaiming her hand and leaving the cloth in her lap so she could touch his cheek. "I like you too. I want to find out how things are with you. Not tonight."

Galen said wistfully. "Probably not tomorrow night, either. Even if everything goes smooth as silk, there's going to be a lot of talking about it after. And waiting around to be talked to. And probably people looking disapprovingly at things."

It made him come across as a rather scolded puppy, and Lydia patted his shoulder. "I'll be with you. We can at least play amusing games on whatever paper's handy while we wait."

That made him laugh again, then glance around. "What do we do for the evening, if we're waiting on - all the everything?"

Lydia considered. "A bit more wine, and tell me a bit more about the Dwellers, the ones I haven't really met yet?" It would be useful, for one thing, even if she were still getting her head around the idea. And talking about the people he'd chosen to weave his life with, that surely had to be somewhat soothing and reassuring.

"Wine and stories. Fine idea."

CHAPTER 34
SATURDAY EVENING, AN HOUR AFTER SUNSET

G alen came out of the portal into a desolate field. It was already past twilight, of course. The one permitted lantern in his hand didn't show him much, even with the waxing moon. The field, a few piles of stone over to the right that might once have been walls. The portal flicked closed and quiet behind him, leaving him apparently alone in the field.

His instructions had said to dress simply, in something clean and easy to remove. No jewellery, even his house pendant. Galen had been grateful for that, honestly. It meant they couldn't take it away from him. And they couldn't see the tiny mark in the metal that marked him as a Dweller if you looked closely enough at the back. On the other hand, he hated how naked he felt without it.

For the moment, at least, he was reasonably clothed in a simple linen tunic that came down to his knees and loose trousers, the kind of ritual clothing he wore when the Dweller work called for it. Nothing remarkable, suitable for whatever magical work might be required, even pockets to hold whatever bibs and bobs might be relevant.

Right now, they had no objects, but there was a location charm sewn on fabric that Blythe had invisibly stitched into the depths of the pocket. Another was folded into the tail of the robe's belt, and two more were tucked in the lining of his shoes. They weren't nearly strong enough to find him from a great distance, but he'd left a little blood and hair for that. More to the point, they were small enough that any of the likely cantrips to show magic on his person would pass them by. Or at least, so Griffin had declared, and Captain Orland.

He'd left Lydia and Blythe and Julius at the house with two Guardsmen, as well as Captain Orland. And Martin and Laura. Captain Orland had apparently deputised to do the on site fussing while Griffin and Captain FitzRanulf saw to things at the Guard Hall or the Hall of Justice. He wasn't entirely sure, and honestly, he shouldn't be thinking about that too much. The amount of Guard time this was getting implied all sorts of things.

Instead, he put his hand up to his head, worrying that the protective charms sewn into tiny hidden braids in his hair had come down. Thomasina, of all people, had done it for him that afternoon, using a blunt needle and thread to attach them. He didn't know exactly what they did. That was intentional. He could say, with a straight face, he didn't know. Some families used them routinely. He gathered, anyway, though he suspected not many. Sewing them in had required him to sit still and deal with his hair being tugged for a good hour.

For a good minute, he heard only the various sounds of the wildlife. Snuffling, what might be a badger or a fox. There was an echoing hoot of an owl in the further distance. He'd never had a gift for birdsong, but he supposed it wouldn't have told him much, anyway. The temperature seemed much the same as when he'd left home in Cumbria, and the degree of darkness seemed about the same, which suggested he hadn't gone substantially north. He couldn't smell the sea, which meant he wasn't immediately near the coast.

Just as he was working through the possibilities, he heard the rustle of someone moving, some sort of heavier-weight robes. It was December, after all. It was a man he'd never seen before, the sort of ruggedly handsome man who should rule the world, according to adventure stories. This one seemed more ruled than ruling. He twitched once in the lantern's light, as if he knew he was being observed.

"Come."

It was ridiculous to resist now. Galen went, without saying anything in reply. The other man led him up an incline, then on a path twisting through a wooded patch. It was perhaps a half-mile's walk, and Galen wished he'd worn shoes with a more solid sole. His feet caught several branches uncomfortably. On the other hand, these shoes were best if he needed to move quickly or quietly. Bruises would heal.

They circled down and around into a second small valley, well hidden from the field by trees and bushes. Galen caught glimpses of light up ahead here and there, but they came out into a clearing that was lit by tall torches thrust into the ground. Suddenly, a tall man, broad-shouldered and - winged? - stepped in front of Galen, barring his way.

"Halt."

Galen had already halted, and he was glad of it. The man had a knife at his belt, the sort of wickedly sharp and curved affair that Galen would never have risked without a scabbard. His mind was chattering along, as if that were the best way to deal with this fear he was having all of a sudden. He wondered if this was what Martin felt like whenever he was doing something worth doing. HIs escort had disappeared, and Galen could see a flutter of bright red cloth, somewhere up ahead.

The man in front of him stamped his foot. There was some sort of charm, because it resonated like the beat of a giant drum, as if the man were immensely strong and powerful enough to shake the ground. Like the hammer at the forge, all that coiled power. Galen knew what to do with that. He just had to figure out how to play this.

For all the Mesopotamian influence that had come out in the former Lord Sisley's trial, they hadn't been sure what that might mean for the ritual. The usual assumption, the one they'd been working with for lack of better information, had been Roman, with an outside chance of French, one of the lines of magic that went back to Melusine and the Merovingian court.

He didn't know what to do with a winged man in a kilt. And yet, here he was, with a far-distant cosmology in front of him. He could only hope that their plans would work, given this. Mesopotamian, of some form, was not an area most folk in Albion had any meaningful knowledge of. All the things Galen knew, all he could remember in that moment, had to do with Tiamat and Ishtar, and great and terrible destruction.

When nothing happened, he hesitantly looked up. The challenge in front of him was a good head taller, which meant he was near six and a half feet. No one Galen had ever seen.

"Why do you come?"

In a kindly run initiation, they would have told him what to expect here. Or at least hinted. The Dwellers, for example, didn't give you a script - the mysteries were the mysteries. But they also felt the mysteries protected themselves well, and they'd suggest things to think about. What to say, what to offer, what not to give up. Here, he suddenly realised he was walking across a precipice with even less of a guide rope than he'd expected.

He was invited. He was willing. He was a foolish stripling who had got in over his head. He was resolute. He was here. He was curious. Invited might work. Willing or resolute. The others, no.

Galen took a breath, then let it out. The Dwellers had drilled that into him. When asked anything in ritual, take a breath and count to three or five before answering. It gave you time to think, and it looked much better to anyone judging you. "I am invited."

It was not the answer that was expected. Galen could tell that immediately. "Why do you come?" This time, the tone was sharper, edging toward harsh.

He could feel the pull of magic around him, that what he said here would be something he might well be held to. "To learn." That was true enough. "To seek the mysteries." Also true. Then he took a breath and let it out, letting all the nerves show, the real ones, that hovered so close to the surface. "To see what I am made of."

There was a long silence, so long that Galen wondered what had gone wrong. Then the man thumped his bare chest with his fisted hand. "Well said. Go forward." He stepped aside, just enough Galen could pass, and waited. Galen half-bowed, offering the nod of the head that showed respect, and walked on.

He came to the edge of the torch-lit circle before anyone

269

stopped him. Then, there was Perks. Right, he must be magical, then. Acting as second in the ritual, Galen thought, because he could see what must be Nico waiting in the centre. Wearing a hood, all decent secret society rituals involved a hood somewhere. But the height was right, and the posture.

"Set aside all your worldly goods." He had a knife as well, and he gestured with the point at Galen's throat and waist, for him to undo his tunic and trousers. Galen let himself hesitate, the way someone who hadn't been through this before would. Then he began to undo the tunic carefully. Someone must have done something about a warming charm, because he did not instantly freeze in the December air.

When he was fully naked, he folded his clothing up and balanced it on his hands. Perks gestured at the side, where there was a basket. "Leave your old life behind."

It was, well, textbook initiation stuff. They'd certainly talked through the basics in ritual class. Not the specifics. And not until fifth year, when he'd already been through his own initiation. And more to the point, been responsible for helping with the three years behind him. There, he'd learned rather a lot more about how this sort of ritual worked behind the scenes. Martin had had pride of place, their last year, and Galen had been his second.

It was harder work than it looked to be the second. The head ritualist had to make an excellent show of it, keep the attention on him. The second saw that everything else happened, smoothly, and with no disruption. Perks wasn't bad at it, but he wasn't nearly as polished as Galen expected. It was as if he'd only done one or two. That had all sorts of implications, and Galen didn't like any of them much.

Galen bent to do as he was told, placing his shoes and clothes in the basket, and setting the lantern beside it. How were they this unpractised? How many things had changed in the spring, when Sisley was arrested? He began to wonder if others had backed out, or been discarded, or injured somehow. How had they not gotten themselves together since? When he stood up, Perks had stepped back and gestured him forward. "Approach and kneel."

There was, at least, a rug in place, three feet in front of Nico's feet. Galen took small steps, feeling every rock under his feet. Possibly also a worm, something that was far more spongy than earth should be. He kept his hands folded modestly in front of his hips, and his chin down, though he glanced around to get a sense of where people were in the circle. Nico, plus he could see four sets of feet. Five, if the guardian had followed him up. That made a circle of seven, then.

They were either desperate for numbers or setting him up as a patsy. Possibly both, honestly. By this point, he was at the edge of the small rug, and he knelt. It did what it was designed to do, make him feel smaller, less in control. On an entirely practical level, it would make it harder for him to move. He couldn't run, even if he'd wanted to. Not naked and without shoes on rough ground.

"Look up." Nico's voice was a smooth, amused drawl, as if he were a cat playing with a bird. Galen blinked once, then looked up. Nico stood with his feet slightly apart, braced, looking down. "You must prove yourself."

This was the trick of it. And it was the piece they hadn't been able to guess at, not really. Galen kicked himself, for not thinking through this better, for spending more time on how they might frame the ritual, given the actual evidence.

He didn't know what they were going to ask, and he was just going to have to make the best of it.

"How may I prove myself?"

"Blood, sweat, and secrets." Nico just looked down at him, and the smile now had a wicked edge to it, like the winged man's knife. Uncomfortably like.

CHAPTER 35
SATURDAY EVENING

Lydia was pacing. She was sure it was irritating everyone else in the room, but she couldn't help that. Something was nagging at her. More than it had been all day. Laura had gone off to help Blythe make tea, the cook was done for the evening. It made for an awkward gathering. Julius was, she gathered, nearby, but given that the library had Martin, Lydia, two Guards, and Captain Orland, that was a lot of new people.

Martin was curled up on one end of the couch, tapping fingers on his thigh. She didn't know him well enough to read him the way Galen would have, but she was sure he was also uncomfortable. It didn't need trained observation skills. He wasn't being subtle about the general state of his distress. When she turned back to face him, she stopped and tilted her head. "What do you think of all of this?"

"I don't like it. I think it needs doing. Galen's a good one to try it. I can't think of anyone better. A couple who might do as well, very differently, but he has an in and they don't." Whatever else Martin felt, he seemed to be honest about it, even with those clipped sentences. "You?"

"I like it less and less the longer it's been." And in reality, it hadn't been terribly long at all. Twenty-five since they'd seen him off at the portal. "I feel like we've missed something, an important something."

Martin grimaced. "Can you. Wait. First. That feeling is bloody normal." He then hesitated. "Pardon, Captain."

Captain Orland waved a hand at him. "I've heard it before and worse. Don't mind my ears." She was settled at one of the tables, with the map set out in front of her. They'd known where he was going, the portal, and she was monitoring the various charms linked to the map.

"I know we talked about it. If he might be taken to some third place. If they'd make him strip."

"Oh, likely the stripping." Martin's voice was half-amused now. "For one, it makes a person vulnerable. They do it in gaol, for that reason. But a number of initiatory or gateway rituals use it as a tool. And if everyone else around you is clothed, well. It gives them control. Also, warmer feet."

His voice had wavered a hair on the 'in gaol' but everyone in the room was polite enough not to take obvious notice of it. Galen had mentioned Martin had spent more than a few nights there, after various arrests. Galen rarely had. His family had money, a competent solicitor, and the ability to raise much more of a fuss.

"That's the thing, I - I feel like we've missed something about what they might ask."

Martin looked at her, then pushed himself upright, suddenly focusing on her. "Walk me through it. The information. Your notes. One more time." He was younger than she was, but he had, in that moment, the makings of a terrifying editor. She wondered if he knew that.

Lydia settled down on the other end of the sofa, pulling

her notebook over to her. She thumbed through the pages, slowly. "What do you remember about the reporting? I saw the court transcripts, but you were there, two days, weren't you?"

"Filling in for Helios." Who was, to be fair, a grand court reporter. He struck the right balance of information and interest. "They weren't key days, though. Mostly that muddle in the middle about who else was connected. Aimtree had testified already, the day before, and they were working along to the others." Martin stretched.

"None of the others stood out much as, well, notable. Sisley had influence, certainly, and a title. And a nephew on the Council, of course." Which he might have expected would protect him from the ordinary sort of problems, and many less common ones. "And Sisley couldn't name his contacts. Always met with hoods and cloaks and glamours."

Martin nodded. "Which makes naming names tricky. Possibly, also something in their oaths. I mean, there are reasons the Dweller oaths obligate truth telling in proper court settings. We realise it's a difficulty."

Lydia wanted to ask more about that, but there would be time in some future later, or so she very much hoped. Then she frowned. "Wait. Were you in court the day they were talking about. Who was it? An Orion."

"So many Orions." Martin grimaced. "Um. Upworth. Undistinguished family, gentry."

"Wasn't he a member of another society? And hadn't they, blast, I wish I could find it." She thumbed through her notebooks, now more certain that there was something there. It wasn't just her nerves, she could feel the zap of connection, the inspirational moment that ran through her best work, making a leap from point to point.

Martin blinked at her, and then he was launching himself out of his chair, and to his bag, rummaging for his own notes. "The Nine Muses," he said, just as Lydia finally found the spot in her own notes.

"Do you have shorthand about what he said?" Lydia's notes were a summary. She'd not been able to take the transcript out of the morgue.

"Something something, they asked if he was a member of any other group. Yes, the Nine Muses. Editorial note, highly respectable, publically known to be a member for some time. Question: Did any of the Nine Muses show any interest or knowledge of his new commitments? Answer, No, not that he knew about. Question: Was there anything else unusual around that time? Answer: He consulted his diary. 'Bunch of us came down ill.'" Then Martin fell silent, thumbing through the transcript.

Lydia waited, but she felt like they were on to something. Thirty seconds later, Martin looked up. "Captain? I'd appreciate your insight. He talks about being in a chamber choir with other members of the Nine Muses, and all of them getting run down. He didn't make the connection directly, but it began not too long after he went through the ritual with the cult. It wasn't an obvious single illness. Everyone getting a cold they passed around is common enough. This was a malaise, lethargy, more prone to minor illnesses but not all the same ones. When they pressed him about symptoms, he admitted to boils and some other skin conditions. One of the others had a cough that wouldn't go away. Nothing dramatic."

"But consistent. My notes had something about that too, everyone being mildly ill. Nothing life-threatening, just tedious. They were all relatively young, too. Twenties. There was a comment someone picked up, in the file, about another person at the trial assuming it was too many late nights and cocktails and who knows what else."

Martin frowned. "Are there other examples? I suppose we can't find out now, can we? Only." He grimaced. "There are magical contagions. So to speak. That's part of the - the goldwasser touched on it."

Lydia had picked up some bits about it, of course, everyone at the paper had. It had involved scandal for some up-and-coming families, and it was a disaster barely averted for various people. But she didn't know all of it. "How do you know?"

"Laura. She was in with that crowd until she had the sense to get out." Martin's voice turned deeply protective.

"I won't press her." Lydia put her hands up. She glanced over at the table, and Captain Orland was peering closely at something. "Captain?"

"I'm wondering about the location." She tapped the map. "We'd been assuming that the initial portal might be a transit location. Remote portal to somewhere else. We can trace them, of course. But here is the marker for the locational charms in his clothing, and they've moved, oh, half a mile, at the outside?"

"Even through the blood link?" Lydia had been trying not to think too hard about the small vial with several drops of Galen's blood and an alchemical reagent that sat in a holder on the map.

"Mm-hmm. Though there are ways to fool that one if they've got someone with the knack for it. Not easily, and not for long, it takes ongoing concentration. Unlikely, though. It's a rare skill." That was a piece of information Lydia hadn't known, and it made her wonder about a case she'd heard about last year, a kidnapping. Or not quite a kidnapping, but someone gone missing, unexpectedly.

Lydia pursed her lips. "We know they want to make sure there - that there isn't another war like the last one. Can we assume that they've got a fair range of skills handy?"

"Yes and no." Martin looked up from where he was skimming through his notes. "I mean, look at the people who we know about. Lord Sisley, who - well, land, title, posh, yes. But not, I gather, the most magically gifted egg in the basket. Not incompetent, exactly, but not the sort of person you'd look to for rare magical skills."

"He had connections at The Research Society, though. And their library and archives and storehouse." Which might be a good reason to recruit someone. "And there was a fuss about Aimtree. The bit in closed court."

"I didn't even hear any gossip about that," Lydia agreed. "They locked it down tight." She glanced up at Captain Orland. The older woman gave nothing away. Lydia had expected that. You didn't get to be a Captain in the Guard without having an excellent poker face. Or tarrochi face, or bridge, whatever her game was.

"And none of the others named were standouts. Do they keep those for Lind's circle, do you think? Or is the whole thing puffing itself up as more than it actually is?" Martin tapped the notebook. "Galen said there were seven circles, which - well. Is what I'd expect. Fourteen each, though perhaps it's a different number for the central circle. So who do they need to replace there? Any recent deaths?"

Captain Orland tapped the map again. "That portal's on the line between two sets of demesne lands. Lord Waxton holds this part, here, to the south, and the Dowager Lady Millflurry holds the northern section as regent."

"Recently a dowager, then?"

"They've a son, not yet sixteen. Her husband was rather

a lot older. He died, mmm. Within the year." She half-closed her eyes and added, "April 17th."

Lydia appreciated that precision. "Do you know her, then? Would she be involved in something like this?"

"She is one of the pillars of the Albion Inheritance. I believe mostly for the gossip. She's actually quite involved with The Ladies Auxiliary Society for Services to Orphans of Magical Catastrophes." The long name rolled off her tongue, with a note of some amusement. "She's one of the more sensible of that lot, actually. Not that that's the highest bar."

Lydia frowned for a moment, then risked a question. "You don't approve?"

"I don't disapprove, exactly. But they often - oh, they'll go on about the proper colour for fabric for frocks for children who need them, endlessly. Until half the children have outgrown the measurements they have. And they'll raise funds, but then not use them as efficiently as they could. They come from families that - well, the bulk of my work is inheritances when things get complicated. And that often brings out the worst in people, who becomes regent, who gets to reside in the entailed lands. All that."

It was diplomatically said, while making Captain Orland's priorities tidily clear. Lydia appreciated that bit of skill rather a lot, even if it was also rather frustrating.

Martin had kept flipping through his notes. "Do you have anything about the area in yours, Lydia?"

She looked, flicking through the pages of her notebook, then stopped. She looked over the page, then looked up. "How quickly can we get there, please?"

CHAPTER 36
SATURDAY EVENING, AT THE RITUAL

G alen swallowed hard. Blood, sweat, and secrets. It was what he'd expected, more or less. But now he was here, in this moment, he didn't know how to move forward with it.

Or what to say. When he'd sworn to the Dwellers, he knew, more or less, what he'd be asked to swear to. Not all the ritual, but they had gone through the oath, the expectations, how they defined the terms. As you'd expect, from moral people with good ritual training. He'd wondered, throughout his classes, why they harped on clarity of purpose.

It was because it was so damnably easy to abuse. To weave someone into a net they couldn't get free from, with the oaths they'd made. Griffin and Captain Orland had talked him through this, but it wasn't the same. That rationality and logic seemed distant, not in this space with the torches and the people around him, not wishing him well.

Now it was about the ground under his knees, and the fact they'd make him bleed. There was a scent of something from the torches that made him suspect there was some alchemical addition. More likely, there would be a cup to drink before he made the actual oath. The easiest way to make sure he did what they wanted.

The silence went on. Galen finally said, his voice cracking once, "What must I do?" That crack embarrassed him, and he could feel himself flushing. On the other hand, it went well with the persona he had been presenting. He ducked his chin, took a breath, and ran himself through the exercises Griffin had taught him. He could feel the magics around him, tunnelling through to find his own foundation and connection with the deep burning forges of Hephaestus up to the celestial lights of Apollo's divine fire.

He lived between them, with the fire brought down as a splendid gift, a force for change, by Prometheus. Galen knew that. He remembered that. He was of the forge and the hammer, companion and friend to those of good will. Another breath, and another, and he dared a glance up.

Nico had been waiting for that. Galen could see his face, that sharp smile. He held out his hand, an unspoken order, and someone put a large chalice into it.

"Drink it all down, and then we will speak."

Galen didn't have a choice. He'd known this going in. There were potions you could take that would blunt the effect of whatever they gave him. But there was always a risk it would show. That would be even more dangerous. He reached up and took the absurdly large chalice. The one the Dwellers used held perhaps a cup of liquid. This was at least twice that. And drinking, then, had seemed like it took forever.

There was nothing for it. He had to drink, and so he did. Galen tipped the cup to his lips. Wine, first, a robust red, the sort that hid all sorts of additions. When he paused for breath after a half dozen swallows, he could feel it begin to course through him. It wasn't a burning, not exactly, though there was a sense of a desert heat. It was more like a vibration. Not the hammer at the forge, how that ran through your bones. This was more like a sistrum, he'd heard that once at a ritual they'd been invited to his last year at school.

Only this wasn't purification or blessing. It wasn't benefic, certainly. It was insidious, whatever it was. He didn't like the feel of it, and he could only hope that the Guard had some method for negating the effect as soon as he was done and away. He drank again, and again, forcing himself to it, until he hit the dregs. There was something bitter in them, sharp and full of the taste of bile, and then a burst of something sweet in the last sip, like a reward. That worried him even more.

Galen handed the chalice back, holding it up on hands that seemed to tremble. He closed his eyes for a long moment, feeling for those connections down and up. He wanted to reach for his fellows, to that line of magic that spread out like the far-flung roots of the yew, renewing the Dwellers over and over again. But Griffin had advised against it, and Galen now understood why. If he did that, if he let himself do that, these men could follow that line. He wouldn't do that. He couldn't do that.

Nico made some gesture, one that seemed blurred to Galen, and the winged man stepped up, placing his hand on the back of Galen's head. There was a rootedness to his power, and Galen suddenly wondered if this was one of the local Lords. It had seemed unlikely at the time, but the portal was right on the boundary between two demesne lands.

When the older man spoke, Galen was sure. It was the oath that made the speaker tell the truth, or at least made it clear if they were not. Galen could feel it settle around him, the prickle of the Silence oath as it came to rest on him like the worst and most dangerous cloak. He could feel the burning fear of betraying the Dwellers, and particularly Martin, before a flash of Lydia shook him. He let himself shudder. They'd expect it, they'd be watching for it.

"Magus, he is yours." The winged man stepped back.

Nico's hand came down, tracing along Galen's jaw line. "Look up, look up."

Galen did. His head was more or less at Nico's waist, and Nico was fixed on him, like a snake on his prey. "Tell me truly, why have you come?"

"To know what I am made of." That was true. He felt only the slightest prickle from the magic.

"Fair enough." It had judgement in it, for all the words were neutral. Then there was a tap of a finger against his skin, what felt almost like the prick of a sharpened nail. A fang. Only Galen knew it was no such thing. "You will speak truth to us."

Galen looked up and blinked, then sucked in his breath. "I can feel the magic." He hesitated, then risked, "Magus." That made Nico's lips quirk in a flash of a smile, perhaps just a hint of approval that Galen had dared.

"Tell me about what you love."

Galen sucked in his breath. He might just be able to thread the needle here. Talk about what he loved, even if it was not a complete answer. "My brother." That was the truth, through and through.

"Despite his -" Nico hesitated, and Galen hadn't expected that. As if Nico had been about to say something different. "Despite his injury. What would you do for him? If you had the power to heal him?"

Galen knew that wasn't on offer. It truly wasn't. The

best of the healers had tried, they had been able to help but not mend. Julius would always have pain, always have wounds that pushed others away. He swallowed. "I wish he could be healed."

"And what would you give for that? Tell me a secret, if you would enter our number. One that could be used against you and all you hold dear."

"A secret." That finger tapped on his cheek again, where the worst of Julius' injuries were, and Galen suddenly wondered if that was deliberate. They'd talked through what he could offer. It had been clear to everyone what they might ask. As he delayed, he felt the magic press on him again, as if someone had tightened the ropes binding him, and he grunted with it.

"It will get worse the longer you delay. The first thing that comes to your mind."

One of the Dwellers had been telling stories, at one point, about a Russian novelist, about not thinking of a white bear. Galen's mind flashed to that, dancing among the other thoughts he did not want to speak. Martin. Lydia. The Dwellers. In that order. He bit the back of his tongue, where it wouldn't show on his face.

"You know about my parents." Galen was sure they did, or at least Nico did.

"Not that secret, no." Nico looked almost amused. "Let me inspire you." There was a purring venom to his voice now, as if he were part way into the sort of Dionysiac trance that grabbed at some people. Ecstasy wore many faces, and for all there was no shouting or dancing or drums. Galen could hear his heart beating loudly and feel a change in the air around him.

"Inspire, Magus?" Galen dared another look up, another title.

"I have many gifts. Many powers." Another tap of the finger on Galen's cheek. "I can see great potential in you if it is properly harnessed. A depth of potential, roots that go down forever, a magnificent palace."

Palace. Not temple. Other people would have said temple. Even Martin, who was not the most religious of people, outside the Dweller's rituals. Palace implied a different kind of power, a different focus. Palaces were for men who wanted things. The sort of man Galen didn't want to be.

"You can?" It was the logical question here. "Magus, I am nothing special."

"They have neglected you, your gifts. Your brother was the shining one, and now..." Nico shrugged, the folds of his robe shifting. "Now it is your turn. If you will simply do as we ask. Tell the truth, shame your family, and join us."

Galen sucked in a breath. Then, softly, he said something that was true. "I never measured up. Not in my head."

"Tell me more." Galen noticed something with the part of his mind that was not buzzing with the drink and the cloak of magic he wore pricking at his skin. Nico was keeping this intimate. Not drawing any attention to the others there. He wondered what they were doing, not that he could do much about it. He couldn't even get a glimpse. Nico wore nothing reflective, not where Galen could see.

Then it hit him. The Silence oath that was pressing on him, his worst fear was giving up the people he cared about. Martin. Lydia. They were going to have to talk about how much he cared about Lydia, given that. The Dwellers, in their many ways. He could not simultaneously tell the truth and avoid that punishment.

"I have always been chasing something." True again. He still was. He always would be, he hoped. "A way to belong.

To be welcomed. To have my skill respected. Needed. Wanted. I want to matter. To make a difference, somehow."

"Ah." Again, that neutral note that held judgement by the bucketful. Then the shine was back, the tempting one. "We can give you that. Do well for us, and all will know your mettle. Your power. Your reach." Nico's voice took on a purr. "You have such reach. You've touched something, did you know? It spreads out from you, long trails." His other hand spread open, then closed, like he was reaching for that. "A secret. Tell me a secret."

This time, the magic closed tight around Galen, making him grunt louder with it. When it relaxed enough to allow him to speak, he swallowed. "I've made other promises. To other people. My - my - magic is not my own. Not entirely."

Nico's chin came up. "Have you, now?" That had a rumble of a threat in it. "What do those bind you to?"

Galen couldn't see a way through this. He had to tell the truth. The path to the truth got narrower with every word he said. But he couldn't give up his fellows. He closed his eyes. "I was young. I felt alone, like I'd never be good enough. No matter what I did. I met someone. He changed everything. What I could do. What I could learn." He swallowed.

"A lover, then?"

Galen threw back his head and laughed.

CHAPTER 37
SATURDAY EVENING

Whatever script Nico had in his head, Galen was certain he was not following it. Not remotely. The look on Nico's face as he laughed was something Galen would treasure for the rest of his life. However long that might be. He could feel a shift around him, as if none of the others knew what to do now.

"You have unexpected depths, don't you?" Nico had gathered himself enough to bring that confident purr back to his voice. Or hiss. Perhaps it was a hiss. The drugged wine was really having an effect now. His mind kept wandering off on the sort of tangents Lydia would disapprove of. They weren't useful investigative points at all. Especially not him thinking about her expression, when Galen talked about Martin, how she knew there were things there that they'd never share with anyone else.

"You love him." Nico's voice cut through the growing haze. "And are unrequited. I know the look."

It was a wrong assumption. Martin loved him, just not that kind of love, not the sort people meant when they talked about love in English. Greek had more words, Latin didn't do so badly. Brothers, that was a good word, true brothers, blood brothers. Oh, right, Nico had mentioned blood. That was going to be a complication. And Nico had said something. He'd want an answer. Nico was the sort of person who expected answers about things that were none of his business.

Some small part of Galen recognised how much the wine was affecting him. And part of him felt he was in so deep that it wasn't going to matter. In the end, he settled on shrugging one shoulder. He let it show. "Can't make someone love."

Nico pounced on that, with a speed and near-violence that shook Galen, even though none of it was actually physical. "What if you could?" That was seduction now, Nico's own particular brand. It had nothing to do with care or respect or mutual affection, and everything to do with power.

"What do you mean?" This was at least getting into the territory of something decidedly illegal.

"This - this man, we don't mind that, very Greek." Nico waved a hand. "He scorned your interest. Hurt you, I'm sure. Drove a knife into your heart and twisted. We can give you his heart, to do with as you choose. A willing slave, devoted to your every need. Ready to please you in bed, if you wish. To wait for any scrap of your time you deign to give him. Everything you wanted, one tidy package. Break him to your desire, whatever that is."

Galen sucked in a breath. That seemed the worst sort of abuse. It wasn't just the physical power, but the idea of twisting someone's mind, so they enjoyed it was awful. The idea he might twist someone's actions but leave someone seething inside their head. That was just as awful.

The rational part of him knew that sort of magic was

vanishingly rare, especially for any length of time. People might manage it for a day or two, but it took a tremendous amount of raw power.

"How?" Galen looked up, doing his best to track Nico's expression, wanting to burn them into his mind. When it came to testifying in court, he wanted to be sure of what he was saying, to get every detail.

"Will you take the oath? Become one of us?" Nico waved a hand. "It needs only that." Nico presented it like it was a triviality, a minor detail, like washing one's hands before supper. "Once you do, I'll tell you all the wonders we can teach you, share with you. How we can bring this man to your bed or wherever you want him. If you want him embarrassed, made a fool of, doors closed in his face for the rest of his life, we can do that too."

"How?" Galen let the world roll out of his mouth, uncertain.

"Oh, we have connections in many places. The War Office, our Ministry, the Temple of Healing, any number of businessmen. The one with their eyes on the future, not on the past. Willing to take risks, to stretch out their hand."

Galen swallowed hard. "So many?"

"Oh, we have such friends. That is, after all, part of how we got so curious about you." Nico tapped his face again. "Will you swear and have your revenge?"

Galen spread his hands out. "What do I get if I swear? Besides that. You can't offer revenge to everyone."

"Power." Nico's voice curled into power, smoky rooms and low voices, people making choices for hundreds or thousands or millions of people with the flick of a pen. The sort of man who had sent others to war a decade ago, or decided that poor quality boots were fine for men who'd die within the month. Galen knew so many reasons to hate such a man. Suddenly, he lifted his hands and intoned a word, the power in it ripping through Galen like a sudden thundering storm that came up out of nowhere.

He could half-feel the others around him step back, and Galen spread his knees slightly on the ground, settling back on his heels. It made a tripod, steady and certain, and he leaned into that rootedness. Whatever these men thought of him, he knew who he was and what mattered. Better than most, anyway.

He almost reached for his oath to the Dwellers. He'd always seen it in his head as a wrought-iron lamp, the glow and the shimmer of it, illuminating everything he did. It felt like it was hovering above him and a little to the right, where he could just see it out of the corner of his eye. Now, though, when he reached toward it, he could feel something else reaching with it. Dark vines, tendrils that promised nothing good.

Galen wasn't skilled at this. He'd never been a duellist. But he put himself, as best he could, in his mind's eye, between that rude and grabbing reaching and the fire he was sworn to. One tendril jerked back, as if it had been burned, before another one got behind, as if reaching for the fittings of the lamp. Safer, enough safer that Galen suddenly felt a pull on his magic, radiating out from him to everyone else who'd made that oath.

And especially to Martin. The strongest of the lines. Oh, there were plenty of others, a spiderweb of constellations, shifting and changing but always shining. Points of light, resolute against the darkness. Touching, despite the distance. Martin, he knew it was Martin, was closest and brightest and most at risk.

He grabbed on to every bit of lore he'd ever learned, every drill in ritual class and the duelling salle. Most of all, he clung to his oaths. He could feel the pulse of power pushing past him, but then Nico's magic pulled back.

"You're fighting me. Why are you fighting, youngling?" That had a nastiness to it, the sort of sugary-soft tone Galen's mother got sometimes, when she was about to do something he particularly hated.

Galen looked up, opening his eyes. "I'm making the oath. Not them." Part of him thought he was revealing too much, but likely Nico had figured that out.

"Deep roots." Nico huffed out a breath. "We will just have to persuade you." Then his voice called out, sharply. "Perks. Wills. The supplies."

A hand grabbed one of Galen's hands, his right, and held it up, gripping hard enough he'd have bruises later, if there was a later. There was a flurry of activity. Galen couldn't track most of it. Some was in shadow, some was too fast, some was hidden by Nico's body. Then everything went still and quiet, waiting.

Nico spoke. He'd used a charm, so his voice resonated, carried halfway up the hill, in all likelihood. "Brothers. Hear now the cry of the Magus, who of old has held dominion over man and over magic. Let the weak fall like chaff. Let the labourer trudge in the field like the dumb ox. Let the spinners and weavers of thread bend over their work until they are old and blind. Let all who oppose our might be bound, hand and foot, tongue and mind. Ours is the power, ours the right."

That last sentence was echoed by the others. It was not an impressive sound. Five men thumping their chests was not the sound of dozens of the Dwellers gathered to welcome their new fellows with cheers and joy. Galen did not like where this was going, one bit.

"We few are made for mastery, put upon this solid earth

to rule and tame the world around us. We are not like other men, those thieves and knaves who crawl upon the ground, unseeing. We are the magi court reborn, the first in all the world. Our fingers drip with poisons and our tongues with fire. We rise in our palaces, never again to be crushed under heel or sent forth to fight at another's word. Ours is the power, ours is the right."

Again, there was the echo, and Galen noted one straggler. Too small a group for proper pomp, too many for the intense intimacy of a private ritual.

"We are come to make another one of us. To give the one kneeling here a glimpse at the power and paradise that might be his in time if he is stalwart and loyal. For he who would learn the truth of magic, but who has not yet won its secrets, he is one who Marduk will teach, if he gives blood and soul. Ours is the power, ours is the right."

Another thump, another chorus, slightly weaker than the last. Then Nico's voice rang out. "Present the candidate." Galen felt himself jerked upright until he was standing. He had been kneeling long enough one of his feet had gone numb, and he wriggled his toes instinctively. It reminded him of the ground beneath the rug, and he shifted one foot back just slightly, until it was touching proper earth.

"Naked you have come into the world, naked and nameless. What will you give?"

Ah, there was the rub. He could give his word. His blood. His oath. But they thought they had taken everything else from him. It didn't work like that. Galen knew his ritual theory well enough for that. He could be made to swear, but Galen could not be made to open to whatever initiatory force might be on offer. There was power swirling around Nico, a chaotic jagged edge of it, like a gathering thunderstorm, but he could fight that, perhaps.

All he could do was draw this out, give him a better chance to fight whatever was coming. "What gift is wished?"

Galen's voice cracked again, as Nico threw back his head and laughed. Then the laugh turned into a roar. "Blood. Sweat. Tears." All at once, Galen felt a rush of something, radiating pain up his arm from where it was held. It made him scream, forced him to it, even before he felt the blade score the palm of his hand. They forced his hand over a cup, and Nico's magic gathered over it.

"Swear that you will keep secret all you have seen and heard, here and in any other gatherings of the magi. Swear on your magic that you will reveal none of our arts nor powers to any other not properly sworn."

Galen was about to refuse, whatever the cost. He would not be forsworn, for one thing. Before he could answer, he heard something behind him, a rumbling thunder like an earthquake gathering, prepared to shake the world to pieces.

CHAPTER 38
SATURDAY EVENING

Things moved very fast, all of a sudden. One moment, Lydia had been sitting, watching the growing flurry of Captain Orland and the Guard making plans, scribbling back and forth in the magical journals. Then, Martin was clutching at his chest, as if he had been struck with a bolt. Lydia had seen someone like that, who had been shot and whose heart had stopped.

Laura had just come in with more food, and she nearly flung the tray aside in her rush to get to Martin. Everything was chaos for thirty seconds, and then the Guard were charging out of the room, their boots rough and loud on the wooden floors. A moment later, Martin was surging up out of the chair, taking off at a dead run behind them, leaving both Laura and Lydia blinking at where he'd been.

Laura reacted faster, slipping as she took off after him. Lydia glanced around, and grabbed Laura and Martin's cloaks as well as her own, before setting off herself. She was at least wearing her laced boots today, so she caught up to them when they were not quite halfway to the portal, with Laura most out of breath.

The three of them came up as the Guards were getting it open. Captain Orland turned. "You can't come."

"We'll follow, anyway." Martin panted, then took a breath. "We can help." He tapped his chest. "That was magic. Awful magic. Through the Dwellers, I think."

Captain Orland frowned, making a decision. "Laura, let the others know. Hot water, broth, I don't know what. Here."

Laura looked stubborn for a moment, but Martin murmured something to her and she subsided. "Let us know what's up."

Captain Orland nodded. "I expect much of it will be over quickly, and the mopping up is ours." She gestured. "Follow me through, stay behind us, and touch nothing until we tell you. Either of you have healing skills?"

Lydia spread her hands. "A bit from the War. Basic first aid, staunching wounds, stabilising someone until a proper healer can get free. I learned how to lend my vitality."

"Ah, that might be handy. We'll have a Healer coming from Trellech. Martin?"

"A bit of rough and ready tending, the sort of thing needed in a strike or a brawl."

Captain Orland nodded once and then stepped through the portal with no further comment. When Lydia came out on the other side, the space in front of it was rather packed with people. A dozen or more of the Guard, at least two with trained dogs, consulting with Captain Orland about the likely location. One middle-aged man in Healer's red, and two people, a man and a woman, who she suspected were Penelopes. No uniforms, but clothing and satchels that looked full of pockets.

Captain Orland turned around briefly. "We will use various measures to avoid being heard until we are right near them. We'll be casting the same on you, or you can't come. Keep quiet, stay behind us, and don't come into the midst of what's going on until I or Evers, over there, signal it's safe."

Lydia nodded. So did Martin. Journalists had an uneasy relationship with the Guard, given how often they went against the accepted way to do a thing to get a story. On the other hand, the Guard knew their work and Lydia certainly didn't want to get hurt. Or worse, risk Galen.

Within three minutes, everyone had formed up, with a plan that had been decided mostly in gestures, murmurs of the Guard's Tongue, and a few raised eyebrows. That middle one left them well out of it, which was part of the point. Lydia was shifting from foot to foot, eager for any news or warning. Then there was a nod, and they set off. Martin glanced over at her, and then they picked up a trot behind the others. They were close enough to use the same light, far enough back to give space for whatever happened.

That wasn't too much of a challenge. Once everyone started moving, they set a quick pace. More than Lydia could manage, and she suspected more than Martin could, especially with that shock from earlier. It was rough ground for some of it, and in the dark, she didn't want to sprain an ankle, or worse.

They could see the flares of magic well before they caught up, rather like fireworks against the night sky. Some were a blood-red, something nastily vibrant, some were a sickly green, with shards of a bright copper. The Guard magic was steadier. Shades of blue shot through with a silver-white that seemed almost cleansing, and bursts of deep green. Lydia wished she had some idea what it meant, especially since it seemed to make some sense to Martin.

That was a Schola education for you, making it possible to diagnose magic at a distance.

He must have caught her frowning, because he leaned in. "Defence magics there, that's the Guard. The silver is the Penelopes, I think. That amber gold definitely is. Focused - there. Oh." His voice went hollow. "That's Galen." They could see the figure, crouched on the ground, with flashes of vivid magic going all around him. Then, suddenly, one of the Guard did something. It brought the central standing figure down, forcing him first to his knees, silhouetted against the torchlight, and then down on his face in the dirt, his hands above his head.

The two Penelopes went forward fearlessly, making a series of gestures and calling out specific instructions. It was as if they were scolding the magic like a wayward puppy, chivvying it back into order with a combination of bribes and threatened punishments. One of them clapped three times and stomped his foot, then slammed down a staff of wood into the ground. The stone at the top crackled briefly with light, then subsided as the rest of the Guard surged forward. Under a minute later, all the ritualists were bound and seated, even the one who had tried to run away.

Martin was rocking forward and back on his toes, like a runner about to begin a race. When Captain Orland called out, "Come down!", he was off like a greyhound, with Lydia barely able to keep up. By the time they got into the ritual circle, Galen was sitting up, rubbing his face badly with one hand. He held out the other. Lydia saw the line of blood, the perilously sharp line, about when Martin and Captain Orland did. The Healer came over, immediately, at a barked command. One of the Guards brought over a blanket to drape around Galen's shoulders.

She hadn't seen him naked before, and she certainly

couldn't look properly now. There were rather a lot of other people around, even before she got to the ritual circle part.

By this time, Lydia had made it up to Galen. He blinked up at her, like he wasn't sure she was real, distracted. The Healer cleared his throat. "Sir, may I check your injuries?" Galen nodded, absently, reaching with his other hand to rub his nose, leaving a smudge of dirt. Martin knelt down, and a moment later, Lydia joined him, while the Healer cast a charm light and examined. The surrounding bustle almost faded away, the Penelopes sorting through things, the Guard documenting what they saw and monitoring their prisoners.

Martin was looking Galen over, head to toe, as if he were ticking off check boxes in his head. "You're - is that the only thing? Did they use any charms on you? Make you eat or drink anything? Are there oaths we need to worry about?"

Lydia could see Galen's eyes go wide, and then how he was overwhelmed with it all. "One thing at a time." She didn't look up. "Galen, anything to eat and drink?"

Galen managed a nod at that. "Wine, cup. Bottle there." He gestured vaguely with his thumb and the Healer grumbled immediately. Captain Orland made a gesture and someone went to investigate it.

"Oaths?"

"Middle of that. Didn't agree. Don't think I agreed? Not sure. He. It was an exceedingly badly done ritual."

That, somehow, made Martin snort and relax. "Galen has opinions about that sort of thing. As he should."

"Healing first, and then we'll see about the rest of it. Charms?"

Galen shook his head, then looked like he regretted that choice. "Nothing specific other than truth-telling. Someone who could require it." A moment later, the Healer was peering at his hand, and then saying, "May I check for other injuries, sir?"

Very polite, for a Healer. Lydia was much more used to professional brusqueness. Then again, she usually saw a Healer at one of the Trellech clinics, never the same person twice, always very busy with a long line of people to tend to. Galen nodded absently, but now he was looking from Lydia to Martin. "How did you get here?"

"Portal." Martin was brief, but smiling more now in visible relief. "Captain Orland allowed us."

"You did point out you'd come through anyway. Which was true." She then bent down. "Safe to do a memory-preserving charm, so he doesn't forget anything until we can go through it properly?"

The Healer did a bit more testing, then nodded. "Safe, but if you could wait on the questioning itself until that potion clears. I think I can put together an - oh, right. I'm sure there are things at his house. You're Julius Amberly's brother."

Galen blinked owlishly, then nodded. The Healer stood. "It'll just be five or ten minutes to put together, I'm sure."

That meant Captain Orland left them alone for a moment. There was all sorts of bustle around the circle, decisions being made about where to take the prisoners, what to do about all the items that were out. Martin hesitated. "How - what did they do?"

Galen shrugged. It was a shrug Lydia knew well from the inside, about being too tired and too tangled up. Like they'd been the night after the ball at the house party, full of complications.

"You want to go home." Lydia asked it, but she knew

the answer. Galen nodded, looking at her. "Well, all right. Let's see how we do that. Can you stand up?"

It turned out in the end that Galen could. Lydia got permission for the three of them to go back, with one of the Guards and the Healer. Captain Orland promised she'd be along in half an hour, probably with someone else, to do a proper interview. Galen could stand, but it turned out, not really walk, even when they'd found his shoes in the pile of his clothes. They ended up in an odd procession, with Lydia on one side of him, Martin on the other. The blanket folded around him like a wrongly shaped toga, held in place with sticking charms.

Blythe met them at the door, looking worried, but the Healer immediately had questions for her, for Julius. The man apparently knew Julius well by reputation, which was rather reassuring. They went off down the hall together. It left Martin and Lydia to steer Galen into the library, and Martin to go up the stairs two at a time to bring down a dressing gown and some other clothing from Galen's rooms. Or so she assumed, anyway. Lydia turned her head and closed her eyes for the part where Galen got dressed, of course, much as she sort of wanted to look.

Ten minutes later, before Galen had managed to do anything other than dress and drink some fresh, cool water, Julius came out. He was bearing a potion bottle and handed it over silently. His eyes, above the mask, looked worried, and Galen immediately drank it. Once Galen swallowed it down, he shook his head, a bit like a dog shaking water from its coat, then let out a long breath. "That feels good. Cleaner."

Julius nodded and patted him on the shoulder, before disappearing back out down the hall. The Healer came round and knelt down to peer at Galen. "That's better. Your eyes are less dilated already. May I check your pulse?" Galen held out a hand, obediently enough. The Healer felt it for thirty seconds. "That's better too. May I get a better look at your hand?"

That took them through another few minutes, piece by piece, until there was a knock at the door and Captain Orland appeared, followed by Captain FitzRanulf. "Ready for us?"

The Healer stood. "He should have something nourishing." He glanced past them to Blythe. "Broth, or something of the kind, cheese, crackers."

That took a little to arrange, but within ten minutes, they had tucked Galen up with a blanket and a warming charm. The two Captains had chairs pulled up near the sofa, and Lydia and Martin had taken up seats on either side of Galen.

CHAPTER 39
SATURDAY EVENING, IN THE AFTERMATH

"Tell us what happened, please, from when you went through the portal."

Galen sounded resolute, stubborn, as he began talking. He mentioned the field, being led down the path, the challenge by the winged man. Captain FitzRanulf had a question, about the style of the wings, if they seemed to be attached by anything. Galen described seeing something that might be a harness, but of course the light had been behind the man, and he'd been distracted.

The way he pointed that out, that had an exhausted good humour in it. It reassured Lydia that Galen was at least sounding more like himself. From the other side of him, she could see Martin relax too.

The rest of the tale, however, made her blood curdle. Martin barely restrained himself as Galen got to the part about the ritual language, or Nico pulling on the magic. Galen realised there was something there, pausing, twisting, to look at Martin. "What happened? What did he do?" Galen's voice was fierce, though he was still weak, and it came out more like a small ferocious kitten.

"'m fine." Martin murmured. "Now. Healer checked. But it - it felt like a heart attack must. Just everything draining away to black, not being able to go on for a moment."

Captain Orland cut in, "Griffin will want a proper report about that tomorrow." She peered at a pocket watch. "No, still tomorrow. Go on, Galen, the sooner we get the basics down, the sooner we can let you get to bed."

It struck Lydia, the more Galen kept talking, that some of his feelings about this had to do with the ritual itself. Not just that it was distasteful or evil or men with power grabbing at more, though those things were true too, but something else. She did not know how to ask about it.

Eventually, they arrived at the point the Guard knew about and the two Captains glanced at each other and nodded. "That will do for tonight. Can you come to the Guard Hall tomorrow? Say, eleven, we'll feed you luncheon if we go more than an hour." A minute later, they'd swept out, taking the Healer and the last Guard with them, who had been taking notes.

Once they were alone, Galen grimaced. "I'm done in. Metaphorically." He put his hand up. "Need sleep and a wash, not in that order."

"Need an arm up the stairs?" Martin asked. Galen nodded, as if he wanted to say something in private, then he turned. "Um. Lydia, mind waiting up for me to wash?"

She blinked. She'd expected to go to her room and stay out of the way. "Um. Sure?" A minute later, she was trailing upstairs, after Martin and Galen, and going off to her room. Laura and Martin were apparently staying the night two rooms down. Maybe three. It was a large house. She wasn't entirely sure how many of those doors were rooms and how many were cupboards or something.

Laura came up behind her while she was still standing

in the doorway. "I suspect Galen wants a word. Want to wash up quickly? There's a bathing room across the hall here." She gestured, making reasonably free with the house.

"Now you mention it." Lydia agreed. She took ten minutes to give herself a good wash with a washcloth and the water from the sink, changing into an enveloping nightgown. Lydia couldn't face running a bath, and she assumed there was only so much hot water. She used a charm to clean her hair, then retreated to her bedroom, pulling out a notebook. Ten minutes later, it had only a few scribbled notes, and there was a knock on her door.

"Yes?"

Martin stuck his head in. "Galen'd love your company." He kept his voice low, but it seemed warm enough, not judging. "For a while, you might want a dressing gown or whatever?" She was less sure what to make of that, but she nodded as Martin added, "Thank you. For helping." Then he disappeared back down the hall.

She gathered up a dressing gown, slippers, and her notebook. When she knocked on Galen's door, it was slightly ajar. "Lydia? Come in, close it behind you?" Galen was sitting propped up in bed, looking freshly washed, but pale again.

Lydia closed the door quietly behind her and came over. "Here?"

"Please." Galen gestured at the bed. It was certainly big enough for two. More than big enough. Lydia shifted to settle and perch, her feet hanging off the edge, tugging the dressing gown around her. "It - you don't mind? If you don't want to be here, I mean, you don't have to..." He suddenly sounded worried, his words tumbling over each other.

Lydia shook her head. "I don't know what you want."

She might as well be blunt. She wasn't sure she knew how to do anything else. Not right now.

Galen swallowed hard. "I don't want to be alone. Not tonight. I don't have any right to ask you to stay, just."

He was asking her. Not Martin, who clearly would have, even if Laura were just down the hall. They surely had done that on other nights. Some of the other Dwellers had mentioned they'd share a room if things were tight there, and something ran late. She turned to face him better. "Why wouldn't I?" She reached out a hand, almost touching his arm, not quite. "We were really worried. Even before Martin..."

Galen grimaced. "I hadn't realised Nico could do that. Could do it so well. It was..." He bit his lip. "Come closer?"

Lydia didn't hesitate. She slid off her slippers, and stood just long enough to tuck herself under the blankets. Galen was wearing pyjamas. She had on a nightgown and a dressing gown. They were well beyond any conservative standard of modest behaviour in general. But she wasn't going to start worrying about that now. She was more worried it would be more than he wanted.

Instead, though, he moved his arm, so she could lean against it. That felt good. Warm, even if Galen was not precisely radiating heat. The bed was, rather. It must have charms on it. That was clever. And it felt so good. She'd spent so many nights with a cold room and colder sheets. The thought distracted her until she felt him squeeze her shoulder. "Get comfortable, please?"

She shifted until she was on her side, mostly facing him. Not quite touching his body, but her head was on his arm, on a pile of sinfully soft pillows. Galen looked back at her, blinking. "I like this." Then he hurriedly added. "I don't want you to do anything you don't want to. Even if I ask.

Please say no if it makes you uncomfortable? I - I don't think I trust my judgement tonight."

"So we should treat it as if you are more than a bit tipsy, and talk about it in the morning?" She tried to keep her tone light, but it came out rather sharper around the edges than she expected.

Galen snorted. "Exactly like that. Have you ever done complex ritual work? It - well, tipsy is an excellent description. Especially when it's badly done."

"Was it, tonight? I started wondering." She wasn't sure how to ask about it. "And not much."

"It's not telling secrets to tell you that the Dwellers, like any sensible secret society with a knowledge of ritual magic, have initiation rituals. We take a lot of care with ours, that they're done properly. People can get hurt if you don't. And not just the ordinary sort of hurts, burns or cuts or whatever." He glanced at his other hand, the one with the healing cut on it, now tidily wrapped up in a neat white bandage. "Magic can mend a lot of those. But inside someone's head, if the ritual goes wrong. The same way the War hurt some people."

Lydia considered that. "And people still want to do the rituals. I mean. You were serious about it, earlier? Being an option for me?"

"Oh, still very serious. I asked Martin earlier, and he'll be glad to second it. Or have some sort of contest with Thomasina for the privilege of proposing you. We agreed that I'm a tad biassed here. And also ..." Galen shrugged. "Whoever proposes you has a particular role in the ritual, and I want someone you trust doing that, but not me."

There were oceans there of things she didn't quite understand, but she could ask about that later. Thomasina might even tell her useful parts. "But people still take the risk?"

Galen contemplated. "I am not, you know, up for a detailed discussion of ritual theory and safety practices. Being, as we have agreed, the equivalent of moderately tipsy, I'm not sure any of it would make any sense, anyway. But it's like horse racing. Sometimes you fall, but there are steps you take, so it's less likely, so it's less dangerous. You learn skills. You pay attention." Galen shrugged. "Of course, sensible people also warn other people about the track conditions. They dumped me into the ritual with no preparation at all."

"Which you expected." They'd talked about it, of course. Though Lydia realised now she had missed dozens of implications.

"More or less. But not like it came out? I was expecting..." He huffed a breath. "Nico is powerful, when he acts on it. More than most people I've met. Charming, despite being more like a snake than a person has a right to be. The sort of charming that holds you. Stories go on about cobras. Like that."

Lydia nodded, blinked at Galen and watching him closely now. The little changes were fascinating, in a way she was less and less able to track. The warm bed made her drowsy. The day had been far too many different things, including the sudden terror that Galen had been seriously hurt. "But the ritual?"

"The ritual was sloppy. A lot of showy bits. Honestly, I'm surprised they didn't have illusions and fireworks. Even if we were out in a bloody cold field well away from any houses in December. Maybe that would have come afterwards, when they'd blackmailed me, but why show off then? That's a waste of energy." Galen was rambling along out loud now, and Lydia found that fascinating and charming in equal measure. "I don't think the rest of them had much experience with the ritual, and isn't that curious, if this had been a going concern for a while."

Lydia grimaced. That highlighted several gaps. "Has Nico been in charge all along? Did he start being in charge after Sisley and all of them?"

"Good questions. I suppose we'll find out, eventually. I hope so, anyway. That there's enough for some sort of trial. The nice thing about being in the middle of the mess is they let you hear the outcome. And besides, I'm pretty sure Griffin will tell me if I ask. He won't approve of the messy ritual magic one bit. It doesn't do anyone any good."

Lydia nodded. "Why was it messy, though? Did they not care, or not take it seriously?"

Galen slid his hand a little further down her arm, holding her more securely. "I think he thought I needed cowing, rather than trusting the ritual, whatever it was, to catch me up. I think he wanted to use me, and he got greedy. If they'd run me through the ritual, and let it be, they'd have hooked me far more securely." He grimaced. "Though on the whole, I'm glad he didn't do that. As it was, I don't know. I need to ask Griffin some questions. Maybe a few of the Dwellers, the proper ritualists. But it felt like that oath collided with it. Silence oaths don't."

"But your Dweller oaths... they're explicit about cooperating with Silence oaths, aren't they? Questioning by the proper authorities."

Galen turned a little to kiss her forehead. "They are, you're right. I don't know how that works out. I expect we can find someone to explain." He let out a long breath. "You're comfortable?"

"Sleepy, even." It slipped out before Lydia could mind her tongue.

Galen beamed. "Oh, good. I like this. If - if you need to leave, that's fine? If I'm too hard to sleep with. Nightmares can be a thing, they warned us in school, badly done ritual. But I'm hoping you'll be here in the morning. And, uh. More talking after we've been to the Guard Hall?"

Lydia nodded. "We don't need to rush." She hesitated, then realised she should be clear. "I want to stay. If I need to do something else, I would. But this - this is, I like being right here with you."

Galen smiled, then dismissed the charm lights. As they faded out, she could see him nestle down in the pillows, his arm still under her neck, and she wriggled slightly to get comfortable herself. He was asleep almost immediately, giving her just a minute or two to enjoy his steady breathing before she drifted off herself.

CHAPTER 40
SUNDAY MORNING

Galen woke with a pounding headache the next day, to find a note on the side table from Lydia. It said that she'd been called into the Halls of Justice and they wanted him to follow when he was up and about. As he was putting it down, there was a knock on his door, and he frowned. "Come in?" He was reasonably clothed, still.

Blythe pushed it open, followed by Julius, who was carrying a bed tray full of food, making Galen realise he was starving under the headache. "It's half ten, and they were hoping for you at eleven or so in Trellech."

Galen rubbed his face. "That ..."

Before he could finish the sentence, Julius tapped the small bottle. "Headache potion. Made fresh." So he'd been up all night, then. Galen didn't know whether to feel guilty or grateful. Both, really. Loved, certainly.

He certainly would not turn it down, and as soon as Julius set the tray on the bed, he reached for that, drinking it in two gulps. Julius's potions tasted decent, because he had to take them often enough himself to invest time in making them palatable. Unlike far too many people. Then he set it down, looking at his brother a little uncertainly. "Lydia?"

"Went in at half nine. She didn't want to leave you but they really wanted her statement before yours." Blythe was amused. "Oh, and Master Kendric's there already. Witness for her, and he'll sit in on yours, of course."

Galen rubbed his face, letting that information wash over him. The family solicitor. "I don't. I don't know, I've never. Not like this." It wasn't the questioning that worried him, exactly. He was on the side of the angels this time, or at least sufficiently so. It was how to talk to Lydia.

Julius settled down in the chair beside the bed, leaning to peer at him through the mask. "Go. Do what's needed. Then talk. To her." He hesitated, as if gathering strength. "Fierce. Strong. Good ideas. Her."

"All of that." Galen smiled weakly. "Here?"

"We'll stay out of your hair. Ring for a meal, or we can have a hamper of things up here. Let you take your time?" Blythe stepped back after saying that. "And you can let us know when you want to talk to anyone else. Need anything else up here? I'll see about fresh sheets and clean towels and all that while you're out."

Galen was not entirely sure what he thought about his almost sister-in-law having that much idea of what he might get up to. But he supposed it was unavoidable, given the circumstances. He nodded again, feeling clumsy and slow. "Um. Thank you."

Blythe grinned and then held out her hand to Julius. "Come on, then. We'll let you eat."

Left alone, Galen ate and peered at the newspaper one of them had included. There wasn't a story yet about last night, just a small piece about news to come. Someone, probably Julius, had also made sure there was more than enough sausage and eggs to fill some gaps in his stomach, and a full pot of tea. By the time he finished, the potion had finally kicked in, and he could stumble through the rest of getting ready. He made it to the Halls of Justice by half-past eleven, not too much later than expected.

The next two hours were, however, gruelling. First, he was shown to one of the small courtrooms, and he could feel the permanent enchantments pressing on him. It was a weight on his shoulders, like always being visible. He had to sit in the witness box, the centre of all that magic, with just a glass of water.

Griffin was the one leading the questions, but Captain Orland and Captain FitzRanulf sat in, and two other Captains who introduced themselves, but whose names he immediately lost. He'd have to ask Master Kendric later. He, at least, was taking notes, writing intently. Galen saw several hours going over those as matters progressed. There was a court reporter, too, with a little machine instead of a shorthand pad, something like a typewriter.

First came the formal calling in of truth. Griffin did it, wheeling his chair to the proper spot in the centre of the room, calling in the magic and making it real and solid. He did it deftly, though, more so than the judge for Galen's parents and their trial last year. Certainly more so than some of the questioning Galen had been at. This felt like truth was on his side, on everyone's side.

He began at the beginning. They'd organised it brilliantly, even Galen had to admit that. They ran him efficiently through a series of questions that laid out what he had been looking for, what he had been offered, and why he had gone to the ritual. All done without ever focusing on the fact he was helping Lydia. There was no leaving her out of it entirely, but it was all general "Had a friend who was curious about what happened in the aftermath of other events."

Finally, Griffin banished the enchantments, and brushed his hands off. "There. That will do nicely for a record. Thank you, Alesya. Soon as you can manage, the transcription would be grand." That was to the court reporter, who nodded and packed up her device, leaving before Griffin said anything else.

"Do you have a moment, sir?" Galen asked. "Privately?" Master Kendric raised an eyebrow, and Galen added, "May I call tomorrow, Master Kendric, unless there's something with more urgency?"

Griffin nodded, and the Captains packed up their notes, retreating to the doorway. Master Kendric cleared his throat. "No further questioning of my client, I presume."

"No, no." Griffin shook his head. "And Galen, you are not in any trouble here. You might have been, if you'd gone without talking to us about it, but since you did..."

Galen swallowed. "Sir," he agreed. Once everyone else had left, Griffin tilted his head. "My office, or is it quick?"

"Here's fine. Can you - do you know enough yet, to know what they would have done? Bound me to?"

Galen was fairly sure he would not get a complete answer. That was a ridiculous expectation. He could see half a dozen thoughts across Griffin's face, then a decision. "Not enough of it yet. But they'd have used your magic, used that of your fellows. Not all at once, but with long-lasting effects. We're still piecing together the details of the ritual, though you have an excellent memory for most of it. That's a help with some gaps we had this morning. That's currently the piece we know will mean a trial, but I'm expecting we'll find a number of illegal acts as we question them and dig further."

"And the money?" Galen knew a first rule was following the money. "Not mine, directly, I mean, though if I can get it back, I'd not mind. They did lie about the pedigree of the horse. But generally speaking."

"The information you've provided already has given the analysts quite a bit to work with. We're still sorting out the details, but it appears that the Paxmans were deep in debt and desperate to get out."

"And Darley?" Galen knew Martin would ask, at the least. Presumably Lydia already had, but perhaps she'd have been unsure if she could.

"That will take more unravelling, but there appear to be a series of companies arranged to pass money through and cover their tracks. There is some war profiteering in there, almost certainly, and more recently attempting to take advantage of situations in the Empire. It is looking promising for our counterparts in the non-magical Ministry to bring charges."

Galen nodded. "So the charges - partly abuse of magic, in varying ways. And partly financial? Do you know why Nico was so - well, so." So venomous a snake, and so hypnotic, too.

"That will also take more research, and questioning. We wanted your statements first, under oath, so we could structure his better. Making an educated guess, based on experience, he had an experience during the War that made him want to reach for all the security he could grab, and he didn't much care who he scrambled over in the process. On one hand, it's understandable." Something compassionate, the sort of compassion that was as tough as hot-forged iron passed over his face. "On the other hand, not the sort of thing we allow to continue like that."

Galen let out a long slow breath. "Oh. And the charges?"

"Magical coercion is likely to be the central charge, quite possibly a number of others. For everyone at the ritual, and we'll be tracking down the others in the magical circles."

"And is Lydia, is she..." He didn't even know how to ask.

Now Griffin's smile was kinder. "She did nothing wrong, either. We had a fair number of questions for her, about her background research, but Editor Morris was here for part of it, and the paper's solicitor. I think she was using one of the spare meeting rooms to write up some of her notes. Whoever's on the desk can tell you. Can I take you to lunch, or do you want to get away from here?"

Galen ducked his chin, amused. "Away, for now. But perhaps lunch sometime, if you don't mind? I'm - I'm getting the sense you know a lot of things."

"More than a few, and that's quite understandable. Both you and Lydia are welcome, of course. Let me know a good day, and if it's not pure crisis around here, I'll see about getting away. And we're down to only about one crisis a fortnight, so your chances are decent."

Galen snorted. "Not that different in the Dwellers, actually. I'll write when things settle."

"I don't need to remind you to drink water and not too much alcohol or any of that. And I'm sure Julius knows the proper potions for a badly done ritual." Griffin said it easily.

Galen nodded. "He's been right on top of that. Thank you. Later." He went out, asking the woman at the desk where he might find Lydia. When he got to the proper door, the same one where they'd met Griffin, it was propped open. Lydia was sitting at the end of the table, the light shining through the window and over her shoulder. She looked like a painting, something out of the Renaissance, and he wanted a photograph of that very badly.

Instead, he just cleared his throat. "Lydia?"

She blinked up at him, and he could see her mind switching gears. Then she flung herself out of the chair, and at him, to hug him, before she backed up as she kept hold of his hand. "Are you all right? Are you done? You must be. Did Griffin want to go to lunch?" She then gestured back to the table with her other hand. "I - I really need to be at the paper this afternoon."

Galen wanted desperately to talk to her, but this was the goal she'd been aiming at. "All night, too?"

"Merlin and Nimue, no. They want my copy by half-four, for a piece in the evening edition, and a full spread tomorrow." She ran her hand through her hair. "Probably done by half-six?"

"Come out to the house and tell me about it?"

She cocked her head to the side. "Not the Dwellers?"

"Not tonight. Tomorrow, in triumph, when you can talk about what's in the paper. I'll let Martin and Laura know. Anyone else? Thomasina?"

"Thomasina." Lydia nodded, counting through her head. "The people who helped, can you do that? Tell them we'll tell them more tomorrow? Together."

"That sounds grand. I'll arrange a suitable feast, too." He could do that all by journal, rather than risking someone surprising him with questions. "I'll be back home, all right? Whenever you get free."

Lydia looked him up and down. "Are you all right? You were - you slept deeply last night. The sort that's worry-ing." There was an edge to her voice now.

"Had a splitting headache when I woke up, but Julius

brought a potion up. Might have a nap if I have to wait for you." A nap, a long bath, the rest of the paper, and maybe some sort of comfortable reading would do well.

"Right. That's a plan then. Can you walk me up to the paper?" Lydia dropped his hand and turned back to go gather up her papers.

"Of course." He let out a long breath. "I - you're sure you want to come back tonight?"

She looked up, a slow smile on her face. "I didn't put in all that worrying about you to go wandering off now. Whoever convinced you that you aren't interesting in and of yourself, Galen?"

Galen shivered once and shrugged. "My parents, mostly." He realised how ridiculous it sounded. "Yes, I know. I'll walk you down to the paper. Anything you'd like to have on hand, I don't know, bath things or pastries or chocolate?"

Lydia slid the last of her notes into her satchel. "Surprise me. Nothing extravagant." She considered. "Something that doesn't take pots of money. Something simple. More than I'd buy myself. But the sort of more where I'd want it, and save my money for other things."

His expression must have been amusing, because she grinned unrepentantly. "There. That challenge will keep you busy for the afternoon and stop you fretting more than is good for you."

Galen could feel himself shiver, and then he was grinning, without knowing quite how he got there. "You do know me." he said, finally. His brain started ticking over. Something nice for the bath, a book, some interesting tea, maybe. She hadn't said he couldn't get multiple things. Though choosing a book or two would likely take him all afternoon.

"There." Lydia shrugged her coat on. "And I will come

and spend the evening with you. The night?" Her voice now had a note of uncertainty.

"I certainly hope the night, though if you prefer your own room, I'd understand." He took her hand. "May I escort you, then?"

"Yes, please."

When he left her at the door to the Moon, she was grinning. Also clearly raring to go write the story of her lifetime, or at least the first instalment of it.

CHAPTER 41

SUNDAY EVENING

Lydia didn't get to Galen's house until nearly half seven. Martin, thankfully, had popped up and offered to send a message when it was clear she wasn't getting out of the editorial meeting until far later than expected. And then of course she had to write an article, get it past Editor Morris, and wait for the final corrections. No pressure.

She was pleased with the result, though. More than pleased. She'd been promised a series of articles, three over the next few days. Then there would be the trial coverage, where she'd be able to go into detail about the investigation and the background. It promised to sell a great many papers if they did their work right, and be meaningful besides.

That was the part that got her. Nico had done a lot of damage already to other people's lives. It was going to be trickier to bring charges in the non-magical community, but they hadn't done themselves any favours there either. She couldn't help thinking about people who'd lost money or worse, because of all of them. All the people who'd had magic sucked away from them.

She was still thinking through some implications they'd discussed that afternoon when she got to the door. It opened as soon as she got to the great stone top step. Blythe waved her in. "Galen's in his room. Go right up. There are clean clothes in the room you've been using if you want to change or wash up."

Lydia did, rather. Her hands and wrists were all over black dust from the ink and the pencil lead and the printer's proofs. She detoured by the bedroom, finding a beautiful blue frock laid out, loosely fitted and made of a fine linen she didn't dare touch until she'd washed her hands. And up to her elbows.

Ducking into the bathing room across the hall, she had a good scrub with the washcloth, and with joyously hot water. Plentiful hot water and smooth fancy soap that smelled like the best parts of winter baking, vanilla and a hint of spices and sweetness. She crossed the hallway, discarding her clothes on a chair. She'd have to figure out laundering them later. The frock, though, fit her perfectly. Longer than fashionable, of course. It was the sort of house dress you kept for comfortable evenings, but it swirled around her ankles as she spun.

When she came out into the hallway, Galen was leaning in the door to his rooms, silhouetted with the light behind him. Taken with a sudden impulse, she didn't even look for slippers, just ran to him. He picked her up, swinging her in his arms into the room, into the light and the warmth, before grinning at her. "May I kiss you?"

"Oh, please." She braced one foot, feeling giddy and drunk on the world, even before she added Galen himself into the mix. A moment later, he had one hand behind her back, steadying her, and he was leaning in to kiss her. He was a fast learner, in this, as in many other things. His earlier awkwardness had melted, and while he wasn't demanding, he had a curiosity that enthralled her and encouraged her. He'd explore what she did if he kissed this way, gentler or more passionately, as his hand shifted on her back. He bumped the door closed with one hip, before leading her in a series of steady spinning twists over to the bed.

Then he paused. "What - how are you?"

She leaned to kiss his cheek, a tender kiss, before resting her head on his shoulder. He was exactly the right height for it to be comfortable and sturdy. "Story's ready for tomorrow. I'll be busy with followups the next two days, then eventually the trial. Whatever that looks like." It seemed real, now, telling him, and he squeezed her in a hug for a moment. "You, Galen? Are you all right?"

"I've been here all afternoon, had a chance to unwind. I don't know..." He hesitated.

Lydia could hear the uncertainty in his voice. "Part of me wants to see what we might find together. In bed." In case that wasn't clear. Goodness, she was doing badly with words now.

"And the rest of you has had a very long day?" The amusement in his voice caught her attention, and she lifted her head to peer at him. "I know what a long day in the pursuit of justice and goodness does to a body. Or at least I like to think so."

It made her laugh. "The question is, I know you don't have experience yet. Do we want tonight to be the start of that? Or do we want to wait?"

Something in the way she put it made him stall and lift his hand to cup her cheek. "We." There was a long shiver, through his shoulder, and suddenly she could feel the change in him, the way he was pressing against her hip, she could feel him wanting. That decided her.

"Come to bed, Galen. For the first of what I hope are many times."

When he stepped back, his eyes were glowing. "You're sure you want me. I don't know what you like."

"I am sure you are interested in learning, which puts you rather ahead of my past lovers." She lifted a hand. "They weren't awful, just I'm entirely sure you're going to be much more - much better and more fun and more attentive. And I want you to have the same. We've already done awkward, at that house party, so let's just tick off that box, and try something else."

Something in that settled his nerves. "How do we do this?"

"Generally, bed is one of the simpler options. Sofas, walls, floors, and other such things are often something of an advanced technique. Also harder on the knees, for one or both of us. Bed, Galen. Both of us. In such a way we can get out of whatever clothing we're still wearing easily." She was sure, for a moment, that she might have pushed too far.

He laughed, throwing his head back. Perhaps no, perhaps this was grand. "May I," Now his voice caught, "May I help you undress?" As if it were the best gift she could give him.

"Not nearly as complicated as it was when I arrived. I left off the complicated underthings when I changed."

The next few minutes were a delight. He undid the buttons of the dress, one by one, revealing the step-in chemise underneath. Then he lowered the straps one by one, until all the fabric fell to a pile in the ground. She glanced up at him, shy for a moment, to find him looking as if there had been some stunning dawn.

She tilted her head and let him look before her fingers itched to get more of his own clothing off. "May I?" Lydia gestured with her fingers. When he nodded, she went to work, steadily undoing the buttons of his shirt, his belt, his trousers, until they were standing amongst their cast-off clothes. He shivered again, and she immediately said, "Warmer in bed."

The next span of time - she wasn't entirely sure how long - was a mix of touching, kissing. Galen's hands on her skin, him letting her guide his touch. The way she made noise, and that wasn't a thing she'd done before. Galen soaked it up, as if the sounds drove him to peaks of passion by the pitch alone.

Galen had been a touch over-eager. The sort that meant they had a round of pleasure, leaving her panting for more, but they'd had to wait for him to recover. The second round, however, was much more evenly matched in pace, with him finding his pleasure as she was coasting through the last clenches of her own.

By the time she noticed again, it was well past full dark and then some. It had not exactly been ecstatically perfect sex. However, she neither expected that, nor particularly wanted it. Perfection was uncomfortable to live with. And it wasn't as if it were something she'd been missing except in the most optimistic and philosophical way.

However, she had a great deal of hope they might progress quickly in that direction. Galen was, as she'd said, a quick learner, good with his hands in a way she hadn't expected from someone who was far more land-lord than craftsman. Most importantly, he was very insistent on doing what she enjoyed. To be fair, she'd done her best to set a high standard for doing things he'd enjoy. She rather got the sense he had had little of that growing up, not in any way that mattered. Maybe sometime she'd have time to ask Blythe or Julius about that. Probably Blythe.

They had ended up in a tangle of sheets and duvet, with Galen dozing by her side. She woke before him, but she certainly didn't want to move. There was plenty of room in this luxuriously gigantic bed, and she suspected if she weren't very careful, she'd never be able to go back to before.

Galen stirred, stretching a little, then wriggling against her, and saying, more to her shoulder than her breast. "Warm."

Lydia snorted. "That's the idea." She kept her voice quiet. This lazy, comfortable cuddling was decidedly new to her. Her past lovers had wanted to get up and get out, which, admittedly, was more of an imperative when you were sneaking off to do the deed.

Galen stroked his thumb along her hip. "Again, later? Is that too much?"

She shook her head. "No. Only." She swallowed. "What - what are we doing here? Besides the sex. The sex is grand. I am up for more of the sex at agreeable intervals."

"Not when you're working." He shifted so his voice was slightly less muffled by her body, though he left his hand stroking her hip. "What will you accept from me, then? For - I mean. While we're making sure it's right."

The way he put that caught at her, a little snare. "You're thinking we will?"

"I am thinking I want that very much. That - this is warm, like Martin's warm. Space for me to be me. Relaxed. Not worried about saying something wrong, or..." His shoulder twitched. "You ask good questions. About what I want to do, or - saying what the options are."

She had, to be fair, done a good bit of that earlier. Galen wasn't entirely illiterate when it came to sex, but he hadn't been at all sure what he'd like in several cases. And truth to tell, she'd enjoyed showing him and exploring it together, the inquisitive, curious twists, rather than either of them making assumptions. It was like investigating a story, being open to what came up rather than assuming you knew it all.

The silence went on longer than she meant to, and he made an uncertain sound before kissing her shoulder again. She patted his ribs once. "Just - thinking how I like how it was like pulling a story together. Strong lede, being open to where the questions led us, and then, mmm. A strong tight finish?" She offered the last part in hopes it would make him smile, and he rewarded her with one of those open laughs.

That she wanted more of. The way Martin saw him, the way Julius and Blythe did. The way the Dwellers did.

"So what does it mean?"

"Right now? We see about sponsoring you for the Dwellers once you're through the rush of things at the paper. I do know how that works, remember, Martin? Fuss and flurry and no time for yourself when the story's breaking. I shan't take offence."

That, in turn, made her smile. "It has been a problem with some people. But of course you'd understand." She let out a long breath. "And otherwise?"

"You're very welcome here. I hope sometimes in my bed, but we've heaps of space. You could have your own room and an office if you want. I don't know what you'd prefer?"

Lydia pushed up onto one elbow. "You know that it's been my typewriter balanced on a rickety end table at the wrong height in the square foot at the end of my bed, right?"

"I suspected. Again, Martin, remember? No reason I can't offer a sturdy desk, with good light. And meals you don't have to pay for, and someone else to fuss over laundry and such."

It hit her, like a rush, what that would mean. So much time back in her life, rather than constantly scrambling. So much room in her brain, not having to keep track of every penny, or when she could pick things up from the laundry-woman when that was open. Company that clearly kept odd hours themselves and wouldn't be offended by hers. And that was before she got into what she'd save in rent and, yes, in food. She could put a good bit by, just in case. Help Mum and the rest of the family a lot more.

"You're sure?" she needed to hear him say it, apparently.

"Very sure. We can talk through the details. With Blythe and Julius, she does most of the bookkeeping for the house. But - we can do that. And you'd do well with it. I know you work hard. You could do more work, changing the world, with a hot meal waiting when you were done."

Lydia let out a long breath. "We'll talk. Right now, um. Bit of a wash, something to eat, and then we might explore new investigations in bed?" The rest of it could wait for tomorrow. At least for tomorrow.

EPILOGUE

G alen shifted from foot to foot, waiting. He'd been through this seventeen times by now, between helping with the rituals at Schola, and the people they'd brought in as adults. He knew what would happen. He knew his part in it, and none of that was remotely helping.

It had taken several months to find a time when Lydia could clear a full day, a full two days, from her schedule. It wasn't just the trial, though that had taken a great deal of time. The charges, in the end, had been significant and serious. Drawing on other people's magic, without their consent, generally was a theft, of a particularly intimate kind. Other parts had been forwarded to the non-magical authorities; Victor and Darley had been implicated in a good dozen fraudulent deals between them. His share of the horse, that had been returned to Galen and all the others who had bought in, already. The other deals would take longer to resolve, apparently.

Lydia had shone, throughout. She'd turned out piece after piece on the implications of the trial, before she'd expanded. Her writing had cut away to the heart of what loneliness drove people to, what the War had changed, and there were a dozen new plans for bringing people together in some better way already. Not all of them would last, but some would.

Finally, things had settled down enough they could plan this. Enough time for the vigil last night, for the quiet preparation today, and then tonight's ritual and celebration. And tomorrow, for the recovery. Diving back into your ordinary life after that sort of thing could be jarring, and even more so for someone who worked in a crowded and chaotic newsroom, like Lydia.

He glanced over his shoulder as Martin came up to him. They'd checked the forge half a dozen times now, making sure that every one of the ritual items was in the proper place. It would be Martin leading the ritual, and Thomasina as Lydia's sponsor. And Galen, well, to be ready for afterwards.

"Thomasina said she's doing brilliantly. You know that. And that she'll see her safe." Martin spoke quietly.

"It's harder than I thought, waiting." Galen ran his hand through his hair, feeling the linen robe shift. "Possibly even harder than not telling her anything about what to expect." That had been unfathomably difficult. They had fallen with such ease in talking about nearly everything else once they'd allowed themselves to.

Around Julius and Blythe - and Martin and Laura - Lydia was clever, thoughtful, insightful, but also curious. She'd ask a question and then listen, really listen, to what someone said. Not planning her next comment or getting distracted. In private, though, she was fierce like a terrier in chasing down something important. Not like Galen's parents were, especially his mother. There, Galen expected problems. Every time he didn't give the answer that was wanted. Lydia wanted the truth, or if not the truth, an honest look at why the truth wasn't an option.

Now, it was almost over. They'd share oaths, the kind he shared with Martin, with all his other friends. Sometime, maybe, they'd share other oaths about a particular sort of relationship, but that could come later.

"Give it one more check and take your place." Martin went to check the table tucked to the side of the forge. Back at Schola, this would have been a fire in the centre of a cave, carefully tended and managed. As it likely had been for millennia by one group of people or another. Gathering around the light and the transformation, both.

Here, though, they had the forge. Half a dozen people had been out here, working it today, the sound of hammer blows echoing through the house. Galen knew full well that Lydia would have heard them, how they rang out. He'd been up there enough times, letting the sound vibrate against his skin, delicate enough to be a butterfly's wing that far up. But Galen also knew the way it got under your skin, how your heart aligned with it, when the forging was done in proper rhythm, as this had been.

There were three cold-hammered tokens to carry, made of copper. And then three items, twisted and formed from hot iron. A scribing tool, everyone got that. And then a twisted circle that could be worn as a pendant or with a pocket watch. Finally, a long slender decorative curved length, tapering into a spiral, for an altar or shrine.

Galen did one more pass, making sure all the items they hoped they'd not need were handy. Buckets of water and sand to put out a stray ember or a small flame, the healing kit, the flask of cool water in case the initiate fainted. Food and drink were encouraged, they weren't the sort of ascetic society who wanted their initiates disorientated and weak. Besides, that was entirely dangerous, around open fire. On the other hand, not everyone found themselves able to eat much.

He let himself settle into breathing, letting the soft sounds of the bellows guide him. Finally, he heard the beat of the drum that signalled Lydia and Thomasina were coming across the courtyard. Miriam, behind him, picked up her own hammer and positioned herself by the anvil, working a piece of iron with lighter but insistent hammer strokes. Enough to ring, not enough to risk deafening anyone, which could be a narrow bridge sometimes. Lydia wasn't blindfolded, exactly, but there was a charm that made the darkness shroud her, until they were ready for the light.

Galen recognised he was babbling along inside his head. Not with his tongue, at least. He kept his hands folded, his mouth shut. Lydia looked gorgeous as she came down the path between the rest of the Dwellers. They'd be sharing phrases from their oaths, from the tales they told late at night or over a leisurely feast. Each one saying the things they'd found most meaningful in lighting their way.

Lydia, though, the glow of the torches and the charm lights made her look like a pearl in an intricate setting. Her hair was pulled back from her face, held back by simple ties, her robe short enough she couldn't trip, without sleeves to catch against anything. Thomasina guided her along until they were in place, then whispered something in her ear. Lydia smiled.

The relief rushed in. The rituals where they smiled were the best ones. The ones where someone was able to step into the magic, into their company, freely. He'd hoped, but you couldn't ever know, not until someone was there in that moment.

Beside him, Martin signalled. Three louder strokes on the anvil called everyone to silence. The others filed in, filling the forge. Near enough forty tonight, an excellent number. Then Martin's voice rang out, and echoing in the stone of the forge walls.

"Do you come to dwell at the forge, knowing all that we may ask of you?"

It was the third time she'd been asked. Once upstairs, once as she entered the courtyard. Lydia didn't show any impatience, just a joy. "I do, if you will have me."

The ritual went on from there. There were the formalities and speeches to get through. The injunctions that the prospective initiate had to hear and agree with, one by one. Lydia replied to each steadily and evenly, loud enough for everyone to hear. They asked the formal questions. First about whether she had come to this freely. Then if any person had pressured or threatened her to join. And finally, if someone had explained to her the expectations.

She named them back. The oath to share the fire of inspiration, the tools shaped by the forge, the community of brothers and sisters who did this work in the world. She promised to pledge her help to any other Dweller who asked within those goals.

Galen was caught up in it, hearing the instructions that came next, of the tools of their society. None of them had been foreign to him, even as a second year, but he suddenly realised her background was quite different, especially around ritual magic. It would be new to her, in an entirely different way.

Finally, Martin declaimed, "Sponsor, lead this one toward the flame." Behind him, Galen felt Owen reach for a torch, lighting it from the embers of the forge. It burst into flame at the same moment Thomasina dropped the charm. Lydia took a half step back, at the burst of light and heat dancing in front of her. She bowed from the waist, never taking her eyes from the fire. That was an excellent instinct, given that all they'd told her was that when she could see, she might wish to choose some gesture of acknowledgement.

Martin led her through the final portion of the ritual. First, he held up the cup of welcome, holding a spark of each of their magic, and some from the forge. Then they began the circle, each one naming off some skill or gift the person next to them had. All of them, everyone who had come to see her made their sister, sharing a sentence or two, and how they fit into the Dwellers. For some, it was some treasure of magic or skill with their hands. For others, it was a mention of "Always glad to lend an ear" or "A genius at bookkeeping - or deciphering someone else's books." A few got everyone laughing, a few got a more respectful silence.

Galen felt, as he did every time he heard this, something settle into place. It reminded him, reminded all of them, of how they were connected, that each of them brought their gifts and talents to share. Finally, it came round to Galen. Owen said, "You know many of Galen's virtues already, but tonight, I want to call out his willingness to do what is needed, even if it looks small or unimportant. I've never known him to shirk."

That took Galen aback, so much so he had to cough and cover. "And Martin, you know him as a journalist and writer. He is also one of the best people I know to see what matters most. Cutting through the fog and confusion." Martin smiled quickly at him. Finally it was a matter of the last few formal phrases, before there was a loud cheer from everyone assembled.

Finally, Galen could step forward and sweep her up, making sure there was room around them before he swung her around. When he set her down, she leaned her head on his shoulder, not wanting to let go. He squeezed her. "Now, we go back to the comfortable chairs and have a feast. Come, take up your new tokens." Miriam was handing over a basket to carry them, and a few other things to bring back. Others were going to tend the forge and put everything to bed so it would be ready to be used tomorrow.

Lydia nodded, glancing around, now shy. Galen knew his part here, and so he led the procession back to the main room, where there were groaning tables of food set out. All the things they'd noticed Lydia particularly liked, and then some. Food in abundance, that was the tradition, to make it clear they were better together, in this as in so many other ways.

The next hours were a mix of toasts and drinks and passing tidbits back and forth. When the others had begun to leave, Galen leaned over to murmur. "Do you want to stay here tonight? Up in the temple?"

Lydia blinked at him. "Can we?"

"Quite traditional. Not something I got to do the same way, but it's grand to spend the night."

She reached for his hand. "I was just thinking I wasn't ready to leave. Though I am a bit tired." She'd have spent the night on a simple pallet last night. Galen caught Thomasina's eye and nodded, and she disappeared to make the space ready.

"Inside twenty minutes, it will be quite comfortable. For both of us." That was less traditional, but they certainly weren't the first pair to sleep up there. Or more than a pair,

333

for that matter. He'd done it with Martin, several times, when they'd need space to think something through.

It was half an hour before they made it up there. Lydia stopped just inside the door, to see it lit gently with charms and brightly coloured pillows and blankets. Earlier today, it had been austere, everything tidied away. Now it was a place to relax and be comfortable. Someone had even left a tray with tea and a bottle of wine, as well as a few final nibbles to fill in whatever gaps they might have.

Lydia was quiet as they found their place on the bed in front of the altar. "I didn't know what to expect. It's not like in stories."

"Certainly not like that gods-awful field. You see why I was complaining about it. I don't mind a ritual ordeal, though I'm glad ours isn't..." He shrugged. "I gather some of the other societies. It's a fair bit more than time to think through what you want to do with your life, somewhere safe and comfortable, even if it's lacking in distractions or amusements. But if you can't choose this willingly, what good is it? You can't trust an oath made under duress."

Galen had come to strong opinions about that, the more he thought about the snake cult. Now, at least, he and Lydia could talk that out properly. For now, he leaned over and kissed her. "Bet it doesn't feel real yet. That's a reason to sleep up here. See what dreams tell you."

"And you're here with me." She settled against his shoulder. "Tell me a few of the stories they mentioned? The myths, I mean. Nothing recent."

Galen snorted. "Nothing recent." He settled down to tell the version they told of Prometheus descending, feeling her warmth beside him, as strongly as they felt the warmth from the temple hearth.

IF YOU ENJOYED *Point By Point* and would like to read more of this series, please sign up for my mailing list to get all the latest news and fun extras. Your reviews (on whatever review site you use) are much appreciated, too!

Read on for a few historical details about this book and the setting as well as an excerpt from the next (and last) book in this series, *Mistress of Birds*. You can read more about Martin and Laura's romance in *In The Cards*.

AUTHOR'S NOTES

Thank you so much for joining me for *Point by Point*. My thanks as always to my most excellent editor, Kiya Nicoll, as well as to my early readers, all of whom made this book vastly better.

Galen, Martin, Laura, Julius, and Blythe also appear in *In The Cards*, along with Hippolyta FitzRanulf. That book also introduces the Dwellers at the Forge in some additional detail. The events of that book get some brief references here, but I've been careful to avoid direct references who the murderer is in that book, to help avoid spoilers. (*In The Cards* is my locked room/remote island murder mystery, because you can't write in the 1920s without one of those, really.)

The Dwellers at the Forge are one of the seven secret societies at Schola, taking in students in their second year with continuing membership into adulthood. I do intend to explore all seven properly eventually!

So far, I've had major characters who are members of Dius Fidius (Isembard and Alexander in *Eclipse*), Animus Mundi (Cyrus in *Sailor's Jewel* and *The Hare and the Oak*), and Many Are The Waters (Rhoe in *Sailor's Jewel* and *Carry On*, and Mabyn in *The Hare and the Oak*), but none of those books have particularly focused on the society aspects.

It was a delight to get to roll around in the details of the Dwellers. And of course, they're very pragmatic about everything from the food to the pneumatic tubes to what they keep handy in their attics. Well-organised progressive action takes a lot of scaffolding, sometimes.

Lydia, of course, draws on the grand history of **Nellie Bly** and the "girl stunt reporters" of the 1880s and 1890s, about 30-40 years before this book takes place. Nellie Bly is the best known of them, but there were quite a few other women who would throw themselves into difficult situations, in order to report on key social issues, abuses of power - and of course those parts of life that made great headlines.

I found *Sensational: The Hidden History of America's "Girl Stunt Reporters"* by Kim Todd very helpful in exploring this bit of history.

(Did you know Nellie Bly also wrote a number of novels? They were reissued in 2021, and I read a few of them while researching for this book as well. They're sensationalist novels of their times, but also an interesting way to dip a toe into how Nellie and her peers saw the world.)

As for Lydia, if you're wondering about that reference to the talisman maker, it is indeed the same talisman maker referenced in *Seven Sisters*. (Farran Michaels is much happier where he is after that, thankfully.)

Horse racing is obviously a theme in the book, though more as a way into the core of the plot than the plot in itself. I'll be honest and say I reread - gleefully and delightedly - a number of Dick Francis novels, for the feel of a racing stable. (Many of them aged far better than I was afraid they would have, and there's a strong thread of kindness and justice through them that I had forgotten since I read them as a teenager madly in love with both horses and mysteries.)

However, if you want a great overview of the history of racing, I also found *Mr. Darley's Arabian: A History of Racing in 25 Horses* by Chris McGrath absolutely fascinating. Through genetic testing, we now know that 95% of modern thoroughbreds in the world are descended from the Darley Arabian, a horse long considered one of the three foundational sires of the breed along with the Godolphin Arabian and the Byerly Turk. They were all brought to the British Isles in the late 1600s through the early 1700s.

This book tracks the history through specific horses, which was both a great way to illuminate a number of the stories, and to show how much breeding and lineage play a role in the sport. It also has some fantastic stories about scandals, gossip, and all the very human parts of the sport. (Though I'll warn you in advance, the chapter on the Great War is heart-breaking, as you'd expect.)

Then, of course, there's Crisparkle. He is an entirely fictional horse, who is related to a real one, Hurry On, who is somewhat older, and who had a good record and who was a leading sire in 1926. (He has a Wikipedia page, if you'd like to check out his details.) He is, however, chestnut, as are most of his relatives.

This is where we get into a bit of equine genetics. If you don't know your horse colours, chestnut is the reddish brown coat, and the horse might have the same colour legs, or perhaps white markings on the legs or face. Bay is the term for a horse that has a reddish brown coat (anything from bright copper to mahogany brown or even darker), with black mane, tail, and legs. Genetically speaking, chestnut is the recessive coat colour, so it is very unlikely (read, impossible) for two chestnut horses to have a bay foal.

Many of the horses in this line are also named for minor Dickens characters, as Crisparkle is (for Reverend Crisparkle in *The Mystery of Edwin Drood.*) There's no particular deep meaning in why that particular name, it just amused me.

This book also meant I got to roll around a bit in some of the **Mesopotamian archaeology** of the period. There were several significant British-run digs just after the Great War. Fairly clearly, Nico was part of them. (There were also some major battles near there during the War, though they don't get nearly as much name recognition as sites elsewhere.) However, this is still a relatively early period for archaeology of the area, so it is easy to imagine digging up sites, finding something interesting, and not being entirely sure what it meant.

Or, if you're Nico, coming up with grand theories about it, and about the expansionist aspects of the culture, and what that could mean. A great deal of our understanding of astronomical (and astrological) magic comes originally from various of the Mesopotamian civilisations, and so that's a thread through everything else, roughly speaking.

Finally, there's a thread in this book of **secret society** ritual in theory and practise. The ritual that Nico runs (and Galen is brought to) is intended to be rather poorly constructed. It's the sort of thing that a skilled ritualist could do something with, but Nico is working with smaller numbers than he wants, and relying on his magical skills to make up the difference.

It would work a lot better on someone without Galen's own experience in initiatory rituals, basically.

Secret societies abounded in Europe, Great Britain, the United States, and the Commonwealth countries throughout the 18th, 19th, and well into the 20th centuries. A number are still around these days, but there were many more, with societies focused on all kinds of particular interests and professions. Most folks have heard of the Freemasons (who have some of their roots in the guilds of stonemasons), but there were a huge variety of others. I riffed on a number of texts from different societies for Nico's ritual.

That's it for this set of author's notes. I hope you've enjoyed these adventures with Lydia and Galen (and getting to see a bit more of Martin, Laura, Julius, and Blythe.) Sign up for my newsletter on my website at https://celialake.com for all the latest about upcoming books, my current writing, and extras for various books.

EXCERPT FROM MISTRESS OF BIRDS

September 1927, London

"What are you working on now, then?" It was the inevitable question, and Thalia tried not to wince. Martha meant well, she really did, but the line between enthusiastic interest in other people's art and pressing on all the bruised and raw spots could be a very fine one.

She was not precisely working on anything. She had had another rejection in the post that afternoon. It had been the sparse 'does not meet our needs at this time.' Nothing but the barren signature.

Once upon a time, last year, the year before, she'd at least got a little personal note of encouragement, asking her to send the next thing along. Worse, she was neither longer young enough nor new enough to be interesting to most people, especially not editors.

Selling that story would not have put food in the larder, or paid her rent, but it would have been reason to keep trying. As it was, she was down to bread and cheese and a few tinned things. And whatever she could snag at a party like this one. She'd spent too much on books again this month.

To be fair, the food was rather good here. Anna and Una were eccentric, even for artists, with a giant wolfhound, three cats, and rumours of a parrot. But they also knew how to feed artists with more inspiration than sense. Lashings of tea, heaps of sandwiches, and there were still some of those salmon pasty cup things that Thalia particularly wanted more of.

The illusionist who'd been performing across the room was quite good, actually, and there was someone doing intricate little designs in light and colour charms in the near corner.

None of this answered the question. "Honestly, town's so draining this time of year, isn't it? All the humidity." The post had brought something else, she remembered she'd wanted to see what her friends thought. "Actually, that's the oddest thing. I had a letter from my parents today."

"Surely not terribly odd? You actually get on with them well enough, right?" Martha settled back, sprawling a bit in an oversized armchair. She didn't get on with her parents at all, and honestly, given her parents, that was probably better for everyone. They were rigid polemics of the first order, refusing to recognise that Martha really did have a fair bit of talent as an artist.

"Well enough." Thalia considered. Well, they got on better when they were most of an island apart, to be fair, but that wasn't that unusual. Even if it were a smaller island than some. "Actually, it was about my great-aunt."

"Who's she when she's at home?" Peter leaned in over Martha's shoulder to grab a roll from the side table. He had washed up before coming along to the party, but not terribly well, and he had a large smudge of charcoal behind his ear. Once he had more food, he perched on the arm of Martha's chair.

"That's the point. She never leaves home. Large house, the land goes back near enough to the Normans, looks more like a castle than a house should, crenellations and everything." Thalia waved a hand, and asked "Could someone snag some of the salmon things and another sandwich, I don't care which?" She heard a noise behind her of amiable agreement.

"You are dawdling in your story, love." Hilaria shifted to prop one of her feet up on the chair Thalia had claimed. She was grinning, the sort of grin that meant she'd come home from the party and be up all night sketching. She had the flat next to Thalia's and they had been best of friends since Hilaria had moved in five years ago.

They were not quite of an age - Hilaria was thirty to Thalia's thirty-three. Hilaria was stylishly dramatic, with dark black hair, pale skin, and a fine touch with cosmetics. Beside her, Thalia often felt a bit washed out, especially when they made a fuss for a night out. Medium brown hair, medium brown eyes, pleasant complexion. None of it made much impression. Like, apparently her writing. She yanked herself away from those thoughts, to continue.

"There is a certain amount of obligatory dawdling. See, Mother and Father have been trying to get her to go for a cure in the south of France for years now, and she's kept refusing, but now her health is actually worse. There's a housekeeper and all that, but Great-Aunt Avis won't go unless someone from the family can come stay at the house. For months, through the winter, most likely. And of course Mother and Father won't, and my sister is horrified anyone would ask her to give up the social season, and you can fill in the rest."

"Will she feed you?" Hilaria gestured at the plate someone was holding over her shoulder.

Thalia looked up, grinned at Oswald, and put the plate in her lap. "Ta, appreciated." She then waved at it. "Food is a considerable incentive. Yes, she would. But I've got the flat, and..."

That was the trick. You gave up a good flat, you'd never find one when you needed one again. Not that it was a particularly excellent flat, she thought about moving at least one week out of four, and more like four out of four when the fogs were bad. But it was up above the worst of the fog and the smell of London, the light was quite good when the weather obliged, and it was hers.

All right, and it was also tiny, draughty, the loo and bath were shared with the entire floor, and she had only a small gas cooker, enough for tea and soup, but not much else. A writing desk, her bookshelves, double and triple stacked with books, and her bed. But still it was hers, earned by the work of her own hands. Mostly her fingers, to be fair, since she did secretarial work to pay her bills.

What was good about it, though, was the location. The building itself was full of her friends and artists and writers. All magical, so no one had to watch their tongue in the house, but with plenty of others to talk to in the nearby cafes and parks and theatres.

There was always someone to talk to, even when she really should be writing. And it was only minutes from the British Museum and its enormous library, and from any number of used bookshops. And new bookshops, but her funds didn't usually stretch that far.

Hilaria tilted her head. "Would you be up for letting it out? Tammy has a sister who's got a job working on a show that's likely running through the winter. I mean, if you had to come back early, she could sort something out, but she really didn't want to share."

"But the books..."

"There's space in the boxroom. And yes, even for the number of books you have. Remember, Bruce finally moved all of his sculpture wire out of the corner? We could stack them very neatly, you know it won't flood, and I think Polly has plenty of cedar blocks to keep out moths."

"Cedar's for clothes, not books." Thalia said idly. But the idea was beginning to grow on her.

"Would your aunt object if we came round for a bit of a hol?" Martha leaned forward.

"It's not near anything." Thalia said immediately. "And great-aunt, and she probably would."

Hilaria snorted. "Might do you good. Some peace and quiet and a different library, and climate. And you still haven't really got over your cough from last winter."

Thalia hadn't. Thalia kept trying not to think about that, to be honest, it wasn't like there was anything to do. She'd talked to the Healers after her mother had taken her to lunch and been very alarmed. It wasn't TB, it wasn't anything in particular, just the smog. Everyone coughed in London. Admittedly, some more than others.

"Might." Thalia let out a breath, then added to Martha. "Maybe she'd be all right with a small number of people? I can ask. But it's a long way from everywhere. It's not so bad getting to Newton Abbott, but then there's a smaller line up to Bovey Tracey, and then it's, I don't know. Four miles? Six? From there. Long winding road, I remember that, and a pony cart."

"When's the last time you were there?" Hilaria leaned back, kicking her feet up.

"I was seven. No, maybe I was eight. Most of the

347

summer, that was when my great-uncle was dying? Father's uncle. But the house has been in Great-Aunt Avis's family for yonks. There's no one around closer than the village except for the house and maybe a gardener's cottage or something? I vaguely remember his grandson was about my age." She hadn't thought of him in decades.

"So. On one hand, no distractions except maybe whatever the library has. Pleasant environs, if a little full of moors, and free food. On the other hand, you've been hating the current secretarial work, you can let your flat to Tammy's sister, and we'd miss you terribly but perhaps come and visit. Paint and sketch and opine about the desolate moors. People have built writing careers out of far less."

Hilaria spread her hand, nearly knocked over three wine glasses, and one of her rings collided with a fourth, ringing out a pure and clear sound until someone grabbed it to keep the glass from toppling over.

Thalia shook her head. "Are you that interested in being rid of me?"

"No, darling, never. Just - you know you're stuck. And you'll be in a foul mood all winter until something unsticks you. One couldn't possibly." She had a knack for voices, and this one was pure cut glass.

Like Thalia, Hilaria also came from money, the sort of money that would grudgingly pick you up if you got really desperate, and would send urgently needed pound notes on the obligatory festive occasions. Often a nicely large one. It was part of why they got on so well. Both of them would have turned into brittle society wives if they'd done as their parents wanted, and that was particular kind of hell, or so Thalia thought.

She lifted her glass. "Well. I'll think about it. Write my

parents and see how long they think I'd be wanted. And to Great-Aunt Avis about what exactly needs someone there."

After that, the party turned to other topics. A bit of satirical poetry, an awful limerick contest that Thalia managed to win with a well-turned phrase about a recent political cartoon Oswald had done. It made him blush, in a way that meant she walked out with Hilaria an hour later, arm in arm. She didn't want Oswald to offer to walk her home. He wasn't a bad sort, but she was sure he was more interested in her, in ways other than artistically, than she was in him.

Hilaria had drunk a bit more than was probably good for her, but there were potions for that, and they even had some. Thalia wondered, suddenly, if she could get Great-Aunt Avis to run as far as a stipend, since she wouldn't be working. Or maybe her parents. Guilt could be a powerful incentive, and then she could put a bit of money away.

"You should go." They were coming down their street now, but Hilaria stopped, deeply earnest. "No, really, you should. I can feel it. Something important."

Hilaria got these moods. Thalia didn't really believe in messages from beyond, or whatever you wanted to call them. She wanted nothing to do with them, in fact. Not since her mother had fallen in with a whole nest of spiritualists after her brother had been killed in 1917. Most of them were predators, and the exceptions weren't much help to anyone, as far as Thalia could see.

On the other hand, one of the principles of their lot was letting people do their thing and see where it led. So long as it wasn't actually hurting anyone.

"I'll write, I promise. Tomorrow, though." If she wrote tonight, Father would be disapproving about her handwriting. Which, of the things about her life he could disapprove of, was actually one of the better options, but still tedious.

Hilaria patted her hand. "Do. I'll miss you. I can come visit." She took a couple of steps, then stopped again. "Didn't you have another letter in your cubby?"

Thalia sighed. "A rejection from The Second Pan."

"Oh, Thal." Hilaria turned and flung her arms around her shoulders. "No wonder. You should definitely go. You have such good things in here." Hilaria tapped her head. "You need to let them out. Figure out how to open the door. A bit of county would do you good."

"You really will come visit if I'm there for ages?"

"Couldn't keep me away with a stick. Come on. I have some cocoa and some milk left. We'll curl up and talk. Oh, I heard the best story from Una, I simply have to tell you."

That would, at least, be an agreeable end to the evening, up til all hours, until they fell asleep.

Printed in Great Britain
by Amazon

32975876R00202